Meet . . .

CLAIRE

She follows a lost love to California—only to discover her own dreams come true . . .

HILLARY

Spoiled, rich, prisoner of her own drives, destructive to herself and to all who know her . . .

MADELEINE

She's got all the guts and talents she needs to be a star, but still she's compelled to disgrace herself to get ahead . . .

They are the

California Dreamers

California Dreamers

Norman Bogner

BALLANTINE BOOKS • NEW YORK

 Published in the United States by Ballantine Books, a division of Random House, Inc., New York, and simultaneously in Canada by Random House of Canada, Limited, Toronto, Canada.

Library of Congress Catalog Card Number: 81-253

ISBN 0-345-30266-4

This edition published by arrangement with Wyndham Books

Manufactured in the United States of America

First Ballantine Books Edition: August 1982

With love for Lori and my friend Jim Parks

1

Claire always seemed to be in a hurry and the characteristic she prized most had vanished. She had lost her capacity to organize her time and with it her security. Each day was more chaotic—she could blame it on Drake's and the pressure of spring business, but the fact of the matter was that her job at the store had never been a burden. She knew what she was doing. But now strings of scabrous salesmen hawking closeouts, along with their more respectable brethren, the manufacturers' reps, lined her office complaining bitterly, stubbing their cigarettes out in coffee containers and glaring at her secretary. She overheard low irritated voices rasping theories that she was behind in her work.

"She's shell-shocked from the season."

"It's her monthly."

"Maybe she's going for an abortion."

"They're eating double knits three times a day. Drake wants her to tell her story walking. Hey, I've seen them come and go . . ." This from a wiseguy sales manager dealing markdown polyester patchwork print blazers. "Remember," he told the anxious men surrounding him, veterans of such ordeals, "I was at Ohrbach's for ten years buying coats when they pinkslipped me the day before Christmas. They docked my bonus and told me to go skiing."

The men in the room nodded. Many of them had been on the other side as buyers and merchandisers. They saw the writing on the wall, could spot trends, sniffed around personnel, ragged sales assistants to see if their line was moving. Claire was out on her kiester. They just blinked at her when she went out to lunch or to a meeting. No more big hellos for Claire Stuart. A buyer without a pencil was in a class with a mountless jockey. She'd been scratched.

However, they were all wrong—to a man. It was true that Claire did not have her mind on business, only half heard what her associates and friends said, stood dazed while they waited for replies and decisions. She had occupied that ill-defined no-man's land of being engaged for more than a year; and in two months—on June 30, 1979, at St. Alban's Methodist Church, to be exact—she was about to be rescued from the waiting room. To make matters even more frenetic, the groom, one Bobby Canaday, AIA, was heading west to Los Angeles that afternoon to seek his fortune as an architect, and she had decided to follow the irascible master of her fate to the continental shelf if he landed a job. Her position at Drake's, thus, was uncertain not because her departments were collapsing under the weight of markdowns but as a consequence of Bobby's being adrift.

The mall outside Westport, Connecticut, where Drake's was located was a shopper's paradise if your taste ran to vinyl loveseats, simulated butcher-block dinette sets, squares of marbled mirror, and plastic ceramic-look tile. Several shops featured unpainted furniture, and wherever the eye rested there were hardware stores. The area, with its lumberyard and home improvement centers, was a wonderland for the do-it-yourself weekend handyman who cut corners because all the promises he had made to redo the house with a decorator had come to nothing. Claire knew the people well. They were her customers at Drake's, fighting over sale clothes, lured by cheap house brand TVs, washing machines that blew the lights and flooded the kitchen when installed. No Sony or Maytag ever found its way into Drake's, which is why the store enjoyed such success. The policy of buying cheap and selling bargains was a formula that worked. Turnover was the name of the game, and if a customer was dissatisfied with his new appliance, then let him write to Gary, Indiana, or some such hinterland and squawk to the manufacturer.

Claire was a natural redhead with shoulder-length hair. She had a slim high waist, pale blue eyes, a small backside, long legs, and an unselfconscious but taunting voluptuousness. She was five-eight with solid, compact breasts. With her straight nose, full lips, and slightly freckled skin, she exuded good health and a careless outdoor beauty that was unhampered by fussiness or vanity. Despite the bounty of nature it was her voice, deep and resonant, that people picked up on. It carried a weight beyond her years and had an insinuating quality. Men had flirted outrageously with her since she was a teenager, but women seldom evinced jealousy. Claire had a way about her of allaying suspicions. Perhaps it was because there was nothing cheap or frippery about her; her natural poise attracted women to her. She simply was not the sort to encourage wandering husbands or hook boyfriends. She had a flair for dressing, always off-center, seldom aping the vagaries of fashion. She often shopped for antique clothes in funny, out-of-the-way thrift shops or at costumers who were having sales. In some respects, she looked like she belonged to another period, when all men assumed women were respectable.

Her intercom buzzed and she finally answered it. Her middle-aged secretary was aggrieved. She couldn't handle the traffic.

"I've got a half hour, so send in whoever was first." Claire bought and merchandised all of the women's wear at Drake's, so she knew well the grisly lines of girdled salesmen, as well as frenzied separates reps whose desperate pinches occasionally reverberated in her nightmares.

A hawkfaced man in a plaid doubleknit sports jacket filled her office with the hacking scent of Hai Karate. He opened his sample case and handed her his card.

"Look, Miss Stuart, I know you're busy, but give me a little time. I just took over Gruskoff's line for the East Coast and I'm writing orders like crazy. By the end of the year they may have to make me a partner 'cause my commissions have been so heavy." He pulled out some lingerie, diaphanous panties in garish colors—chartreuse, primrose, scarlet, and of course black—and bightened it along on his arm like a towrope, then seized a pair and placed them across his broad hips. "Nobody's going to get near these up here because I'm giving you an exclusive."

"The crotch is missing," she observed. "Did you run out of material?"

"Hey, this is the latest thing on the Coast. In San Francisco they've reordered six times, and in L.A., Lily St. Cyr, the gal that used to strip in Vegas, runs a lingerie boutique that sells a gross a week."

"Mr. Kreb—"

"Sol, please."

"Sol, this store sells basically conservative fashion knockoffs to married women and college girls as well as the woman who's into sports."

"The Westport women'll go for it."

"*They* don't shop here. This store is for the workers, not the boutique browsers. Our customers aren't putting on sex shows."

"Trust me."

"Absolutely not. If you've got normal bikinis and briefs in cotton or nylon, I'll have a look, but do me a favor, don't bring any of this kind of gear in again."

She wound up buying a gross of slightly irregular flesh-toned front clasp bras, which saved his day.

Kreb disappeared from her life to be replaced by a servile jobber who had bought out a bankrupt, suicidal manufacturer of separates. Implausible as it seemed, the jobber, wheeling out his dirndls, kept insisting that "These were cut from original *Anne Klein* patterns."

She had a headache and the bullshit was getting on her nerves. Just because she was twenty-four, what made these high-pressure schleppers imagine she didn't know her business? She had been at Drake's for five years, having left F.I.T. after only one term when she realized that designing haute couture clothes was really a tedious exercise for self-proclaimed geniuses.

"With all due respect, these skirts couldn't even be described as sisters-in-law to Anne Klein. They're badly cut, the seams are crooked, the fabric wouldn't make it as drapes in a lunatic asylum."

She closed out the salesman. Kreb had left behind a pair of the passion bikinis in a modest fuschia. On a whim, she removed her own panties, shoved them in her handbag, and put on Sol's *délices*. She was feeling mildly crazy, up in the air, and she was late. She was taking Bobby to the airport and she had him for only another four hours.

Claire whipped into the reception area of her office and the salesmen rose, bellowing they were next. "Sorry, it'll have to wait. I've got to make a pit stop," she said pertly, then dashed out to the elevator.

It was a warm humid April day and shoppers with their infants in strollers clogged the parking lot. She got into her eight-year-old, newly painted white Alfa Romeo and prayed that the goddamn mechanic who'd soaked her two-fifty for a tune-up and a new clutch hadn't jobbed her. The last time she'd had any repairs she'd had to be towed off the Merritt Parkway. She drove through the center of town, past all of the boutiques, to Ash Avenue to the Canaday house, a green-shuttered Cape Cod that stood on a corner lot, American flag flapping in the breeze. Bobby's father was a stockbroker who'd recently acquired the local American Legion account; with the Lions and with the Rotary Club already in his hand, the place with its medallions, emblems, and plaques resembled something AAA would recommend. She pulled into the driveway behind the Canadays' new gas-saver, a sardine-can Fiesta, which they used in place of the '64 Rolls when state dinners at the country club were not called for.

Bobby's room, or apartment as his mother called it, was above the garage, with its own staircase and entrance. Claire hooted, and Bobby came to the dormer window.

"Come up, babe, we've got time," he called.

"The traffic . . . ? Is your mother home?"

"Yes, she is," Lynn Canaday said, stepping out of the front door. "Where's the fire?" She was dressed for cocktails at the Plaza in a lilac suit. She'd hit fifty-five, flushes, anxiety, and no vermouth or olives in her martinis. She was seeing a psychiatrist in Greenwich twice a week and she dressed for the occasion. Bobby had traveled only to Vietnam, and whenever he took a plane she imagined he was about to be spirited off to some old Asian global scenario of Kissinger's.

Claire kissed her mother-in-law-to-be, told her to drive carefully—Bombay was on her breath—and said, "It's only a couple of weeks. Pretend Bobby's going to Camp Berkshire and he'll come back a lifeguard."

"He's never been to California," Lynn replied, frowning. He was the male heir of the Canadays; two sisters had preceded him. Corruption and his cock were still his mother's concern.

"Where are you?" Bobby shouted.

"On my way." Claire turned to Lynn. "There's nothing to worry about. Either he gets a job or I'll keep supporting him. Your son's a genius."

Mystified, Lynn hugged her and slid into the Rolls at the curb. A state occasion.

"I wish to hell I knew if it was Wednesday or Sunday."

"Tuesday."

She blinked, waved farewell, flooded the engine, then rasped despondently, "Robert, tell your father he can reheat the brisket and I'll be back in time for the Fonz." She'd Visine'd her eyes. "Claire, nobody gives a rap about me any longer," she observed with the appropriate lachrymal additive, then burst off with a spew of hellish carbon backfiring. Halfway down the block the Rolls played octaves, sounding like Horowitz on the comeback trail, and was gone.

"Silence." Bobby beckoned, smiling delightfully innocently. "We can fuck before the plane."

Claire blew him a kiss. Life had become enchanting again.

"Wait'll you see what I've got for you. I didn't buy it—it's on appro."

She climbed the stairs, reentering the wonderland the two of them had woven. Her mother had come in from Vegas for a visit, and Claire had been driven out of her own apartment. She had a tingling sensation, vaguely wanton, when she reached his door. He had seduced her above the garage a couple of years ago, and the experience had come as a culmination, a fulfillment of the romantic fantasies she had entertained since first seeing Bobby in the high school corridor when she had been a freshman and he a senior. He had been a gangling seventeen-year-old with long wheat-colored hair, fair skin, eyes of such penetrating cerulean blue that at times they seemed metallic. He was saved from prettiness by his nose, which was a bit flat, and a massive-boned jaw. He had boxed on the school team and in the PAL and he was on his way to Dartmouth on a Westinghouse scholarship. She had been thirteen, light years away from him, but the memory of his face had come back to her repeatedly, even after he went on to college. They had never dated; as far as he was concerned, she was one of many familiar faces that he nodded to when he came across it in Westport when he was home on vacation.

They had never spoken until one day when he had come into Drake's looking for a portable radio. She had been managing Small Appliances in those days and he was doing graduate work at the School of Design at Harvard. She switched him from a Drake's own brand Meteor to a G.E. Two years later he asked her for a date when he ran into her at a charity fashion show she had organized at the country club. She never revealed to him that she had fallen in love with him at first sight in the school corridor, but he would have understood and not chided her about it, for he was blessed with majestic tenderness and sensitivity that at times made her feel that she was unworthy of him.

He put his arms around her and kissed her in the small messy living room that he worked in. Mobiles hung from the ceiling, blueprints and drafting paper were scattered behind the old sofa, and a drafting table was filled with mathematical notations. On the bookcases were awards he had won in architectural contests: the room was loaded with models of buildings that were never to see brick or mortar. His was the destructive idealism of excellence, and he accepted rejection with the tranquillity of a saint. The world was full of schmucks who took the safe way out on projects he declined. So be it. Now he was embarking on the last journey across the continent to find work or settle for a teaching appointment and choke on his principles. He was a complicated piece of machinery; although she had from time to time attempted to temper his ideas with the pragmatism she had been born with, she soon gave up, realizing that gifted people operate under different laws.

"What's your surprise?" he asked, stroking her hair and pulling her to the sofa.

"Christ, I'm going to miss you."

"Me too."

She prayed that he would be offered some kind of job in California or that she could be with him in order to blunt the natural disappointment of being passed over. She had no confidence in his diplomacy. He was blunt and abrasively honest and she knew there was no saving Bobby from himself or his character.

They sat still, close in each others' arms, too tense to talk about the puzzle of his future. It was a time for hope but she was held back by the despondency of his prospects. He was twenty-eight, going nowhere and meant for another time. He needed a patron but the period of the master builder had passed. Robert Moses had gone, corporations picked architects like Philip Johnson, and unless a developer took a liking to an architect, he couldn't expect to be anything but a drone in a large firm's back room, drafting plans that were modified or thrown out at the partners' review meetings.

She pressed her lips against his ear and he gave her a sleepy smile.

"Nervous?" she asked.

"I guess." He sighed, stretched his arms. "I wish the hell I knew if this was the right thing. If by some miracle I get a job, what're you going to do?"

"Come out, and, well, I'll find something at one of the department stores. Bullock's or Neiman's. They can always use a pro. Hey, let's not worry about it." She lifted her skirt, revealing the bare target area.

"Looks like you're ready for L.A."

"Right. I'll dance topless or become a call girl."

"I'll pay you a hundred," he advised her.

"Give me your Visa number and I'll phone and get an approval."

"Claire . . . you make me feel so good. How the hell do you put up with my shit?"

"As long as you're not gay or making it with my girlfriends, it's a cinch."

She got him to JFK without a tear or a scene, but on the way back to Westport she stopped off at the Red Lion, dropped a pair of vodka martinis, and felt her guts being wrenched when she thought of him flying out of her life, even for only two weeks. She phoned the caterer, who invited her to drop by his office to settle the final details of the wedding reception. Hors d'oeuvres were on the agenda. Fresh shrimp and a selection of pâtés and terrines appealed to her, but cheese puffs and anchovies on deviled eggs were less expensive. But her wedding day was one that she'd always remember and why, she asked herself, foul the air with platters of dry salami on crackers that broke in your hand or the runny egg salad that invariably oozed onto people's shoes and lapels? She'd have to find other ways to cut corners.

She parked on Papa Micelli's enormous lot. Acres of parking space gave the caterer's vaulted Gothic banquet hall a sepulchral character. With the hills surrounding the mock-brick building, it might have been a crematorium. However, Micelli's postcards and ads featured it from a low angle; the amenities had intimations of pastoral weddings with multi-tiered cakes "baked on the premises," and one expected a bride and groom to be followed down the hill by a procession of angelic choirboys. Meanwhile, the green M in the neon sign was blackened and a workman on a ladder cursed as he tried to coax the long fluorescent tube out of its bracket.

The caterer, Micelli, made her nervous. He was a man who lived on deposits and she had shared a lie with him. She, not her mother, was actually paying for the wedding. Bobby and his family had been told that Milly had received a large settlement from husband number three, a Vegas pit boss who'd vanished, relieving Milly of her jewelry. The groom, as was traditional, would pay for flowers, musicians, liquor, and the minister.

Micelli was in his office, smiling beatifically as he repeated his spiel to someone on the phone.

"It's once in a lifetime, a never-to-be-forgotten occasion—" He beckoned Claire to a velvet bench. Overhead pictures of brides, ushers, and solemn priests provided a kind of spiritual crazy-paving. "Just send in a thousand-dollar deposit," Micelli cajoled the customer. "Of course it's returnable. Listen, Papa Micelli and Sons didn't start yesterday. We're established since nineteen forty-five."

On Micelli's wall, Claire observed the milky expressions of sailors, soldiers, and marines along with their post-war Ann Sheridans. Micelli had been holding receptions since the end of the Second World War. He was a pudgy man with geometric ripples of fat under his chin and a ruby pingy ring; he nipped his cigars with a gold Dunhill instrument, which he wore on a keychain along with a cross, a Shriner's pin, and the keys of the world. His carnation was always white and crisp. After half a dozen meetings with him, she had come to dread his unctuous avuncular manner. He clasped both her hands in his whenever they shook, crooking his gray leonine head to the side as though admiring a long-lost grandchild. The benign relative was holding two and a half grand of her money. Sweet-voiced, solicitous, he pointed out his hors d'oeuvres facsimiles. He reminded her of a mortician merchandising his caskets. Quiche hoods loomed behind greaseless gold-patina'd egg rolls in the opened display case. Meatballs were soldered in tomato gravy in a deep chafing dish; a favorite trick of his was to lift the bowl and attempt to spill them on his figured oriental carpet. He guided her hand to the shrimp, which did not of course smell and which had the consistency of marshmallow. She marveled at the ingenious use to which rubber foam had been put.

"Just like the real thing. Shrimp always give color and class to an affair." Weddings, parties, confirmations were always affairs. He had a culinary version of a wax museum and a movie short to go with his presentation, which Claire had been subjected to at their first meeting. "They're running me ten-fifteen a pound, and that's wholesale, honey."

"How many pounds do you think we'd need?" she asked.

He whipped out her file. "Fifty couples. Ten pounds would be chintzy, twenty gives you color and depth. It also protects you."

"From what?" She saw it coming, another of Micelli's knuckleballs.

"You always got some freak who can gobble three-four pounds before dinner. He just stands at the cold table and rakes them off the ice. He doesn't need a plate. He's like a kingfisher with the trapdoor jaw open and then your guests start asking what happened to the shrimp."

"Ten-fifty?"

"That's *my* price, darling . . . for you it's twenty a pinky ring; he nipped his cigars with a gold Dunhill instru-Inflation! Oil! What's a few bucks more on the most important day of your life?" He was already making a note at the bottom of the contract and getting her to initial it. "I hope your fiancé appreciates the type of human being he's getting in you, Claire."

Micelli recapped the menu to see if he could inveigle her into anything else. Baked Alaska or Cherries Jubilee instead of the three-flavored ice cream cake. Claire's mind drifted. If only her mother hadn't lied, it would have been possible to have a more modest wedding in keeping with her financial position. As it was, it would cost Claire ten thousand dollars. Every penny she had saved. Her boss, Gene Drake, was going to lend her five thousand.

"The hell with it, Mr. Micelli, let's shoot the works. Baked Alaska."

He made additional notes on the contract as though adding codicils to a will.

2

Sandwiched between the Bistro, battalions of real estate agents, and a triumvirate of antique shops specializing in Tiffany lamps that began at a modest thirty thousand dollars for one of the master's spindly creations, the firm of Hayward Associates, Architects, had its brass plaque on a pale sandstone two-story building. This was to be Bobby's last interview and Hayward had kept him waiting three days in a Holiday Inn closet in Santa Monica—the rates were cheaper at that end of town. He'd been depressed at the frequent postponements, fearing that the job he was up for might already have been filled. His frustrations had begun the moment he arrived in Los Angeles.

Prepared to accept the conventional high-handed Eastern appraisal of the city, he had discovered that the place was charming, architecturally interesting, adventuresome, unconventional, and replete with a dizzying variety of possibilities. He liked the proximity of the ocean, the flowing mountains, the vistas from the hills, the breathtaking flow of life, all heightened by dazzling sunlight. For years he had disapproved of the place as strangers do. He preferred to accept it as a cultural wasteland, a fairyland of sham without any distinctive character. But, damn it, he'd never been more wrong about anything. He was crazy about L.A., finding the place congenial, uninhibited by preconceived ideas except for some overdressed, Spanish *finca* styles. But it had a grace, a relaxed wayward indolence, and he was convinced that he'd rather take a chance living here than return to commuting, overcoats, the desolate grayness of a Manhattan skyscraper where he spent his days in a windowless back room wondering how he'd screwed up his professional life. He did not detect the tensions or the revolutionary extremes the city had been celebrated for, nor did he find it lacking in grace. He embraced its openness, discerned that the landlords were up in arms over rent control and were rushing through condominium conversions. He easily imagined himself and Claire living in an apartment, working, recreating their lives. Just twenty minutes from Beverly Hills, in the Valley, people kept horses; and a mere five-minute drive from the Holiday Inn, he could sail. No wonder, with this extraordinary range of choices, people from the East found complaint and dismissed it out of hand.

But as he headed for his appointment, he realized that more than anything was the imperious wealth of Los Angeles and its precincts that was breathtaking and made the Fifth Avenue co-ops, the Madison Avenue townhouses of New York appear cramped and dispiriting. The lavishness of the homes, from Santa Monica, Bel Air, through the pastoral climes of Beverly Hills, was unprecedented. Scarsdale, Greenwich, the estates in Westport he'd visited were by contrast playthings without substance. He parked his rented Pinto on a lot beside the Hayward office, marveling that if he stayed all day it would cost him only three-fifty, the price of one hour in a New York lot. Notwithstanding the ubiquitous smog, of which there had been no sign during his stay, and the serpentine traffic jams on the freeways, it was a place in which convenience had become so deeply ingrained that only visitors noticed it.

Deeply polished rich hardwood floors began in the vestibule at the receptionist's desk. He gave his name to a pretty blonde manning the switchboard who was dressed in jeans and a tank top. He was wearing his three-piece Oxford gray Brooks Brothers job, a rep tie, button-down blue shirt, and he gave off the aura of a trainee in term insurance. The girl pointed him to a waiting room adjacent to her corner where three other men around his age, none of them wearing ties, but casual in sweaters, cords, loafers rather than his winged cordovans, appeared to be applicants, judging from their portfolios leaning casually against the wall. They were all talking about the position and he felt out of place, foreign, a stranger to the good life. Bobby did not join the chat. They were his adversaries, sure of themselves, possibly talented, glib, loose, and he thought he detected behind their mannerly facades the same deep-rooted anxiety choking him.

He'd been bumped early at his interview at the University of Southern California. His notion of teaching a survey course in the history of architecture did not meet with departmental approval. He thought that the chairman of the department considered him radical when he praised Saarinen's precept of "the style for the job" in his design of the TWA terminal at Kennedy airport. None of them were keen on symbolic attitudes in architecture. So he'd been blown out immediately.

A meeting with a developer from San Diego who was proposing to build a retirement community in Coronado proved equally disastrous. The developer and his syndicate had high-density barracks in mind, outrageous management fees, and were wedded to pre-fab in construction. He was sorry he'd wasted three hours with the man, whose philosophy was summed up at the very beginning. "These people are sixty-five plus, so how long do they have to live? We're selling shelter, Mr. Canaday . . ."

Hayward had written him an encouraging letter, setting up the interview, but the way his luck was running, he had little reason for optimism. What burned him was the prospect of returning to Claire empty-handed, the understanding look on her face and her gritty response to his failure. Well, if he busted out again, he'd take some deal with a Long Island builder of instant slums, hit the Dunkin' Donuts, Seven-Eleven circuit and grind out a living. He'd take his fine notions and shove them for good this time. Two aspirants were seen before him, and he marked time, reading about acreage for sale in the back of the *Times*.

When he was finally called in to see Hayward and two other men lounging in his office, he had just about given up and decided he had nothing more to lose by firing from the hip. Interviews always offended Bobby, brought out an aggressive streak that had the effect of altering his personality. Rather than behaving guardedly, capitalizing on his natural charm, he usually became antagonistic. But with the sunlight streaming in on Hayward's glass and chrome desk, the apparent openness of the tanned faces confronting him, he relaxed. Hayward's walls were filled with honorariums, obscure civic awards that reminded Bobby of the sort of endorsements he saw in his dentist's office. Several prize renderings of developments, hospital wings, and condos struck him as pedestrian. An arcade of shops on Rodeo Drive still in the model stage and called Rodeo Puerta had a kind of sleekness that had become fashionable in European reclamation schemes. None of the work on display indicated any originality and he hoped to hell no one asked him to offer an opinion. He was sweating through his flannel, felt a positive schmuck for having dressed incorrectly, especially when he saw the Gucci loafers worn without socks by Hayward and a man who was introduced to him as Leonard Martinson of the Martinson Development Corporation. The office was done in casual earth tones, all very elegant and unfussy and slick. The third man, Gary Rubin, was in his worried fifties, clearly junior. Hayward invited him to be seated, looked through his portfolio and handed Leonard his resumé.

"Why don't you take your jacket off?" Hayward suggested. He was dressed in blue linen slacks, a Lacoste shirt, and he had that studied neatness of a man who organized his life around tennis and lunch dates. "You've got a helluva background," he said affably, stroking his sculpted conquistador beard. "Why'd you resign from Cummings in New York?"

"It was a dead end."

"You were there for four years," Rubin observed. He was short, intense, stoop-shouldered, but his face had a humorous cast. "What happened?"

"I wasn't happy with most of the things they wanted me to do . . . shopping centers, mini marts, that sort of thing. Yeah, occasionally they threw me a house or a building conversion."

"Bored you?" Martinson asked. He had opalescent gray eyes, a fine slim build, a cavalier manner, which went with the gleaming white-gold Patek Phillipe watch on his wrist.

A pale blue cashmere sports jacket was slung carelessly on the back of his chair; when he leaned back he crushed the collar, but it didn't appear to trouble him.

"Most of the time I felt the other people in the office could do a better job," Bobby replied. "When a franchiser comes to you he's already got his design package laid out and it's like following the numbers in a kid's drawing book. They don't really want any suggestions and they resent it when you tell them they're wasting space or the materials are wrong."

"You stepped on toes?" Leonard asked.

"I'm smart enough not to go out of my way to do that, but after a while I began to think that nothing interesting would come my way."

Rubin shook his head assentingly. He too was a specialist of the ordinary, the unimaginative.

"What do you think your real strength is?" he asked.

The three men were attentive and Bobby sensed that his answer would be pivotal.

"In some respects I'm waiting to find out."

"Don't hedge," Hayward said. "There's no right or wrong answer."

"Fair enough. I like doing houses, but I think I was meant for office buildings. I like large sites and the feeling that what I'm doing is part of the environment—which isn't to say I'm hysterical about environment and ecology. But there doesn't seem to be much continuity or any real planning that architects do when they're given a project. Just bang out something the client wants and come in at a price. All of that's reasonable, but when you think of someone like Le Corbusier and his concern for the relationship of the various parts, city planning, well there's no reason why it can't be done on an individual basis as well."

Bobby got the impression that Rubin was on his side but without the power to make a commitment. Yet he was moving the other two. No demurrals or offhand disagreements. Martinson picked up his jacket, carelessly dragged it along the floor.

"Tim," he said to Hayward, "why don't I run Mr. Canaday over to the house I bought on Alpine and see what kind of ideas he has." He smiled at Bobby. "Provided you don't mind."

Part Two of the test, Bobby thought as he followed Leonard out to Cañon Drive where a canary yellow Rolls Corniche was parked at the curb. A chauffeur sat behind the wheel dressed in a blue blazer. Leonard told him to grab some lunch and he'd drive. Along the way, Leonard explained that most of Tim's work came from him. They'd been friends for twenty years, the developer and the architect, a comfortable marriage. Leonard had a wonderful relaxed quality that seemed to epitomize the seductions of Los Angeles.

They headed north from Santa Monica Boulevard and stopped on a wide tree-lined street just below Sunset Boulevard. Leonard pulled up in front of a rambling stucco Spanish house whose facade was striated with large damp patches. He opened the trunk of the car and his social life—Borg racquet, Lynx Predator clubs, several swimsuits, and a broken croquet mallet—leaped out at him. He located some musty blueprints.

"Here's a set of the original specs," Leonard said. "Why don't you wander around . . . no hurry. I'll be back. Key's under the mat."

Houses . . . to suggest that they were mere brick and mortar, shelters, would be to deny them the spirits, the souls that had conceived them. Most of them were imperfect because the men who built them compromised or had faulty vision. But even as a boy, they had fascinated Bobby, conjured up visions of families living out their most intimate moments. To the untutored eye, the abject soul, they were inanimate objects designed to serve a purely functional purpose as dwellings. But in that role they were devoid of romance, a hodgepodge of materials, beams, carpentry, plaster. Constructions. Yet as far as he was concerned, they possessed magical essences. Unlike office buildings, which were hives of commerce where men fell from grace or fulfilled their destinies, the home was a holy place in which dreams and aspirations, the ultimate communion of love might flourish without any need for justification. Finally, the home was to him the last sanctuary of privacy in a world of eavesdroppers.

The front garden was overgrown with giant weeds; massive pampas grass fluted around the entry and gnarled wisteria snaked around the windows. Bobby opened the door and found himself in a drafty vestibule, heard rats scurrying and saw their black droppings on the faded terra cotta tiles. There was a formal living room, dark and dank, which led to a dining room the size of a banquet hall. An unhinged door lay against the wall; its doorway led to a narrow musty kitchen. Small barred windows gave the place a portentousness, and heavy oak beams—decorative, not structural—overwhelmed the heroic proportions of the ground floor, giving the house a claustrophobic effect. Sunlight had been excluded. He walked up the wide staircase to the rooms upstairs. There must have been eight or ten bedrooms, all poky with small prison-cell, grimy windows. He peered out and saw an expanse of untended garden. It was not so much a house as a place of incarceration. But he had a vision of how he could change the house by adding windows, enlarging the rooms, and introducing color to the flat-toned terra cotta. He'd window an entire wall of the living room, treble the size of the fireplace, expand the kitchen by reducing the size of the dining room.

Bobby passed through the service porch into the back garden, then walked along a narrow courtyard, finally reaching a listing fountain tiled with Aztec markings. It was filled with blackened rainwater, dead birds, and decomposed leaves. He saw Leonard sitting on a tree stump.

"I bought this horror for six-fifty on spec."

"Incredible," Bobby said, aghast at the price.

"I bought it at the top. . . . I don't think I outsmarted myself."

"I don't know what to say . . . almost three quarters of a million dollars. It sounds steep."

Leonard motioned him to follow and they surveyed the acre lot in silence.

"I'm going to give you a lesson in property values. If this place were anywhere in the country it might go for two hundred tops. It's a monstrosity and only some guy with imperial notions would consider it. He'd have to pour money into it. He'd get equity loans and it'd bleed him to death. But here in Beverly Hills—and this is prime flats—

money has no value. People pay for an address and the privilege of saying they live in Beverly Hills. There's no logic to it. I'm prepared to put another five hundred thousand in it . . . pool, north-south tennis court will run a hundred and a half. So I've got three-fifty to play with. Any architect can do a job on this place and I'll put it up for sale through Tim, save the six percent broker's commission that way and net a million. But if I had an architect who had some inspired ideas and could work within the budget, I'd pull out a million and a half to two million. Believe me, Bobby, walking around, house hunting, is some guy and his wife with so much money and so little imagination that if it's done right they'll think they got the bargain of a lifetime. See, there's not just the snob appeal of living in Beverly Hills but the special cachet, the vulgar pleasure of telling your friends you paid three mil for a house."

He respected Leonard's analysis and thought for a minute of how to respond.

"You're selling ostentation for that price, not good taste, and it's a helluva challenge. Okay, we're dealing with a house that's dark and has only one good-sized room. The rest of them are broom closets, so let's consider the heroic proportions that would emerge by having a two-story entry with a skylight and an open gallery to the bedrooms. We'd gain vertical space and still have something that was functional. Open the rear wall and go with a twenty-foot floor-to-ceiling window. You introduce light and the outdoors into the house and with some work on the garden with a good landscaper, you'd have a feeling of living with nature. The rooms upstairs—I guess there must be ten of them—we make four of them into a master suite with a sitting area, sauna, double bathroom, and a couple of huge closets. Three other bedrooms with baths en suite. A new kitchen, which we widen and fill with skylights and greenhouse windows. The guest house in back can become servants' quarters. Basically that's how I'd approach this job . . . but I'd think about the amount you've allotted for improvements. Good plumbing fixtures and new electrical work can eat you up."

"My people are non-union, illegal aliens," Leonard informed him. "We look for skilled craftsmen, tilers, and we stay away from the unions. That's how we can bring it in lower and still be up to code."

"You're the contractor. Just don't cut corners in workmanship and you've got a chance to get your price."

Leonard pondered his suggestions. There was something so likeable and yet circumspect about Bobby that he wanted to continue the discussion even though he'd be late for another meeting in the Valley. He went to his car, called his office from the car phone and rescheduled the meeting for later in the afternoon. Any architect could build new, but to take a derelict house and give it new life required extraordinary talent and imagination.

"I don't mean to contradict myself, but there's one thing you shouldn't lose sight of no matter who does the house for you. The rockbed principle of a house is always a family—sharing their lives together. It contains secrets. It should provide them with intimacy despite the size and so it should be thought of in a spirit of caring. There has to be a union of space contained by time. Do you follow me?"

"Not exactly, but I like the sound of it and I like you. Are you doing anything for lunch?"

'No," he admitted. "I'm just going to hang around until I find out if Hayward wants to hire me and if he doesn't I'll catch the next plane back East."

"This job means a lot to you?" Leonard asked with concern.

"Well, frankly, I'm not sure what the hell I'll do. I don't really want to teach. I've been doing that part time at the New School in New York. Two nights a week . . . and I don't like the idea of hooking up with any number of developers who offered me work."

"There's a short list. Another man and you," Leonard informed him. "He wanted to get rid of the Spanish look and do a total revamp with wood and glass. Ultra modern."

"It'd be a mistake. This house is part of tradition . . . forget its condition. You'll find someone who wants the Spanish look. A good contemporary house can be tough to sell. You need an educated buyer, someone with imagination. For three million, a buyer doesn't want wood and glass, he wants bricks."

"That's what I told the other man."

* * *

It was seven o'clock in the East when he got through to Claire. He could not contain his elation. He'd gone back to Hayward's office with Leonard Martinson and been hired at a starting salary of twenty-five thousand a year with a review in six months. He'd also been offered a half percent commission on any work he brought into the firm. Leonard was calling the shots and Bobby would be involved in his projects at the beginning.

Claire looked at her mother across the room. A Vegas cashier, she was waiting for news as though it were a keno win. There was no extension in the apartment so she winked at Milly as if to say, I'll tell you later.

"It finally happened."

"It's a fluke," Bobby said. "We're going to be in L.A." His room at the Holiday Inn looked like an acrobat's changing room. When you booked in for a week, they left it a slaughterhouse. Marmalade was still on the washcloth he'd used for the continental breakfast he hadn't ordered. Some guy's jungle green blazer with a "Buick Dealers" patch had been hung in plastic with a $7.95 bill on the doorhook. "Hey, how are you? And what did you do with the panties?"

"They're in cold storage for the time being," she replied, noting that her mother had the Yellow Pages out, searching for some divorced guy who'd kept her for eighteen days before he sold his pizzeria and became a restaurateur. "Bobby, I'll have to work out my notice at the store." He told her to wait until he'd signed the contract. It wouldn't take more than a week or so, and Leonard Martinson, whom he described as his patron, had asked him to begin work on the plans and renderings of a house conversion. The news galvanized Claire. All of her hopes for Bobby were about to come to fruition. She rejoiced, spiritually embraced her man; destiny had smiled, blessed their union. "I love you so much," she exclaimed.

"Claire, it's not a dream, it's real. You'll love L.A."

"I can't wait to have you back."

"Darling, I've got to go . . . speak to you soon."

He was a young man in a hurry, on the move, and indeed he was running late. Leonard had invited him to his home for drinks and an informal supper party where he'd meet some of his colleagues from the office. The world had suddenly opened up for him and he eagerly embraced his opportunities.

He had a map of L.A. and carefully followed Leonard's directions. He drove through the Bel Air West Gate along tortuous roads, passing large estates which he glimpsed out of the corner of his eye. Fortunately it was still light or he would have gotten lost in the maze of streets. Just above the Bel Air Country Club on a knoll was Bellagio Crescent and at the end, behind fences throttled with bougainvillea and oleander, were high wrought-iron electric gates. He pressed a button, announced himself, and the gates glided open silently.

He drove up a long used-brick driveway through a parkland that might have been a game preserve to the top of the knoll. There were a dozen or more cars. Ferraris, Rolls-Royces, and Mercedes slanted on the hill. His gray Pinto was a conspicuous anomaly. Spreading out below him were perhaps five acres, green houses, a croquet lawn, a lighted tennis court where a doubles match was in progress, and a majestic tiled pool where twin alabaster fauns guarded the entry. He was utterly dazzled by the grandeur of Leonard's domain. Outside the house—a mock French château upon which ficus had been trained—stood a large fountain with goldfish and a variety of other fish he did not recognize.

A servant wearing a striped French country apron opened the highly varnished front door.

"Mr. Canaday," he said. "They're all in the library. Won't you come this way." He walked along miles of polished pine floor, occasionally broken up by brass inlay. On the walls, he saw tapestries and an astounding collection of paintings. He paused in front of a Murillo depicting a street urchin gobbling a shrimp. Leonard lived like a Renaissance prince and he had gained the patronage of this remarkable man, would be working with him; Bobby's vision of the future became tangible, the possibilities illimitable.

The room was indeed a library but it was also a screening room and contained one of several bars scattered strategically through the house. A six-foot Sony screen revealed Walter Cronkite's sagacious, calming face and his voice came from concealed speakers. A few people were watching the news, while several others lingered at the bar, among them Tim Hayward. Leonard and an attractive woman in her thirties stood on the terrace just outside the library, drinks in hand; they were talking with, it seemed to Bobby, some hint of anxiety. Leonard's face was red and his eyes troubled, but the expression altered when he saw Bobby.

The woman's name was Ann Shaw and she was English with a fine-boned face and a gracious friendly manner. She was Leonard's personal assistant. Bobby was asked for his drink order by another servant, also liveried, and in a moment he was brought a Chivas on the rocks.

Bobby wondered how Claire would react to these people and the awesome wealth that appeared to be so natural to them. She'd probably be unimpressed and see them as mortals rather than gods. Leonard took him around the room, patiently introducing him to his guests. It was clear to Bobby that a real affinity existed between the two of them. Leonard had plans for him.

He returned to the terrace where several benches and a piece of modern sculpture were arrayed. The game on the tennis court was over and the foursome made their way up the hill in two golf carts. He recognized Rubin's lugubrious face. He was sitting beside a hatchet-faced, scowling woman whose skin was the color of a date. In another cart were two other women who, on their aqua bench seat, appeared to him like wildflowers fluttering on a pond. They seemed to inhabit a different planet in which they made the laws as they went along, and the conjunction of their beauty amid the rolling acres of the Martinson estate overwhelmed him.

He met the older of the women first. Her name was Ellen Dunlop, a tall lithe woman with long, tanned legs, an athletic body, chestnut hair which she wore up. She was wearing a lime green Head tennis outfit and on her left hand was a diamond ring the size of a Brazil nut. Her brown eyes had a certain amused worldliness and she was attached to a pugnacious stocky man who he learned was Frank Dunlop, *the* Frank Dunlop, chairman of Marine Mutual Insurance. He looked Bobby over as though he had dared poach on his territory; he had the malevolent dark eyes of a Krait, the hooked nose of a bazaar trader. He made the people around him, including Leonard, uneasy, radiating the tension of the malcontent, out of tune with the Martinson universe.

The blonde girl with Ellen did not bother to greet Bobby or anybody else, but announced that she was going up for a shower. She had a remoteness about her and since there was no Martinson wife on the premises, Bobby naturally assumed she was Leonard's mistress. She was buxom, with that prepossessing health of California girls he'd seen in movies and TV shows, but at the same time there was an aura of restless energy and disquiet in her movements.

"How was your game?" Leonard asked amid the clinking glasses and the silent waiters who wove in and out with hot Chinese hors d'oeuvres. The mini spare ribs were gloved. The girl winked at him and leaned over and said in a voice that only Leonard and Bobby could hear:

"We kicked ass."

"You played with Ellie?"

"Against her . . . and Gary."

"That doesn't help the cause," Ann Shaw suggested.

"Who can play politics on a tennis court? I'm beyond it." She ordered a shooter and Bobby waited with curiosity to see what she would be brought. It was something straight—he assumed tequila since she bit into a hunk of lime before downing it. He realized that the girl studiously ignored him and he thought that she had an instinct for knowing who was heeled and who overdrawn. She gave off a scent of knowledge, money, and unpredictable excitement. He'd never come across, at least in the flesh, any woman with a greater sense of her own sexuality and the flagrant power that accompanies such natural gifts. She breezed through the room, saying "Hi" to a few of the men who interrupted their backgammon games to greet her, recognizing her importance.

Rubin, solemn and sweating, strained to smile at him. "We'll talk later. I'm glad you got the job."

"I appreciate that . . ."

"That was Leonard Martinson's daughter . . . and it's a no-no."

"Thanks, but I'm engaged. You ought to see Claire."

He pointed to two men in the corner of the bar, red with drink, playing poker dice.

"Hillary was engaged to both of them . . . at different times. She broke up with them and they hang around here. They've become friends. I guess they like to suffer."

Gary Rubin looked like he had a keen appreciation of their predicament and Bobby thought he might have been on thin ice somewhere along the way, but he was too happy to inquire, inasmuch as troubles were out of place in this pantheon of great barons. Bobby was just coasting, enjoying the scenery, privileged to be in attendance at such a gathering. For all he knew, Sinatra might walk in for a drink at any minute. Leonard asked him if he was enjoying himself, meeting people, then lost his ebullience when Dunlop crooked his finger. There was a certain outrageous coarseness about Frank Dunlop that had lurid magnetism, entirely unique in Bobby's experience. He certainly had the capacity to make Leonard jump and Bobby was struck by the power structure he was beginning to detect in this society.

The buffet dinner that was served at eight-thirty was pulled out of a magician's hat. Leonard's chef had learned his craft and sauces at Trader Vic's, whence he had been spirited by the epicurean developer who knew his gastronomy. Apparently it didn't hurt to compare the fare he served with the barbecues and chili that his associates and friends dished up at their evenings. Bobby kept a low profile during dinner and sat listening to a few of Hayward's staff discuss with the boss the traumas caused by Dunlop over the design of the new Marine Mutual building in Century City. Hayward, as befitted the firm's principal, told them to keep plugging away. Bobby had heard all this before. Clients were invariably disgruntled because they didn't know what they wanted and only came to their senses when presented with something that bore some flimsy relationship to a vague notion they had.

A screening of *The Godfather* was to take place after dinner and although Bobby did not want to ruffle any feathers or appear to be ungracious, he preferred to shoot pool by himself in the billiard room. He'd always enjoyed the game and was extremely skillful. He'd once run four racks in straight pool and when he was at Harvard he'd hustled in a few of the Back Bay pool rooms. The game settled his mind, closed off the rest of the universe, and the sound of the balls making contact had a placid music all their own. There was the counterpoint of the bank shot, the harmonies of a three-ball combination, the fugue of the kiss shot, all of it intensely satisfying, good for the soul.

From one of the darkened patios, onto which the billiard room opened he heard the sound of applause and then, as though by some breathtaking act of sorcery, Leonard's patrician blonde stepped into the light. Her face luminous, her skin coppery from the sun, her manner idolatrous.

"I've never seen a shot like that. You're sensational . . . just sensational."

"Thank you." He bowed his head with self-assurance.

He had made a ball in the end pocket, then drew the cue ball the length of the table to make a ball at the opposite end. He put the cue stick back in the rack and sat on the edge of the table. A kind of effulgence and gratitude shone in her crystal blue eyes.

"Are you good at games?"

"Not really. I don't play backgammon."

"That's half the people's social life out here."

"What's the other half?" he inquired.

"Avoiding the people who play backgammon."

"Are you really that cynical?"

"Not as a rule. It's just that I don't like these gatherings thrown together at a minute's notice, but it's my father's way of doing business. I'm Hillary Martinson," she said, extending her hand tentatively. Obviously her rejected suitors under the same roof had unnerved her. "Who're you?"

He told her his name, explaining he would be working for Hayward and that his first assignment was the renovation of the house her father had bought. She evinced a surprising interest in the project.

"I work for a firm of interior designers and we've got the job. Nepotism, but who cares . . ."

"I've heard of worse things."

For some reason she had become deeply curious about him and he got the impression that this was her technique with new faces. There was nothing he could detect of the spoiled mistress of the manor about Hillary Martinson. She exuded an exciting vitality that obstructed the tutored poise of the rich.

"What made you decide to become an architect?"

He laughed unselfconsciously and she joined him as if the question weren't so much absurd as superfluous.

"I didn't make any decision. It chose me, which is why I guess I've had problems."

"Like what?"

"Getting ahead, doing individual stuff. I make people uncomfortable. I'll have to make up my mind to play office politics."

"Kiss ass?"

"No, that's impossible, Just be a little more diplomatic and not look for trouble. See, most of the problem about being an architect today is that most of them have moved away from humanistic qualities. They've forgotten that people have to live and work in their buildings. It all boils down to giving the client what he wants at the right price. Maybe it's naive of me, but I know I'm part of a tradition, a historical line. I want to do what's good for people's spirit. I care about the people who are going to spend their lives working in something I've done—do you understand?" He absent-mindedly took a sip from her glass of brandy. "Look, modern life is so filled with anxiety and people silently traveling to work every day who want to start screaming—'I'm going crazy and I can't stand my life . . .' Well, I sure as hell haven't got any answers for them . . . no message, but the least I can try to do is make their surroundings as pleasant as possible. I've tried to do this since I got my stamp, but it doesn't work. Hayward's giving me a shot. Maybe I'll bust out. Who knows?"

He was overcome by a certain inexplicable numbness. He did not like to discuss himself. It always sounded brazen, querulous, and he was genuinely disconcerted by Hillary's reaction.

"Bobby, you're terrific."

"We'll see." Yet the compliment intoxicated him—he thought a girl like Hillary who'd grown up amid this splendor would be niggardly about her endorsements. The scowling put-down would be more in keeping with her style, he judged from her behavior after her tennis match. But the warmth she showed contradicted him. He liked her perfume, was tempted to ask what it was called, but did not, fearing that she would laugh in his face, and his gaucheness would be revealed. Yet she had the ability to relax his inhibitions and he could not understand why he was beginning to feel a strange loyalty and obligation to her. Was he that insecure? Rubin had warned him about Hillary. Yet breaking through the caution was the girl's bounty, the pleasure of her voice, the satisfaction of having a woman so carelessly magnificent assume that he was important.

"Can I ask you a tactless question?"

"If we're going to be friends, why not?" she replied.

"What's it like having two ex-fiancés together?"

"Oh . . ." She sat on the edge of the table, blocking his shot. "Maybe it should be exciting—provocative, you know? At another time when I was somebody different, it would have been a turn-on, but now . . . it's . . . they're sort of furniture. One is the shopping center king of Orange County—the one with glasses—and the other has a bunch of tostada franchises throughout Southern California. They do a lot of joint ventures with my father and I guess that's why they're here. Leonard suckles people like them. They're both too old for me and I'm not cut out to be the wife of a businessman who throws pool barbecues for his executives at home and has conventions in Hawaii for his salesmen. Frankly, waking up in the morning and not feeling suicidal because you've got to face guys like them is what it's all about. The two of them became friends. My father brokered it," she noted bluntly. "What about you, Bobby?"

"I'm engaged."

"Don't make it sound like preventive medicine. You going to get married?"

"Uh-huh."

"First or second?"

"First, naturally."

"You're in L.A., Bobby, so the question shouldn't be so surprising. This is a place of encounters."

Not to be outdone, he said, "So's New York."

The screening had ended and the guests began to say goodnight. Cars revved in the driveway. Dates for exercise class, tennis, lunch, and weekends in Palm Springs were made provisionally and would be confirmed when diaries were consulted. Leonard came into the billiard room, smiled enigmatically at the two of them.

"Hill, people want to see you before leaving." He regarded Bobby with benign majesty. "You enjoyed yourself?"

"Yes. Thank you, Mr. Martinson."

He was the last to part from Hillary. She walked him to the car. Insects buzzed around them; the grounds were light with hundreds of green and yellow spots and Bobby felt that he had touched the genie's bottle and been awarded an evening in the garden of enchantment. When Hillary suggested that they get together for lunch one day, he casually agreed, shook her hand, and perceived that this gorgeous object of worldly delight might be his for a time, days, who could be certain, if he made the gesture.

3

Plagued by Bobby's absence—ten days had passed—Claire found herself with time to fill. She had never thought of herself as fragile or vulnerable, but she was gnawed by insecurities. She and Bobby spoke every day. He hadn't gotten around to apartment hunting; he was being kept busy working on the plans for the house he was renovating. Claire found herself inhibited about asking how he was spending his evenings. He had dinner with Madeleine, her closest friend who had moved to Los Angeles six months before. She desperately missed both of them and the presence of her mother intensified her loneliness. She could not confide in her mother and they shared no common ground.

Milly had settled in Las Vegas several years ago to work in the casinos and Claire knew that her trip back East had a dual purpose. She was checking out Atlantic City to see if she ought to make a change. But she found the weather intolerable, an affront to her permanent desert suntan. Milly had come to be with her for the wedding and would attend the shower the girls from Drake's were giving her that evening.

Yet Claire was glad when, just after six, laden with goodies from Bloomingdale's, Milly made an exuberant appearance in the living room. She dropped her packages and pirouetted around the room.

"Well, what do you think?"

"I'm not sure," Claire said, staring at the new hair color.

"Just call me the Silver Fox. Regine's, Vegas, Miami, here I come."

"What made you do this?" Over English muffins that morning, Milly had been a honey redhead.

"It was a compromise. Buddy wanted me to go straight platinum." Buddy was the latest in the interminable line of men who had been her mother's suitors and lovers. He was in tax shelters, buying property not yet built and selling it to people who filled out the ads he placed in provincial newspapers. He had a phone in his white Continental and carried a wafer-thin Sharp calculator in his breast pocket and was always calling a special number to get sports results. He had been Milly's "numero uno" for three weeks. She'd hooked up with him in Vegas when her shift was over at the Sands. She'd been a blackjack dealer for two years, then retired to the sanity of the cashier's cage when the four A.M. graveyard shifts blew her social life.

"It's a little brassy."

"Well, in Vegas it'll look subdued. And I'm off to Miami in a day or two with Buddy for the condo show. Then back here for the wedding. We'll hit Vegas by July fourth for Wayne Newton's opening."

"I never heard of a condo show."

"Well, they have car shows and shows for hardware, so why not condo shows? All on Uncle Sam. It's a tax write-off for Buddy."

At forty-eight with a thirty-eight D cup, her principal asset capped teeth from Dr. Slakoff, husband number two, a philandering dentist, Milly still had the kind of rolling hills and scenic byways that attracted men. It also helped that Milly enjoyed sex, and bore a faint resemblance to the late Jayne Mansfield, especially now that she was in her silver period. Claire had given her *Passages* to read and she'd handed the book back after ten minutes with the scornful comment: "It's a lie. Other people have passages, babe. I have sex with younger guys when I can get them."

"You're on a good time."

"That's what it's all about," Milly observed, dropping into a chair, heaving off her shoes and sipping Claire's gin and tonic. "When it's there, grab it, because before you know what's hit you, you're on the table for a bypass and the doctor's looking for veins."

Milly's was an uncomplicated world view and Claire realized that all through her life she had reacted against her mother's loose practices. Not that Claire was against pleasure, but casual liaisons, paying bills late, flim-flamming men for weekends and gifts offended her. She took pains not to judge her mother harshly, but at the back of her mind she was aware that there was a cheapness, a lack of style about Milly. Milly seldom made any reference to her father. Milly had been a war bride and when Joe Stuart had been killed in Korea just before the cease-fire, Milly had been torn between getting an abortion and having the child of the man she would never see again. The fact that she was in her fifth month decided the issue. Claire heard the story when she was sixteen, one evening when Milly had been tearfully drunk because one of those faceless men who populated the girl's life and her mother's bed had walked out. Claire tried to suppress her anger and the resentment of discovering she had been unwanted. For a long time she succeeded in burying the hurt. But every now and then, when Milly was feeling her oats and setting off on one of her forays, Claire found herself growing irritated with her mother. At best, Milly was not a tramp but, as she liked to describe herself, an early freedom fighter for women's rights. That she took not the slightest interest in the women's movement never impressed her as a contradiction.

"Heard from Bobby?"

"I'll speak to him later tonight."

"Frankly, babe, I don't know how you're getting by without him," she said with a suggestive smile. "And what about him?" she continued, pawing at Claire. "Sitting on his hands every night."

"Lay off, will you, please." Claire went to the kitchen, fixed them gin and tonics in tall glasses. She squeezed a piece of lime into the drinks and brought them back to the living room. Milly had the singular talent of touching the delicate nerve, hurting her confidence.

"Just be philosophical about men and don't ask questions. They stick it in and forget about it. Just roll with it."

She's an unconscionable bitch, Claire thought, watching her strip to her panties. She was trying on a yellow silk backless evening dress cut provocatively low in the front.

"It's bra-less . . ."

"For you, you're kidding, Mom. You're not Charo. But I guess for a condo show in Miami, anything goes."

"I bought it for your wedding."

"I don't believe it. What're you expecting to do there, turn tricks?"

"Don't be rude to your mother," Milly said, somewhat subdued.

Difficult to be sore at her, Claire reflected. The woman's a flake.

"Come on, seriously. You can't go to church looking like that. Bobby's family will freak out—and speaking for the bride, well, honey, I love you but this time let's shoot for a little dignity on our side of the fence."

"Babe, let's be honest about one little thing. The Canadays don't like me much and I can't stand them. I mean to say . . . what the hell's so special about them, for Chrissake? Bobby's father is a broker on Wall Street who used to make passes at me at the country club bar . . . and as for Lynn, Jesus, I don't think she's been laid in ten years."

The digs, the insinuations, the odious malice that her mother demonstrated had its roots in the past. She was one of those women who had missed her moment. She slavishly courted men, and when they did not respond, she found them and not herself lacking. It had been a relief to Claire when she finally moved to Las Vegas. Westport was too small for her act. And Claire saw that amid the surreal middle-aged bombshells who worked the coffee shops and casinos with their skintight hiphuggers, platinum bird's-nest hairdos and customized Dr. Tippet breasts, Milly had located her destiny. All that counted was a guy with a roll, preferably single, who luxuriated after a win in his suite with champagne and played out the charade of king for a day. They usually grabbed for the younger hustlers, but for the price of some drinks and an occasional dinner, they hooked up with indefatigable warhorses like Milly. It no longer upset Claire to know these things about her mother.

"What makes you so resentful?" Claire asked.

"Is that how I strike you?"

"I accept you for what you are."

Milly's churlishness faded and a softer, more resonant image of what she might have been like twenty years ago gradually cleansed the tarnished patina of her face. The thick, viscous lipstick, the eyelashes dank with mascara, gave way to an exhilarating sunlight of innocence.

"What's that?"

"You're my mother . . . I want a different life, not the one you had."

"I don't blame you one bit . . . It's just that being back here chokes me. I wanted to break out years ago, but you were at school and I didn't think—"

"Let's not waste our time on guilt trips."

"Fine. I'll get dressed and we'll get loaded with the girls." She rose, walked to Claire and fondly stroked her chin.

"I'll change the dress, babe."

At the back of the Cheshire Cheese, one of those Connecticut steak houses masking itself as an English pub, there was a small party room, which the girls at Drake's had hired from seven-thirty to ten. Forty of them had chipped in, something like ten dollars a head for the Cheshire's special Dr. Johnson's Roast Beef dinner served with Yorkshire pudding. Drinks of course were extra and the atmosphere of gaiety and raunchy girl-talk took Claire's mind off the scene with her mother. Milly had ambled out of the room to talk to the piano player brooding at the bar between sets. Claire was surprised by the number of gifts the women had bought her.

"Satin sheets for the Saturday Night Special," Leah Mann, a tall elegant woman in handbags said. She was involved with a married retailer and had adopted the sensible attitude of praying that he never left his wife. "He's got a spoiled twelve-year-old son," she had told Claire. "One of those big-mouth *gifted* children. And his idea of fun is going to the trotters five nights a week and cheating on his wife."

Lingerie had pooled in for a Spode service for eight. The irrepressible group in the Bargain Basement presented her with a silver-plated tea service; on the tray next to the creamer was a diaphragm. Sweaters and Blouses had selected a set of bone-handled steak knives and forks. Linens naturally gave her six king-size sets of Bill Blass sheets and pillow cases as well as an assortment of towels.

By eight-fifteen the girls had loosened up and those not

completely pissed were well on their way to oblivion. Tales of bedroom heroics made the rounds and despite the fact that Claire usually disliked smutty stories, she was genuinely amused by Patsy in Ties who had mistakenly slept with twins.

"Not at the same time, naturally, but on the second date, how was I to know?" Patsy began. "I came up to his apartment while he was in the shower and I slipped in with him. He looked at me a little funny, then he smiled, and we started soaping each other. By the time I was shampooing we were—how shall I put it—kind of attached. We never even left the bathroom and I'll tell you I had the shock of my life when we went into the den and there was Tony—my guy?—mixing a batch of martinis. He starts screaming at his brother, the twin, Joey, that he was a two-timing so-and-so, then he turns on me and says: 'Patsy, you got rocks in your head. Didn't you even notice that Joey's the one with the tattoo on his arm?' "

Claire was rolling with laughter and her drink shook in her hand. "You can't leave us this way," she said.

"Come on," the other girls bellowed. It was becoming a smoker, and why not, Claire thought. She felt free and filled with enormous expectations.

Patsy wriggled her rounded ass, downed her highball.

"Hey, I don't want any funny looks at the store and if any of the guys in Shipping find out, they'll drive me nuts. Promise?"

Voices rang out with "Promise."

Her gray eyes opened wide with excitement. "Well, the thing was, the whole idea began to turn me on. We had Tony's martinis. Three of us sitting there uptight watching Mike Wallace grill some termite religioso on *Sixty Minutes* and I'm thinking, well, this is not exactly fair to Tony. I've been with Joey when I should've been with him, then what am I going to do with Joey who is really a nice person while Tony and me are inside trying to do justice to the situation? So I took both their hands and I said: 'Look, I hate people to quarrel, especially brothers, more especially twins from the same egg, so let's square everything. Tony goes first because Joey's been there, then both of you if I'm still moving.' It's what I called a memorable evening in my diary."

Dinner was about to be served and over the fruit compote Leah proposed a toast.

Her glass of Taylor New York State Champagne in hand, she rose to her feet and grandiloquently observed: "Some of you girls only worked Drake's. Others of us have been around for years from Klein's on the Square to Macy's to Gemco and back and we're here to tell the story. We've worked good and bad seasons with merchandising people and buyers climbing on our backs, but none of us ever had a better boss than Claire Stuart . . ."

Milly squeezed Claire's hand with pride. "What people only think of you, babe?" Claire nodded. She was overwhelmed by the affectionate response of the women at Drake's.

"So from all of us, Claire"—the girls rose to their feet—"have a happy life with Bobby, but please stay with us and don't go to California."

There was a babble of cheers and amens, which resounded as stiff, grim-faced waiters were pulling away the fruit cups and dealing out salads. Leah left her table and embraced both Claire and Milly. Claire's life had become a festival.

"Claire, honey, you walk and half the girls go with you because they'll bring in some Nazi. You just tell Bobby if he starts pulling that housewife number on you that with the money you bring in, he'll be driving a Caddy for life."

Claire was in a quandary, which could not be resolved until Bobby returned. She had to give Drake fair notice and begin her buying for the winter season. Drake had promised her a new contract, stock options, and a complete package of benefits if she remained with the organization. She wasn't sure what she ought to do.

For the main course, a baron of beef was set up and the women formed a line beside a carver who hacked away cuts and placed them on their plates. It was like a cafeteria, and Claire's thoughts revolved around the elegance with which Micelli's corps would perform at her wedding. She had seen them in action at another wedding and knew that behind Papa's bluster, a really efficient group of professionals would be at work.

During lemon sherbet, demitasse, and Schrafft mints, a familiar face appeared at the doorway.

Mr. Eugene Drake himself. He was a self-assured man in his mid-sixties who had started out as a door-to-door tie salesman in the Depression, when executives were cutting their throats and he knew he could survive just about anything. He had introduced the dollar tie to New Yorkers; then, when he seemed to be at the peak of his success and was fondly known as Mr. Tie in the city, he had sold out in order to apply his cutthroat retailing techniques to the innocents swelling the arteries of suburbia. He had five stores and well over a thousand employees. From the moment he had met Claire, he recognized a natural, made her his personal assistant and then gave her control of the women's wear in the store. The figures jumped eighteen percent in her first year. Now, after five years, she had doubled the business and volume was running at somewhere over four million a year. Her impending marriage gave him sleepless nights.

"I feel like I'm losing a daughter," he informed Milly.

"She's not quitting so soon," Milly retorted with a smile. "So don't panic."

How, Claire wondered, could her mother be so astute and at the same time a willing victim to the fly-by-night nobodies who conned her so clumsily?

Drake cleared his throat and raised his arms in a gesture familiar to all the women who attended the monthly store meetings, which were like seminars on how to succeed, conducted by Drake with evangelical fervor.

"Ladies, forgive me for intruding on your evening for Claire, but I felt that the management of Drake's ought to be represented for a few minutes. Your executives and I felt that it would be only fitting to show what we think of Claire. So I wish to present her with a check for one thousand dollars on behalf of the management and you know I share your hope that she will enjoy her new life . . . but that we can expect her back for the July Fourth sale."

Claire kissed him and said, "Gene, that was lovely of you."

He was about to linger when Thelma from Lingerie, with a double brandy in her hand, rose and shouted: "You better get lost. We're bringing on the male strippers and blue movies."

For a moment, convinced she was serious, Drake nervously joined the blithe tittering, then rather uncermoniously galloped through the tables. After the previous year's Christmas party, which had turned into a drunken, frenzied orgy in the Packing Department, organized, he had heard, by this same Thelma, a sylphlike black girl rumored to be the Thursday late-closing mistress of his revered Mr. Sanderson in Personnel, just about anything was possible. Christ, without Claire at the helm there'd be anarchy. He dreaded the prospect of her leaving, even for her honeymoon.

Claire stood at the entrance of the room, kissing the girls goodnight, listening to last-minute dialectical advice: how to hold a man; never to douche herself dry; to schedule the silver on her insurance floater; to have kids; not to have kids because they all grew up to be selfish bastards and drug users; to keep thin.

Finally she was left with her mother. Milly's eyes crinkled with smoke from her low-tar Merit and her breath was malevolent with gin.

"Buddy's still in the city. Another business deal. That's his story and he's sticking to it. So I'm going to have a drink with the pianist. Laughs, you know. Don't wait up for me."

She watched her mother walk to the lounge where a slight, jaundiced man in a maroon shantung dinner jacket anxiously took her hand.

Claire made three trips in the elevator with her presents. She stacked them in the hall closet and decided she'd wait until Bobby returned before opening them all. It was past midnight when she tried to call Bobby. She felt her pulse quicken when she was told that he had checked out earlier that day. There was, however, a number where he could be reached. She put through another call and was surprised by the apprehension that stirred within her. An unfamiliar voice answered at the other end, startling her. He introduced himself as Gary Rubin and got Bobby to the phone.

"Where are you?" she asked.

"A man at the office invited me to stay with him. The Holiday Inn was getting depressing and expensive. How was the shower?"

"Okay," she muttered, suddenly joyless. "When do you think you'll be back?"

"A week or two."

She was thunderstruck.

"That means you'll be away a month."

"Don't make it sound like an accusation. There's a rush on this job. Before they can begin, my plans have to be approved . . . permits pulled."

"I'm sorry. It's just that I miss you so much and I'm so damned confused about when to give Drake notice. He gave me a thousand-dollar check and I was afraid to tell him. I won't deposit the check."

"Don't be naive. You're entitled to it."

"Are you okay for money?"

"A little tight. But I can make it juggling my credit cards."

"What's Mr. Rubin like? Gay?"

She heard him bellow with laughter.

"God, no. Just in the middle of a divorce."

She wanted the assurance that he loved her, but pride would not allow her to ask him. The separation was draining her, giving her the jitters.

"Love you, babe," he said, then hung up with what she imagined to be abruptness. She was tempted to call him back. Her mind was playing tricks and when she got into bed, she felt an irreparable loss as though the distance between them could no longer be measured in miles.

4

Rodeo Puerta, the shopping mall Leonard was building, had formerly been a parking lot. It had taken all of his resources to purchase it and begin development. It was lodged next to the American Savings Bank and was at the source of the three golden blocks that made up the shopping district of Rodeo Drive. The fight for retail space ensured that if he could continue to patch up his financing, he would be the major property owner on the highest-priced street in the country. Not even Fifth Avenue could get away with charging fifteen dollars a square foot for a store. The forty thousand square feet he would have when the project was completed meant that his property would bring in six million dollars a year. It would open new sophisticated techniques of maneuvering and leveraging his money, which would get him out of trouble.

Sitting in the site office, surveying the work, he faced the future with equanimity. Rodeo Puerta was on the east side of Rodeo Drive; there was easy access from the Beverly Wilshire Hotel, and it would catch the traffic from the major department stores on Wilshire Boulevard. Thus, when shoppers had had enough of Neiman-Marcus and Saks they could cross over and shop at any of the twenty stores Leonard was developing.

After considerable doubt, Leonard had decided to go with a Mediterranean-style development. He had liked the small *paseos* he had seen in Marbella, which provided a quiet haven for people who did not want to be hurried when shopping. There was the further advantage of not having to cross Rodeo with its permanent stream of traffic. The facade of Rodeo Puerta was in terra cotta; the stores would be uniform with red peppermint awnings, walkways done in gray-veined travertine marble, accented by black slate. An escalator would take customers to a second level where there would be a Spanish bodega with tables outside.

Rodeo Puerta would have a unity and become the premier development on Rodeo Drive, and Leonard reveled in his triumph. He had made his money in grotesque shopping centers and cheap housing developments in Orange County and the Valley. He had believed that the market would never dry up, but inflation and soaring interest rates on mortgages had virtually driven him into the ground. He had some eighteen hundred unsold units speckled through his developments and the carrying charges had brought him to his knees. His cash flow had dried up and he was becoming desperate.

However, many of his anxieties disappeared when he considered the astonishing change in Hillary. She had never been happier, more fulfilled, and when he saw her and Bobby crossing the street arm in arm, he felt secure. Hillary had made great strides in the year that she had been with Disegno Contemporaneo. She had a new sense of purpose, was learning the business. He knew that his financial problems would have been over had she married either of the two men he had introduced her to, but he took comfort in the fact that her relationship with Bobby possessed a solidarity that had been absent in her previous entanglements. Maybe it was for the best that she should be interested in a penniless architect who had talent.

As long as she was happy, nothing else mattered. In the weeks since she had met Bobby, there was new life in her and the past appeared to be buried. He wondered, though, if it would come to anything. Bobby was engaged and apparently determined to get married and he wasn't sure if Hillary could accept Bobby's warmth and friendship, let him go, and possibly find herself fighting another period of manic depression. He dreaded the prospect of seeing her ill again.

He left his office and walked out to meet them. The look of adoration on Hillary's face as she and Bobby approached him was clear evidence of her infatuation. He was glad to see that Bobby had adopted a more informal way of dressing. He was wearing beige jeans, a short-sleeved striped shirt, and tennis sneakers. Hillary had taken him shopping at the Gap when it was apparent that he was running out of clothes. He had gone through Bobby's latest set of drawings that morning.

"We've just been to the house," Bobby began, "and I changed my mind again."

"Nothing major, I hope," Leonard asked. He leaned over and kissed Hillary. "How's my honey?"

"Couldn't be better." She glowed; when she was with Bobby the girl gave off a profound sweetness that was mesmerizing in its vibrant beauty.

"I want to do a cathedral ceiling in the bedroom . . . let it make a statement. Since we've got to redo the roof completely, I don't think it'll add more than a thousand to the cost. What do you think?"

Since Leonard was already in debt for something like seventy-five million dollars, the question had a certain absurdity. However, he respected Bobby. He had adhered to the budget, knocked himself out coming up with inventive solutions that would not soak Leonard. There was about Bobby a probity and idealistic innocence that he had come to cherish.

"You're the boss."

"No, you are," Bobby said. "It'll be worth it, setting off the master suite. The other thing is, I think we ought to move the Habitat unit to one of the end rooms. See, if you can have a room with climate changes, the buyers will want to show it off to their friends without taking them into the master. Sometimes people don't make the bed . . . the maid's taking her pregnancy test or having root canal, right?"

Leonard and Hillary laughed. Bobby had that knack of putting people at their ease. He was always a bit off center and he never ruffled people with a remark, but without trying he made everyone aware of the fact that his point of view was a bit different; this very lack of effort enhanced his charm. They were idiots in New York not to have given someone like him an opportunity. He'd draw more business to Hayward than any of the guys working under Rubin.

"Go ahead. I think you've done a helluva job in the time you've had."

"Gary said he'd get one of the juniors to pull the permits."

"Fine. I can line up a crew to begin by mid-June."

"Sounds good." He looked from Leonard to Hillary and there was a hesitancy in his manner. "Well, then, I can make my plane reservation this afternoon. Head home and tie things up and be back by the middle of July if it's okay with everyone at the office." Hillary stood transfixed, speechless with disappointment, then turned away. "One other thing, provided you're not busy tonight. I'd like to take you, Ann, and of course Hillary, to dinner."

"Of course."

"Any place you prefer?"

"Wherever you like," Hillary finally said.

"I've heard that Giovanni's is excellent."

"I'll make the reservation," Leonard advised him. "If Giovanni doesn't know your name, he'll tell you he won't be able to seat you until eleven o'clock."

Disegno Contemporaneo was one of those outrageously expensive showrooms that specialized in modish Italian designs, giraffe-like stainless steel lamps, glass tables inlaid with brass, poured-concrete coffee tables, modernistic all-glass backgammon tables that went for five thousand. However, the purpose and principal business of the operation was its resident interior design department.

Once a customer found her way inside and showed any confusion, one of the staff immediately made an appointment to visit the naïf at home where drawings, color schemes, fabric coordination took precedence over the retail side of the business. The designers worked on thirty percent of whatever was purchased and would arrange visits to all of the "to the trade only" showrooms where everything was tagged in code. Hillary's function was to attract customers from her father's set, develop leads, and allow one of the pros to get her hooks into the victim. She performed this task with peerless skill and had earned close to fifteen thousand in her first year. But no one, she least of all, took this very seriously. She was Leonard Martinson's daughter, came to work in a Rolls Camargue, and had a personal allowance of five thousand a month which she found impossible to spend; she unwittingly practiced thrift because when you have the freedom to buy anything and have had entrenched wealth, it no longer made any difference whether you spent a few hundred for a dress or a couple of thousand from a designer collection.

Hillary kept no regular hours and had most of her appointments outside the showroom. She usually lunched with other decorators on Robertson, went to auctions at Sotheby's and occasionally visited a client at home to "open" for one of the high-pressure specialists at D.C. She enjoyed the work. It was not taxing but in the last three and a half weeks, since meeting Bobby, her hours had become a joke. She appeared once a week with an empty order book but no one dared say a word, for Leonard could open the golden pavilions of the rich; in any event Hillary was exquisite decoration, and brought with her the cachet of knowing the Ahmansons, the Tapers, the McCullochs, the Chandlers, all of the grand old money of Los Angeles. Introductions she effected were worth their weight in platinum commissions. The firm entertained hopes that, when Leonard began construction of the Marine Mutual Insurance building in Century City, Disegno Contemporaneo would get the job. It was impossible to calculate what this would be worth.

To her credit, Hillary had no illusions about her position; when she returned home and called the manager to inform him that she would not be in for the rest of the week, there was no demurral at his end, just a servile *"Senz'altro, s'immagini."* It was an ideal way to conduct one's business life.

As she dressed for dinner in her white kid-glove-leather St. Laurent jeans and a lime green Courrèges wide-stitched cowl neck sweater, she thought she had never looked more attractive and desirable. For comfort she often wore a bra but this evening she wanted to be free, loose, and make certain that Bobby could glimpse her breasts through the knit. He was waiting downstairs with Ann and her father, having cocktails in the living room, and when she appeared he rose, shook her hand with tenderness, and there was no hesitation when she offered her cheek to be kissed. Rather than disconcerting him, as was her intention, she became flustered—this was the first time he had kissed her.

They sat opposite Ann and her father. She was pleased to see that Bobby was enjoying the Beluga caviar canapés she had told the chef to prepare, and he had evidently enjoyed the Perrier-Jouët champagne she had insisted be served. She liked the gay artwork on the bottle and it seemed appropriate to mark the occasion of his departure. Ann was examining his drawings of the house with approval. With Elton John singing softly on the perfectly balanced Bang & Olufsen speakers, and Hillary smiling, no one could have detected the anguish tormenting her. She fought valiantly to combat the grief welling up inside her.

Everything she thought she ever wanted in a man was about to be taken from her by a force of circumstances she could not control or come to terms with. It was as though the gods had decreed that she must never be happy, know the exhilaration that comes with falling in love. Everything that had happened to her before Bobby was meaningless, and that she could not have him appeared to be some mystical expiation of sins she had committed.

"We'll be sorry to lose you. You've become one of our little group," Ann said with genuine affection.

"It's only for a month or so."

He had intended to add that they would adore Claire, but the wistful look on Hillary's face prevented him. He had trodden a dangerous line between friendship and the natural tenderness that Hillary had inspired in him. Their behavior had been circumspect, blameless, and he could not suppress some regret for his fine resolutions. Sitting beside her, he found it difficult not to reach out and touch her. The civility of Leonard, the kindness of Ann, and the way he had been made to belong to this glamorous dream life, which he had never before imagined, intoxicated him. To repay Leonard by seducing his daughter was beyond him. At times when he was alone with Hillary he felt trapped by his mortality, but he would not permit himself the luxury of conjuring up the possibilities that existed. He was free, he had choices to cope with, and he wished that he were capable of the turbulent involvement that lay before him like the Waterford crystal champagne tulip.

He'd turned his car in and Ann had taken him to the house, and when Hillary asked him if he needed a lift to the airport he was tempted to give in.

"Gary's taking me . . . but thanks."

There was a vague hint of pain in her eyes, but she shrugged it off. When he was alone with her in her car on the way to Giovanni's, there were things he wanted to say, but could not bring himself to utter. Hillary drove slowly, unusual for her, he thought, and he got the impression that she wanted to prolong what little time they had left alone.

"I'm going to miss you," she said as she turned onto Rodeo Drive and stopped at a light. "I guess I shouldn't be telling you that."

Ahead of them carhops were dashing like relay racers to and from cars outside of Giovanni's restaurant. A small pink sign, designed to the owner's signature, was lit by two soft spotlights above the entry.

"You know my situation," he said finally.

"People change their minds, don't they?"

A carhop leaped to get Hillary's door open and knew her by name. Bobby waited for her at the curb. A doorman opened the door for them and they were thrust into a charming Italian albergo that had waiters in dinner suits and a quiet dignified formality about it. At the entry stood Ed Giovanni, a tall elegant man with those cherubic perfect features of child film stars. He had at one time been a bit-part player and women constantly thrust themselves upon him.

"Good evening, Hillary. Your father is in the bar." He kissed Hillary. Above them on the balconied second floor people leaned forward to see if they recognized a famous face.

Hillary walked a few steps ahead toward the circled bar with its covey of minuscule tables and Bobby whispered:

"Would you see that I get the check, Mr. Giovanni?"

"Sure. It's Ed." They shook hands and Bobby gave him

his name. "Your table's ready whenever you are . . . no rush, though."

Ann and Leonard were at a small table crammed in with friends talking and they waved to them. Ann said they were going to have another round. Hillary had found a corner at the bar.

"A split okay with you or do you want to switch?" Bobby asked her.

"Champagne's fine."

The bartender brought them Veuve Cliquot, wrapped it in a napkin and deftly popped the cork. Bobby and Hillary clinked glasses and she said: "Here's to goodbyes."

"I won't be gone that long."

"But when you come back, it won't be the same, will it?" He nodded. "Can I ask you something?"

"Naturally. Anything."

"You've been here almost a month. It seems like a day."

"To me as well."

"Bobby . . ." She leaned close to him and her mouth was inches away from his. "Have you, even for a second, thought it would be nice to stay here, you know, not go back . . . sort of pretend that you didn't have another life?"

Several people stood behind them, closing off Leonard's view of them and Bobby pressed close to her and lightly kissed her.

"Yes, you have. What's stopping you—no, forget I asked that. I retract it. Nothing would make me put you on the spot. It's not fair. It's just that all this has been so unexpected and I can't help how I feel . . . caring for you."

He was faced, he knew, with an insoluble dilemma. No matter what he did he could not justify himself.

"I have loyalties. I made a commitment, Hillary, and I have to live with myself," he said without persuading himself that he could overcome the ambivalence piercing his mind. "Is it possible to be in love with two women?"

"Anything's possible." She sipped her champagne and her face became reflective and more beautiful, he thought, than he could remember. "I trust you. You'll be able to resolve it."

"It's not that easy. You know about Claire, but she's not even heard your name."

"Do you compare us, I mean mentally?"

"No."

"Because you've slept with her?"

"That's part of it . . . experiences."

"Shared?"

"Uh-huh. She's a wonderful girl. I've had my periods of not knowing what to do . . . especially when I quit my job and she hung in, believing in me . . . and frankly, Hillary, there was nothing that I could believe in or hang on to except her."

A look of resignation came over her face and Bobby clutched her arm, unwilling to hurt her.

"It doesn't sound romantic."

"How can it be . . . all the time? People have lives . . . disappointments, the hassles of pulling yourself together."

"I know about that. Money isn't some invincible wall that insulates you—from breaking. I've been there. Nobody to blame but myself. My father's a reliable backboard and he's had hell from me; and believe me, there are times when we could strangle each other . . . and the other men I've known"—she laughed—"after my crazy period, well, they weren't you. I never felt as though . . . it's hard for me to put into words . . . I could surrender." She rested her chin in her palm and propped her elbow on the bar. "Claire. She must be something else."

"You're very different."

"It's ridiculous to admit it because I don't believe it myself. But the minute I saw you, the first night when I came off the tennis court, I fell in love with you. Love at first sight in this day and age! It's not supposed to happen. We're all too smart and experienced. We know better. . . . My father's signaling us for dinner."

As he held her hand and led her through the smoky bar penetrated by happy gabbling voices and the chamber music Giovanni's played discreetly, he felt powerless, caught in some insufferable schizoid pattern of modern life without any idea of how to extricate himself. Had he fallen in love with Los Angeles, a way of living represented by the Martinsons, or what? But at the bottom of it was Hillary, elusive to everyone but him, oddly vulnerable and yet with a self-assurance he admired. Bobby's head was swimming as people looked at him, nodded, waved as though they knew him, recognized his face. He was in Beverly Hills, all right.

"No one's allowed to have everything," she said with girlish sweetness while Giovanni took them to their round table in the center of the room, displaying them to everyone in the restaurant.

"The trouble with us is that we want it all," he said, yielding to bewitchment, enthralled by the moment, the prisoner of Hillary and time.

Giovanni's menu consisted of sonorous arias of Northern Italian cuisine, followed by an emblazoned challenge: "Just ask for it and we'll do our best." There were no prices on his menu, a first for Bobby. He deferred to Leonard on the choice of wine with dinner and felt himself caught up in the reckless lark of a society dedicated to pleasure. It was a relief for once not to skimp, to do things first class and to be treated as if he were someone special, a man of substance. His face flushed with drink, he listened attentively to Leonard's plans for Rodeo Puerta and how the future would be laid out and belong to him once he was able to persuade Frank Dunlop to approve a design for the sixty-five-million-dollar Marine Mutual Insurance building.

"It's something you might think about," he suggested to Bobby. "Tim will show you the specs." He groaned and Ann touched his hand.

"Don't worry. It'll turn out all right."

"I'd like it in writing," Leonard said with distaste. He leaned over to Bobby. "See, Frank Dunlop's a thug. He doesn't belong here. For two years now, since he came out here, he's been trying to break into society, using me as his stalking horse. Christ, the guy donated ten thousand dollars to SHARE so he could get his name on the *Angel* page following Johnny Carson's. It's lunacy, of course, but Dunlop expected to be accepted socially by all these people. He's had parties which no one shows up to except Hollywood riffraff, but he never relents. Sinatra, Carson, Norman Lear are regularly invited. Then he phones Tina Galick at the *Times* and George Christy of the *Reporter* with his guest list. I think they once went to one of his *dos*"—Leonard pronounced the word with such acidulous disdain that Bobby almost had some sympathy for the luckless Dunlop—"and the only noteworthy people were a couple from *Hee Haw* and some people who'd appeared as contestants on the *Gong Show*. They marked Dunlop's cards after that. I am, unfortunately, saddled with the man. He brazenly tries to poach my guests, then complains to me when they don't come to his house. But I need him," he lamented.

"Leonard, I'll look at the building plans. Have you got any idea what he wants?"

"No. Nor does he."

Medleys of light pastas appeared as hors d'oeuvres, accompanied by a couple of bottles of silky Meursault, petit limestone salads with honey mustard dressing, and then bass poached in fennel, fragrant white veal with rosemary, and more wine. Bobby had never eaten such a dinner, and as he approached his espresso with Cointreau he was prevailed upon to assess the magical feathery light zabaglione. However, no one ate very much. They *tasted*, then moved on. It was, for Bobby, a lesson in dining, somewhat different from the country club prime rib and baked Idahos filled with ponds of sour cream and chives.

During dinner, Hillary remained attentive, a bit distracted, and he was faintly relieved that they were not alone. He did not wish to make promises either to her or to himself that he could not keep. The idyll was fading into a new dawn. The captain presented him with the check, just six bucks and change under three hundred, and Bobby magnanimously handed him his MasterCharge. Leonard shook his hand, Ann kissed him, and they thanked him without effusiveness. After all, he'd become one of them, a blossom in their arbor. They diplomatically bid him goodnight and left him with Hillary to wait until the transaction was over.

She and Bobby waited some time, almost thirty minutes, before the Captain reappeared. He brought Hillary another Cointreau.

"Could Mr. Giovanni see you for a moment, sir?" he asked Bobby with nervous cordiality.

Bobby followed the captain to an alcove behind the bar where he found Giovanni sitting at the owner's private table. Giovanni smiled warmly, displaying magnificent actor-only caps. He beckoned Bobby to sit, offering him a glass of Poland water from his bottle, which Bobby declined.

"Is something the matter?"

"Nothing important. I just didn't want it to be awkward for you."

"In what way?"

"Well, Bobby," he said the name as though it were part of a mellifluous lyric, "I was with a party, otherwise this wouldn't have happened. But our cashier has to get an approval on anything over a hundred dollars. And . . ."

"Oh, Christ, I haven't been home for weeks. I must be over my limit."

"Sure," Giovanni noted amicably. "Happens all the time. But since I wasn't on the spot, things got a little out of hand. A MasterCharge supervisor got on the phone and instructed her to cut the card. She had no choice." Giovanni pushed over an envelope and Bobby found his card, snipped into small pieces. "It's part of our contract with them. If I were there, I wouldn't have allowed her to do it. The hell with MasterCharge. I'd have covered it."

Bobby felt shaken. He took out his wallet and displayed American Express, Visa, and Diners, then thought better of acting precipitously.

"They're probably over their limit too," he said with consternation. Why hadn't he let Claire wire him a few hundred? "I've been out here and things obviously piled up at home. I'll be working at Hayward and Associates." He fished out his razor-thin pack of traveler's checks. He had sixty dollars left in the folder. "I'll be coming back in July."

Giovanni did not lose his amicable expression. "You're an architect then?"

"Yeah . . . who pays his bills late," he added with self-reproach.

"Don't let it worry you. The rich pay late. That's why I don't have house accounts any longer."

"Can I send you a check?"

"Don't bother with a check. You'll settle when you get back."

"Are you sure it's okay?"

"Certainly. These things happen. In fact, I owe you an apology."

"Don't be silly." He looked around, hoping Hillary would not appear and witness his ignominy. "What's a fair tip, Ed?"

"Thirty-five for the waiter and fifteen for the captain. I'll add it in for you."

"Shall I sign it?"

"It's unnecessary." He offered his hand and Bobby shook it eagerly, then returned to Hillary, who was staring languidly at her reflection in the gold mirror across the room.

"You ready, Hillary?"

"Any problem?"

"No. Ed wanted to ask me a few questions about enlarging the restaurant. He's got to be one of the nicest guys I ever met."

"It's his business. He's *the* ladies' man in town. God knows how he keeps it up. He's almost fifty."

Rubin lived in a small garden apartment conversion on Spaulding in south Beverly Hills near the high school, and when Hillary found a spot beside the building Bobby invited her in. Gary had a date with a lady in Marina del Rey and would be staying over. The moment Hillary was inside the apartment, Bobby knew that he had made a mistake by asking her in. The look they exchanged left no doubt for them.

She sank into Rubin's Castro Convertible and regarded the surroundings without interest. He sat beside her and reflexively held her hand.

"A lot's happened to me, Bobby . . . before I met you."

"So? Does it matter?" he replied good-naturedly, reflecting on Giovanni's smoothness and how he'd helped Bobby avoid an embarrassing scene that would have destroyed Hillary's illusions and closed the evening on a sour note. He broke away from Hillary, went into the small kitchen and located a bottle of Drambuie. He held up the bottle and she nodded.

"I keep thinking about Claire . . . you and her."

A nervous pulsation throbbed in his temple.

"I do all the time," he admitted.

"How do you feel?"

"Lousy." He handed her the drink and fell opposite her. If only they could suspend time, moment, they could both escape. "But someth pened to me."

She pushed the shaggy forelock off his forehead, leaned down and kissed him. Before he could think, his hand had moved around her waist and she was pressing against him on the floor.

"Do you belong to Claire or yourself?"

"Myself."

"Then I can have part of you. There could be room for me in your life." She lay on her side and guided his hand under her sweater along the silky filament of her breasts and he kissed her neck. Her white breasts were now exposed. Neither of them could protest. They had found the harmony that had been intended for them and they could not turn back. There was a smell about her of honey and he was intoxicated by her body, the deftness of her fingers and mouth. He had his trousers off, then his shirt, and he went back to the sofa and sat down. She wriggled out of her jeans—she was wearing white satin bikini panties—and she sat across his bare knees and fed her breasts into his mouth while stroking his cock. Then she bent down and with her tongue tantalized the head of it. His fingers groped between her thighs and she was wet. She shuddered repeatedly and finally he eased inside her while she sat up, facing him, delirious with excitement.

"Don't hold back," she whispered, "give me everything."

When he could no longer resist, his body shook wildly and her frenzy increased, then she turned on her side. Come dripped down her thighs and she covered her fingers with it and licked them voraciously and at the same time began to lick the head of his cock. She moved his fingers into her vagina, one by one, until to his disbelief his whole hand was inside her and he wanted to stop, fearful of hurting her. "Make a fist," she pleaded and under her spell, he did as she asked and his whole hand, fingers clenched, was jammed in. She rested on her knees, eyes closed, and held his wrist tightly and rhythmically pumped his fist further and further into herself. She lost control of herself in a spate of wild multiple orgasms. The experience was so violently erotic that he found he could not stop. Anything to please her excited and thrilled him. Finally he removed his hand and she seemed in a trance for a few moments, then she began kissing him all over, her voice trilling words of endearment. She lay beside him on the sofa, exultant, and he embraced her, could not keep from touching her and returning her frantic sentiments.

She spent the night in his arms on the sofa, clinging to him, and at dawn she stirred, found some instant coffee and made a small pot. She was not self-conscious and she had shorn him of any modesty he might have possessed. The two of them sitting naked watching the sun come up seemed natural, so much a part of nature, that he marveled at the power of their intimacy.

She watched him shave and they squeezed into the small stall shower together, soaped each other's backs, kissed and made love standing under the water. It was all he could do to throw his clothes into his bag and change into a pair of jeans.

At seven, Gary Rubin called and told him he was driving back from the Marina. They planned to have breakfast and stop by the office before leaving for the airport. Without complaint, Hillary accepted the arrangement. She was thoroughly composed and Bobby felt another surge of tenderness for her.

"This had to happen to us," she said.

"I know that. I guess we both did. No regrets?"

"None . . . there couldn't be." She smiled bleakly at him, a captive of the defeat that engulfed them. "But life has to go on . . . you and Claire. She'll never know and maybe if she's the kind of person I think she is, if she ever found out I hope she'd understand that this wasn't just a cheap lay. . . convenience, that sort of thing." She had a quality of stoicism in her observations that touched him so deeply that he could have wept. "Funny to imagine it, but the next time I see you, you'll be a married man."

"I do care about you."

He kissed her neck and her mouth and the feel of her calmed the upheaval he was experiencing. She had pinned her hair up after the shower and her neck had a melodic grace. Her eyes sparkled. He had seen her swallow some pills in the kitchen, but he did not comment. He'd heard about California vitamin freaks. She was lucid and not as overwrought as he had anticipated. He was the one with the flutters.

"Of course you do," she said, holding his hand against her face. "You're the real thing, Bobby. I knew it the minute I saw you." She lowered her eyes. "The last thing I intended was to disrupt your life . . . and even though you love Claire and you're on your way to getting married, don't ever feel you were unfaithful."

More than she, he was aware of his lack of guilt and shaken by the depth of his commitment to her.

"Hillary, I'm so goddamned confused, I can't think straight."

"Don't be. You've got an opportunity out here and you'll do just fine. We'll see each other from time to time and it'll be fine. I'm not going to climb on your back and make a nuisance of myself. Honestly, Bobby, don't worry about me. I'll be just fine. We'll be friends." Her eyes told another story. "I better get going now." He walked her to the door, holding her tightly. "I'll always care for you a little, but don't think about it. It'll just be there . . ."

She closed the door and he stood silently staring at it, then he rushed out, caught her at the car and held her for a final minute.

"I feel exactly the way you do . . . but it's over," he said.

"Don't fret. It was good while it lasted."

5

He was in a cold sweat during the flight to New York, drinking too much, unable to concentrate on the design plans he had picked up at the office for the Marine Mutual building. Leonard was not one to procrastinate. Having mentioned over dinner he had problems with the design, he had a portfolio of rejected plans waiting at Hayward's office when Bobby stopped by for his paycheck en route to the airport. He'd forgotten to telephone Claire with his flight number. The fact was that he preferred not to be met, but rather to head up to Westport, collect his thoughts, and then see her. He couldn't face an emotional reunion, lie to her, lead her on, pretend that he was the same man who'd left a month ago in search of a job, restless, insecure, with no vision of the future. He had in effect put aside a life he had developed in Los Angeles, and although he might have been guilty of rationalizing, returning to Westport was a step backward.

He caught a bus to Grand Central from the airport, bought his ticket, catching the commuter train, and he found himself light years removed from the men shoving at the bar for their martinis. The latest Steinbrenner/Reggie Jackson civil war on the Yankees occupied the men, along with moans about inflation, the shellacking everyone was taking in the stock market. It was another man's life, no longer his.

Peering bewilderedly through the grimy train windows at wives picking their husbands up in station wagons, he imagined at times that he could see Hillary, waiting expectantly for him, her open face creased in a fervid smile. That she was a continent away agitated him, burst through the web of fantasy he knew would collapse the moment he stepped off the train and entered the familiar world of his past.

It was close to six and Claire would be leaving Drake's. He decided to take a cab back to his house and call her from there. More than anything he wanted to sleep, to readjust, but he had to see Claire.

When he arrived home, he discovered that the Rolls was out of the garage. He walked into the study and amid a mass of Standard and Poor reports, prospectuses for new stock issues, he found his father's appointment book. Turning to May 25 he saw his father's crabbed handwriting announcing: "Lion's Dinner Dance at CC. Drinks 6."

He wished his father were there so that they could have talked over his trip to L.A. Bobby would explain what had happened and his father would listen, quietly smoking his cigarillo, occasionally sipping his bourbon old-fashioned, and in an offhand way give him the right advice. Jack Canaday loved Claire. She was a success, epitomizing the new woman, but there was nothing abrasive in her modernity. Rather, she embodied a genteel tradition that agreeably blended with the women's movement. Jack was crazy about her and Bobby sensed that his father would tell him that the L.A. thing would blow over; give it a few days, get back with Claire, and pretend that Hillary Martinson did not exist. What nettled Bobby was that his father's appreciation of the situation would be the right one, sensible, practical, the honest thing to do—and it stuck in his throat.

He brought his stuff up to the garage apartment, took a shave and shower, then loitered by the phone with a vodka martini. He roused himself from his despondency to call Claire. He felt himself pumped up by the drinks and nervous energy. It would be impossible to sleep in his state.

There was a wonderful elation in her voice.

"Bobby, it's so great to have you back. I can't wait to see you."

"I missed you, babe," he said, meaning it, hearing his father's voice. The image of Hillary receded in his consciousness. She suggested dinner at her apartment. Milly was out for the evening and Claire could throw a couple of steaks on the barbecue. They would be alone, catch up on things. She craved intimacy and something told him to resist it.

"How about the Harbor Inn?" he asked. It was her favorite restaurant.

"Fine, if you're up to it."

"Eight-thirty."

"I'll see you there. I love you."

Claire took a long bath, luxuriating in the smell of the Vitabath, carefully shaved her legs, and slid into the new model flesh-toned satin panties and matching bra that Maidenform had brought out. She twirled on her toes in the full-length mirror, flicked her hair back off her forehead, and thought she was not overstating the case when she said to her reflection:

"Babe, you're irresistible."

Her excitement increased with a straight Stolichnaya she took from the freezer, then she wondered as she browsed through the medicine cabinet in search of her Norell if Milly had ripped it off. No, it was there behind Milly's selection of pharmaceutical wonders. Wedged between Tuinal and Dexamyl, it stood on a pyramid made up of bottles of Valium and the unlabeled bottle of black and orange capsules that Milly wantonly called nuclear bombers. She dabbed the Norell on her wrists and temples, and rejoiced in her sensuality while splashing some along her thighs.

She pulled on a black linen skirt and a red Indian silk blouse, embroidered in black and yellow. She left the top three buttons undone and trickled some more Norell along the cleavage that was exposed.

Driving down to the Sound with the top down, she felt sexy, wild, exultant. She was early; cruising past the Harbor Inn, she parked on a narrow stretch of road that overlooked the Sound. The day had been intolerably hot. It was cooling down. The wind furrowed the water and people in sailboats caught by surprise leaped to their jibs and ropes. The world was gorgeous, Claire thought. She sat behind the wheel of the car breathing deeply the coarse fresh saline smell of the water. The wild flowers clustered around the trees blinded her with splashes of color as the sunlight fragmented into fiery spokes. In a few minutes she'd see him. They'd be together.

She gave the carhops at the Harbor a flagrant smile and the boys, slouched behind the striped blue-and-white awning waiting for cars to arrive, hungrily looked at her. She exuded that confidence of a woman who had everything, mysterious, beautiful, elusive. The restaurant had a terrace, and she stopped at the maître d's desk to see if he had their reservation. Legibly printed next to eight-thirty was "Canaday, 2." Breathless with anticipation, she walked to the bar, which was already crowded. The Harbor Inn drew the smart crowd from Westport and Greenwich, people who weren't afraid to tip their captain five dollars. A few single men sitting at the marine-varnished, parquet-topped bar smiled hopefully at her and in her condition of loving the world she smiled back, fearlessly, aware that she gave off the scent of another man's woman. She could afford to be bold. She was secure.

Bobby was habitually late and she punctual. It was something that she accepted and running true to form while she nursed her vodka martini, she saw that the clock behind the bar had moved to eight-thirty. At a quarter to nine the bartender asked if she was ready for a fresh drink. A few of the unattached men began to wonder if she was indeed on her own and one of them might luck out. She watched a professional singles operator in his thirties conduct a skywriting pantomime with the bartender to indicate that her drink was to be put on his tab; then, lighting a cigarette and scooping up his Dupont lighter, he pulled the seat of his brown seersucker trousers off his rump and set out on his voyage of conquest. She was relieved that the pickup had taken this long. When she was in Manhattan, she couldn't even get through a bar door before half a dozen guys sprinted up to her. In good old gentlemanly low-key Westport, it had taken twenty minutes. He was in advertising, his own brand-new firm naturally, thirty-five, separated, working out the settlement with Godzilla, and he'd come out with his skin barely covering his flesh. He realized how much he'd missed by marrying young, what a burden children were, having interfered with his current pursuits of jogging, dancing at Regine's with models, and racquetball. He amused her, but she wouldn't let him pay for her drink. She was waiting for her fiancé. Ceremoniously wrapping his cocktail napkin around the bottom of his glass, the man retreated.

She was beginning to worry about Bobby. She asked for some change to call him. She walked to the pay phone and caught sight of Bobby at the entrance. He seemed nonplussed for a moment as she ran to him with hands outstretched. Her arms were around his neck and she was kissing his face. Her eyes closed as her lips moved to his.

"I thought maybe you'd fallen asleep," she said, not sure why she felt like apologizing and breaking down at the same time.

His eyes were bloodshot and his pallor gave him a worn harried look at odds with his triumphant return.

"You need some sun," she said solicitously, entwining her hand in his.

"I never got the chance. There was so much going on. I had to bring some work home. I'm not directly involved, but the developer asked me for my ideas."

"I knew it would happen."

The maître d' took them to their table and despite his fatigue Bobby felt a curious and unexpected lift at seeing Claire again. There was an energetic beauty about her, a driving ambitiousness that she communicated to him. He ordered a bottle of Moët to celebrate their reunion and in the glow of candlelight he watched her smiling with such love that he couldn't help but yield to her mood.

"Babe, even when I was down, you believed in me. Why? Blind faith or what?"

"It was just a question of time before you broke out. You're the sort of man who needed rejection to bring out your best. And I think the change of environment did it. You weren't forced to hold back. I can't wait to go out there with you."

They clinked glasses to their new life in Los Angeles. As they had done so often before, they ordered the Chateaubriand with Béarnaise sauce for two, medium rare, no surprises, no unfathomable mysteries to explore between them. They had tailored their relationship to fit their personalities so perfectly that at times they both had the sense of already being married. Just about the only decision they had not reached accord on was when they would start a family, but still they had a loose game plan. Bobby would have to be secure in his position and they wanted to be in a house.

"Madeleine said she'd start sending us the rental section of the L.A. *Times* and she'd check out anything that would appeal to us. I told her we could go to four hundred—with both of us working."

"There's no such thing as a four hundred dollar apartment in L.A.!" He had seen Madeleine for dinner at an actors' hangout the first week he'd been in Los Angeles, then lost touch with her. "I ran into her one night when I was with the Martinsons at a club called Pips," he said with a frown. "I don't know what the hell she's up to, but I kind of felt embarrassed seeing her. The guy she was with must have been in his sixties."

"A producer or director probably," Claire countered quickly. Any innuendoes about her oldest friend tended to unsettle her.

"She's caught up in the whole show business thing. I hope for her sake it comes to something. By the way, you won't recognize her. She's lost twenty or thirty pounds and she's . . . oh, what the hell, it's not important."

Claire was vexed and she implored Bobby to tell her what he meant.

"Hey, I'm no moralist and shit, we've all known each other forever." He hesitated, poured some more champagne, becoming a bit tipsy. "I think she's hustling. It's none of my business."

The prospect of her maid of honor turning tricks dismayed Claire and she quickly changed directions.

"Have you got any idea where we should live?"

"West L.A. or Santa Monica. We could probably find something small for five or six hundred."

"That high?"

"Nothing's cheap in L.A. Unless we went to the Valley, and I don't think you'd like it there."

"I could probably get a job at Bullock's or Neiman's, don't you think?"

"I don't know a thing about the department stores there, babe. Gene's bound to give you a good reference."

"Oh, God, I wish I could see into the future," she said,

flinching. "The thought of giving him notice worries me. I mean, if he asks me to stay on longer and train someone, what do I do? I know I'm going to love Los Angeles, but at times it scares me, starting again, new people, making my way . . ."

"It'll take time, but Claire, you've got a real talent too, so don't you sell yourself short."

"My problem has always been that I want to set the world on fire. I'm in a terrible hurry. I can tell you to be patient, but I can't take my own advice. I've been reading about Rodeo Drive for years now and I've fantasized about how to break into a street like that. Now that we're actually going out there to live, I feel sort of lost and nervous."

At bottom she was a vulnerable small-town girl with high-flown ambitions, which he hoped she'd one day realize. The domestic role as a wife, he was convinced, would never suit her and would ultimately damage her spirit. Among other things, what endeared Claire to him and everyone who came in contact with her was her dynamism and inventiveness. She had that passion which one encounters only in exceptional people and he felt compelled to shore up her confidence. They skipped coffee and dessert and he was aware that he had forced her to have dinner out because he was afraid. She was eager to return to her apartment with him.

When he entered the neat little living room he had a feeling of claustrophobia, of being at the wrong place, of not belonging, of such anxious perturbation that he could barely focus on her face. She had a bottle of champagne in the fridge for the occasion but somehow he could not stir himself out of the morose, benumbed mood that he had settled into. He was a liar, cheating this girl, deceiving her, and his self-immolation became an insurmountable obstacle to intimacy. She had undressed in the bathroom and came out wearing the lime satin robe he had given her last Christmas.

"Don't you like your own taste?" she asked innocently, curling up next to him on the sale couch she had purchased for their future home months before L.A. had figured in their plans.

"I don't even know if I like myself."

"Jet lag."

"A guilty conscience."

She was not put off by the implication.

"You don't have to tell me about it. I'm really not very curious."

They went to her bedroom. It too was smaller, daintier, fussier than he remembered, with its dressing table in a paisley fabric he had watched her sew during the winter as he read in bed or glanced at TV.

"I live in the world, Bobby. I'm a big girl. I don't need pictures drawn for me." She tried to help him, exculpate him from the guilt riddling him. "Fidelity's a mental state."

"It isn't for you, is it?"

"Hey, you know all about my lurid past . . . the two men I had before we got together. It happens, no one's a saint. It's just crazy to have regrets about that sort of thing."

"I don't, but I wish I did," he said bitterly.

He lay naked on her bed, feeling the fine smooth Irish linen, knowing that she had changed the bed after he had telephoned. They began to fool around without any real passion. It was just the playfulness of old lovers.

"You really want me to start asking questions . . . well, I'm not curious," Claire said apprehensively. "All I care about is that you've come back to me. Maybe I'm being too broadminded or too complacent . . . take your pick," she added with great amenability. He remained withdrawn; although he stroked her fondly, it was without desire. His heart wasn't in it. "You feel compelled to confess something. I'd prefer you not to. But we've always been honest with each other and I won't stop you."

"I don't want to hurt you."

"Well, then, stop it, because it is beginning to hurt." She was distressed. She was ill-suited in the role of whiner. She wanted to change the subject and she remembered that she had saved a number of unopened presents from her shower so that they could open them together. They lay motionless, unaroused, and she tried to compose herself. She prayed that he would stop looking at her, close his eyes, doze off, wake up refreshed and purged. His face was strained and to relax him she slowly and timorously rubbed his neck.

"I'm ashamed of myself," he said.

"Don't be. No apologies or explanations are necessary. I understand!" Indulgence offered a measure of safety, a path to the future.

He sat up in bed abruptly. She had never seen him so unstrung.

"Babe, I've got to tell you about it. I'm so fucking messed up."

"What's there to be upset about?"

It was one of those fatal questions which, because they were never guarded with each other, slipped out. One of Bobby's most endearing qualities was his inability to dissimulate; throughout his career as an architect it had caused him trouble. He always spoke his mind.

Haltingly, he told her about Hillary. She listened raptly, a slow paralysis creeping over her until she didn't know what the hell had hit her or even where she was. There was no phantom experience of drowning, as she thought there might be as she was gripped by panic; rather, she imagined herself trapped in an inferno with her hair in flames. Vainly she attempted to save herself from the searing pain by banging her head against a pillow. Bobby caught hold of her.

"Claire, stop it, please, please, baby." She was in a semiconscious state, able to absorb information but powerless to respond to it. "I couldn't help myself. I didn't want anything to happen that could touch us."

Tears of mortification trickled down his cheeks and automatically she touched his face to soothe him. The depth of his agony enveloped her. She had never seen him cry and was jolted out of her submissiveness.

"Well . . . what . . . I don't know . . . what'll we do?" she gasped, not sure of what she'd said.

She rested her head in the crook of his arm, looking into his eyes.

"I'm terrified," he said, "of going ahead with the wedding. Then leaving for L.A. like nothing happened—then seeing *her*. Waking up every day and thinking, am I going to betray you . . . cheat, have a lousy affair and even if I don't, you'll wonder if I am. There's been too much good between us for me to put you through this wringer. And anyway, who the hell am I that I should have so much power over you! It's not fair, Claire."

"She got to you."

He violently resisted the accusation.

"I swear she didn't want to do this. It just happened . . . without any logic or premeditation."

"Do you want to marry her?"

"I'm not sure about anything."

"Oh, Bobby, why did this have to happen to us and spoil everything?"

He gestured fruitlessly, thwarted by his failure to make clear the tragic enigma that had torn them apart. He was no closer to understanding it than she. She left the room and returned in a few minutes carrying a tray with champagne and glasses. She had no recollection of why she had done this. No irony was intended and she was beyond sarcasm or rebuke.

"I couldn't drink a thing," he said.

She sat on the edge of the bed, then placed the tray on the floor. Her mind was vague and a heavy lassitude settled over her.

"The wedding . . . ?"

"I'll pay whatever it is."

"You haven't got any money, Bobby . . . Bobby."

"I'll borrow it."

"I'll see what I can do." She was nauseous. "Look, is there a chance to save us? I mean, you're not going back to L.A. for a while yet. Couldn't we try? Couldn't we . . .?"

"Babe, how can we start off this way? It's you and me—the way we've moved each other—God."

She knew the more she persisted the more ground she was losing.

"Do you love her?"

"I don't know."

"Do you love me?"

"Yes," he replied with conviction, "and that's what makes this so complicated."

She felt worn out. She pressed herself, seeking some compromise.

"Is there any hope for us, Bobby?"

"How can I answer that?"

She knew at that moment he was lost to her, and as she watched him dress, noting every movement, the way he backed into his loafers, hitched his trousers, carelessly mis-buttoned his shirt, that she had never loved him more than at this minute and that life without him would be unendurable.

She lamely followed him to the door. He put his arms around her and hugged her tightly, as though they were comrades about to be separated by a long trip. When she returned alone to the bedroom she fought to keep herself together. Then she spotted the key to her apartment. He had left it on the bedside table. It was a Schlage key and she remembered painting it with red nail polish so that he wouldn't have to fumble with his other keys when he wanted to drop by. She rooted through her desk drawer for an envelope so that she could send it back to him, but she couldn't find any of her stationery. Her mother had commandeered her desk, using it as a make-up repository. In her obsessive search she stopped in the middle of the room, realizing that the task was absurd, a futile, humiliating gesture . . . and then she cracked. She became disoriented and she felt her mind splintering.

The lights were out in his parents' bedroom when Bobby returned home. He wished his father were still awake. On the hall table he found a note from him: "Welcome home, stranger. See you at breakfast." Beside the note was a telegram addressed to him. He shoved it in his pocket, climbed the stairs to his apartment and switched on the light. His mother had unpacked his clothes and made the bed. He sat down at his desk and gazed at the phone, torn between calling Claire and the inertia that crept over him. Could he possibly take back everything he'd said? He couldn't leave Claire to grieve. Yet hearing her voice, the vision of her lovely face weathering the shock with dignity, drained him. He fought with himself, picked up the phone, then laid the receiver on his desk blotter, which was filled with squiggles of insolvent designs that belonged to another day. The sound of the receiver off the hook had a disconcerting squawk. Eventually a martial voice on a recording ordered him to hang up.

He was unaccustomed to receiving telegrams except

from the government—he'd served eighteen months in Nam, in the engineering corps, building ammunition depots.

He opened the telegram and read it:

PLEASE DON'T TELL CLAIRE ABOUT US. I COULDN'T LIVE WITH IT. I LOVE YOU FOOLISHLY.

HILLARY

6

It was nine in the morning and Claire found herself in the bathtub. The water was cold. Her fingers had turned rubbery and she had a throbbing ache at the back of her neck. She had no idea of when or how she had gotten into the tub. She pulled herself out, grabbed a towel, and went into the living room.

The TV was on to a morning repeat of *Hollywood Squares.* A woman contestant, about to X out her male opponent, picked Paul Lynde. Peter Marshall cleared his voice and addressed his question to the show's resident wit. "Now, Paul, what would you think had happened if you woke up one morning and everything was brown . . . the walls, the floors, the ceiling?" Lynde screwed up his puckish face and his eyes gleamed with adolescent malevolence. "What would I think, huh?" He giggled, rolled his eyes like a minstrel man. "Well, of course, the PLO had blown up my maid." Hyena-like laughter detonated the studio.

Claire thought she was going mad. Finally, without bothering to dry herself, she threw on a robe, caught a glimpse of her vacant eyes and did not recognize herself. She was aware that this was a dangerous situation. Milly's bottles of pills were in the bathroom. Maybe she ought to go back and swallow a bunch of them. It would be painless. She wouldn't even write a note. Who gave a damn about her in any event?

She telephoned her secretary and heard a battery of voices in the background. She couldn't face the salesmen.

She told Marcy she'd be in late and to reschedule her appointments. She offered no explanation for her action. She returned to the sofa and listlessly watched the television screen. She had turned off the sound. In the back of her mind, she held on to the tenuous hope that Bobby might contact her. She had forgotten to draw the curtains and sharp needles of sunlight burned her eyes. She wanted to talk to someone but the only one she could think of was Madeleine. But what the hell could she say?

She opened a sliding door, wandered out to the terrace, and fell into a white wrought-iron chair, part of a set. The other two chairs were stored in the basement locker. Her attention was caught by the bright orange Mr. Meat Smoker she had bought on sale at Drake's a few weeks ago. It had a few scratches and had been reduced. She had thought it would be more practical than an ordinary barbecue. She could put on a roast in the morning and it would cook slowly and be ready when she returned from the store so that she and Bobby could have a hot dinner without fussing. The tag was still on the handle. She was tempted to fling the goddamn thing off the terrace.

Anger was a sign of health, she realized, but after the flare-up she once more drifted into a mindless trough of despondency. She tore at herself, searching for a reasonable explanation for Bobby's breaking with her. Why? She had been his willing, adoring lover for two years—his friend! Yet somewhere along the way she had failed him. Perhaps she didn't fit into the society in Los Angeles. She immediately discarded the suggestion. Bobby was not a social climber, nor was he capable of such contemptible adventures.

She regretted never having lived with him. Maybe it wasn't too late. Suppose she went out to L.A., found a job at a department store, took an apartment, and tried to find some new common ground with him. They could both come and go as they pleased. Nothing furtive. Everything out in the open. He'd have a basis of comparison between her and the other girl—Hillary—and then make up his mind. She wouldn't press him. The prospect, however, sickened her. A contest . . .

She went back inside. The blood rushed to her head. The nausea was back, a malaise that came and went mysteriously, ghastly, as though she'd swallowed poison. She lay on the floor, unable to move. The full horror of the situation gripped her, twisting her soul. Bobby and Hillary, kissing, sharing, intimate. Only last night he had been with Claire. Their last desolate encounter and he had turned away, refusing to lead her on.

Finally she managed to get herself dressed, but as she was about to leave for the store she remembered the shower presents. She looked into the closet and couldn't bear to continue the fraud that they represented. An all-consuming compulsion took hold of her and she made trip after trip, loading them into her car. By the time she had finished, she was so numb that she floated on a new plane of impassiveness where nothing could touch her.

When she pulled into her spot at the back of Drake's, one of the men from the Packing Department wheeled his dolly beside the car and asked if she needed his help.

"Returns, Claire?" he asked blithely. "The manufacturers are going to climb the walls." He reached into her car and began lifting the packages from the rear seat. "You got the dockets?"

"It's personal. Just bring them to my office."

She took the elevator to the third floor, all the while shaking inside. She opened her office door and Marcy, her secretary, raised the beaded string holding her glasses and admonished her.

"You don't look well. Why don't you take the day off?"

"Marcy, don't mother me."

She handed Claire a stack of pink telephone messages as well as yesterday's interdepartment memos. She gave the packer a murderous look. "Since when do you load us with samples? We've got no room."

"It's okay, they're mine," Claire said, briskly walking into her office. She closed the door and before she could get to her desk, Marcy had entered. She knew that Claire allowed her to boss her. It was one of those office games in which the secretary appears to wield power. "We're not getting married," Claire said tersely.

"What? You and Bobby . . .?" Unshockable and with the manner of a bodyguard who has seen all forms of human drama, Marcy, nonetheless, cringed against the door.

"That's right—it's over."

"But why?" Marcy asked in a voice filled with calamity. "I didn't mean to ask. Forget it. It's just that I was taken aback. Claire, I'm sorry. This is crazy though, giving back all your shower gifts."

"What am I supposed to do with them?"

"God, I need a Valium."

And that was the general reaction Claire encountered as she started in the Bargain Basement with the silver tea service. By twelve-thirty she had reached Lingerie and returned the Spode dinner plates. She was toughing it out, but the reaction of the women began to wear her out and the physical aura of humiliation that the girls themselves experienced battered Claire. The entire sales staff seemed to be thrown into a state of chaos, and when Claire rigidly moved toward Sportswear, she saw girls huddling at their counters, speechless with outrage. There was for Claire an awful notion that she had been responsible for a community abasement, that in the flowers of compassion she was silently offered, some deadly plague had descended on all of them. She fought for self-control, but despite the struggle, she was weakening. Marcy was at her heels.

"Claire, I'll do it—return everything. You don't—"

"I have to, don't you understand, I have to . . ."

Gene Drake was in conference and couldn't see her at the moment, so Claire left the check he had presented with his secretary. She was in fact magically better, purged, until she returned to her office and was buzzed by the switchboard operator.

"Marcy's not at her desk," the operator said. "It's a Mr. Micelli. Do you want to speak to him?" Claire faltered. "Miss Stuart, are you still there?"

"I'll talk to him . . ."

Micelli's mellifluous voice brought her out in a cold sweat.

"How's my beautiful bride?" the caterer inquired. "Claire, honey, I've got good news about the shrimp."

"Can we talk about it later?"

"Give me a time."

"An hour."

"See you."

When she put down the receiver, she looked up at the

perplexed figure opening her door. Neither she nor Gene Drake could speak. He had the check in his hand and a melancholy look on his face. Although he was hard-driving with the staff and they lived in fear of him, he had a soft spot for Claire. She was his creature, his protégée, and as he stood there, he remembered the lovely, quick-minded, bright girl who had come to work for him when she was nineteen. She had flair and what Drake's lacked at that time was anyone with taste or imagination to run the women's departments. In those days the store had sold cheap house dresses, matronly suits, and had done a roaring trade in foundation garments. Step by step, Claire had reorganized the fashion departments, and in the process she had changed the thinking of the store executives. She had insisted on bringing a young approach to the store.

For months now he had been toying with the idea of offering her a directorship. Contracts expired and had to be renegotiated, and he knew that in the present business climate it was virtually impossible to find real talent in the retail marketplace. In spite of the emergence of the new woman, most of the women in the area did not want to make a career at a store like Drake's. They had families, and kids. They worked for him just long enough to collect unemployment benefits; taking advantage of the twenty-five percent discount offered to all employees, they outfitted themselves and vanished. Good staff were like gold bars, and the prospect of losing Claire frightened him. It was nonsense about no one's being indispensable in a large organization. He knew that without Claire the fashion departments would fall through the floor. Naturally there were experienced merchandisers around. But the girl had smarts and knew how to mark up. She could do it all. From lingerie to separates.

"I know this is painful for you," he began, "but there are lots of people here who care about you." He was a tall, powerfully built man and she could see that his emotion was genuine. She hated commiseration.

"It sort of happened out of the blue," she said, relieved that she had overcome the shakes.

"Claire, we're going to begin summer sales. You've done most of your buying for the fall. You've been saving your vacation for a honeymoon. Take the time off now. A month, six weeks . . . go to Europe. First class." He handed her back the check. "And use this toward your expenses. If you happen to see anything that interests you, buy it, but don't get the idea that you're actually working. What do you say . . . London, Paris, Milan, the South of France." There was in his hooded eyes the sharp-edge hint of a pitch. "Claire, I'd like you to be a director of Drake's. There'd be stock options and a profit participation."

"Gene, I really can't think straight."

"I'm sorry." He sat down on the edge of her desk, anxious to comfort her. "Sometimes a thing like this is for the best. If you start off with lots of problems, in a few months you wind up fighting it out with lawyers."

She could not concentrate on what he was saying.

"I just lost him. If I could figure out why . . . oh, I don't know, would it do any good?" she said impatiently. "I thought we were different, unbreakable. He went out to California to see if he could find a job that would make him happy and he did. I encouraged him. Well, he found the job and a new life that didn't include me. In a month it all slipped away from me," she said in a rage.

Drake welcomed this show of temper. He believed it would be good for her to explode, let it all out. He knew that failure either personally or in business hardened the strong of the world. The weak sisters weren't worth a second thought. No matter what, they'd eventually fall apart. Claire's fury abated too soon to suit him and once again she lapsed into silence.

"I hope this whole ugly experience is going to make you more ruthless."

"I doubt it. I'm not a bitch or a killer. Look, business is one thing. To me it's always been a game, which is why I'm good at it. After all, what's at stake? Just money and I can't take money seriously." He was shocked by the admission, for Claire was as tough as he when it came to driving a bargain or ensuring that her figures were better than the other department heads'.

"Let me know what you decide. I can get the travel department onto it any time you say."

She nodded. She would not get better, she knew, and there would never be any healing process. She had been too deeply committed to Bobby, too much in love with him. It wasn't something she would eventually get over. The savagery of the blow had already taken a toll. She no longer cared about her job at Drake's, or her future, for all of it was tied together, her ambition, her emotional life. One fed the other, but a man would not understand why the two could not be separated. Naturally it was still a man's world because it was simple, mean, petty, without mystery, with obvious emotions and surface desires. Men were incapable of subtle intentions. They were as pragmatic as children. Just give them a good screw and money, and forget those higher regions of the human spirit. In spite of this perception she recognized that Bobby had been different. He wanted more than the material things. He lived in a rarefied atmosphere. He wanted to make something. He was a builder and she had never met anyone like him. She had no idea how she could go on living without him.

Micelli was outside his reception hall, bellowing at two workmen on ladders. They had replaced the M in his neon sign and in the process blown the rest of the lighting.

"See, Claire, I was having the sign fixed just for you." He looked up and venomously shouted: "You get it working today or I'm going to sue." He nervously twisted a thick tuft of his sideburn into a curl. "Show me a black electrician and I'll show you a short." Both of the workmen were black. "And I'm not prejudiced, mind you, but after the years of experience I've had, I know that wires and colored people don't get along."

She hadn't listened to a word, but when his lips stopped moving she finally uttered "Mr. Micelli," only to be interrupted.

"Hey, come on, it's Papa to you, Claire. Have I got good news for you." His voice sounded like an automatic weapon. "Forget shrimp. Anybody can serve shrimp. No style. If Safeway stocks them, where's the glamor? I made a crab connection in Oregon. Crab claws flown in fresh every day. And they're the same price as shrimp. Can you believe that? I don't know what's going on in Oregon, but let me tell you, we're stealing them. You know what kind of impression you make with crab? Guests are going to faint when they see the ice sculpture I do with them. And I put little paper leggings on them so you don't have your hands smelling fishy. It'll be a knockout."

She decided that she could not call him Papa and the image of hundreds of crab claws for some reason frightened her. Her hands flew to her face.

"You all right?" Micelli asked.

"We're not getting married."

"Jesus, I'm sorry to hear that. I mean, this does happen" —he was no longer smiling—"before the plunge. You get mad, he gets mad. It's nothing. I've seen it a hundred times. In my day you kissed and made up but now it's a little heavier. So you work it out in bed and you both walk around with grins on your face." She was not comforted by his suggestion and he suspected a cancellation. "Let's go into the office and discuss it."

"He backed out," she said quietly.

"What's the matter with him? Let me pull the paperwork and I'll give him a call and discuss this. In my time, I've pulled a few maybes out of the water and they're swimming beautiful. Each year *I* get an anniversary card from them. We're like family. Claire . . ." She was staring through him and he didn't like the signs. He would have been more comfortable with hysteria. He could work with hysterics. Talk her back into it, or if the guy was playing up, he'd visit him and his family at home to re-close. This dead fish-eyed unfocused expression worried him. "Stuart-Canaday. Here's the file. Robert John Canaday." He located the groom's phone number. "Is it Robert, Robby, or Bob?"

"Don't call, please."

"Claire, this is going to be a problem for you if I don't get hold of him. You look like you got enough problems." He removed the contract from the folder, leafed through two pages, then came to her side and pointed to the relevant clause. "Claire, you're going to be stuck with a big headache if Robert John doesn't come around."

The small print contained an unambiguous legal statement that apparently was standard with all caterers.

> In the event that the parties in the contract cancel their reception for any reason whatsoever (including death),

they shall forfeit their deposit and no claim will be made against Micelli & Sons, Ltd.

Claire saw her initials scrawled in the margin. Micelli had made her read it. What with consumers constantly suing, he was not taking any chances on being accused of fastballing an innocent prospective bride and groom. Claire's initials were worth twenty-five hundred dollars to Micelli, which represented the twenty-five percent down payment he required to book the wedding. In the first rush of excitement, Claire would have signed anything.

"I lose it all?" she asked, stricken by the fact that everything seemed to be going against her all at once.

"*You* lose!" Micelli was choleric and his mouth became viperish, the professional smile lanced by scorn. "And I'm knocking my brains out for you with crab claws. What for?" He was addressing himself and he thrust his arms out in the posture of a man crucified for his faith. "I got you blocked in on a Saturday night. June thirtieth! Where am I going to find a wedding on such notice? What do you think, I run down to the butcher the day before and put in an order and then send out for some booze? Waiters, ushers, musicians, chefs, kitchen staff, checkroom people, carhops are all involved. I got a nut of forty people before a dinner roll is on a plate. This isn't a beer and pretzel bash at the bowling alley or a canteen birthday party. This is *my* season, understand? I finally got myself a June with five Saturdays! It's a dream come true. A caterer lives or dies by a stinking day of the week. I give you prime time for a hundred a couple. I could have booked two hundred couples at two hundred a head. Volume, that's where I make my profit."

His acrimonious attack stunned her.

"I never thought this would happen," she implored him.

"You should have checked it out with lover boy before you came here. I was going to put the menu to bed at the printer today once you gave the okay on the crab." He paused to reflect. "You know what *Écrevisse d'Oregon avec Sauce Moutarde* looks like on a menu? It's Suzy's column, sister. They send reporters from *Women's Wear Daily* and the *Post* for a number like that. If I don't get a last-minute booking, I can sue your ass from here to Hong Kong."

His venom was inexhaustible and she wilted under the relentless barrage of insults. Good, sweet, paternal Micelli.

She couldn't catch her breath when she reached her car. She pumped the accelerator so many times that without realizing it she flooded the engine. She put on her dark glasses and slumped down in the seat, thoroughly cowed by the onslaught.

7

Claire drove through town in bewilderment, traumatized by the events. She could not bring herself to return to the store and she phoned Marcy from a gas station to tell her that she was not feeling well. She was in no condition to drive. All she wanted to do was to lie down on her bed, draw the curtains and go to ground. She passed a red light and a cop pulled her over. He patiently waited for her to appeal, but she was beyond such ordinary, normal practices.

She kept her speed down on her way to her apartment, and she had no recollection of getting there. She had made up her mind to call Bobby. She simply couldn't give him up without some last heroic effort. Rushing up the stairs, trembling with a shock of hope, she quickly unlocked the door and was about to grab the phone when she spotted an envelope that had been slipped under the door. It had her name on it.

Dear Claire,
I'm on my way back to L.A. Some kind of crisis at the office. There's not much that I can say about us except that I'm also deeply unhappy. I'm enclosing a thousand-dollar check—all I can manage at the moment. If you need more, I'll try to get it to you in a few months when I'm on my feet. I wish it could have been different.

With love and regrets,
Bobby

Nothing was left of them. The check seemed to cancel out the last of his residual feeling for her. She had proved to be unworthy of him, and he had found a new solvency with Hillary.

She was sinking. It would be easy to blame Bobby, hold him responsible, behave as though she had been victimized by an unscrupulous man. But a voice from within needled her, mocked her, until she was virtually clawing at herself. She was convinced that no force on earth could move a man if he were truly in love with a woman. Neither sex nor money could sever a relationship unless the woman had failed the man. Somewhere along the way she had taken a wrong turn. She hadn't been enough for him. Whether it was in bed or in their everyday transactions, Claire knew she had come up short, and as she faced herself in the mirror, there was an element of satisfaction in prosecuting the case against herself.

"A man doesn't take a walk for nothing," she told herself.

The intensity of her self-loathing rippled through her like electric current and in that dangerous territory of self-abnegation she found an unexpected serenity. Searching, probing, examining her motives, she recognized that she had placed him in a position that he had subconsciously abhorred. She had counseled patience when he was working in New York. She had advised him to take jobs with local builders and to grab any work that was offered to him. He resisted, and the chemistry between them had been indiscernibly altered. What had occurred was a growing reliance on her, which opened the way for resentment.

In the strength and the power of her love, she had usurped his manhood. She was the one accustomed to the deceits of the working world, and the range of her experience had persuaded her that Bobby needed to be protected. The insight stunned her. She'd scared Bobby off. He had broken away from her sphere of influence in Los Angeles. Yet these thoughts were at variance with her perception of herself. She was not a domineering woman who had manipulated him.

From the west a flash of lightning illuminated the sky; it was followed by a bark of thunder. Sheets of spring rain violently lashed the windows. She went to the window, saw her car outside with its top down and she didn't care.

She couldn't go on. The public humiliation she had brought on herself at the store made it impossible for her to return there. Oddly enough, in this emotional limbo she found a measure of freedom.

She belonged to no one. The crazy-quilt pattern, the flux of life, had stopped. There was nowhere to go, nothing to do, she thought without sentimentality. Nobody could make things better. Her self-image faded and she made no effort to recapture it or hang onto the center of herself.

Her friends and business associates would remain mystified, unable to comprehend Bobby's reasons for falling out of love with her. Enough that she knew that she had represented compromise, the easy way out to Bobby in their relationship, so that he could never trust her because there was the possibility that one day she might persuade him to betray himself. It went beyond love and the convenience of marriage. He needed a different kind of woman.

She was finished and once she admitted that to herself, the burden was lightened; the pain of loss took on a spectral shape. She listened to the sweet melodies of madness, hummed cheerfully when she went into the bathroom and opened the medicine cabinet. The bottles were an army of defenders. Nembutal, Quaalude, Dexamyl, Percodan, Seconal, Tuinal. There was music in their names. She ripped off her clothes and flung them on the floor.

It was becoming very interesting. Her senses were alert. She had once again become the center of her universe. Bobby was excluded. She had moved beyond pleasure and pain into a new area.

Games.

Fascinating.

She was both hunter and quarry. The pupils of her eyes dilated with excitement and the feverish rush of tension held her in thrall. This was magic, the power of life and death. She felt omnipotent, ecstatic, reckless, as she moved into the God Game. She could do anything. Rules, laws, no longer applied to her. Micelli could keep her money. The traffic court could write all the subpoenas they liked. Gene Drake could find another body to replace her. Businesses were immortal.

She was safe, untouchable. She flicked out several clean Gillette double-edged blades from the dispenser and picked up some of Milly's bottles.

She glided out to the terrace. In a moment she was soaked and she sat down on a chair, smiling. She placed the blades and pills on the table beside her. The rain pelted her. From the grass, eddies of sultry humid clouds danced especially for her. She was feeling so up that her first choice was a couple of Quaaludes to soften her mood. She opened her mouth and fed them to herself, then swallowed some rainwater dripping from the gutter above the terrace. People home from work dashed from their cars to the building. A few of them covered their heads with newspapers.

The pills hit her and she became dizzy but floated with the sensuous fugues playing in her head. She picked up a razor blade and although her vision was blurring, she slashed a thin vertical line from her wrist to the crease in her arm, scoring her skin patiently.

Painless. Everything she'd heard about this was nonsense, propaganda to frighten people. Blood welled out from both sides of the cut and she watched with morbid interest. Then she took another pill from an unlabeled bottle and swallowed it. One of Milly's bombers. A vein of lightning flared in the black-blue sky and she braced herself for the wave of thunder that followed. She sailed right through it, blissfully cutting yet another line on her skin, this time closer to the vein on her wrist, toying with herself, building up to the moment of complete release when the blood would spurt. She was enjoying herself too much to rush it.

The pills, she imagined, were fighting a battle within her for control. Two swordsmen, thrusting and parrying their tempered steel. The rain eased and the sky began to brighten. Claire sat in the chair laughing to herself. Then she slid into a deeper soporific state and added a couple of Seconals to her witches' brew. She had discovered that she preferred the more mellow strains of the game. Downers. She rose to her feet, pitched against the terrace rail. She blinked when unexpected jagged arches of sunlight broke through the cloudbanks. "Get out of here, get the hell out of here," she screamed. "What do you think you're doing?"

The sun now blazed. It was that late afternoon molten heat that spurts and rages demonically when the planet seems out of control, about to scorch the earth. She hated the light, raised her fist threateningly, cursed it. Her drenched hair was matted flat and she staggered inside.

Her vision blurred. Only the outlines of the objects in the room were discernible. She could no longer distinguish colors. She was rocking back and forth, her eyes closed, and in a corkscrew motion she dropped to the floor.

Claire had the sensation of being gripped by the hair and then having it pulled violently. Her mouth was opened and a foul liquid was poured down her throat. She was being supported over the bathtub, heaving.

"Claire, Claire, more . . . bring it up."

Milly filled another glass with warm salt water. Claire was held by a man. She couldn't make out his face.

"Buddy, hustle it—turn the shower on cold!" Milly commanded.

"Jesus, let's call the paramedics or get her to the hospital. Her color's no good."

"Damn it, do what I tell you. She's breathing."

The water was turned on full blast. Milly pulled off her dress and, with Buddy's support, she got Claire under the shower. She held the girl tightly and again force-fed her the salt water. Claire retched. The water exploded in her face. Milly held her under the arms and kneaded the back of her neck with her thumbs, then jammed her on the shower bench and proceeded to slap her face hard. Claire wanted to protest but she had no will, no ability to communicate. Her eyes rolled closed.

"Get up!" Milly forced her to stand and with the palm of her hand banged her hard between the shoulder blades. "Dry heaves. I think she's got most of it out. Buddy, get me more salt water." The liquid went down Claire's throat and bile came up.

Milly, soaking wet, directed the shower head against Claire's temple, all the while vigorously pumping her diaphragm. Large bath towels were spread on the tile and Milly eased her out of the shower into Buddy's arms. They helped her to the floor, dried her, and the two of them carried her into her bedroom. They held her as she sat down. Claire's eyes opened. She was disoriented.

"Come on, babe, we're going to do a few laps around the room. You're not going to sleep."

She and Buddy took turns walking back and forth from the window to the door. Claire's legs sagged and they dragged her.

"Her pulse is good," Buddy said.

"She needs a jolt. Get me my handbag."

Milly broke open an amyl nitrate and stuck it under Claire's nose. Claire felt her heartbeat rush and her eyes opened.

"Wake up the dead, huh, babe?" Milly sardonically observed. "I've been there before. Pulled a few of my friends out of worse holes."

"We'll get you a license," Buddy said. "Next time I have a coronary I want you around."

"Claire, Claire. You're coming out of it. Can you take something in your stomach?" Claire nodded her head. "Terrific. Buddy, over the sink you'll find a pack of beef bouillon cubes. Break up a couple and pour some boiling water into a mug." When he left the room, Milly allowed Claire to rest for a moment in a chair. "We're some pair. I never should have left the goodies around the house. Grown woman too. Jesus Christ, don't doze on me yet, sister. I'll let you sleep when I think you can handle it." Milly heaved her to her feet and took her on more tours of the bedroom, then Buddy came in with the broth. She sat her daughter down on the bed and held the mug to her lips. "Sip it slowly."

The broth burned Claire's lips and tongue. Milly sent Buddy out for a tablespoon. She proceeded to feed the girl with inordinate patience but at the same time retained a hectoring attitude. Finally, she helped Claire into a flannel nightgown and put her to bed.

She sat in the room for hours, frequently taking her pulse, and at about ten in the evening she woke her. She helped her to the table in the dining alcove and insisted she eat the soft-boiled eggs Buddy had prepared.

They sat in silence, watching Claire shakily raise the spoon to her lips. Claire remained dazed, taciturn. Milly made up the sofa for Buddy and bid him goodnight, then returned with Claire to the bedroom.

"Are you going to talk to me?"

Claire was by turns raving and suspicious of her mother, but more than anything she was resentful.

"You don't have the energy for a decent fight. Let it keep till tomorrow, babe." She leaned over and kissed her daughter. "I haven't been a perfect mother by any standards. But I'm no goddamned hypocrite, so there aren't going to be any recriminations."

Claire spent the following day in bed. Milly had called Drake's and informed them that Claire had a bad case of flu and would be out for the week. Buddy was left in front of the TV watching a Yankee night game and she took Claire down to Cos Cob for dinner at the Lobster Pot.

They had vodka martinis at the bar. Except for indifferent monosyllabic replies during the day, Claire had refused to talk to her. She would not put on makeup and was horribly pale. Milly had brushed her hair and twisted it into a ponytail. Claire had been sullen and recalcitrant. Her eyes were expressionless and an uncharacteristic abstraction completely altered her looks. It would be difficult for anyone to recognize her. It was not so much that she had suffered a drug overdose—rather, she gave off a scent of neglect. Her energy evaporated, she could have passed for one of those commune girls with an acid-eroded brain who had a bunch of multi-colored kids she breastfed on TV documentaries celebrating marijuana agriculture.

Milly pushed the cheddar dip and Ritz crackers on the bar toward Claire, who ignored them. A few couples waiting for tables were at the other end of the bar.

"You pissed off with me?"

"I wish to hell you had never come back and had stayed in Miami or Vegas or wherever you were."

"Me too. Small towns never agreed with me. And if Dr. Slakoff hadn't pulled us out of the city to Westport nothing could've shifted me." She took back the cheddar and slapped a glob on a cracker. "How long did that last? Eighteen months, then he moved his root canals to New Haven. If you're trying to needle me about my track record, don't bother. I've always finished out of the money. I've found my level in Las Vegas . . ."

"What am I doing here? I don't even want lobster."

"Then try the scallops."

Inadvertently Claire laughed and caught a glimpse of her transformed looks in the bar mirror. The smile froze on her face. She signaled the bartender for another drink. The alcohol was going to her head, muddling her thoughts.

"There's no reason for you to stay on."

"I know." Milly fiddled with the toothpick on the olive and broke it. "You've made me very welcome. You don't like me much." She snapped her fingers at the bartender. "I'm watching you, so use Smirnoff and not the bar fuel." She turned to Claire. "Caught him."

"You're terrific at that sort of thing."

"Oh, Claire, shove it. I read the note Bobby left." She ran a hand through the parched platinum thatch that she'd annihilated over years of bleaching and teasing. "It's a shame. He was a honey. But look at it another way. It was coming . . . sooner or later. In some ways you're lucky it happened before you were making formula for one kid and shoving Big Macs into another kid's face and your body looked like a steel-belted radial tire that'd skidded onto a soft shoulder."

Claire was revolted.

"The way you talk—"

"The truth isn't crystal slippers." Milly glanced at a menu fastened to a metal frame. "Split a dozen cherrystones? The seafood in Vegas, forget it."

"I'm not hungry."

"You were always moody." She ordered the clams and reminded the waitress who took her order to bring extra horseradish and lemon.

"I'd like to leave after this."

"I'm eating dinner. You can watch me. I ordered a couple of two-pound-plus lobsters before we came. We can have lobster salad tomorrow." Milly chucked her under the chin. "Claire, anyone ever tell you you were a royal pain in the ass when you wanted to be?"

"I'm going to call a cab."

"Oh, shut up and listen to me. Do you want Bobby

back?" Claire's eyes filled with tears. "You're not even drunk, so quit it. Crying's not going to help the cause. Anyway, you've never been a complainer and all this woe-begotten garbage isn't you. Babe, you were stood up, but all is not lost."

They settled at a table by the kitchen, their lobster bibs fixed, with a bottle of house white wine in a carafe beside them. Claire waited in vain for her mother to rebuke her for having taken the pills, but Milly was too cagey. It would be going over old ground. They ate their chowder slowly. Milly never rushed dinner.

"Years ago people tagged me as a tramp," she began. "I've never denied that I am by nature flirtatious and I enjoy the company of different men because I never met one I could tolerate for any length of time. You're very different. Whatever I do, well, you go the opposite way and, Claire, there are disadvantages both ways. *I* can't get let down. On the other hand, disappointment of this kind made you suicidal."

Claire shrank from the cold assertion. But in Milly's worldly eyes she recognized the affinity of pain that had united them.

"I don't know where I went wrong," Claire said.

"He's an attractive guy and all men wander."

"I gave him the chance plenty of times before. He finally met somebody else."

"You gonna quit? He's confused. L.A.'s a peculiar place. It's easy to find yourself lonely. Hell, if I were you, I'd kiss Drake's goodbye and go out there. See him. Maybe you can make it work. If you don't make the effort, you'll never be happy. You'll always be wondering what would have happened."

Claire thought about the suggestion. She tried to visualize herself in pursuit of Bobby.

"He ran for his life."

"He can't face you. He humiliated you. What do you expect? He's human. He got horny. You were three thousand miles away, so what was he supposed to do?"

The prospect of groveling, pleading with Bobby, disgusted Claire. She was an enemy of hope.

"He rejected me!"

"Give him a chance to change his mind. It happens all the time. Men panic before getting married. Coming back is harder for them," Milly advised her.

Actually, Milly had taken things a stage further. She had spoken to Madeleine earlier in the day and Claire would be welcomed by her friend, have a place to stay, a ready-made social life.

"It's a change. And if there's any way of getting Bobby back, you won't do it sitting on your ass in Drake's, chiseling salesmen."

"Did you tell Madeleine what happened?"

"Naturally," Milly said blithely. As a conspirator, her mother was in a class with John Dean.

"Everything?"

Milly smiled, seized a lobster claw and crunched it with the cracker, then daintily scooped the meat out. It looked as though she were swallowing a live salamander.

"I can't think of anything I left out. I'm supposed to lie to Madeleine?" She dunked some meat in the butter sauce, chewed it slowly, savoring the taste. "Madeleine's your friend, so why the hell play games with her?"

"But this was so personal."

Claire pushed her lobster away. A confrontation with Madeleine would be unendurable. At a nearby table of eight, the people were howling with laughter. Claire imagined they had overheard Milly, then realized they hadn't. The drinks had made her queasy.

Milly spat out a piece of lobster shell.

"Oh, yes, very personal. If I hadn't walked in with Buddy, everybody in town would have read about it. Suicides are news in Westport. Young pretty girl . . . Sweetie, you would have been on Eyewitness News—as a corpse with a camera jammed up your ass. So don't hand me any of this secrecy stuff or imply that I've been indiscreet," she said, affronted. "Four people know what happened. In case you haven't heard, Buddy wants to marry me . . . eight hundred bucks he spent as an engagement gift on Louis Vuitton luggage and that's without me encouraging him."

Claire was feeling ragged. A look of deep self-abasement transfixed her face and Milly stopped eating, reached across the table and held her hand tightly.

"God, I hate myself," Claire said.

"Babe, you've been through a gruesome experience. It's got to leave marks. But you're not alone. No one's turned against you." She operated on Claire's lobster, scooping out the soft meat and putting it on a separate plate. She got the busboy to clear the vacant shell and entreated Claire to taste it.

"You loved lobster as a kid, but sometimes we didn't have the money to go out . . . oh, what the hell . . ." Milly lost interest in the enterprise, dropped her lobster fork, and stared across the table at this stranger, her flesh and blood, who had turned inward years before, spurning the friendship Milly had sought and failed to provide. "Claire, Claire, just because I've been a loose woman by your standards doesn't mean that I don't care about you. You quit on Bobby, you quit on yourself."

Claire bitterly snapped at her. "I have to have some dignity."

"Tell me about it." Milly caught the drift. "Or better still, if you wind up with some asshole, have his kids and hate yourself when you're forty, your dignity's going to be real important. All cocks are not the same."

The barbarity offended Claire, made her squirm. She had despised this woman since adolescence, considered her life squalid, a swamp Claire had been trapped in, pulling her down, debasing her. She couldn't consider her mother as a human being with her own quirks and delinquencies.

They skipped coffee and dessert and Milly handled the check with a crisp hundred. No credit cards for a Vegas skimmer, Claire thought. The woman was all flash, a cheap neon sign like the one in front of Micelli's. Yet in her disapproval of her mother there was an element of such passion that she could not restrain her fury.

On the parking lot they faced each other.

"You don't like me much," Claire said. "You never did."

Milly refused to be baited. She'd been there with guys, her kid was easy to handle.

"I think I've got the hang of your car now. I won't strip the gears. Shift cars. They belong to another century."

"Don't give me that casino palm stuff. I asked you a question."

Milly leaned against the hood of the car, puffing out air,

holding back her temper, even though she was exasperated. She wanted to open her arms but Claire had forced her to be combative.

"Jesus, Claire, really. We're not two bums from a bowling alley, having a beef, who've stepped outside."

"You don't understand a thing about me."

Milly dangled the key ring in her fingers. The blood rushed to her head. Finally she lost her composure.

"Claire, you're a pussy."

"Coming from an old whore, that's a compliment," she hissed. "You're nothing. Just an easy fuck. Who the hell are you to tell me anything? What do you know about feelings? You've had more men . . ."

Milly moved away. She never took shit or backed off, but now she was being degraded. She knew she was dealing with someone who was irrational. Her daughter.

"I've never been a professional mother like some."

"I'll testify to that."

"I think you better get in the car."

"Don't ever tell me what to do, you bitch."

She'd pushed Milly to the edge of the cliff, too far for a woman who had gone her own way. Milly put her handbag on the roof of the car, then approached Claire. She whacked her on one cheek, then the other, blowing the girl back. She grabbed hold of Claire by the short hair on the back of her neck and shoved her into the car. Milly was breathing hard. Claire had thrown herself on the floor of the car and it was impossible to start it with her in that position.

"I love you, babe, but you're overmatched." She lifted Claire onto the seat as though she were a butcher's order that had fallen down. Then she strapped her in with the seat belt. "You people with these sports cars who pretend you're racing drivers. I ride around in Sevilles and Lincolns and I can't get the goddamn straps around me."

Claire's head was bent forward, her body listing. Milly realized that the drinks had hit her. Claire grabbed Milly's face from this awkward position.

"You won't raise your hand. You're a fourflusher, babe. I can make them all the time."

Claire released her grip. Milly's pancake was on her fingertips like greasy flour. She was beyond tears. She recognized that she had done something so terribly wrong that she longed to be chastised. Claire made a move toward Milly while she searched to find the ignition.

"Mother, help me . . ."

"You're still a pussy," Milly said, refusing to toady.

"Why?"

"Shit, shit, shit. Where the hell are your instincts? You love him. Go out there and fight for him. Fight, Claire. Fight. Understand?"

8

Going west . . . cut adrift, floating toward the continental shelf was in the nature of a pilgrimage for Claire. She no longer felt quite so alone. She had come back to life, acting decisively once again. She had resigned from Drake's and parted with Gene on good terms. He realized that he could no longer keep her and his arguments lacked persuasiveness. With her vacation money and Bobby's check, her bank balance had shot up to thirty-one hundred dollars. Her confidence had been jarred but it was returning slowly. The girl who had swallowed the pills represented a dark side of her character, which she had buried. She retained a cautious aloofness about her chances with Bobby. So, without any rigorous mental preparation, she bought a thousand dollars' worth of traveler's checks, sold her car privately to Leah at the store for eleven hundred and accepted her note for the debt.

Milly and Buddy drove her to the airport, implored her to keep in touch. Vegas was only a forty-minute flight from L.A. Milly offered to have Claire's furniture put in storage and would settle any hassles with Claire's landlord if he gave her a hard time about breaking the lease. Her mother was a real expert at quarrels when she was in the wrong, employing a clamorous insolence that made people back off. Without really giving it a great deal of thought, Claire was on the plane to Los Angeles.

Madeleine met her in the baggage claim area. It was almost a year since Claire had seen her and Madeleine grabbed hold of her, squeezed her, and noisily kissed her. She was one of those forceful termagant women who have the capacity to create bedlam wherever they are.

Madeleine's late mother had nicknamed her Grub because of her slovenly habits and the name had lingered throughout high school. However, it no longer fit, for there had been an attractive although eccentric change in her appearance. Her hair had been cut short, waved at the sides, highlighted with David Bowie-like reddish tints that screeched. Madeleine had lost more than thirty pounds. Her figure had a tumultuous extravagance that was accentuated by her skintight jeans, which curved over her reshaped hips. Lest there be any doubt about her quest for high visibility, she wore a blood red tee shirt a size too small that had "HOME WRECKER" emblazed in silver on the back and "HOUSE CALLS" across her astonishingly large and firm breasts. Claire laughed. It was like being met by a red fire engine with the sirens clanging—an assault. The plump girl Claire remembered had been totally reconstructed. True, her nose still tilted a bit to the left, but the dark brown gloomy eyes bespeaking a calamitous truckling adolescence now possessed an undaunted bluster. Madeleine wasn't quite beautiful, but neither were billboards nor the Goodyear blimp. Their function was to capture one's attention.

"Well, it's not Audrey Hepburn," Claire said, escaping from Madeleine's grasp and Wind Song.

"I'm pure L.A. I even speak some Spanish. *No está en casa*. This is the new me. You like?"

"Unbelievable."

"I lost five inches of junk food off my waist and I work out with a chest expander every day. Let me tell you something, babe . . . even in L.A. where they've seen everything, a thirty-six D gets attention. They don't bury my car." There was a moment of restrained silence while they waited for Claire's luggage. Then Madeleine linked hands with Claire.

"How are you, babe?"

"Together."

"You of all people. Who knew you were so crazy?"

"It's behind me."

"It should be." Claire's bags spilled out of the chute and

thudded down to the carousel. They wheeled them out on a trolley to the parking lot. It was a cloudy day. June in L.A., the resident expert advised her, usually had few beach days, cool nights, and many divorces, for it was the house-selling season and such considerations were put off during winter reconciliations.

"Claire, you look damned good . . . a little pale, but you can handle any of the competition out here."

"Are you working?"

"I'm out sick today for a change. The big thing," she continued with vaunting stamina, "is my acting. I'm taking classes three times a week, voice training. . . . And I work with a small theater group a couple of nights a week," she added, as though it were the most natural thing in the world for any girl to do. Madeleine was still impregnated with callow dreams.

They reached a dusty brown old Mustang convertible with a scummy windshield and a rash of holes in the top. Madeleine opened the trunk, shifted her makeup case, her laddered leotards, and a bald tire to make room for Claire's suitcases. "I'm not going to wind up at thirty still working at Gucci . . . oh, no, not on your life. Forget it. I'll break through," she added with that synthetic assurance of someone who has just taken an instant sales engineering course daring to be great and is convinced that bravura assertions erase the bogeyman of disaster.

Madeleine had always been convinced that she would eventually be a movie star and at twenty-three the fantasies and the my-time-will-come attitude struck Claire as incongruous. Madeleine had been bitten by the bug as far back as high school where she had taken all the available drama courses and was hooted off the stage by the brave bulls of the football team after an unspeakable performance as Stella in *Streetcar*. The public thrashing had hurt her confidence for perhaps a weekend, Claire recalled. After graduation she had bounced back as a one-woman variety act, but she never got any further than the local Arthur Murray Dance Studio. She was riding high as the sometime mistress of a pasty-faced shuck and jive gonzo who knocked her up. After threats of lawsuits, he was finally persuaded to part with five hundred dollars for an abortion.

Madeleine took it in her stride; there was a hardiness in

her clashes with adversity. She had become a fixture at Rienzi's in the Village, a coffeehouse personality. Ultimately this led to an unpaid job as a stage hand at Cafe La Mama, which brought her into the THEATER! She had wet-nursed and been fucked over by a herd of aspiring actors during this period. To support herself and her commitment to art, she had sold men's underwear at Macy's for three years before bailing out and trekking to Los Angeles to be close to the studios.

The girls had been friends from the age of ten when the two swinging mothers came to an arrangement: if either of them was entertaining a man for the night, Claire or Madeleine, depending on the disposition of the male body, would be shipped to the free apartment to sleep over. The girls' teens became a succession of musical Castro Convertibles, presided over by suspicious "uncles" who doled out five-dollar bills to keep them in burgers, movies, and out of the apartment. Thus, Claire and Madeleine had shared almost seven years of solitary friendship, frozen TV dinners, freighters of send-out pizzas, and they came to participate in those feckless confidences of children planning futures that excluded their roving mothers.

"I'm not letting you go back to Westport," Madeleine said authoritatively. "You'll get a job making twice what Drake paid." She had always been the visionary. "Claire, I've missed you. The friends I've got out here aren't for real—not like you."

"We carried a few loads together," Claire said, filled with enthusiasm. Someone wanted her, needed her, and it would be difficult to renounce this kind of security.

"That's what it's all about. You can't replace the experiences we had—even the bummers." At a stop sign off the San Diego Freeway, she affectionately stroked Claire's hair. "You've been through the wars, babe. Nobody's worth it. Not even Bobby."

"He doesn't know what happened and he never will," Claire said firmly. "I think there's still a chance for us."

Madeleine's impetuousness was held in check by the despair she observed. Claire was hypersensitive, never could roll with the punches, she thought. This last effort to save face was pathetic, and Madeleine let it pass without comment. Claire began to relax as they rolled around jackknife curves on Sunset.

She looked out of the window at the profusion of palms, the wild purple bougainvillea climbing from garden to garden, the intense tropical green of the place, the variety of houses. On one street alone she saw a mock Tudor beside a stately Spanish casa with a pantiled roof and duenna bars, which was opposed by an all-redwood-and-glass ranch with dimmed sunglass, which seemed to be challenging the French Regency on the corner. She lit two cigarettes and passed one to Madeleine.

The sign announcing Beverly Hills seemed like a place where a border patrol might do a lively trade and she was not surprised when she saw house upon house with warnings of attack dogs, Bel Air Patrol, Westinghouse alarm systems—for behind these fortresses, it was becoming increasingly clear, were the stanchions of Midwestern fortunes, foreign millionaires who had fled from revolutions and taxes, the Eastern metropolitans who had had enough of icy winters and muggers. Occasionally her eye rested like a butterfly on what she took to be a pure California home with its used-brick facade, its golden children lolling on the lawn ruled by a Mexican maid whose uniform matched the original pink stucco on the side, which had been retained as a courtesy to a period still too youthful to be counted as the past. It was bewildering, the efflorescence of hibiscus, the meandering roses, the verdant gardens exploding with jungle colors.

"This is *the* street," Madeleine informed Claire as they drove down Rodeo Drive. She pointed to Gucci. "That's where I work." They passed the Beverly Wilshire. "Warren Beatty lives in an apartment at the hotel." She was still a fan, and Claire remembered her as a fourteen-year-old, lying on the carpet, munching a hero sandwich, her face embedded in *Silver Screen* with a pile of film romances waiting in the wings.

It was just after four when Madeleine suggested they stop at El Padrino in the hotel for a drink. At this hour they would be certain to get a table. They walked a block so that Madeleine could save the parking charge.

They settled themselves in the dark bar at a table near

the piano, drinking screwdrivers, like rich matrons whipped after a long hard day's shopping. Madeleine gave her a crooked smile and the expression on her face was girlish and tainted with the sly awkwardness that, Claire knew, indicated a revelation was on the horizon. Madeleine's incisors were irregular and she had a slight but discernible overbite. She was not beautiful, Claire thought again, but strikingly different, a character, and it would be hard to forget that face, although Madeleine hated the look of her mouth. A fearful scene had taken place when Madeleine's mother had closed out her orthodontist in favor of a mink stole. It was tough luck, she told the girl, but looking presentable in the cocktail lounges she frequented was more important than her tubby daughter's choppers.

"Let's clear the air about Bobby," Madeleine suggested.

"I'd like to give him a call tomorrow. I've got two numbers for him."

Madeleine could not contain herself.

"And do what, grovel?"

"I'll just tell him I'm out here."

"No, you won't. Claire, listen to me, will you? If the situation was reversed, would you want to see him? Of course not. You'd shrink from it. You'd feel hemmed in. Forget what you've heard about L.A. It's a small place. You might run into him. Babe, give yourself a chance, take it easy for a few weeks, you'll meet people and you'll find a job."

The advice made Claire terribly nervous.

"I'm afraid. I'm running out of time . . . he's got someone else."

"I know," she said reluctantly. "We had dinner one night when he was here. I've always liked him. What's not to like? But maybe a week later we had one of those embarrassing numbers. We were both at Pips . . . it's a private club and well, neither one of us wanted to acknowledge that we'd seen the other. Bobby was with Hillary Martinson—getting into the driver's side of her Rolls—and I was with somebody who's so uptight and jealous that if I speak to anyone he throws a fit."

Claire couldn't understand her friend. Madeleine was forthright and thoroughly independent.

"Then why do you go out with him?"

"Why? Why indeed." Madeleine had always been straight with Claire but she wondered how far she dare go.

"Hey, tell me."

"Don't take this in the wrong way, but this is a very expensive town and . . ." She paused, exhibiting an affected modesty. "There are times when I need money. I can't live on what I make at Gucci."

"I would've tried to help you."

"Claire, this involves thousands. This guy paid for a broadcasting course at KIIS. He also came up with my tuition for drama school. There's no way I could afford these courses without some help."

Claire failed to simulate worldliness. It went against the grain.

"And what do you do for this—scholarship?"

"Anything I'm asked."

Bobby had been right about her. She was hooking. Claire looked at her sympathetically. Madeleine's destiny had embraced her.

"I'm not apologizing for it. People make compromises. Do you want to hear about it? After all, I'm not the only one. Hillary is the daughter of Leonard Martinson."

"So, what are you implying?"

"Leonard Martinson is one of the largest property developers in L.A. We passed Rodeo Puerta on Rodeo Drive. It's his property . . . all of it."

Claire shook her head with disapproval.

"This isn't worthy of you, Madeleine. No, no, no. Say what you like about Bobby, but don't make him some kind of gigolo. Maybe he fell out of love with me, but don't tell me he sold himself on the auction block. The man was perfectly truthful with me. What you're saying is just indecent."

She had touched a nerve in Madeleine and rather than back off, the connoisseur of mores summoned a churlish attitude. It was so strange. She had longed to see Claire and now she was losing her poise and affecting a belligerence she had not intended.

"Grow up," Madeleine said disdainfully. "Where the

hell've you been all your life? You don't know if you're alive. I'm trying to cushion the blow. Call Bobby. Be my guest. See what kind of welcome you get."

Claire became flustered, aghast at the shabby motives attributed to Bobby.

"If the Martinsons are so wealthy, how would you know them?"

"Last licks, like when we were kids, right, and then let's cut this out." Claire averted her eyes, withdrawing. "I know the Martinsons the way I know Barbra Streisand, Cher, Jack Nicholson, not to mention Allan Carr and Rod Stewart. I *wait* on them. If you came out here to get Bobby back, then forget it, babe. I care about you. See if you like L.A. It beats Westport. Claire, you've got such a lot to offer . . . just stop torturing yourself."

Madeleine had been a child of furnished apartments and it was evident to Claire that a house of any kind would be preferable to her than yet another fugitive gypsy flat. She lived off Laurel Canyon in the Hollywood Hills in a small bungalow cantilevered on a cliff. It contained two small bedrooms, a cramped living room with a wood-burning fireplace. A jittery warped redwood deck hung like a suspended entrail outside the kitchen's sliding doors. The deck was furnished with a corroding hibachi and a plastic beach chair. Claire examined the hibachi. Its blackened grill appeared to have contributed to the recent death of some steaks from Lucky's supermarket. For reasons unknown, Madeleine saved as evidence the Saran-wrapped containers in a rough wooden tub. There was a view of the canyon along with desiccated brown rolling hills that loomed like a birthmark through the widow's veil of smog engulfing the house. An occasional glimpse of the sun gasping in the west gave the outlook no cause for hope.

"You're paying five-fifty for this?" Thoughts of Bobby gave way to jet lag and astonishment.

"View and location!" Madeleine fired back. "It's a bargain. I'm five minutes from the Strip, over the hill to the Valley. Fifteen minutes from work. It's worth stealing not to spend my life driving on freeways."

Claire had unpacked and showered while Madeleine worked the telephone. Like a bookie or a dope dealer, she had a book. It was a school-sized looseleaf affair that contained the names of scores of men. However, it wasn't simply a list of numbers and addresses. It was sociology, in-depth profiles with comments relating to each man's financial and marital status, his looks, where she had encountered him and whether he was a serious prospect. It was, Claire thought, a kind of rap sheet.

Madeleine lounged on the prickly brown hessian sofa. On an unpainted table were one La Costa ashtray filled with butts, a large shell featuring an assortment of roaches, miniature plier-like holders, pipes, flavored papers, and former vitamin bottles with labels: Colombian, Gold, Home-Grown, Shit. She cultivated several marijuana plants in cheeseboxes on top of the refrigerator where there was also a carton with candles shaped like fruits. Considering that Madeleine was a working girl, out taking classes, the place was surprisingly tidy. A happy contrast to the teenager who stored burger wrappers and the flotsam from send-out food in her mother's underwear drawers to spite the gay divorcée. Her eyes were as steady as a mongoose's, never leaving the phone. A black and white Motorola TV played fuzzy local news with the volume switched off.

"Do you think you'll stay?" Madeleine asked, finally off the phone.

"Who knows? If I do, I'd like to split the rent."

"Don't worry about that," she replied, stretching languidly.

"But how much can you take home working at Gucci?"

"Not enough. Eight and a quarter, around there." Claire was puzzled. "The landlord here is a nice guy and he doesn't press me when I'm short. He lives two houses up the road and lets me use his pool whenever I like. His father left him a cufflink factory, which he sold the minute his old man was buried. He lives on the interest of a million or so. Getting back to you, I don't see you running back to Drake's. Babe, it's exile for someone like you. You won't have any trouble getting a job in L.A. They're starved for talent."

"On Rodeo Drive?"

The phone rang and Madeleine counted aloud, "One, two, three," then picked up. Rodeo Drive captivated Claire. They had breezed through it on the way to the Beverly

Wilshire. The street was so loose and informal. She had never imagined that customers just glided in and out of stores dressed so unstylishly. There were no pushing crowds as she saw on Fifth Avenue. Rodeo Drive was decidedly small-town in spite of the presence of Gucci, Van Cleef, Courrèges. Madeleine grimaced on the phone, then said she'd call back.

"Where were we?"

"Nothing important," Claire said. "Do what you want to. I'm going to bed."

"I'll hang in with you and doze off during Carson." Madeleine closed the looseleaf book. "I could have some dates, but I'd rather not. A couple of degenerates. Waste of time. Garter belts and that sort of shit."

"You want to be an actress."

"Yeah, and I'm playing the role of my life. They don't give Oscars for this, either. Oh, Claire . . . I don't like this business. Inflation. Let's blame it on that."

Claire joined her on the sofa, looked through the pages Madeleine had slid cards into, then put the book back on the table.

"What's this all about?"

"I can't afford an IBM computer. I'm still using reinforcements. It's my *book*." Madeleine frowned, reached for the longest roach in the shell, lighted it and took a few puffs.

Claire pointed to the book. "Do you blackmail these men?"

"I should be that smart. Everybody I meet, I give various ratings. I'm not really in the business-business. A few guys pay me when I get desperate. My friend from Pips, and there's this man in Brentwood. He's in blouses and a tit freak. It's a blow job for seventy-five dollars." Madeleine got up and jammed a frozen pizza in the oven. "You're getting some welcome."

"Don't burn the pizza. It's on too high. Start at three hundred and then work it up."

"Oh, babe, it's so good to have you here. I missed you."

"Listen, call the man. If you need the money, then go."

"Ahh, I'd rather talk to you and this week I'm in good shape."

She phoned Brentwood back while Claire nurtured the

pizza. She heated the grill above the range and when it was ready she crisped it up. Madeleine enjoyed her food burnt. Madeleine hung up, told Claire where the hot red pepper shaker might be located, then spread-eagled herself on the couch. They had a beer while the pizza spat demoniacally. Claire felt a curious well-being. Madeleine was wonderful at expunging lies. Claire watched her roll a joint.

"I'm glad I came."

"So am I. I hated to lay this thing with Bobby on you."

"I won't call him." Claire went to the range, took the pizza off, cut it sloppily with a bread knife and found a couple of clean plates in a cabinet. She served up dinner. Madeleine stubbed out the joint. Claire picked up a slice of pizza and smiled at Madeleine. The tired chills hit her and she felt wonderful. "Let me say my piece and we can drop it. I don't feel inadequate because I'm not. What happened with Bobby hasn't got a thing to do with money. Believe me, it doesn't. So don't make him out to be some kind of hustler. He couldn't hustle himself into tomorrow. He didn't job me. It was romance . . . and I love him for it."

9

Just because it was mid-June, the divorce season in Beverly Hills, not everyone went with the flow. There were certain abominable pragmatists like Sylvia Rubin whose lawyers' coffers were already filled with depositions, discovery proceedings, and other legal refuse, who decided that now that she had Gary's balls scrunched in the lawyers' mortar and pestle, it might be a good time to shoot for a reconciliation. Bobby was made privy to the scene at Gary's apartment, and, as he came to realize while assisting Gary and his possessions to Sylvia's new Mercedes 300TCD station wagon, there were modalities to Sylvia's beau geste that to normal people would be inconceivable.

It was Saturday and the usual assortment of Belgian cyclists, Olympic joggers, and skateboard stars were already at their work, clogging up Spaulding Drive. Balding men dribbled basketballs on the sidewalks en route to Roxbury Park for halfcourt games; others, the aristocracy, with more racquets under their arms than Borg would bring to Wimbledon and certainly more fashionably dressed than the Swede, limbered up by marking time at corners while waiting to cross to the park's courts. Dressed in a grayish tee shirt and old khakis, unshaven, Bobby carried the last of Rubin's boxes down to the elegant wagon.

"If you can't stand Sylvia, then why are you going back?" He himself was not favorably disposed to the spouse.

"I love my kids and Sylvia's a very dangerous woman. She uses this against me and she's got a few other techniques that they don't teach in law school. To begin with, our house has been on the market for six months but Sylvia hasn't got an offer she can live with. It's worth maybe five-fifty and she's holding out for eight. With the mortgage market in the crapper, that isn't going to happen. Meanwhile, I'm still supporting the house and making payments."

"So the divorce is off because of the house price."

"Precisely. She doesn't have to sell. You don't fuck with Sylvia. She wants a reconciliation and that means a suspension of legal fees—hers and mine—for however long it lasts. In the meantime, Bobby, you got the apartment on a four-hundred-a-month sublet, so enjoy it."

Bobby shook his hand and smiled.

"I won't change the locks."

"Smart boy. I'll be back. We're having a barbecue tonight and you're welcome to come."

"I'll let you know."

Returning to the apartment, Bobby attended to domestic chores, shoved dishes and glasses into the dishwasher, gathered his laundry in a sack, wrote out a shopping list. He was feeling unexpectedly flat. He had liked having Gary around and they had gone out together frequently since his return. Hillary had taken off for Hawaii the day after Bobby left for Westport. Leonard had not heard from her, nor did he have any inkling when she was due back. Bobby got the message. Nobody meddled in Hillary's personal life, and her father was loath to discuss her. Leonard, despite his continuing warmth, showed little interest when told that Bobby was not going ahead with his marriage. It became clear to Bobby that the man preferred to stand apart as a neutral observer. He had expected to hear from Claire and now, two weeks afterward, there had been no communication. The guilt he had experienced did not magically vanish.

On impulse, he dialed Claire's number in Westport and after a few moments a recording came on informing him that the phone had been disconnected. Perplexed, he called her office at Drake's. Saturdays were holy in the retail business and no matter what kind of week Claire had, or even if she were ill, she would be at the store so that she could see what was selling and which lines to mark down for the following week. He got hold of one of the secretaries in the buying office—Marcy was on vacation—and was told that Claire had left Drake's and no, there was no one who had any idea where she had gone. A call to his parents elicited no further information.

Claire had disappeared. He became convinced that something cataclysmic had occurred. He sat at the kitchen table, staring abstractedly at the sports page. He thought of her mother in Las Vegas and decided to track her down when he returned. He picked up his laundry and pulled his new silver Honda Civic out of the garage. Hayward had generously leased the car for him. He drove down to Pico Boulevard, dropped his laundry off, hit the drugstore for blades and then Owen's Market, where he had opened an account. He wandered down the aisles, picking up the bachelor's assortment: instant coffee, six-packs, a couple of frozen dinners and some Scotch and vodka. Through it all, he was like a man sleepwalking, unable to get Claire's face out of his mind.

When he returned to the apartment, he bounded inside. Christ, what was the matter with him? He couldn't think straight. Of all the people he should've called, the one he had forgotten was Madeleine. He pulled out his address book and dialed her number.

Claire was sitting on the deck and Madeleine shouted that she'd get it. When she picked up the phone and heard Bobby's voice she immediately slammed down the receiver, then took it off the hook. She went out to the deck. Claire was relaxed, drinking a Tom Collins, and had begun to get a wonderful coppery tan.

"Guess who called?"

"No games."

"Bobby . . . what do you think? Do you want to speak to him?"

"Of course," she said excitedly. She jumped up from the chair, grabbed a towel to wipe off the oil and replaced the receiver. She smiled at Madeleine. "God, I'm glad I listened to you."

"Trust Mama."

Bobby had tried Madeleine's number twice more; getting a busy signal, he gave up. He unpacked his bags, opened a Coors, switched on the TV, and was about to watch the NBC Game of the Week when the phone rang.

"It's tougher to get hold of you than Fred Silverman. First your line was busy for ages, then no answer, then busy again," Hillary said.

"Welcome back. No forwarding address?"

"I got the impression that we'd said our goodbyes." Her voice had a tantalizing playfulness.

"I got your telegram. . . . Are we going to see each other?" he eagerly asked.

There was a buoyant resonance in her laughter that recaptured the intimacy he longed for.

"I can't believe what you've done," she said. There was an embarrassed silence. "Oh, Bobby . . . I'm sitting in my bedroom with a mess of dirty clothes on the floor, crying and laughing. I've spilled orange juice on the carpet and . . . are we going to see each other? Forever, as far as I'm concerned." The outpouring, unrestrained affection, thrilled him. "I don't usually give up on what I want so easy . . . oh, what the hell. I'm never going to let you out of my sight. How's that sound?"

"Sensational," he admitted, sensing that their destinies were now welded together. "Tonight?"

"Of course."

"Gary's gone back with his wife and he asked me over for a barbecue."

"Let him barbecue Sylvia without us. Do you like baseball?"

"I've got the Pirate–Cincy game on."

"How about the Dodgers live tonight? We've got season tickets and my father's not using them. Listen, I'll order sandwiches at Nate 'n Al's. We'll have a picnic."

"I'll pick them up. Tim leased a new Honda for me."

"God knows where you can go from there. Come by as soon as you can. Bring your swimsuit. I want to show off my tan."

He rushed through a shower and shave, had the radio blasting away and trilled joyfully along with Supertramp. He threw his gear into an old satchel and as he was about to leave, the phone rang. He distractedly picked up the receiver and heard Madeleine melodramatically ask how he was.

"In a hurry. Can I catch you another time? Oh, yeah," he added as an afterthought, "have you heard from Claire?"

"Is it important?"

"Not really. I just wanted to know if she was okay."

"Is it finished?"

"Afraid so."

The servants greeted him by his last name and he was accompanied out to the pool by a maid. Rising up from a float in the pool was his Primavera. She was wearing a white satin bikini, the skimpiest thing he had ever seen. Her hair was sun-streaked and through the blonde he saw lines that were almost platinum. She agilely paddled to the side, twisted, and leapt to the top rung of the ladder so that she escaped with only her ankles wet. Her bikini bottoms were cut so low that he saw below her navel a small tuft of hair. He couldn't imagine how someone so fair could tan so darkly. Her skin was almost ebony and with her light blue eyes and golden hair, the contrast was so sharp and striking that she took his breath away. She didn't speak but smiled with the gorgeous innocence of a child. She took his hand, led him to a table under an umbrella beside the cabanas and sat down with him. The table was laid with an assortment of cold meats and cheeses, a bottle of Chablis in an ice bucket. She poured the wine. He was again under her spell and slid into the mood of perfect love and understanding that she was able to create.

"If nothing ever goes right with my life again, I'll know that I had this moment with you." She placed his hand over her breast. Her heart was racing wildly.

"What a weird thing to say, Hillary. It's just the beginning for us."

"I never dreamed it would come true. Bobby, Bobby, you don't know."

He leaned across the table and kissed her. She had the capacity to incite such an emotional furor within him that his regrets about Claire were doomed to fade in the glow of her personality.

"Was it awful with Claire?"

"The toughest thing I ever had to do."

"You told her about us?"

"I had to."

"Does she hate me?"

"Claire's not that kind of person."

In her eyes, Bobby detected a strange combination of desire and guilt. He knew that he was in love with Hillary but he had not anticipated anything like the reciprocity of feelings that consumed her. To have fallen in love was one of those flukes, but to have found a girl like Hillary with such natural gifts of beauty and wealth who wanted to possess him left him in a position of disconcerting power. Her adoration was a responsibility like no other.

"Bobby, can I be honest and unkind?"

"You can't be unkind," he teased.

"Sure I can, where you're concerned." He drank his wine and looked at the pool with its French tile surround. At one end a Jacuzzi pulsated, hissing steam as though it emerged from the earth's center. "Bobby, promise me, please, that you'll never see or speak to Claire again."

The request should not have surprised him, but Hillary's face was contorted, abject, and he was shaken by the vehemence.

"I can't promise . . . but it's not really in the cards, is it?"

"You won't promise?"

"Well, how can I? If I run into her sometime, do I just cut her dead?"

"Am I being unreasonable?"

"Sure. Relax, Hillary."

He listened with unspeakable distress as she described the period in Hawaii. She'd been drunk from morning to night, out of her head on Sinsemilla and God knew what else. He shared her torment, despising himself for contributing to her ordeal.

"I haven't freaked out like that in years. I never thought any man could get to me the way you did."

"You made me nervous at times." He pulled her to his lap, stroked her head, coddled her like a parent calming a child after a nightmare. "Hillary, I'm a very mortal guy with problems too. Don't try to make me live up to something that's beyond me. I want to make you happy."

"I want to give you my life," she countered.

The degree of her commitment was harrowing, beyond flattery or mere devotion. She was consumed by him and he feared failure as never before. He was totally unprepared for this baring of her soul and troubled by the dependence she had placed on him. Who could live up to such expectations? Yet there was an element of such passionate yielding that transcended her jealousy that he took comfort in the loyalty that was being offered.

They swam for an hour and he was invited to change and shower in her room. The spectacular lavishness of her suite overwhelmed him. Her sitting room was filled with Impressionist paintings—eight of them to be exact—Degas, Renoir, Manet, and, well, he didn't bother with the others, and he accepted the Louis Quatorze writing table as though he came across such things every day. Her bathroom contained a shower that also functioned as a steam bath. Alongside it was a large Jacuzzi tub surrounded by pink-veined Italian marble. Her dressing table was a Chippendale washstand that had been marine-varnished so it would be water-resistant. The three rooms were painted in various hues of pink. She slept in a four-poster bed covered with an oriental tapestry. Her terrace overlooked the pool and there were a wicker swing, chairs, lounges, a table. God knew who she entertained there or what happened when it rained. If it ever came to that, the prospect of keeping Hillary was so wildly implausible that he giddily dismissed it.

An entire wall of the bathroom was mirrored with small inlaid plaques; another wall supported an eight-foot French country armoire in which there were stacks of towels along with the perfumes and makeups of the world. He picked up a bottle of Norell, recalling the scent.

"Do you like it?" she asked, whirling around the tub in a lather of bubbles and sweet oils.

"I used to."

"Remind you of anyone?"

"Not really."

He learned how to use the amenities, the Mr. Steam in the shower, and he luxuriated in the convenience, washed his hair with something called Jojoba which Hillary recommended. He was about to towel-dry his hair when she handed him her Clairol blower. They'd switched to Wyborowa vodka, straight from the freezer in her sitting room. With all of the cosmetics available, he was surprised to see her just rub some Swiss Performing Extract moisturizer on her face, put on some Fracas, and comb her hair straight back. As he passed the dryer to her, she rubbed his ass.

"I like walking around naked with you," she said. "It feels so natural."

"It does, doesn't it," he agreed.

They heard the sound of a car pulling in and she went to the window.

"My father's back. Maybe you ought to get dressed," she suggested without any sign of tension.

"Good idea."

"It's not that he's a prude, but—"

"You don't have to explain."

In a moment he had his clothes on and took his drink into her sitting room. He found a single copy of *Architectural Digest,* several months old, and noticed that there was a place mark in it. He turned the pages and saw Hillary's suite in the center of the magazine, in living color. Going with her to a Dodger game struck him as marvelous. The simplicity of the girl despite the wealth was one of those fascinating unexpected attractions that Hillary possessed in abundance. She came into the room, her eyes glowing with love. She had on a pair of Mac Keen blue jeans, a tank top, and a light blue cashmere sweater. Just one of the gang, he thought.

"I left my bag in the bathroom," he said.

She kissed him lightly on the mouth. In this relaxed, composed mood, Hillary captivated him.

"See you downstairs."

He packed his wet swimsuit and the rest of his gear, then sniffed the air. An overpoweringly heavy sweet smell permeated the steamy room. Beside the dressing table he found several empty bottles of Norell in a china wastepaper basket. The odor, however, was strongest around the toilet and he saw that the perfume had been poured into the bowl.

He went downstairs, vaguely unsettled by the discovery. Hillary was possessive and she had been forthright enough to declare herself. He understood her point of view. She was responsible for the breakup of his engagement and guilt had tainted the claim she had staked out. Bobby was bemused, never having considered himself a prize. Except for his work as an architect he was without pretensions or vanity.

He found Leonard and Ann in the library. Stacks of folders were laid on the coffee table and Leonard wore a dismayed preoccupied expression, although he was affable enough. It was clear that this was not the moment for socializing and Bobby declined a drink invitation that was offered half-heartedly.

"I'll make a game one night," Leonard said. "By the way, we've got season tickets for the Rams if you like football. It's their last season in L.A."

Bobby had that boyish thrill when he opened the door of his new Honda for Hillary. She was the first woman to ride in it.

Appearances can be more than deceiving and in the instance of Leonard Martinson they were downright lies. Surrounded by the panoply of a wonderland of money, he was no longer solvent. The estate he owned, his collection of paintings, his Rolls-Royces, and La Puerta on Rodeo Drive could go under the hammer in thirty days and he would be powerless to prevent such an unpleasant process. By the time his creditors were satisfied, he would still owe fifty million to banks and insurance companies, and how such a man could sleep at night and manage not to drive off a cliff on his way home from the office was a tribute both to his tenacity and his belief in the Arcadia he envisaged for his tottering empire. Leonard, Leonard Martinson of all people, had been skillfully playing the property game for thirty years until he got caught in a tight market, and this painful fact accounted for the presence of Ann Shaw in his life.

Until recently, Ann had worked in the commercial loan department of Barclays Bank in Beverly Hills. She earned twenty-eight thousand a year as assistant to the vice president and through her hands daily passed requests for loans running into the hundreds of millions. Her recommendation during the preliminary screening process had a life-or-death effect on a loan.

When she had met Leonard a few months earlier at a cocktail party at the Bistro, she had seen the opportunity she had been waiting for. Two days previously she had acted as his executioner, placing his head on the pike with Machiavellian adroitness.

Leonard was well known, a publicity-minded millionaire. His reputation as a philanthropist, art collector, and property developer was as prominent as the HOLLYWOOD sign. He had spent years cultivating the image of art patron while building tract horrors in the Valley and Orange County. The only problem Leonard faced was that he was not creditworthy. He had overextended himself.

Embracing the boom in Southern California, he had bought land like a wildcat prospector, and his bid to build Marine Mutual Insurance's new headquarters in Century City had been accepted by Frank Dunlop, Marine's chairman. Leonard had a few problems, however. He did not own the property, he just had an option on it, nor could he raise funds for the construction loan.

Ann realized that if Leonard had turned to Barclays rather than U.C.B. or Bank of America, he would have to be in serious trouble. When she analyzed his pro forma she saw blood on the statement, and as she ambled up to him at the Bistro, holding her martini, she saw a glum and worried man. She introduced herself and he immediately perked up when she told him who she was. The familiar charm of the borrower asserted itself. He suggested dinner at Ma Maison. He was wrong to expect a miracle from Ann for a decent table at the restaurant and an introduction to Patrick Terrail, the professional charmer who owned the place.

Toasting the beginning of friendship, one of his favorite openers to naively suggest that he was sexually interested in her, she decided to find out just how good a punch he could take. He was a dapper man with a full head of thick gray hair, a tan on which the sun never set, a small frame with fine bones and a patrician Roman nose. He was about as good looking as any man approaching sixty could be, still vigorous, and counting on immortality.

"I hope you're serious about friendship."

"Sure. I hear that you're very well thought of at the bank."

"I'm afraid that's true."

He looked up over the salmon mousse he had insisted that they order for an appetizer and took her remark as calculated British modesty.

"Tell me a little about yourself."

"You haven't got forever," she said pointedly, "so I'll just tantalize you. I've been here just over a year. I spent six years as a property consultant in London with a financial group. We're still in close touch. They're looking for opportunities in California and in an unofficial way, I act as their adviser. I wanted a change from London."

Leonard was falling in love, she knew without a doubt.

"Are you happy at the bank?"

She detected a job feeler.

"Not always. Especially when there are certain unpleasant things that come across my desk. Like any loan officer, I naturally look for the merits of a case, rather than try to rip apart a P and L before it goes to the loan committee."

Leonard hadn't yet picked up. He was one of God's chosen, designated by the Almighty to blight California's landscape with cluster developments and ratty shopping centers. His project on Rodeo Drive would change all that.

"I can sympathize with you."

Another bottle of Blanc de Blanc appeared and the waiter poured the champagne. She hoped Leonard was not about to propose a toast again.

"Getting back to the rotten part of my job . . . if I can speak off the record . . ."

"Ann, I think we're going to be very close. Just a feeling. I trust my instincts."

She nodded uncertainly.

"I don't know about your instincts, Leonard. But the fact is, you're in over your head. You've been buying undeveloped land all over the place like an amateur."

His mouth turned down at the corners and he suddenly looked older, sallow, worried.

"I don't get your drift."

"Well, I had to turn you down. Your application was thrown out by the loan committee on my recommendation."

The veal chop in sorrel sauce had arrived. Leonard

could not contain his shock. He was about to be exterminated.

"I can go over your head," he said defiantly.

"Try it. We're beyond game playing," she snapped.

"Just who the hell do you think you are?"

"Someone who can make you liquid. If you don't honor your commitments to Marine Mutual, Leonard, you'll be making tents in Afghanistan. Do you get *my* drift? I did a careful analysis of your holdings, and if you don't want my help, then taking a Chapter Eleven is going to make a lot of your dear friends spend their lives avoiding you."

She got down to business with the veal chop, tender, white, not overcooked; the vegetables were crisp and the merry faces of George Hamilton and Kirk Kerkorian sitting at nearby tables provided a happy visual interlude while Leonard attempted to regroup.

"I am in over my head," he admitted.

"Tell me about it," she said, attempting to revive him.

"I saw a boom coming and I lost control. Imagine, after all the years in this business, I . . ." He couldn't go on. The specter of disaster was written across the face of this astute Englishwoman. "You mentioned helping me." His voice had lost its vintage-Burgundy timbre. He sounded as if he were in the intensive care unit.

The waiter arrived and Ann listened to the aria of desserts.

"Chocolate mousse, please, and espresso. Leonard?"

"Black coffee."

"You'll share my mousse, won't you?"

The waiter nodded sagaciously and withdrew.

"I can't remain at the bank and work full time on your behalf. In any event, even though I could do some things on the quiet, it would be a conflict of interest. I don't want to sully my record. A dignified resignation. Then I join you in the position of financial P.R. You pay me fifty thousand, plus expenses."

"How long for?"

"A few months."

"I've only got till July first."

She approached the mousse delicately as though undertaking a transplant.

"Oh, I know that. By June I'll be in a position to deliver my private sources."

"What sort of terms?" He lit a True cigarette and recoiled at the taste.

"My man will deliver twenty-five million in cash for a half interest in Marine Mutual. With that amount in your company account, any bank will co-finance."

He shook his head in refusal.

"That's robbery."

"Well, then we'll pick it up when you're in receivership."

He raised his hand aggressively and glanced furtively at the room. Army Archerd of *Variety* was listening to different musical agonies and studiously checking a story.

"Not so loud."

"First time I've been told I'm loud. It's the onset of financial paranoia, Leonard. I've seen it in London. For my part, I will have a contract drawn up by my attorneys, Mayer and Glassman, granting me a finder's fee." She smiled sweetly at him. "I never negotiate on my own behalf."

Leonard had a burst of hope, but it was tempered by the jitters.

"How do I know you can deliver your people?"

She twisted the lemon peel into her espresso and ordered a Calvados. She liked the coarse rough peasant taste of the brandy after a rich meal. It reminded her that she was the daughter of a Yorkshire smallholder who still rose at four in the morning to tend his farm.

"They trust me. After all, I did the same thing for them in London. We bought half a dozen property companies on the stock exchange before the City knew what hit them. Oh, they listen to me, love."

Leonard was relieved to have Hillary and Bobby out of the house, and now as he faced Ann he could not restrain his anger. She had made him sweat since their dinner at the end of March. Her story about the investors she had lined up no longer was sufficient to allay his fears of being had. What had set him off was a casual remark he overheard at the Dunlop buffet that afternoon. Two bankers, formerly friends, were ahead of him on line and one had observed that he was finished. The other placidly agreed and both had an air of complacency about having judged his position prudently and turned down his loan. He quickly left the Dunlop house without bothering with lunch, phoned Ann and told her to hustle her ass over to his house.

"Do you think Hillary's serious?"

"I didn't ask you over to discuss my daughter's love life," he snapped. She looked at him patronizingly. She had one of those fine facial bone structures that withstood time. Her skin was pink, not tanned, and her constantly surprised blue eyes had the effect of exasperating him.

"What is the crisis?"

"The crisis is five million dollars that has to be put into the escrow account by close of business next Friday or I lose my option on the parcel in Century City. Frank Dunlop sues me and I go under."

"That's not going to be a problem."

He threw up his hands in frustration.

"Nothing's ever a problem with you."

To secure the property for the Marine Mutual office he had already paid five million dollars. The price was fifteen million and he had two more payments to meet, July 1 and September 1. The contract called for breaking ground no later than December 1, but he could hardly build on ground he didn't own.

"You'll have a check this week and the loan agreement."

"God, how can you be so casual about this?"

"Leonard, my principals have things they're looking at all over Europe. It's impossible to pin them down."

He had never done business in such a haphazard fashion and it offended him deeply that the financial community had turned against him. His life was in this woman's hands. The placid dizziness she used like barbed wire drove him crazy.

"Where's the money coming from?"

"Either Switzerland or the Bahamas . . . whatever suits them," she noted indifferently. "You're getting a very good deal."

He almost choked on the assertion. He had been forced to give up a half interest in Marine Mutual for the money.

"Ann, our agreement isn't the usual kind. You people have me by the throat."

"If you don't like it, then put up your collection of pictures for auction."

"I've already borrowed against them for the initial down payment. The interest is eating me up."

"What's happening to your staying power? You're caving in," she said scornfully, testing her pigeon.

He ran his hands nervously over his face, slumped back into the soft folds of the settee. The pressure had gotten to him. He was trembling. The life he had so meticulously built would be torn away and he would face the ignominy of a bankruptcy court; and if the failure was as massive as he expected, the Justice Department and the IRS would send teams of agents to investigate. They would find things, irregularities. Without huge sums of money to put lawyers on retainer, his citadel would fall.

"Leonard, listen to me," she began, knowing that she had reached the right psychological moment. "You'll get the ten million to complete the purchase. But I think you ought to be prepared to negotiate in good faith for the fifteen million you'll need for the construction loan."

He was baffled. Hadn't he already given up half of his developer's profit?

"But I thought that was part of the package."

"That was months ago. Interest rates have gone crazy all over the world. They can get twenty-five and thirty percent for their money."

"What would they want?"

"I have no way of being sure, but I would think they'd be prepared to discuss some kind of participation in La Puerta."

"Give up a piece of Rodeo Drive? Never."

10

Madeleine did not like the signs. It was seven-thirty and Claire hadn't spoken to her for hours. Spending Saturday night at home did not appeal to Madeleine. If you had your ass glued to a seat watching TV with a bowl of guacamole dip and tortilla chips at your elbow, nothing significant could happen in your life. She had thought of dragging Claire to Joe Allen's, her usual haunt when she wanted to connect with someone also struggling to be discovered, but she decided against it. She had made a reservation earlier that afternoon at Giovanni's. Never mind that an officious voice had told her that they could squeeze her in at ten-thirty on the balcony and no one important would find her at that altitude. However . . . an hour or so at the bar might prove rewarding. In L.A. you never knew when your moment had come. Just have enough exposure and the right timing.

"I'm not going to let you drag ass all night," she boomed. "Get into the shower, makeup and dress to kill. Bobby's out of your life and to put it bluntly, the fucking you were getting was not worth the fucking you were getting."

She pulled Claire off the sofa and strong-armed her into the bathroom where the shower was blasting away. She pointed to the towels and pulled open the shower door, spraying them both.

"You've exactly got one hour."

"Why not?" Claire replied.

"You got the message at long last. You're twenty-four

and—not that I'm interested in ladies although the thought has occasionally crossed my mind on a one-shot basis—you're a striking piece of ass, not to mention the smartest pussy I know."

"Not pussy."

"The word is disagreeable?" she said grandiloquently, about to launch into her one-woman improv number that she had used at a tryout for new talent at the Comedy Store. She had not been booked.

"I've heard it too often lately."

Claire dumped her clothes in the hamper and adjusted the shower. One of the faucets needed a wrench, but she got it into mid-range so that the water was tolerable.

"We have cocktails and flirt with Telly Savalas and Dick Zanuck, and, who knows, we might even wind up at the Daisy afterwards."

"With a hairdresser?" Claire asked, jumping into the shower.

"Hey, I live here, not you. I'm supposed to know."

Claire closed the door. She was beyond tears or even mere disappointment. She could survive only if she accepted the fact that she and Bobby were finished. Hope was the enemy and she resolved to abandon it finally, since it would destroy all of those good moments she might encounter.

Claire wore a pearl gray trouser suit with a bright red silk blouse and red shoes. She put her hair up and spun curls around her ears. She had never been given an engagement ring and she only had a wristwatch, a cameo necklace, and a few pieces of inexpensive costume jewelry. She had a nineteenth-century look and although she never consciously compared herself with other women, she was convinced that she could hold her own with Madeleine or anyone else. Madeleine resembled a cream puff in her white dress with a low plunging neckline. Claire wanted to suggest that she put on a small scarf so that not quite so much cleavage was on display, but changed her mind.

She found it awkward on her first night out cruising, but she realized that it was the only way she could regain her self-esteem. As she took in the bar at Giovanni's, oblivious to the interested stares both she and Madeleine were getting, she reflected on the craziness of the situation. Both she and Bobby were finally together in Los Angeles and going in different directions. Despite the momentary surge of desire that had welled up when Bobby phoned earlier that day, she refused to allow herself to be carried away.

He would not come back and what they had had was irreclaimable. Actually, she had no wish to see him again. She recognized that going after him was foolish, naive, at variance with the last night they'd spent together. She was no longer cowed by her decision to get away from Westport. She could break new ground for herself and in the process get conveniently lost in the shuffle of transients and loners who migrated to L.A.

On Madeleine's side, a few men had gathered and were pitching her. The air was filled with the babble of TV pilots, the action in cable programming, and divorce settlements. There was an enormous vitality about the restaurant along with smooth service. A man with dark bully-boy good looks found an opening beside her and the bartender without being asked opened a bottle of Poland water, twisted a lime in a glass, and served him. His face was familiar and Claire could have sworn that she had seen him on TV or in the movies. He had a magnificent suntan and an attractive litheness. He emanated a charged virility without being offensive. He was on the verge of talking to her, but held off, and Claire liked the smooth reticence he projected.

"Are you meeting someone?" he asked after a few minutes.

"No. It's just girls' night out."

"Do you live here?"

"I've just made the big move from the East and I think I'm going to stay."

"More and more people are doing it. In a few months you'll wonder how you ever tolerated those winters." She let him continue, noting that there was a strong seductiveness about him as he tried to persuade her that she had endured a geographical tragedy until the wonder of California manifested itself.

"Where would the world be without the miracle of skateboards and hang gliding?" she said.

He laughed with a certain convivial artfulness as though he were accustomed to this kind of antagonistic remark.

"Just give the place a chance. You've been reading too many articles." He sounded very secure, slick, once over easy in the small universe of the restaurant. "First you have to meet some nice people."

"First I've got to get myself a job." She explained that she had been in charge of women's wear at Drake's, making the position seem to have a grandeur beyond the monolithic cut-price mall where it was situated. She might have been talking about Bendel's.

"Maybe I can help you," he said without bravado, nor was there any implication that he expected anything for his trouble; she took it as the casual line that strangers at bars exchanged and then forgot. "What time's your reservation?"

"Ten-thirty."

He caught the maître d's eye and the suave, handsome Italian approached them, beaming.

"Yes, sir."

"Carlo, you've got a two for ten-thirty?"

"Yes. The Gilbert party."

Claire didn't quite understand what was going on.

"There's a two breaking soon downstairs. Nice booth facing the room. Give it to this lady and her friend."

"Yes, Mr. Giovanni."

"I didn't know you were the owner," Claire said.

"Well, I expect to see a lot of you."

Claire introduced herself and Giovanni warmly took her hand. "It was very thoughtful of you. I appreciate it."

"Well, I think you're a sweetie, and," he smiled luminously, "there's always a practical reason for things I do. I don't like single women sitting at the bar. It opens the way for misunderstandings. A couple of guys might get pushy. I don't have incidents like that in my place. And you're too pretty to get lumped together with the women in the meat market joints."

It was evident that he liked her and that he was a bit ruffled by the men circling Madeleine, who had three rounds of drinks stacked up waiting for her, bought by her fans. Madeleine leaned over and asked Claire if she'd like to go to Pips after dinner with two of the men voraciously sizing her up.

"You go."

"Do you mind?" Madeleine asked, her mind already made up to accept.

"Come on, don't be silly."

Giovanni nodded approvingly and led Claire to the table while Madeleine feverishly confirmed her arrangements. Claire wasn't quite sure if Madeleine was hustling or just operating. Giovanni sat down opposite Claire, waved to a few customers at adjoining tables, then concentrated on Claire.

"I guess you're not in the mood for company tonight."

"Are you asking me or telling me?"

"That sounds encouraging. Shall we hook up after dinner?"

"Can I believe that a man like you hasn't got a date—or rather a selection of fine wines in young bottles just waiting to be drunk?"

"Nicely put. You assume right." His eyes had a sincerity and gentility that appealed to Claire. Whether it was the professional manner of courting or genuine didn't seem to matter to her. She was being picked up and she relished it. "I like new faces," he admitted, "and I'm a snob. I was watching you ignore the cattle stampede."

"I didn't notice."

"Which is why I noticed."

"Are you married?"

"My teeth should fall out first."

Over dinner, Claire learned from an expansive, slightly high Madeleine that Giovanni had been a small-time character actor. He had opened the restaurant ten years ago, parlaying an interest in cooking and his natural arrogance into Beverly Hills' most fashionable restaurant. It was then that Claire realized why she had thought she had seen him before. Indeed, he had been wounded or murdered on episodes of *F.B.I.* and God knew what other tripe when she had been a kid. His was the body lying in the gutter after he'd fired shotguns into the faces of people the Mafia had marked for death. Ed Giovanni had the distinction of being the groovy hitman who checked into obscure hotels with his assassin case and whose subsequent death was bereft of mourners. Claire recalled reading an article about him in *New York Magazine* about personality innkeepers. She had been in the dentist's reception room waiting for a cleaning. In person, he was engaging and not the stiff recoiling from a bullet wound between the eyes and then hitting the pavement while Jack Lord or Robert Stack looked on smugly.

Near eleven-thirty she joined Ed at the bar while the last of the customers were leaving. Claire had no idea what either of them expected. She was open to suggestions. After thanking him effusively and kissing him on both cheeks, Madeleine had been bundled off to Pips. Giovanni had not presented them with a check. He'd picked it up himself. Inasmuch as the menu had no prices, Madeleine would have been prepared to show her gratitude in a more practical way. Departing, she had whispered, "You got yourself royalty tonight."

"Beginner's luck."

Giovanni's house was perched in a cul-de-sac behind the Beverly Hills Hotel and Claire had no idea how much this lack of pretentiousness was worth. A ranch house was a ranch house, she thought when Ed pulled his Mark I Jensen into the driveway.

Before entering the house, Ed keyed the burglar alarm, then opened the door and led her through a foyer with a highly polished wooden floor inlaid with teak and oak squares. An animal skin rug that she could not identify was in the center. He switched on the lights in the living room, adjusted the dimmer, pressed another button and music came from four speakers, which surrounded them. The living room was unfussy; leather chairs, a masculine tweed sofa, and a chocolate brown carpet contrasted well with the glass coffee table and chrome lamps. It was a subdued room and in its simplicity it projected warmth and comfort. There were some modern paintings on the rough cast walls and congeries of Mexican artifacts displayed in a glass cabinet.

Claire settled at the picture window framing the garden. Steam rose from the spa and smothered the satin aqua pool water. His bar was filled with the largest variety of bottles she had seen outside of a restaurant.

"Gifts from wholesalers," he explained, pouring two Marcs in balloon glasses. He was studying her. The intimacy they had established earlier oddly vanished and Claire was guarded, and unsure of herself.

"I may as well get this over with—"

"No explanations necessary," he interjected.

"I'd like to tell you so you don't think I'm a yo-yo. I've been engaged . . . seeing one man for the last two years."

"No marriage?" he suggested.

"That's about it."

"Are you still cut up?"

"I'm trying not to be. It won't get me anywhere and frankly it bores me to walk around and behave like the world's come to an end."

"Did it?" he asked sympathetically.

"Yes."

"So I'm the first man you've been out with in years and you don't have any idea of how far you can go. Is that what's bothering you?"

"Kind of." She noticed that he was receptive.

"It offends me to push anyone. Just because you came back to my house doesn't mean that you've got to sleep with me."

"I don't like playing games."

"I liked the look of you the minute I saw you. But, Claire, we're civilized people. We do what suits us," he said agreeably. "There's no pressure. We've started off honestly. I don't expect you to stop thinking of the past."

"I want to."

"Give it time," he said coolly. The prospect of nurturing a protégée appealed to him. He'd bring her along slowly and the sweet possibility of a revenge screw stirred his vanity. She was not very experienced and her candor touched him. Inexplicably, he liked her more than such a short acquaintanceship warranted and since he was a worldly man who had been slickly undulating in and out of affairs for most of his life, the discovery moved him, made him realize that he was not invulnerable. Apart from the enormous physical attraction she inspired, there was a quality about Claire that he could not easily pinpoint. Perhaps it was the fact that she had no idea of how beautiful she actually was, or how resonant and musical her voice was, or that she embodied certain small-town virtues that one lost sight of in the sophisticated circles he moved in. That she did not crave an acting career greatly enhanced her desirability. He'd been through hundreds of starlets, avoided them now like lepers. They were bad-news mooches, like her girlfriend who laid it all on a plate. The prospect of educating Claire, introducing her to people around town tantalized him. He knew that guys would say behind his back, "Where does Ed find them?" and he found himself motivated by gallantry. His manner had always been benevolent, but Claire brought out a tenderness he'd imagined himself incapable of giving.

"You look a little lost," he said. "Is there something you'd like to do? I've got a few hundred movies on tape. We could watch one."

She hesitated, then shook her head negatively.

"This'll probably sound outlandish . . ."

"Go on, ask," he encouraged her.

"Well, I've never been swimming in a pool at night. Is it complicated? Like, well, would you have to start turning on all sorts of machines?"

Gorgeous. He was won over. For all he knew, she'd never seen a private pool in someone's home.

"It's heated to ninety degrees, day and night. I've even got a batch of swimsuits in the cabana."

He took her outside. The night was balmy, surprisingly warm and windless. She stared at the free-form pool with delight and he was tempted to put his arms around her, offer himself as her protector, but he worried about scaring her off. He couldn't quite believe the feelings of affection and consideration that took hold of him while he waited for her to change. His houseman had the weekend off and he was pleased to stock the table with Marc, a bottle of Chablis, soda waters, anything his new little toy wanted. After the thousands of nights he had spent at his restaurant and the countless pickups who'd been easy bangs, nothing had prepared him for Claire.

"I found one that fit." She had on a one-piece black suit and he smiled decorously.

She had an extraordinary fluid body with graceful long legs, firm shapely breasts, smooth shoulders. She was small-boned despite her height and she gave off an aura of unselfconscious femininity. And she did not want to be an actress, would not pester him for introductions to producers and agents. How lucky could he get.

She tested the water with her toe. "It's perfect. You coming in?"

"No. I'm going to sit here and enjoy myself by watching you."

She stood beside him and then impulsively kissed him on the mouth. He did not embrace her, simply let her call the shots. He took hold of her arm and touched the long zigzag scar, still red, that had formed on her arm.

"I'll have to teach you how to carve the roast."

"Yeah," she said, grimacing, then dove into the pool and swam with long powerful strokes, turned perfectly underwater.

How was it possible that some man had given her a hard time? he thought. Human nature mystified him even though he considered himself a peerless judge of character. He was not about to let this honey out of his sight. She rested on the side of the pool just under him.

"Do you play tennis?"

"No. I've spent the last five years building a women's wear department. I haven't had time. My big accomplishment," she said sardonically.

"Well, Alex Olmedo has a new pupil. I'll book a course of lessons for you."

"Why? We don't even know each other."

"I think it's a good investment. One day I expect you to be a doubles partner."

"Don't make plans."

"You're right, Claire. But, sometimes, well, you have a compelling urge to do things for someone without worrying about consequences. I'm afraid, honey, my time has come."

She did not respond. It was beyond her at the moment and she found herself caught in the first conflict of her new single life. What wasn't there to like about Ed Giovanni? Yet she suspected when it came to that inescapable confrontation in his bedroom, she would run. She was attracted to him, had no doubt that he would be skillful and ardent, but how could she rationalize the fact that this was anything more than a one-night bash? He'd add her to his list, then abandon her. It was in the nature of conquest.

She had never conceived of the possibility of a man other than Bobby touching her. There had been no provision for change in her life plan and she was thoroughly baffled by her position as a target for other men. It no longer mattered that Bobby had walked out on her. The problem was more insidious and revolved around her adjustment to new circumstances. L.A. was foreign territory, and Ed, for all his generosity and the splendor within her grasp, represented danger, the unknown. Could she spend the night with him, then walk away as though nothing had happened? All around her were women who, without flinching or losing face, carried on with different men, and nobody thought any the worse of them. Patsy at Drake's had regaled the girls with her story about getting it on with twins and the girls had laughed and congratulated her.

Ed, sensing her anxiety, had offered to take her home. But she had decided to stay.

"There are three bedrooms, so you can take your pick. You're a little curious about how it might be with another man, aren't you?"

"No question about it." She dried her hair with the towel. "If I ever have a pool, I'm going to swim every night."

"Until you do, you're welcome here."

"Why do you like me?"

"I haven't the vaguest idea, but I do."

"I'm not used to turning men on sexually. It's like I'm standing outside, watching someone else. Do you understand what I'm trying to say? The image I have of myself is changing and I can't get hold of it."

"In California, honey, it's called growth."

He invited her to change in the house, keeping his distance, concerned that any precipitous move would intimidate her. Convinced that she was worth the trouble, he decided to maintain the detached posture of statesman and guide. Reflecting on the number of women who had passed in and out of his bedroom, he had a sense that Claire would be special, requiring delicacy. She'd been demoralized and he saw as his task rebuilding her confidence. She had a virginal quality that captivated him and when she came out of the bathroom, jacket slung over her shoulder, her bright red blouse clinging, outlining the shape of her breasts, he was hooked. She embodied to a remarkable degree a natural sweetness that he had never before encountered in a woman.

She sat down beside him, leaned her head on his shoulder, but he detected a wariness in her eyes.

"You seem kind of uncertain."

"Tonight's been such a pleasant surprise—meeting you." He fondled the back of her neck, touching the still-wet hair she had missed with the towel. "Ed, would it spoil it for you if I went home?"

"Of course not. What do you think I am?"

"Oh, I wish to hell I knew what I wanted to do. I mean, one minute I think I'm ready, the next . . ." She moved away, sat up straight and regarded him with intensity, searching for an answer. "Really, what's the big deal?"

"I'd like it to be a big deal and not something we forget about. Understand, Claire. This is the wrong time."

He was forty-eight and Claire had the effect of returning him to a period in his life when he was a struggling actor in love with an extra who eventually left him to marry a director, and to his dismay became a star. He had been guarded with women ever since, enjoying the freedom that his successful restaurant brought with it. He traveled to Europe every spring to eat at the great restaurants in France and Italy and to see if there were any dishes he might add to his menu. He would spend a pleasant week in Bordeaux buying his wines. Let his competitors serve and swear by California wines. Giovanni's served haute cuisine and the wines that went with them were French and Italian. He had a condominium in Aspen and spent a month skiing every year. It was a happy, controlled existence and wherever he went, there were women, both single and divorced, with great wealth who courted him, proposed, flaunted him at parties, made desperate efforts to capture this will o' the wisp.

He had never had any yearnings for a normal domestic life and he considered children a nuisance. He wasn't missing a damn thing and the notion of settling down held no appeal whatever for him. His reputation as a rake suited him and had a certain factual basis, but more important, it enhanced his position as Beverly Hills' prince of restaurateurs. He reflected on these aspects of his life while negotiating the blind curves up Laurel Canyon. He turned into Woodrow Wilson Drive, drove slowly down the narrow canyon street until he finally located the small house. He parked and turned to Claire. Like a boy parking with his girlfriend, he reached over to hold her.

"Ed, have I disappointed you?"

He kissed her neck and forehead, loving the taste of her, the purity he perceived.

"I thought we were over that hurdle. You'll never disappoint me except if we don't see each other."

"Oh, I want to see you very much," she said exuberantly. The specter of Bobby was slowly dissolving.

"We're closed on Sunday and there's a brunch out in Malibu. Would you like to come?"

"Yes, What do I wear?"

"Jeans . . . anything. Don't worry. Bring a swimsuit."

"Ed," she said nervously, "if you'd pressed, it would've happened."

"It wasn't appropriate. Fact is, I'd like you to fall in love with me. It looks like I may be going through my one-woman passage."

11

More than a month had passed and Claire was growing increasingly tense as no job offers came in. She had made the rounds in the midst of a heat wave using Madeleine's battered Mustang which had no air-conditioning. The machine pinged, evacuated hellish fumes, groveled up hills, broke down in parking lots, and drove Claire half crazy. Tempestuous Santa Ana winds transported charred flakes from raging fires in suburbs outside of L.A. Weather forecasters interrupted top-forty stations, giving reports of conflagrations from Ojai to the Hollywood Hills. The smog and the heat were malevolent and Claire would arrive at interviews wobbling, sopping wet, then be chilled when she reached her air-conditioned destination.

Neiman-Marcus wouldn't even give her an appointment; a series of interviews at Bullock's came to nothing; she came close at Ohrbach's but was passed over; the important personnel people at Robinson's were on vacation and the girl she saw there suggested her experience might be useful for K-Mart or Zody's. Her one offer came as a trainee at May Company downtown, at minimum wage since Claire did not speak Spanish and most of the store's customers were Chicano and Mexican. She resisted using her credit cards because she was behind in her payments. Her bank balance had shrunk to fourteen hundred dollars and the routine of rejection was making her desperate.

"Why not speak to Ed about a job?" Madeleine counseled. "He's wired. Don't stand on ceremony—use him.

For Christ's sake, you've got the man standing on his head for you."

And that was precisely the trouble. She was disinclined to bring business into their affair. It struck her as shoddy, intruding on the intimacy of their relationship. She was grateful to him for cutting her loose from the moorings of the past.

Whenever she chose, she could lunch at L'Esplanade, the food boutique he operated. It was connected to the restaurant and was filled from morning until closing time at six, when Giovanni's opened. The boutique offered everything from organic health foods, Shelton Farm chicken, to redoubtable hero sandwiches and salads. In the foyer were showcases with homemade pasta, cheese, caviar, real Scotch salmon, smoked eel flown in from Holland. Ed's business did not merely flourish, it proliferated through catering to parties to which he was invariably invited, and which as his companion and good and dear friend, she had been attending. However, she felt bogus, lost in these circles, and she had the disconcerting habit of telling people she was looking for a job, dispelling the illusion that she might have been a model or an actress.

She drove Madeleine to her job at Gucci each morning and dutifully picked her up at closing. Although she realized that not finding a position at a department store comparable to the one she had held at Drake's was discouraging, her heart was in Rodeo Drive and she was drawn to the street. She charted the progress of Rodeo Puerta, fascinated by the clean lines, the elegance of the development. The name Martinson on a large board had become so familiar, she no longer saw it.

More than anything she admired the boutiques, which weren't merely in business for a quick buck but to make a statement. They had spent millions outfitting their stores with gorgeous facades, antiques, splashes of color, crafted woodwork that would not offend a Chippendale, and they charged exactly what they pleased. If a customer expected to get a good buy, he had to look elsewhere, for Rodeo Drive clearly was established on the principle of individuality. If one expected to get something cheaper, he couldn't go down the street for a bargain. He had to get into his car and try the Century City department stores, the cheaper stores in mid-Wilshire or west Los Angeles. There was no compromising when it came to style or taste.

The boutique section of Rodeo Drive—which, she learned, had a mere five years ago been a sleepy pleasant village street servicing Beverly Hills—had become the most expensive place in the world to shop. It was three short blocks, running from the Beverly Wilshire to Santa Monica Boulevard, and anyone who wanted to spend a hundred thousand dollars during an afternoon shopping spree didn't have to walk far. It was a magnet to everyone but the poor and middle class who could only be outraged by the knowledge that people could actually afford a five-hundred-dollar skirt at Céline, eight hundred for a sports jacket at Mr. Guy, and would make an appointment for the privilege of a fitting for a suit at Bijan for four thousand dollars.

If there was one place to make it, Rodeo Drive was it as far as she was concerned. She had investigated other areas—shopping malls in Fox Hills and in Northridge—and they were no different from Drake's, just characterless expanses of concrete over which a Sears, J.C. Penney, or Ward's presided. They provided the daily needs of people who wanted to do some comparative shopping and find a place where they could save a buck on Levi's.

Claire had spent years at the lower end of the market and it was time to elevate herself and discover the world that Bobby had entered. The raw awesome power of wealth that every store on the street represented fascinated her. She'd start from the bottom, just another shopgirl, but eventually she hoped she too might make a statement that would be heard and influence the rest of the country.

Beverly Hills from Linden Drive to Cañon was an enclave of unparalleled but sedate power. Claire had taken to prowling the streets and discovered that every major brokerage firm in the country was present. Banks dominated every block. In a few streets all the financial and fashion power of Europe, Wall Street, and Fifth Avenue had a base. The concentration of authority gave the entire village an atmosphere of sovereignty as though in this democratic country a court actually existed. What was vested in miles of most cities was just across the street in Beverly Hills. You could walk to your bank and withdraw money, buy stock from your broker, a diamond at Van Cleef's, eat at restaurants like the Bistro, Giovanni's or La Dolce Vita, all without getting into your car. It was a miracle of fortuitous planning and the relaxed faces of the people who seldom carried cash, just small handbags with credit cards, emphasized one essential fact to Claire. Hollywood had chosen a stage to shop and live and they had outdone the sets they showed in films by constructing this palatial village.

Nothing in her past had prepared her for the studied elegance of the place and she gained a certain insight into what had attracted Bobby. The world could open up for her too. The rich, the famous, and the beautiful strolled around these few symmetrical streets in jeans and tee shirts because people made it a point to dress down. She remembered how as a girl when she went to New York with Madeleine and their mothers, the women took elaborate pains to look just right, smart, hoping to blend into society. It was absurd to wear your best clothes when all you planned to do was window shop and visit a few stores or have dinner at a cheap French restaurant that disguised canned onion soup and specialized in coq au vin falling off the bone in a swamp of red wine.

She reached the end of Rodeo Drive and was still astounded by the railroad crossing where occasional freight cars of the Southern Pacific crunched along and islands of Rolls-Royces and Mercedes waited until the outlandish train, whistle blaring, finally passed. The insouciant unstructured life she was leading did not agree with her. She had to be doing something and reluctantly she started back down Rodeo Drive to L'Esplanade.

Giovanni was sitting at a corner of the bar and the doorway was packed with people. She squeezed through the traffic to reach him. He left the bar, signaling Mario to take over, and went up to her. Embracing her affectionately, he took her to a window table reserved for him. Heads turned when he kissed her on the lips, demonstrating pride of ownership.

"The suns shining, we're alive, the cash register is ringing, so what're you looking so miserable about? Admittedly, you can't breathe the air, but that'll pass."

He was wearing powder blue linen trousers that fit perfectly, a navy Lacoste shirt, and white loafers without socks. Lean, with a flat stomach, and beaming with loving kindness, he enveloped her in his aura of leisured serenity.

"Want a drink?"

"No."

"Yes." He caught Mario's eyes and ordered two Camparis. "What's bugging you, Claire?"

She could no longer hold back.

"I need a job but I want it to be on Rodeo Drive."

"To be near me," he said expansively. "What's next?"

"I have to get a car. I can't keep using Madeleine's."

"Very serious problems." He leaned back, attempted to be serious, but couldn't help but smile.

"To me they are, Ed. Stop making fun of me."

"I'll make a few calls on the street. Shouldn't be a problem with your experience."

"That's what I thought."

"Hey, Claire, you just don't want to listen to me. I've been telling you that a department store isn't for you. You did that number. Reach. Half the people on Rodeo Drive don't know their ass from their elbow. They've got big finance and except for a few of them, they don't know what they're doing. Okay, that's settled. Now what kind of car—a 450 or 280Z? Which do you like?"

"What about a Pinto?"

The drinks arrived and he ordered Salade Niçoise for their lunch.

"I have to admit that I'm glad you finally came around. You've got these middle class ideas that asking for help isn't done, demeans you." He extended his hands. "You have to learn to accept graciously. Frankly, I'm amazed you lasted this long. Because who the hell do you know in this town except Madeleine and she's some help, and me, and people I've introduced you to? L.A. looks like a soft touch when you come from the East, people playing golf and tennis, running to the beach, it's a playground. This is a tough, mean town. When you told me you were thinking of working at May Company downtown, well, babe, I was just going to keep my mouth shut and let you do it. You don't like people interfering, so I wasn't about to cross swords with you about it."

He was not imperious or offensive, but rather an astute businessman who knew his way around, she realized.

"I didn't want to seem to be taking advantage of our relationship," she said indignantly.

"Why not? It makes you beholden to me? Listen, I have no control . . . suppose next week you tell me you've met some young kid and you're sleeping with him. What do I do, take you to court?"

They settled on a Toyota Celica in a creamy color at a dealer Ed knew on Ventura Boulevard. Ed had him knock five hundred off the price, unheard of in view of the demand for the car, but Ed held out the carrot of a table at sea level rather than upstairs in the Himalayas to the dealer, who ate at the restaurant a few times a month and never before ten-thirty. She signed a thirty-six-month open-end lease allowing her to buy the car at the end of the period. Despite her protests, Giovanni prevailed when he co-signed the lease and wrote out a check for the first and last months. The car would be delivered to his restaurant the following day.

"I feel like a kept woman," she said, throwing her arms around him outside the showroom.

"Then do me a favor, move in and let's enjoy life." But he knew she had no intention of doing anything of the kind and one of her attractions was the independence she guarded so fiercely. He had insisted that she use him and not the other way around, a first for Giovanni and preferable to the clinging girls who mooched for cash and credit cards. He was convinced he loved Claire, but realized that he must continue to be patient, allow her to regain her confidence before he pressed her to make a commitment. All that counted was the happiness she brought to him, the purity of her intentions. He had stopped running.

"There's a screening at a friend's house tonight. Al Brockman's an agent at ICM and we used to bum around together—before I met you, naturally."

"Can I bring Madeleine?"

"If you must," he replied, thoroughly disenchanted.

"Ed, please, it would mean so much to her."

"Okay, okay, just tell her to wear clothes."

She thought Madeleine was about to have a convulsion when she gave her the news. Her face turned chalk white and she began to hyperventilate.

"Al Brockman! Claire, do you know what you've done?"

"You're going to a screening is all. I think there's a buffet or something. He and Ed—"

"Al Brockman!" she shrieked. The top of the car was down and they were stuck in a line trying to catch the filter up to Laurel Canyon. People stuck their heads out of car windows, thinking Madeleine was having a fit or a stroke. She sat up on top of the seat like a madwoman and stuck her feet over the windshield.

"Madeleine, stop it, will you?" Ed's resigned look came back to haunt her.

"This is my launch. He's vice president of talent at ICM, that's all."

She was still out of control when they reached the house, raving, singing, intolerable, impossible to handle. "Claire, you're lucky for me. I just knew it . . ."

She rushed into the bedroom, flung all of her clothes onto her unmade bed, and then began discarding what she thought wouldn't bring down the house. Her boots, shoes, sandals, were dumped in the middle of the living room as she ran frantically back and forth, holding up a dress or a blouse for Claire's opinion.

"Something informal, highnecked—conservative."

Madeleine shook her head, deep in rumination, considering the suggestion.

"You just might be right. Play against character. Don't worry. I'll get it synchromeshed."

In the face of this counterfeit glamor, the pathetic helplessness Madeleine evinced made her squirm. The time they had lived together had been a trial, what with her practicing lines from *Picnic*, which she was due to perform in some warehouse on La Brea, to her infernal singing on the tape recorder, her comic routines and imitations of Bette Midler, Tina Turner. Streisand she left alone. Her biweekly sorties to Brentwood, walking up to her north-south landlord a few houses up, stark naked because that was the way he liked to receive her, her chiseling dental bills for periodontist treatments, along with her dates with her sixty-five-year-old Palm Springs patron who called for her at the house, sat rigidly in the living room stroking his liver-spotted hands, never speaking, eyes darting everywhere for a grandchild who might betray his secret. It was he who had sprung for her ill-fated broadcasting course and drama lessons at what was called Tomorrow's Stars Workshop. Well, it was all beginning to unstring Claire, convince her that her tolerance level was not without limits.

Cackling laughter emerged from the bathroom and out came Madeleine, her face dipped in the green slime of minty face mask, searching for a roach and holding it with a wire clip like an entomologist turned cannibal. The smoke was virtually toxic. Claire declined a hit. She'd gagged the last time.

"Al Brockman!"

"God, what have I done?" Claire muttered.

"What?"

"Nothing. It'll be all right, won't it?"

"What a question. Wait till he sees *me*." A loud obscure chortle. "Before he left for vacation we met," she continued with demonic excitement. "I sold him an attaché case at Gucci. Beige pigskin."

"Terrific, you can talk leather all night."

"Claire." The poor girl was turning deathly serious, heavy-lidded, auguring a confidence of which Claire had had a bellyful. "I can't go on the way I am. Just another piece begging producers for interviews and when I get one —with a production manager—these guys hang me up till twelve-thirty when their secretaries go to lunch. First thing that happens is the production manager pulls me over to the sofa and unzips his fly. I was meant for better things than lunchtime blow jobs. If a man like Al Brockman would represent me, no one would dare come on to me." Tears squirted through the squinting pockets of her eyes and there was no more laughter, just smirches of green dribbling down her neck.

"Madeleine, it'll be wonderful—don't carry on," Claire pleaded.

12

Madeleine was on her best velvety behavior, keeping her infernal nattering to a minimum at Brockmans' house on Camden in the flats of Beverly Hills. Indeed, in her pale pink jeans and flowered yellow blouse, she might have passed for a Bonnard boudoir pastel. She mingled, smiled discreetly, and really did her best to cultivate the pose of mysterious woman. The only problem was that she scarfed the Chinese hors d'oeuvres voraciously and the bar waiter circulating was always one drink behind her.

No matter whom she happened to be talking to, her hawkeyed gaze homed in on Al Brockman who, rather than moving from group to group, found himself leaning against the fireplace mantel while members of his inner circle paid tribute, whispered in his ear. And what an assortment they were—people connected with long-running series, studio and network executives, actresses, a director. Although there couldn't have been more than thirty people, it had the appearance of a premiere for Madeleine.

Brockman had shaken her hand when she arrived and that was it. He had screened a two-hour movie for ABC which was actually a back-door pilot. If the ratings were good, the network would pick it up and make a limited series out of it. It was called *The Cast-Offs* and concerned runaway teenagers living at a halfway house run by an ex-prostitute junkie who had seen the light and was helping to straighten out a collection of pregnant girls, gays, and a juvenile angel dust chemist. Since Angie Dickinson was not available for the leading role, they had cast a woman who resembled her. On screen the viewer would imagine for a second that it was Angie, then Jill Vickers would open her yap and out would come a throaty Method voice that sounded like Bacall gargling.

There was no question in anyone's mind that ABC had another winner for their fall schedule. Since Brockman had packaged it with his director, actress, writer, and producer, he was being treated as if he had just made *Annie Hall.*

Every room in the house was painted Navajo white and the furniture was one or another hue of brown. Madeleine thought his decorator must have been a genius. There were photos on the piano of Brockman with Zanuck, Jack Warner, and Fred Silverman. Al was a short man in his early forties with wispy black hair laid straight across his skull like a decoration, a small nose whose nostrils resembled mosquito wings. He wore pink-tinted glasses, spoke in such a low voice that even his entourage had to strain to hear his wisdom. Although a number of the ladies in attendance made overtures, he clearly was not interested.

A Chinese caterer announced that the Mandarin's special buffet was about to be served and the guests strolled through the French doors into the dining room, where Brockman's red-lacquered Oriental pieces with matching table and chairs beckoned them.

Madeleine stayed away from Claire, who had been talking to an older woman most of the evening. Advised that she wasn't in the business, Madeleine had kept her distance. Roving around the perimeter but never able to breach the Swiss Guard surrounding the imperial Brockman, she waited for her opportunity. Observing a gradual dispersal while Brockman checked the supplies of Meursault at the bar, she closed in.

"Is there anything I can do, Al?"

The question seemed to puzzle him.

"Like what?" he whispered.

"Well, you haven't got a hostess and I thought . . . you know, seeing that everyone's got a drink and food."

He was taken aback by the offer.

"That's very thoughtful of you, but I think the waiters can handle it."

She had never been close to a powerful man *in* the

business and a rush of adrenaline made her giddy. Behind the bar, she recognized the go-between that had effected their introduction—the Gucci attaché case.

"How was Mexico?" she asked, having overheard his vacation plans in the course of the sale.

"Too many tourists." He raised the pink glasses and she got a glimpse of a single drab brown eye. "You're errr . . . who?"

"Madeleine Gilbert. I came with Ed Giovanni and Claire."

"Do we know each other?" he asked in a muffled tone.

"Gucci!" she chirped. "I gave you some advice on your attaché case. Remember now?"

The shared experience apparently possessed less magic for Brockman. He made a timorous move to leave his corner prison.

"Have you had any Peking duck?" he murmured and when she indicated that she hadn't, he quickly took her arm, guided her to the buffet table and said: "Chef, fix this lady a plate, please," and before she knew what had hit her two smiling Chinamen had her in tow and seated at a small carved table opposite the pimpled angel dust chemist who had been reformed and reclaimed by Missy, the den mother of *The Cast-Offs*.

The kid was about sixteen and immediately came on to Madeleine. He asked if she liked to be eaten and when she pretended not to hear, he slipped his hand on her knee and solemnly informed her that she should accompany him to the bathroom where he'd give her a blast of Bolivian Rock. She left the kid at the table and sought refuge at the bar where brandies and after-dinner drinks were being distributed to a claque of men. To her consternation, she heard them rave about the monstrous boy's performance and his star quality. Everyone at ABC was searching for a project for the youthful lunatic.

From time to time, Claire glanced at Madeleine; to her relief, Madeleine had caused no disturbances. Claire had spent most of the evening with an attractive woman in her late thirties who had disliked the screening as much as she did.

"It's a joke," the woman said to Claire. "But Frank got us on some kind of list for screenings, which he doesn't enjoy either. I guess they got the idea that he's a potential investor, and the reason he insists on coming is he's afraid he might miss something."

Ellen Dunlop was a sleek, panther-like woman with an intriguing face, high cheekbones set off by intelligent brown eyes. She wore her chestnut hair in a bun which was held fast by a diamond comb, and the ring on her finger had the intensity of a comet. She had a cunning mouth and she treated her short antagonistic husband with a mixture of indulgence and artfulness. His name was Frank Dunlop and he seemed to be in a flap about some slight all evening. Edging from group to group, his location made clear by a snorting derisive laugh and a strident voice, he would return to Ellen, bark another name to be included at their next party.

"Frank doesn't like to admit it, but he collects people. Actually he doesn't have much success. It takes people a long time to get to know him and he tends to pressure them, which doesn't work in Beverly Hills . . ."

However, Frank's other venture did not meet with the same dismal miscarriage. He had a company, Claire learned, called Marine Mutual Insurance, the concept of which had a treacherous brilliance. Frank insured computers and company chairmen, and boats of all kinds so long as they did not carry oil. No airplanes, health plans, workmen's compensation had ever been covered by Dunlop. They were headaches. Just give him a Shah, a Peron, Indira Gandhi. Give him an executive like David Rockefeller or Ross Perrot who wanted fifty million worth of insurance to protect him against kidnapping, assassination, or other untimely death, and Frank was off and running, the umbrella man for steel corporations, chemical conglomerates, financiers with enemies. The reason this type of insurance was so vital had to do with estate duties and taxes. For these Tiffany policies, Frank was able to charge astronomical premiums.

Midway through Ellen's explanation of these arcane matters, the Chairman stood to the side of Claire gauging her interest, studying her as though she were a slide under a microscope.

"Your husband's a genius and who gives a damn, with a mind like his, if you get invited to the right parties or not?

What's right? Tonight? Your favorite table at Giovanni's or La Dolce Vita? Who cares?"

Frank Dunlop hooked her arm and for the first time that evening an expression of pleasure erased his habitual snarl.

"Here's the way it works, honey. Years ago I met an IBM computer and I named her Lori. Well, Lori told me that I couldn't lose doing this. It's a house game and I'm the banker." Claire noticed that with his pulpy fat neck and simian arms, just buying shirts would have been an ordeal for him. He was a man out of tune with the universe in his aggressive posture and he could never come to terms with the wretched vanity that obscured his truculent intelligence. Gaining her attention was all that he needed. He seized both women, escorted them to the bar where there were three empty stools, plopped them on seats and asked for Grand Marniers.

"Frank, her name is Claire."

"Put her on the list."

"I already have," Ellen replied.

He crinkled his eyes devilishly.

"Stuart's the last name, right? I never forget."

Claire told him his memory was admirable, not realizing that he had drunk a bit too much.

"Every day I wake up, Claire—okay, Boss?"—he winked at Ellen—"I pray that the PLO should be okay and healthy and that the IRA stays in business, that the Red Brigades in Germany and Italy should get their cars filled with gas and keep up the violence. In Milan it's a problem." He gulped down his drink, elegantly waved his glass in the bartender's face for a refill, and then lighted Claire's cigarette with a platinum lighter, the likes of which she'd never seen. Between the diamonds on Ellen and Frank's rare metals, Claire was dazzled. She looked at Giovanni, but he was always busy, moving like a bee from one flower to another, never in repose. "The more important, frightened people there are in the world, the bigger I get. Last year, I paid just fifty thousand in Italy for a shoe manufacturer's thumb. He'd been kidnapped by kids. He'd been insured three years with Marine Mutual at four hundred and fifty thousand a year. We didn't lose money." His raucous laughter made the bartender jump. "I mean, what's a thumb worth if it's not on your tennis hand?"

It was no problem to understand why Frank Dunlop was not popular, Claire thought as he battered her with his accomplishments. The Dunlops, after leaving Chicago in 1977 and having paid three million for the Verona estate on Lexington, had not made the splash in society Frank had promised. "And that's before the market went crazy," he told Claire while Ellen drifted off to join Ed. "Right now, it's wavering between eight and ten. How'd you like them apples? And I'm building the largest skyscraper in Century City."

She wondered why Frank with his fortune couldn't calm down, and she decided to use her approach.

"I've got four interviews tomorrow."

"Don't talk to me about movies."

"They're store jobs, selling, on Rodeo Drive. I've got to learn . . ."

He was signaling Ellen for a Kent Light, which she kept for him in her purse. Failing, he found a Carlton on the bar, examined the warnings, and finally lighted it.

"Notice, Claire, I never leave my lighter on the bar . . . just shove it back into my pocket." With a boyish smirk, he raised her hand and kissed it. "Listen, do me a favor—and believe me, I don't ask total strangers, but when you get yourself located, call Ellen and come to the house for lunch."

Drunks did not agree with Claire, despite the fact that she had warmed to Frank.

"Why? To show your house off?"

"No. You're honest and eventually I'm going to have a piece of Rodeo Drive."

"I can't call Ellen. It'll look as if I'm after something."

"Isn't everyone?"

She kissed him on the forehead indulgently because she didn't want to send a pest home with the headache he'd arrived with.

"You need shirts, Frank. Yours doesn't fit. Christ, at Drake's we couldn't've fitted you, but on Rodeo, surely you can find something."

"Call Ellen." He flung a card on the bar amid the melted ice cubes which had slicked the top. Claire left it there, then caught the any-time-you're-ready-to-leave signal from Ed.

* * *

She and Ed were hooked up to different emotional terminals, Claire thought on the way home. She held herself aloof and remained uncommunicative. During the evening, Ed had freely roamed around, doing his charm number with several women. Ellen had mentioned that they were all previous connections of his, so she kept her distance. For his part, Ed was expansive, full of romantic sentiments, as well he might be. He had never had an evening in which four women he had been intimate with were all under the same roof. Not quite a gaggle, coven, or minyan, but nothing to hang his head in shame about. The only man he had ever met who had achieved this feat wound up on Terminal Island for extortion.

They crossed Sunset, hit the familiar dip, which busted speeders' axles, when she said: "Let's forget it tonight."

He reacted as though he'd been caught in an ambush.

"What've I done?"

"Home, please."

He pulled up at the curb, reached across for her, but she pulled away.

"I felt like I was part of your crowd tonight."

"Oh, I see," he replied, inordinately flattered by what he took to be jealousy. "They were never important."

"At times you're such a—guinea."

He loved the remark, keyed up by the possibility of a bout of lovemaking based on solace. He'd be delighted to provide Claire with such a service. He couldn't take her refusal seriously.

"I was being sociable."

"Really?" She wished he had been covert. "You were so smarmy—all that cheek kissing. What do you take me for? Isn't this commonly known as being fucked over?"

"Claire, you're crazy."

"Ed, you've got a night off. Call one of your ladies and go bowling or shovel pasta, whatever suits you."

Impossible to explain. She wasn't even that sore, just discouraged, a number totaled in the columns of his sex ledger that demonstrated that their relationship was merely a sham. He took her back to Hollywood, appealing to justice and logic.

"You can't hold the past against me."

"Why not?"

"You're jealous."

"For your sake, I wish it were true."

His position had suddenly become insecure, vulnerable. She had wounded him. The weeks with Claire had been the happiest caprice of his life, an infatuation that showed no sign of disappearing, rather deepening, possessing him. Her vitality and charm seduced him, not to mention that she was the most incredible lay he had settled into. Even in fatigue, when he was convinced he'd had enough, he went back for more, and he knew enough about himself to differentiate between desire and gluttony.

"It won't happen again."

"Ed, don't give me this much power. I'm not entitled to it and it becomes my responsibility rather than yours. You've invited me. I'm in your debt."

He wouldn't tolerate a kiss-off.

"I adore you."

"I'll think about it. Good night."

He was beside himself, watched her turn on the lights in the house, draw the curtains, ignoring him. He hung in for ten minutes in case she cracked. Being out in the cold, dismissed, was a first. When he got home he tried to call her, but her phone was off the hook.

Never one to waste an opportunity, Madeleine had stolen up the stairs before the last of Brockman's guests had departed. Her brazenness had climbed to a new pinnacle. Wearing the tops of Al's coffee-colored French poplin pajamas, she sat on his bidet, studiously reading *Zen and the Art of Motorcycle Maintenance,* imagining it to be a do-it-yourself albeit quirky manual that the agent consulted when fixing his bike. That it contained no illustrations further demonstrated Brockman's extraordinary versatility.

The john itself was a work of art, giving her new insights into the workings of the inner Hollywood, containing as it did a library with several hundred books, a telephone with a WATS line, a TV, stereo, sunken tub, piles of scripts filled with readers' reports, a contraption that enabled him to hang up his trousers and that at the push of a button would press them, a refrigerator stocked with Gelson's own fresh O.J.

As though this weren't enough to confirm her high opinion of Al Brockman—agent to the gods—she located between the Royall Lyme and Aramis a pair of two-gram bottles filled with transparent shining crystals the size of fingernail clippings. Her first vision of Peruvian Flake cocaine suffused her with a desire to wrap Brockman in her arms. The only blow she'd come across had been stepped on by a mule and would have served a more useful purpose sweetening coffee. Her ablutions completed, she continued reading, aspiring to be intellectually worthy of Brockman should a question arise concerning manifolds, double stroke engines . . . pistons.

Languidly stretching, yawning quite musically she thought, Brockman unsuspectingly wandered into his privy, saw her, and recoiled as though in the presence of the dreaded violin spider. He backed up and she detected a lessening of his phlegmatic posture. He was becoming really loose. She went to him, smiling from ear to ear.

"We're the same size," she informed him gaily, lovingly anticipating the moment when he would brutalize her.

"People like you shouldn't be allowed into Beverly Hills without a visa."

She thought the moment hilarious. Brockman had raised his voice.

"See, you don't have to whisper all the time. I knew you could talk louder if you made an effort."

He was so taken aback by her imperturbable submissiveness and immunity to sarcasm that he plopped into a chair next to his library of scripts, closed his eyes, waved a hand at her as if this would cause her to vanish.

"What gave you the idea . . . ?"

"Listen, Al, you don't have to spell it out for me," she mocked him. "You're with a sharp-shooter. You're a wonderfully neat man," she said without cloying but in a true spirit of admiration.

"Do you look in people's drawers?" he asked as though condoning such investigations.

"Only two until I found your P.J.'s . . . and the medicine cabinet, of course, for an antacid. That kid you introduced me to really burned my ass. What a mouth on him, like a degenerate."

Brockman appeared to be dozing so she reminded him he had a guest. Massaging the frail chicken neck, she assured him that it was a perfect method of relieving tension. She was extremely adroit at misunderstanding a man's intentions, since she had already signed herself to the role of willing, anything-goes hostage. Al must have been preoccupied with business. He was very definitely not coming on to her and these low-range sexual acoustics fueled her insecurity. He stood up and walked into the bedroom. She followed him uncertainly.

"Something wrong . . . are you offended?"

He removed his glasses. His moist brown eyes avoided her scrutiny.

"Possibly." Well, was he or wasn't he? She was not designed for ambivalence. "This town," he observed in his characteristic muffled tone, "is built on confidence, real or imagined. People have postures."

She felt as if she were back into the weirdo motorcycle book.

"I'm not following you."

"Let me put it to you this way—when I was a boy growing up in Rego Park my mother used to work and after school I'd have to do the shopping. I particularly disliked the butcher—all those fatty blood-red chunks of beef in the showcase . . ."

"Yes?" Maybe he was into cuisine. Nothing about him would surprise her.

"You remind me of a slab of meat on the butcher's block. All that's missing is the sawdust on the floor and the butcher's grubby apron."

"That's quite a hello, Al."

"Your name is Madeleine or something in that area." She agreed. "Don't you understand that finding you in my bedroom is embarrassing and the infraction is compounded because you have no idea of the impression you've made? You're an imbecile. I've come across impudence before, but you're in a class by yourself." Ignoring her, he went to the bathroom, undressed and returned. She magically found something opaquely positive in his comments, a cultured pearl of sorts. He had put her in a class by herself.

She was still in the race, not yet disqualified. In his absence, she had unbuttoned the pajama top.

"You're smothering the world with your tits out of ignorance—not that you don't give off the scent of a hired hand . . . by the hour or day." There was no abrasiveness in his honesty, just a world-weary fatigue. He might have been an art critic exposing fake Rembrandts. "What do you want from me?"

She was flabbergasted by his directness, overcome by the naked yet serene way he had put the question. No flimflam or romance. He was dealing and picked the game.

"Help," she gurgled.

"Help?" He repeated the word and it had an ominous register. "On the way to stardom?"

"Yeah." She felt battered, psychologically fouled, snuffed out.

"How old are you?"

"Twenty-three."

"You don't look your age." He paused, raised her chin like a surgeon examining a patient. "You look older. You've got mileage on you. Twenty-eight on your best day—on your best side."

"You're making me feel like a used car," she complained.

"Madeleine, I'm trying to be a nice guy by cutting through the fog of bullshit this town is covered in. You're a schlepper and you'll stay one until you get it through your head that you have no talent."

The suppurating wound that had developed during his pronouncements finally gushed open, exploding in a helpless shriek emanating from the soul. He could have called her a tramp, a lowlife, a piece, but to climb so wickedly into her head, gouging her very brain cells, was inhuman.

She threw herself on his bed and mercilessly beat her hands against his thick quilted spread, releasing motes of dust. He pulled her up from her prone position and she leapt into his arms. Unwittingly, he found a nipple braced against his palm and like a reluctant fence appraising a hot ruby he examined her flesh for defects. None were evident.

"You've made me feel so worthless."

"I'd call that fortunate. I should have thrown you down the stairs and had the maid vacuum you out in the morning." He was becoming perversely enthralled by the depth of her stupidity. In high school the pale scholar had eyed all the beautiful pubescent heavy-breasted girls, never daring a feel. Strange how women now gravitated to him, for he had not really changed. He had a power base and that made all the difference.

Recovering her composure, she noticed that his hand had not left the moonstone and she reveled in the triumph that her very weakness enabled her to achieve. She had been held in disdain by men before but never savaged quite so meticulously. And yet he was not a purebred bastard. She might have forgiven him if he were and she could attribute his contempt to a character defect.

"I haven't had a chance," she protested. "And . . . you've got no right to tell me I'm no good. You've never seen me work."

He sat down on the edge of a cane chair, regarding her patiently and with sympathy, like a teacher listening to a senior plead for a passing grade. He was somewhat dazed by the manic scope of her ambition and its ability to absorb abuse and still survive in its rounded pristine state.

"Where am I supposed to see you work?"

"Don't you ever go to the Improvisation or the little theaters?"

"Not if I can avoid it."

"Then how," she pondered, "do you find talent?"

"They come to me."

"Well, I've come to you."

She had, without realizing it, put her head in the noose.

"Not exactly," he said in a tone of rebuke. "You've presented your ass as a blue-plate special. That's somewhat different from calling me for an appointment at my office and arriving with your composite, a résumé, and your reel."

She gave him a bleak anguished look. Her face was like a special-effect explosion done in a slow motion. It seemed to be collapsing in stages.

"I haven't got them. Just a few head shots from years back." This had been the work of the Arthur Murray teacher who had tried to convince her to pose nude for him.

"Not even a composite?"

She started to cry again because he was right about her

unprofessional approach, and now it was unnecessary for him to castigate her. She had demonstrated that she was in league against herself. Brockman was a gentleman and he would not succumb to a fast hustle. She was in over her head.

"Where do I start?"

One of those nefariously brilliant packaging ideas occurred to him. A discreditable character by the name of Eugene Roth had once been a client of his. A promising director without staying power—everything had to happen overnight—Roth had become a still photographer, lurching in the footsteps of John Derek. A mettlesome item like Madeleine might appeal to his bizarre tastes. It would give Al an opportunity to get back in touch with him. Christ, he'd love to sign Roth again. But this time he'd structure his career, start him back off in commercials and then whip him into a TV pilot.

"Suppose I give you the number of a photographer who'll do a decent job for you and won't charge a fortune. He used to be a client of mine . . . very talented. No one in town can light better than Eugene. You'll get your pictures and we'll take it from there. End of business discussion."

She raised her sulking eyes to him and there was an implicit recognition between the two of them that crude as her tactics had been, she had succeeded. She accepted her lack of grace as one of those wondrous personality quirks that could be fashioned into a weapon.

"Do you want me to stay?" she asked when his attention wandered.

He shrugged indifferently.

"I've got an early breakfast meeting and I don't like girls sleeping over. It creates the illusion of permanence. So you'd have to leave." The way he put it, there seemed to be an element of doubt in his ground rules.

"That's okay with me." In the abyss of her humiliation she found an intangible source of strength. She had hit rock bottom, but as far as she was concerned, it was like tripping off the curb and falling into the gutter. No big deal. "Al, I'd like to tell you how much I appreciate your—"

He raised his arms like a conductor demanding silence. "Don't. I'll never get it up on gratitude."

13

Leonard Martinson was not quite sure how he had survived the first two weeks in August. He invariably had a distracted expression in his eyes, forgot the thread of conversations, and began losing regularly at tennis to Frank Dunlop, who played like a human backboard. He had his annual checkup with his cardiologist, who wasn't pleased with the results of his treadmill. Leonard had developed an anxiety neurosis and Dr. Herbert Stein suggested some time off and prescribed Inderal when he had an attack of paroxysmal tachycardia. Twice Leonard thought he was dying. His left side froze, pulsations occurred in his autonomic nervous system, and the starlet he saw twice a week noticed that her ministrations were to no avail. Leonard couldn't get it up. He was in a pressure cooker.

He had sold off a couple of developments in the Valley to a Saudi at thirty cents on the dollar so that he could keep up with the interest payments on Rodeo Puerta, which he was determined to have completed by the end of March the following year. However, the building inspectors were insensitive to his plight and constantly turned down the underground parking plan he presented, revised, and resubmitted.

Tim Hayward, his friend and conspirator for twenty-odd years, was growing concerned about him. Their fortunes were interlocked and the signs of an impending disaster were becoming evident. Tim had his loyalties—he was

Leonard's house architect—but he was not about to be pulled down because of friendship.

Hayward and Associates were skillful imitators who went to any lengths to please their clients. If someone wanted a farmhouse, a turreted mini-castle, or an all-redwood beachhouse smack in the middle of Beverly Hills, Tim had a silky smile for his victim. "No problem. For the money you're spending you ought to get what you want. You worked for it." Seldom flustered, a good hand with a wine list, he roved from the Bistro to Ma Maison to Le St. Germain with his sheep. He grabbed checks and closed contracts with equal facility. What he did offer was structurally safe construction and he came in at cost.

Conservative to a fault and indecently derivative, he naturally enjoyed an excellent reputation. Outrageous people might live in Beverly Hills but when investing millions in a dwelling they tended to be reactionary. What Tim hadn't counted on was an opportunity to do a major office building in Century City, and from the moment Leonard made the proposal for Marine Mutual Insurance, Tim was dubious. Leonard had used his usual arguments about sharing costs, how they could whack Dunlop, zip him in a plastic bag, shortcutting. On a fifty-million-dollar building, not including overages and final appointments, Hayward was looking at a seven-and-a-half-million-dollar commission. Sure, he'd have to kick back most of it to Leonard, but the prestige of the firm and the profit margin overcame his reluctance.

Now, sitting behind his desk, his gaunt face rigid with fright, he averted his eyes, unable to look at Leonard. Leonard drinking brandy at three o'clock in the afternoon? Leonard's constantly boozy breath and the black saucerlike pockets under his eyes made Tim uneasy. Ann had delivered the first five million for the parcel and now they were waiting for the second five so they could close escrow.

"I don't want to bring this up," Tim began sipping his iced Sanka, "but I had a meeting with my lawyer yesterday. Stan Finberg told me I'd be liable for damages if Dunlop doesn't approve of a design. See, he could prove that we've been fucking him around. The litigation could cost a fortune. I've told you time and again that Dunlop isn't the sort of guy to mess around with. He's an animal. You thought you could promote him and outfox him, but I'm scared to death."

The fact was that any firm of architects in the country would have been elated to have the commission, but Leonard had demonstrated that his own architect could do the building as well as Johnson or Luckmunn. Leonard had brokered the deal for himself and Tim. They were bound like Siamese twins—packaged. Both would be liable.

"My money man is coming in from London at the end of the month," Leonard said, trying to pacify his conspirator. "They came through with the first payment."

Hayward swept the pile of renderings of Marine off his desk. His skepticism had turned to disdain.

"I never liked Ann. I think she's getting us in deeper."

"I had no alternative."

"She knew it. But that's history." In the future, he realized, his symbiotic relationship with Leonard would have to be broken. Like doctors and lawyers, they would go their separate ways and discover that they were antagonists, not allies.

"Naturally. She's a professional finder. We just have to keep Dunlop bottlenecked."

Tim thought he was beginning to sound like Nixon during Watergate and he foresaw no triumphant outcome.

"I've got Frank coming at four-thirty."

"Let him scream. You can't give him anything he might approve before I tie up the finance."

Tim had a variety of recommendations given to him by his attorney. He was not prepared to be trapped in fraud. Other architects in the firm had been briefed, taken notes during planning sessions. The assignment had been handed to Gary Rubin, whose experience encompassed shopping centers and heavy-density cluster developments. Why give Gary this project? It was like telling a pediatrician he was now going to do a heart transplant. Architects did not operate in this fashion. The only legal stance he had was that Frank had rejected eight or ten other architects' plans before meeting Leonard and being sandbagged.

"I'm going to suggest, diplomatically—as only I can—that Hayward and Associates and he are having creative differences and bow out. Our lawyers can work out a settlement and no hard feelings." Tim was looking for a middle.

Leonard's jaundiced tan faded.

"You blow me out then. I've got no fallback position. I'd have to resell the deal to him and it can't be done. I'm dead."

Hayward was being boxed in. Until his recent disaster, Leonard had been able to sell anything. In previous years, before they became a respectable presence in Beverly Hills, the two of them had, in their developments out of L.A., blighted landscapes, contributed to divorces, crime, and who could predict what further havoc to hundreds of thousands of people. Their markdown-priced high-density housing excluded all human privacy. No green patch had ever found its way into any of Leonard's works of art. Fast easy mortgage money, cheap bright carpets, a wallpaper-painting allowance, cottage-cheese blown acoustic ceilings, space-saving Formica kitchens with bottom-of-the-line appliances that exploded and flooded the place, improper drainoffs, playgrounds that were unusable and always closed because of accidents. Leonard had been an early adherent to nonracial housing. So long as the price was right, black and white blue collars thought they'd found paradise. They just couldn't live together in these conditions.

"How could this happen to you, of all people?"

Leonard rose. It was ten to four and he didn't want to run into Frank in the office. He was in bad shape. Seeing Frank socially, when he had to, usually enabled him to tread water. In the office, it would be another ass-whipping.

"I got greedy and you came along with me, Tim—to lick the plate."

"Who the fuck do you think you're talking to?"

Leonard retreated. He'd shot his load. He was devoid of energy.

"I'm in a bind, Tim. Two more weeks. Bail me out, for Chrissake."

"Don't you understand? I can't keep feeding him these negative ideas. He's seen through me. I can't go on stroking him."

"I beg you."

He saw his former patron to the back door so that he wouldn't have to pass through the office and suffer any further humiliation.

"I'll do my best," Tim said, immediately regretting his acquiescence. Leonard had sold him again.

He checked with his secretary to find out if Dunlop had arrived and was relieved to learn that he would be an hour late. Tim had no recourse but to bring in Rubin and ask for help. It might mean making Rubin a partner and formalizing the conspiracy. For a moment, before buzzing Gary, he sought another solution, but short of revealing his problem to a brother firm, which presented another scenario of dangers, he had run out of choices.

Rubin was apprehensive and unhappy. His work had been shot down for months by Dunlop, sapping his confidence. His marriage was still shaky and the arguments at home were ceaseless. He regretted going back, should have washed it out. When he appeared, Tim invited him to have a drink, put his feet up. The warm reception disconcerted him. He ran a hand through his wiry hair and took the Scotch the boss offered him.

"We're in something of a pickle, Gary."

Rubin thought he saw disaster coming.

"I admit I've been struggling with Marine."

"It's taken you away from the condos in Sherman Oaks and your remodels."

"I've had to pass them over to Bobby and Slater." The latter was another middling architect. "Tim, you yourself suggested a conservative approach with Marine. The client has other ideas. Besides, I've never dealt with anyone so bad-tempered, who takes exception to whatever I say."

It was becoming clear to Hayward that his office workhorse was seeking a way out of the dilemma and was not making any effort to save face. No need to tip his hand about a partnership.

"I agree that you've bent over backward to accommodate Dunlop. But we're not up against a reasonable man—he's an egomaniac."

"I'm in a muddle about this project," Rubin admitted.

"Then you wouldn't be upset if you dropped it?"

Rubin bolted down his drink. This was the best news he'd had in months.

"I could get back to my own stuff. The shopping center on La Cienega is dying without me."

"Is there anyone in the office who could come up with an approach for Dunlop fast?"

They reviewed the workloads and the competency of the twelve architects in the firm and rejected most of them on the basis of original conceptual thinking. Hayward lost his buoyancy.

"What about Bobby?" Rubin said. "I've discussed my problems with him and I know he's been playing around with a few things."

Hayward's next question astounded Rubin. He realized that his employer was hazy about most details and his judgment was often capricious. However, his inability to assess another man's work was beyond Rubin's realm of comprehension.

"How good is he?"

"Bobby has imagination in design, a first-class knowledge of structural mechanics and engineering. He has a tendency to be outrageous and might have to be tamed, but frankly, Tim, in spite of his age, he's the most complete architect we have."

Hayward became irresolute. A project of this size for a new boy would be asking for more headaches.

"He's certainly not a traditionalist."

"That's why his work is exciting," Rubin informed him. "He's searching for a style."

"That's what makes him so risky. Could he take the pressure?"

"I don't know." Gary hesitated. Criticism exasperated Hayward. "I have to tell you that he thinks most of the work we do is rubbish. He hasn't said it in so many words. He's diplomatic and he doesn't want to hurt anyone's feelings, but he's intimated that the concepts we've done for Dunlop are old-fashioned and dull."

"You're not offended?"

"No, it's the truth. I've been uncomfortable with my work."

"You've persevered. Gary, do you think I ought to bring him in at my meeting with Dunlop?"

"It's a crapshoot. Bobby can be very independent when he's put on the spot."

"Get him."

There had been five messages from Hillary, none of

which Bobby had time to return when he was summoned. Gary had given him a general briefing of what to expect. Although the work at the office was untaxing and routine, he had come to enjoy it, mainly because of the deepening relationship with Hillary. He was convinced that he had made the right choice about Los Angeles and her. In a way, the two of them went together, harmonized.

Dunlop was already in the office when he got there, fulminating. He and Bobby had seen each other a number of times at Leonard's house and had avoided discussing business.

"How are you, Frank?" Bobby said, nodding to Hayward who was behind his bar fixing drinks, out of harm's way.

"Just pissed off with your boss as usual. The stuff he's been showing for months looks like we're putting up a mausoleum."

"Come on, Bobby, speak your mind," Tim said.

Although Bobby agreed with Dunlop, it would be unethical, not to mention dangerous, to criticize his brethren. He wanted to have his own office before he was fired. The prospect of taking part in Marine Mutual had been suggested by Leonard, then dropped. Apart from a few renderings he'd been toying with, he had not thought about it seriously. He'd kept his notions to himself rather than step on heads, but the opportunity to start fresh intoxicated him. Tim brought him a Scotch.

Dunlop's porcine eyes followed him as he walked around the office. Despite his hectoring manner, Bobby had come to respect him. The man was out front, never dissimulated, had a sense that the ideas foisted on him were unsuitable. He saw that he was an hour late meeting Hillary and sighed.

"I've seen most of the renderings prepared by Gary and his staff and I think some of them are interesting," he lied. "But maybe part of the trouble is that not enough thought went into the preliminary discussions."

"Come on, get to the point," Dunlop snapped.

"You see, Frank, before you get into a distinctive shape for the building, there are certain things you ought to consider and I'll suggest them to you. First of all, you've got a superb site that is going to be a part of the skyline of

Los Angeles. The office buildings in Century City don't offer much competition. They're conventional, and Marine Mutual can be unique and make a statement like the Hancock in Chicago and the TransAmerica pyramid in San Francisco."

Frank Dunlop listened intently, as did Hayward, and Bobby was filled with a sense of freedom, liberated from all the mealy-mouthed little dealers he'd met in New York. Here was a man who was prepared to take risks and might respond eventually to a dramatic concept. Like most of the multimillionaires Bobby had met recently through Leonard, Dunlop was searching for an identity which his fortune had not brought him.

"What I'm getting at, Frank, is this. When people come to Century City your building shouldn't be like every glass box in the area. Nobody knows one building from another. They park in the wrong garages like I do. The Tiger building is a maze and so are the others."

The lines on Dunlop's ruddy, high-blood-pressure face relaxed. He turned to Hayward and held out his glass for another drink.

"Go on, Bobby, I'm enjoying this."

"Now, insurance companies have a lousy image with the public. They hassle people with claims and it doesn't matter who's right. Usually buildings they have designed look like fortresses—to give people confidence. Well, it doesn't work. It's forbidding. The minute you hear 'insurance' you think of dying, disaster, and being fucked over. So what you ought to determine is how this is going to reflect on you. And I've got some odd thoughts on this. Is this building going to be Marine's headquarters, the corporate monolith, or is it going to be something else?"

"Like what?" Tim asked, intrigued by the nuances of Bobby's patterns. He was unaccustomed to discussions of this kind.

"Suppose, Frank, you thought of it as *home* office. If you did, then you could reach out, allow yourself to be distinctive, and get away with it. Now, that's really the crux of it. You can't have it all ways. It's either another ice cube or something individual. And home can be inviting and open or you shoot for privacy, play into the notion that conspiracies are taking place and the public has to be kept out because you don't want them to know what's going on."

A tremor of excitement played on Dunlop's face.

"No ice cubes," he said vehemently. "Home."

"I've missed something," Hayward said, growing uncomfortable.

"It's a question of whether the company's *family* is going to reside in the building or if you want to tell people that its troops are there, manning the guns in a citadel. You have to make that decision, Frank. Whatever I do"—he looked over to Hayward—"if I'm put on the project, depends on your feelings. There's nothing intellectual about this. Go with your gut instinct. You'll never be pleased with what anyone does on this job unless you come to terms with this. You're a self-made man. You built your company from nothing. Do you want to show people what's inside or hide?"

Dunlop followed his line of thought closely and became more exacerbated with Hayward than ever.

"Why the fuck didn't you put me together with Bobby at the beginning?"

"Unfortunately, he wasn't working here when we started."

Bobby was wound up. He could discuss concepts forever. He was in his element and he now knew he had been right to turn down the shoddy mini-marts and developments he'd been offered. He was an architect with a vision. Like a painter facing a blank canvas, he had to interpret space so that people could function.

"Just to give you another point of view: Is this the kind of place that Ellen would be glad to come to, have lunch or dinner with you and friends and business people?"

Dunlop was awed by the possibilities available to him.

"I love it," he said.

"Well, then, why shouldn't there be a really marvelous restaurant in the building? I mean, does it have to be a coffee shop or Hamburger Hamlet that opens and closes during business hours? Why can't there be a variety of restaurants like at the World Trade Center in New York where people can come to?"

"Movie theaters—a complex," Tim shouted.

"You're competing with Plitt then," Bobby informed him patiently.

They continued the discussion and Bobby, who had not read the original specs and proposals, learned that Marine only employed six hundred people and could be accommodated on the top three floors of the twenty-five-story skyscraper. The big profit would be in renting office space. The possibilities of converting it into short-term office condominiums with graduated increases had never been considered.

"We can't zone for condos," Tim explained.

"But why can't we operate on the same principle?" Dunlop fussed. "I've got companies in England and France in property and we do it there. The key is freehold. If I've got that, then you can structure ground rent with it. It's a tax deduction to the tenant. We can finance the mortgages with endowment policies. Tim, don't you realize the kind of thing this could be? I'm personally financing the building. The board of directors are my lawyer, my accountant, Ellen, and a few retired hacks who served some terms in the House of Representatives. Marine isn't a public company. I don't control it, I own it!" he shouted.

Hayward had never known this ratty, vicious man in an amenable mood and he wanted to rejoice. He and Leonard still had their pigeon. Christ, as soon as Dunlop was on his way, he'd call Leonard, come out a hero, beat him down to a half of the kickback and still put some color into Leonard's washed-out cheeks.

"Don't rush into this," Bobby suggested to Frank.

"Why not? I'm excited."

Bobby had seen projects disappear overnight and he was not prepared to get to work until Dunlop had the time to reflect and could provide his own input.

"How long will it take to get me some renderings?" he asked Bobby.

"That depends on Tim."

"Don't give me any shit about office politics," Dunlop said, rising slowly.

Bobby caught him before he was about to lace into Hayward.

"Frank, there's a proper way of doing things." He observed that both men appeared let down. "Look, Ellen is very important to you. She's a highly intelligent woman. See what she has to say."

"I make the decisions," Dunlop stormed, gesticulating like a maddened chimpanzee.

"I'll still be here tomorrow."

When Dunlop finally left at six, Tim fell on the sofa, exhausted. He could have murdered Bobby and kissed his ass at the same time. What further disturbed him was Bobby's eagerness to leave rather than chew things over. Tim insisted on another drink. Bobby had a wariness that disconcerted him and after watching his performance, Tim wished to give him a lesson in business.

"Just this quickie," Bobby said, raising his glass. "Hillary's been waiting for two hours at Alpine for me and I haven't called."

"Fuck Alpine."

"What're you talking about? It's Leonard's and my first project. I love the house."

Hayward was beside himself. Bobby had a screw loose. He needed counseling and an education.

"You are without question the best salesman I ever had. Why the fuck didn't you close Frank? It would've given us more time and we could've done a number on it."

"I'm an architect, that's why," he said. "I don't peddle ideas."

"You had the man in a gas chamber."

The image revolted Bobby.

"I don't think you understand me. If Frank goes with my idea, then I'll send you a memo with my demands."

"What are they?"

"Very simple. Principal Architect."

Tim was a bit high but he had his senses, could still read a balance sheet or do a costing. He decided not to press Bobby. Just please him. That was all.

"Forget about the house. Gary'll do it."

"No way. I'm going to finish it." Bobby was appalled by the Machiavellian techniques he was being dragged into. Sure, money was important, but what had happened to the idea of hanging in, doing a job well? The pleasure of the act, like lovemaking, was inexplicable to Hayward.

"How long've you been here?"

"Since May, give or take. What's that got to do with anything?"

"I haven't got the sheets here, but what're you making?"

"Twenty-five with a review and option to renew my contract in six months."

Mardi gras time for Tim. He observed Bobby's anxiety to leave and although he was an unemotional man, he hugged him.

"You're up to thirty-five—retroactive. We got you cheap and if you're Principal Architect on completion of Marine, you'll get a bonus."

Bobby shook his hand. Money might be important to the world he lived in, but all he wanted really was an opportunity to fulfill his lifetime ambition. The money would come sometime. He didn't need a great deal. The Dunlops of the world had different goals. Just let him build and he'd be satisfied.

"I appreciate the raise. But if you forget about it, I won't worry."

Sitting on the grass, smoking a joint, Hillary savored the last of the sunshine. One of the Chicanos on the job had laid some primo on her while the guys were passing it around in the back garden. She'd been cultivated before and she wasn't ready to be a mark again. She was cured. Still, the Sinsemilla had loosened her up and, surprisingly, not wasted her. It gave her dreams and although they might be dangerous, there was Bobby to fall back on. He had changed her. Yet she couldn't quite identify the malaise that slowly ate away at her. Some part of him still eluded her, remained separate, would always be owned by Claire. He was disarmingly open and affectionate but a bit too tentative when Leonard was around.

They made love in his apartment almost every day, compulsively. Surprisingly, he never encouraged her to stay the night.

Bobby was more than two hours late and her mood shifted to anger. She was about to leave when she caught sight of his Honda tearing up the street. She rushed to the car, opened the door and threw her arms around him. His eyes shone and he squeezed her tightly and with such a flood of love that her insecurities vanished.

"Sorry I was late . . ." He was breathless, his face animated. "But I think I've got my first real commission. Marine Mutual! Dunlop practically begged me to do it.

And Tim bumped me up ten thousand on my salary. Hillary, do you know what it could mean to me?" She was chilled by his exuberance. It emanated from a source she had no connection with. "What've you got to say about that? Thirty-five thousand a year! It hit me after I left the office. I was so calm and laid back about it. Caught up in my ideas for the building that nothing else registered."

"Including me."

"Who could I share this with but you? Let's go somewhere and have a drink to celebrate. Hillary, I'm crazy about you."

"Are you really?"

"Haven't I proved it?"

They wound up at the Bistro Garden, took a table outside on the terrace. Occasionally he had lunch there on the firm and he was greeted by the maître d'. He belonged to this society now and he wondered how the subtle transformation had occurred. He had not been consciously working at it.

"Baby, what's bugging you?" She had withdrawn and her face lost its candescence.

"I'm pleased for you." She raised the glass of champagne. "Here's to your future."

The joy left him. There were many times when he could not fathom her mercurial temperament. Their affair had heightened elements that defied explanation, but then she would lapse into an impenetrable melancholy. Whenever they were together he found that his raw lust for her was like a drug, addictive. Then she would vanish—the girl he loved—and a strange other-worldly impassiveness would intrude during which she retreated to another plane.

"What is it?" He clasped her hand, raised it to his lips, stroked it.

"I knew you were going to get somewhere . . ." Her eyes were unfocused. Why couldn't she rejoice with him, enter into the palmy future within his grasp? "One of the guys at the job laid a joint on me. Grass doesn't agree with me. I'm past it." She disengaged herself. "I've always been lonely but since we've been together it's worse because I want you with me all the time. We met almost five months ago . . ." He picked up her line of thought and was beset by ambivalence. "I'm in such a weird situation . . . I don't know how to broach it," she continued, dejected and remote. "Do we have any future? I hate putting you on the spot. Are you afraid?" She drank her champagne, then, losing her self-control, angrily blurted out, "You're still in love with Claire."

He frowned. The dazzling excitement coursing through him gave way to sorrow, snapping him in half. He hadn't thought of Claire for weeks.

"Why bring her up? What the hell're you suggesting? Be logical. People fall in and out of love. They break engagements or get married and then divorced for sure," he said lightly.

"You *never* would've divorced Claire. Bobby, I know you. You have loyalties. You two would've stayed married because you would've stayed in love."

They polished off the bottle of champagne, skipped dinner. When they arrived at his place they didn't notice his grubby kitchen or the laundry still on the sofa that he removed piecemeal from its blue wrapper without ever putting it into the bureau, nor the summer daddy-longlegs bouncing along the walls and ceilings in a reckless gavotte.

Her skin had the texture of a ripened apricot. He couldn't hold back—none of those complacent evenings when they had both gone to the bathroom, emerging with Vitabath bubbles on their ears. He gripped the side of her neck, impatiently seized the buttons on her blouse, burst the snap on the front of her brassiere, pinched her nipples involuntarily, then thrust the whole of her breast in his mouth, leeched at it. Then he put his fingers inside her and rubbed her other breast with the honey. He licked her nipple, going back and forth insatiably. Her pussy had never been so hot and moist.

He couldn't get enough of her. His sex drive had never been stronger, the meshing of their bodies inebriated him. Their stomachs thrashed together almost painfully. Her nails clawed him and there was a wanton unregenerate extravagance in the frenzied pitch they achieved, spurring them on.

She cupped his face in her hands.

"You belong to me—only me," she insisted breathlessly. "Always, Bobby."

He had no doubts about the claim. They had gone too far.

14

Rodeo Drive was filled with zealous ladies on motorized tricycles writing tickets. They wove from spot to spot with the precision of assassins, checking parking meters for red flags. It was a balmy Saturday, which brought tourists and locals to the street, some of whom would buy and others who would return to Cleveland or Minneapolis and report that they had actually seen a human being purchase a fifteen-hundred-dollar handbag or a skirt for seven hundred.

Good as his word, Giovanni had arranged interviews for Claire at Polo, Ted Lapidus, Theodore, and a few other stores, all of whom offered her jobs. She settled on a boutique called Minerva for two reasons. She liked the clothes, most of them English imports, and the salary range offered her greater opportunity. She was being paid eight hundred a month against a six percent commission, seven percent if she sold over twenty-five thousand dollars, and there was a forty percent discount on the clothes.

The store was financed by a syndicate of British investors and operated by the frosty twice-married Minerva who despised the clientele, sneered at them. Her finest scorn was reserved for black music producers and their charges who sidled in with their diamond rings, earrings, gold chains, and pastel clothes and seemed to have a lock on Rolls-Royces equipped with phones, TVs, stereo systems, and bars. They all had chauffeurs who came into the store to carry out the packages so that sir and madame wouldn't have to do any lifting. She referred to them as Kaffirs or wogs, depending on her mood, when they were out of earshot.

Minerva's was located a few doors down from the Beverly Rodeo Hotel. It had a used-brick exterior, arched windows, and the most magnificent woodwork and counters Claire had ever seen in a store. The floor was inlaid with Brazilian hardwood. Unlike most of the stores on Rodeo Drive, Minerva's had a dress code. Shop assistants, six women, dressed in black skirts and white blouses. About a quarter of the store was given over to men's wear—hacking jackets, Norfolks, Church shoes, cashmere sweaters by Bernhard Altmann, shirts from Jermyn Street. The rest of the selling space featured classic tweed skirts, suits, blouses, sweaters, and handbags crafted by a tanner in Canterbury. No polyester or synthetic fabric ever found its way into the store. Wool, linen, and Egyptian cotton.

Peering from behind tortoiseshell spectacles attached to a gold chain, her long fibrous nose tilted in the air, Minerva might have been head sister in a British nursing home for the titled. Although in business for only a year, Minerva regarded the store as an institution, and her reputation among the other store owners as the rudest woman on Rodeo was well deserved. However, she had a point of view that Claire respected.

"We're selling tradition—that's our gimmick. Let the other people peddle the flimflam fashion stuff that's *out* in a fortnight. I did that at Biba's for years and it's too chancy and cutthroat."

She wore her gray hair in a short man's cut, dressed in suits, deplored air conditioning but was grateful for it during the fierce hot weather. Virtually nothing could alter the scowl graven on her thin mouth except counting the day's receipts or a visit from her friend Ann Shaw who, contrary to policy, also received forty off on her clothes.

The hours for Claire were long and arduous. She was on her feet more than forty hours a week and when the store wasn't busy she checked stock, unpacked merchandise in the back, and forced herself to remain busy. She had been at Minerva's for a month and with the help of several customers, she had sold twenty-eight thousand dollars' worth of clothing, which brought her total pay to just under two thousand dollars. It was a hard buck and although she was entitled to a five-day week, as an act of good faith and because she wanted to learn, she hadn't taken any time off. She was anxious to get over the financial hump. Payments on her car and insurance ran two-forty a month, rent two-fifty; buying clothes and stocking the refrigerator with basics put her in a bind. She still owed Giovanni close to five hundred dollars and was determined to begin repaying him when she collected her check at the end of the day.

Waiting outside the small office in the back of the store, she remembered Minerva's pronouncements: "Rodeo Drive is for people who don't know what to do with their money. Give them something they can't buy in the department stores and you've got them." But Claire thought that the stability of the business also depended on regular customers and not the one-time walk-ins from out of town who gorged themselves and begged to be loaded. Continuity expanded a business. That was the key element at Drake's. Claire was last in line for her check. She was the new girl and younger than the other five women.

Minerva had a bottle of Beefeater's and some bitters on a shelf. She drank pink gins after Saturday closing. She waved Claire to a small wooden stool below her desk and punched out her sales receipts on her Canon adding machine while Claire checked her sales book.

"What do you make it?" she asked.

"One thousand, nine hundred and sixty."

"Not bad. You're twenty dollars off," the shopkeeper announced proudly. "The exchange you made wasn't equal. So you've shortchanged yourself."

"Error in my favor, that's a relief."

"Claire, you finished number two. I'm really delighted with your attitude and your abilities." She indicated the bottle of gin. "Rinse a glass and join me."

"Not straight."

"There's a bitter lemon or tonic in the fridge."

Claire went to the bathroom, washed a glass, found two ice cubes in a plastic tray, wiggled them out and refilled the tray. Minerva had given Claire a monster shot and Claire poured half back into Minerva's drink.

"I've got to drive home. Have a heart."

Minerva ran the check through the machine, signed it, then handed it to Claire.

"How're you fixed financially?" she asked.

"A little tight this month."

She shook her head with august theatricality.

"I thought you might be. I am not by nature given to reckless acts of generosity nor do I debase myself by ingratiating myself with the staff. As an old Roedean girl, I am unaccustomed to favoritism. However in view of the references I've received for you all through the month from a variety of manufacturers and Mr. Drake, I propose to make an exception. The three-month trial period is hereby waived"—she raised her glass to Claire—"and I'll take out your Social Security and withholding taxes next month if that's agreeable."

"Thanks. I can use it."

"You're a pro," she said, exploding with a cough and glaring at her Rothman cigarette. "Are you going to stay with me or is this a stopgap?"

"Fair question."

"You've given it some thought, I take it."

"I'll stay . . ."

"You sound tentative. You're waiting for a better offer. Filling in time?"

"Not at all, Minerva. Just until I can open my own store on Rodeo Drive."

Minerva's husky laughter brought on another coughing fit, the lofty headmistress, complacent and secure in her office with an affected, unrealistic student.

"My dear Claire, I'll have you till you're fifty. You'll give me your youth. And I ask nothing more than your best years. Until Monday, pet."

Driving home in the stream of traffic on the Strip, Claire was pleased with herself. Free from pain, alive, beginning again, she had a smile on her face, amused by Minerva's posturing. The check in her purse gave her security. She had regained that invigorating spirit which had been demolished. No, she wasn't a loser. Maybe it was just bluster with Minerva, but Giovanni had assured her that if she had a really original idea for a business, he could arrange financing for a store on Rodeo Drive. He had people with cash looking for a way to bury it legitimately. They'd form a syndicate, back her all the way. Just find the concept, and be able to execute.

The restaurant closed the last two weeks of August, like all good French ones, and reopened after Labor Day. Ed usually went to the south of France, Eden Roc, for his vacation, but at the last minute he had canceled because she had refused to come with him. She had turned down La Costa, Puerta Vallarta, and Rome. It wasn't that she had such a high opinion of herself or that she thought she could do better. She just had no intention of being kept. The idea was so alien, so contrary to her own image of herself, that even though they had overcome their rough patch and saw each other constantly, she held back emotionally.

Giovanni was not going to break her heart. She wasn't playing games with him or leading him on in the expectation of a serious commitment. Finally she was becoming her own person, retaining detachment and a renewed purpose. Maybe it was presumptuous, but she was reaching out for something more, which she couldn't quite identify and which would have been preposterous, beyond her, if she had remained at Drake's.

Madeleine was already at home, glum, worried, puffing on the joint stuffed in her mouth.

"Easy Ed called," she said sarcastically. "He's sitting by the phone. Boy, you must've done something to him. When he says your name it sounds like he's coming."

"Lay off." Claire threw off her shoes. Her feet were swollen and she wanted to sit in the bath for an hour with a drink and read a magazine.

"I think it's a party at the Colony."

"I might stay in."

"Just who the fuck do you think you are? A party in Malibu and you behave like it's Shakey's."

Claire couldn't believe the animosity that Madeleine thoughtlessly conveyed. The girl had been so foul-tempered for the last week that she didn't know what to make of her. As soon as she could afford her own apartment, whether it be a one-room convertible on Fountain Avenue or a loft in Studio City, she'd be out the door. Sharing, even with a close friend, presented such a host of problems that she vowed never again to allow herself to be inveigled into a similar predicament. It just wasn't worth it. The accountability, the money-splitting, the cleaning, all got on her nerves. Claire decided to go out. She couldn't tolerate an evening with Madeleine enviously glaring at her. She wrote a check for half the month's rent and left Madeleine still blazing.

It had been a rough month for Madeleine. Even with Claire's money, she would still be behind in her rent. Her situation at Gucci had become increasingly dangerous. The assistant manager was suspicious of her and she was forced to curtail her little sideline until things cooled off.

Madeleine had been selling bags that had been brought in for repair to a few private customers who had the repairs done at a small shop on Third Street. This brought in as much as five hundred extra a month, but when there had been a rash of complaints and a store meeting with a factory representative, she froze with panic. Then she learned that an insurance investigator would be taking statements from all the girls and keeping an eye on them until this little racket ended. The management made no bones about it: Whoever was "shortstopping" the returned bags would be prosecuted and the charge would be grand larceny.

Without an extra few hundred there was no way Madeleine could survive on her salary. If only she could quit, find some wealthy guy like Giovanni to keep her so that she could continue with her acting classes. She had given up calling Brockman. He was always out to her, but she ceaselessly pursued the photographer, gritted her teeth when he did not respond to her messages. Eugene Roth was her ticket to a new future. Why wouldn't anyone give her a break? What had she done to deserve such officious treatment?

She had left messages at least a dozen times with Roth's service. It galled her when the operator assured her that he checked in daily and had been given her name and number repeatedly. Yes, she was pushy, but who ever got anywhere in Hollywood without leaning on people?

She dreaded another encounter with her landlord. The last time she had gone over to his house, he had a friend in. He was going through his adventures in living experiments and she had taken on the two of them; the experience had left her shaken and disillusioned. They'd buggered her brains out and she'd been sore for days.

She considered heading down to Joe Allen's to see if she could connect. The phone rang and in a sour mood, expecting it to be Giovanni, she answered gruffly.

"You've been lighting a fire under my service," the voice said. "This is Gene Roth."

"God, I'm sorry, Gene. But our mutual friend, Al Brockman, begged me to keep trying."

There was a pause at the other end.

"Bullshit," Roth replied. "We haven't talked in over a year."

"Honestly, he gave me your number."

When Claire appeared, beautifully dressed and made up, Madeleine waved her hand approvingly and smiled radiantly. Claire knew she had a trunk full of personas, none of them convincing. Madeleine obviously had a live one on the wire. Perhaps her Palm Springs mentor was in for his monthly session. Madeleine beckoned her to wait and pointed to the joint in the ashtray.

"How soon can you get over to the Valley?" Roth asked.

"An hour."

"Bring a bikini, boots, sexy lingerie, leotards, shit like that, and I'll see what you've got."

He gave her the address and hung up unceremoniously.

"Claire, it's happening," Madeleine gushed. She darted up from the nest of crushed pillows she'd been camping on and whirled Claire around the room.

"A producer?" Claire exclaimed.

"Better than that. A director! He's asked me to read for him." She released Claire and rushed in the direction of the bathroom, bellowing: "There better be some hot water."

Her professional cosmetic case with battery lights, stuffed with her pots, grimy tubes, liners, eyebrow pencils, bounced on the passenger seat, and Madeleine petted it at every light, communicating positive vibes to the chemicals. Swishing back and forth was her costume bag, a black vinyl sack in which she'd dumped her underwear drawer. She had even washed her oh-so-sheer lace bra and the

French-cut satin panties her Palm Springs connection had bought for her at Trashy Lingerie during his last visit. If Eugene had an iron or a blow dryer, she was in business. The ensemble would be dry in five minutes.

She crossed over Laurel Canyon to the Valley, and then headed west on Ventura Boulevard through the maze of cruising kids and the frenzied commerce of fast food franchises whose neon lights formed multicolored serpentine ganglia for miles along the undulating street. She didn't know the Valley well and she got lost when she reached Van Nuys. She drove through batteries of singles apartment complexes, all with their underground garages, coffinlike terraces, and concrete-decked pools where bored tenants gathered for their Saturday night barbecue mixer. Then she ran into Miranda Street, locating a small ranch house with weather-beaten shingles and a broken front window.

A rusty, mud-caked pickup truck was parked in the gravel driveway. The interior light of her car was broken and she turned her Bic lighter to high to check out her face. She toned down a few extra blushes with pancake, grabbed her makeup and wardrobe bag, and breathlessly clattered down the uneven path.

The brass lantern above the doorway was tarnished. She rang the doorbell and tried to compose herself. A barechested, bearded man with opaque blue eyes, wearing cutoff jeans and smoking a joint, stared at her for a moment, then waved her in. She found herself in a large living room furnished with beanbag seats, a torn Naugahyde sofa, faded orange drapes, and two small plastic fold-up TV tables on which mayonnaise jar tops were littered with cigarette butts.

Eugene Roth had a big nose with a camel hump at the bridge, square yellowish teeth, and the mien of a biblical prophet. A gold Star of David the size of a sovereign dangled on his neck. He was just over six feet, thin, with a tendency to stoop, but he projected an insouciant sensuousness that rather teased Madeleine. He had long black hair, tied with a rubber band in a micro ponytail.

From two Tanoid speakers a Kiss track resounded. Through the sliding doors leading to the back she saw a redwood hot tub. Roth sat down on the floor beside the fireplace, stuck his feet on a beanbag, and raised a bottle of beer to his lips.

"Al Brockman . . . how the fuck is that old lady?"

"Al's just terrific . . . deals, deals, you know him," she said, brimming with confidence. "He discussed you constantly."

"I'm impressed," Roth observed skeptically. "What're you standing there for?"

She gave him her poised, military carriage walk, no simple task over the broken lino in the living room.

He sized her up.

"There's some wine in the refrigerator if it's still working." He pointed to a corridor. "Left and left."

She ambled through the passageway and arrived at the ruined, desecrated temple that had once been a kitchen but had become a place of anarchy ruled over by beer cans, chipped glasses, and a busy line of ants scurrying through the freeways of garbage. A bottle of Cuervo tequila with two inches left in it was on the counter and rather than investigate his stores any further, she grabbed it and fled. A bunch of glasses nested on the mantelpiece and she took one.

"Some people never quit," Roth observed.

"If you're going to survive in this business, you can't," she informed him with great earnestness. "I've got my convictions—"

"Convictions." His laughter was acerbic. "I'll tell you what you've got—big tits."

She was blown out by his directness, but refused to knuckle under, a master of all manner of dramatic situations.

"That's part of it. Why not use what I have?" She poured herself a short drink and tossed down the shooter. "Al has enormous respect for you. He said you could light better than anyone."

"He's an agent. What does he know about lighting? Jesus, you believe everything you're told."

She was becoming flustered. Roth was one of those contrary men who criticized as a reflexive action. However, she was prepared to tolerate his ill temper. She had him in the crosshairs and he was going to take her pictures. She would draw him out.

"How did you and Al get together?"

"Years ago, before he was at ICM, he had a one-man office and he represented me for commercials. I got fed up shooting the same shit over and over again. I was waiting for something in TV or a feature. A couple of scripts came along and I was approved. But the scripts were so moronic that even in my desperation I passed. I got tired of waiting and Al's promises, so I quit. I didn't give a fuck."

Just what she needed to build her ego. She explained about how she and the illustrious Brockman had met at Gucci and embellished the tale of relentless invitations to his parties. Ultimately, she gave in, responding to the urgency of his demands that she get a composite so that ICM's modeling division could properly launch her and structure her career with Al masterminding every move in the thrust leading to stardom.

Roth closed his eyes, suppressed a yawn, then advised her: "I've never heard such a crock of shit. What do you take me for?"

"You're a terribly difficult person, Eugene."

"You're not my mother, so don't ever refer to me as Eugene. I do mostly beaver for tit and ass magazines so if you're ready to take your clothes off, I'll explore the Andes and see if the Panama Canal doesn't fog my lens."

"So you write poetry in your spare time?" she said, biting her lip, utterly distraught.

He led her into the scruffy garden where there was an open corrugated iron shed to the side of the hot tub, which could hold eight or ten people. The water gurgled invitingly. He turned on a light and she observed a small makeshift studio with white background paper and a few Nikons on a work table. Hanging on a clothesline, held fast by metal clips, were a batch of prints of a naked girl. She had a moment of indecision watching him set up his lights. He jammed a meter next to her face. His detachment offended her. She hated to admit that there was a striking roughhewn virility about him that attracted her. He was the sort of man who controlled women like her by treating them badly. Abuse was his tactic. His foul mood waned when he explained that he had been shooting a layout for *Hustler* in Carmel for five days and they had decided against using it because they didn't like the girl. Instead of making three thousand for it, he had settled with them for a kill fee of a thousand and expenses.

"Al thinks the composite is vital."

"Then tell your pussy to smile."

"Just what is it with you? Why do you have to be so brutal? Look, I haven't done anything to you." She was close to tears. The men she saw paid her, treated her with respect. She did a Lude or something to take her mind off those assignments and left with her dignity. He continued rejigging the lighting while she sat on a bar stool. "I'm not going to spend my life on Rodeo Drive wrapping handbags and kissing ass at Gucci."

"What's wrong with it? You might luck into a guy between divorces and wind up with community property."

His cynical assessment of her worth was humiliating.

"I'm going to be an actress."

"A straight session," he said, ignoring her, "will run you six hundred."

"I thought—"

"Consult the Yellow Pages for passport photos." He shoved the joint into his mouth. "Figure two-fifty for prints and internegs."

She leapt off the stool and confronted him. The lights had made her perspire. He turned his back on her, suggesting she should change, and asked if she wanted another shooter. Protesting, she rushed alongside him in a canter. The scrub grass was worse than the lino in her heels.

"Gene, I can't come up with that."

"Cash."

"You're tearing my eyes out."

He got the bottle of tequila, fell into a flattened beanbag, bottle in hand. He took a long swig, then regarded her without compassion.

"We're running out. Why don't you hit the Liquor Locker on Van Nuys?"

"Don't they deliver?"

"I owe them a few bucks. They'll try to collect."

She opened her purse—a Gucci evening bag with a long gold chain meant to be worn on the shoulder and destined for the avaricious wife of an accountant. "I've got sixty-three dollars."

"No change for meters?" He reached up, touched her earlobe gently. "Run down there. Come on, show good faith. Pay a few bucks on my account."

"Are you serious?"

"Sure. Listen, it's Saturday night and there hasn't been a rape on their parking lot for about four hours. You're home and dry. The cops are all around. Who'd want to fuck you in any case?"

She pulled his hair and he smiled incorrigibly, did not make a grab at her.

"See the way I did those pictures hanging in the studio? They wouldn't take them because of the way I lit. This ostrich has a grand slalom course under her tits, not just ski tracks. Moguls. She had plastic surgery over her caesarian scar—another bulge—and I have to shoot close, so I worked low angle with my ass on a dolly and they kill it."

"And you're taking it out on me."

She made the liquor purchase and paid ten dollars on account; the clerk with his sing-song Latino accent invited her into the back for a sampling of Mezcal, which she declined. He held the door open for her, waved at the black-and-white ensconced in the darkness at the side of the lot, and helped her into the car. Was she free for the bullfights tomorrow in Tijuana? She drove off in a fury. Eugene Roth was a lunatic.

He was adjusting his camera lens in the studio shack while she unpacked the half gallon of Cuervo Gold, six-packs of Beck's beer and nacho-flavored Doritos taco chips. His cynical treatment of her was repugnant. She had hoped that a friend of Al Brockman's would encourage her, inspire her to reach out in acting class. Instead, he flattened the dreams that had shored up the bleak nights when she left class and cried in her car. How could she explain that without the fantasies that sustained her, elevating her, she might as well head back to Macy's underwear department, eat her lunches at the Blarney Stone, and die.

"I can see you're a director," she said blithely.

"Really?"

"Certainly. The way you have people on the send."

"I'll need bashers for your eyes. Get that awful makeup off your face, will you. It looks like Pennzoil."

"Gene, you owe me thirty-four—" She pulled out a receipt.

"Would you talk to Stanley Kubrick this way? Whip your clothes off and put on a pair of leotards." He shoved a Polaroid film pack into an SR-70 and checked his light meter. "You want to smartass me? Believe me, you're in trouble. I'll give you an invoice before you leave. I don't work on spec. Cash, ass on the table."

She would've liked to smack him but apparently he was serious, stepping over cables, checking shadows in the room, moving floods, oblivious of her.

"Gene, you're talking about eight hundred and fifty dollars. How do I come up with that?"

"I'm not a financial counselor. Get your shit together and we'll see what you look like. I'm certainly not going to work it off you in trade."

"Bastard."

"Listen, dum-dum, the reason I want your top off and no sludge on the eyes is to see if you're interesting. Okay?"

His bathroom was piled high with towels from the Holiday Inn, Sheraton, The Concord, The Dunes, and other rest stops. She gave up the inventory and put on her bra along with fishnet stockings, garter belt, and her canary yellow peek-a-boo panties. The leotards were run to death and seemed obscene to her, so she threw them out of his bathroom window. She removed her eye makeup with J&J baby oil, and did her eyes with a liner and mascara. She put on a pair of his old beaten slippers and gracefully slinked out to the set. Thank God it wasn't raining.

He placed her against a piece of white backdrop paper, raised her shoulders, instructed her to look directly at the lens of the Polaroid three or four feet away from her and informed her that he was testing the lighting. No smile necessary, no poses, nothing.

"It's hot," she complained. The lights hit her, burning her eyes.

"Sophia, try not to blink. And wet your lips since you're paying for the film."

He popped off half a dozen shots, laid them on the work

bench and inspected them. He was pleased with the lighting and the way she photographed.

"Take off the bra now."

"Jesus, do I really have to?"

"Pretend I'm your gynecologist."

"Oh, well." He posed her leaning against the stool. "Gene, I can't pay you in one clip."

"Keep quiet, I like the expression. You look scared. We'll discuss money later."

He ran off another batch of Polaroids. She thought that she had seldom been less animated. Her allure was gone and she dreaded his criticism. She became apprehensive. It was one thing to have her clothes off when she was making love, but this raw exposure was eerie.

"Major tits," he informed her, "and they haven't been tampered with."

"I do exercises."

"Very exciting." He set up his Nikon on a tripod and moved in close. He barked instructions at her. The camera shutter clicked repeatedly and she heard the whir of the automatic winder. He changed angles and her pose every so often. "Now drop your panties."

She shuddered. Her spirit of adventure was gone and this cheap exploitation was humiliating. She began to cry and he switched off the lights. He offered her the joint and also poured two fingers of Cuervo for them. He patted her comradely on the cheek, the first time he had touched her.

"What's the problem? Never had your pants off?"

"You're so abusive. What have I done?"

"It's my character. I've been mangled. Don't take it personally."

"Gene, I've just got to have the pictures."

"You want to negotiate?" he said lightly. "Let's give your agent a ring. Let him earn his commission."

"Christ, no."

"Madeleine, I don't like working on the come."

He explained that he would complete the session provided she agreed to nude pictures. He would try to peddle them to skin magazines and split the money with her. It might be difficult, for what was moving in the trade were lesbian scenes with black and white girls. She was revolted. The characteristic bravado she displayed with men vanished as he battered her with setups that made for easy sales. She might get a few hundred out of it.

"But it still won't be enough," she said plaintively.

"What kind of sex have you had?" he asked with detachment.

The question boggled her. No one had ever been so adamant and severe with her, challenging her for personal details. She had never reckoned that there was a squeamish side to her.

"I've had some affairs," she admitted reluctantly.

"Ever made it with another girl?"

"Are you kidding?" The suggestion frightened her, attacked her deepest sense of femininity. What kind of sewer had she fallen into? Having occasional *dates* for money with men was not central to her life, a kind of part-time work she forgot about. "I couldn't handle it with another girl."

"Listen, there's something off-center about you." He tried to think of how to put it. Madeleine occupied that strange territory of silliness and sexuality in which Goldie Hawn might believe she was Laura Antonelli. The mixture propelled an unexpected sexuality on film. Even the Polaroid snaps were good. She had a variety of faces, which the camera, much to his surprise, fell in love with. "I might be able to get you as much as five hundred for a film. You've got a freshness . . . I'd print some stills and move them to the magazines."

He let her chew on that, pulled out his last gram of coke and chopped some lines on a mirror. He picked up a small plastic tube from the table and offered it to her. She did two of the lines and dabbed her gums with a few crystals.

"It's laced with a little speed and procaine for those sultry summer nights."

"Gene, it's good."

"That's why I can't pay my liquor bill."

She mulled over his proposal. In his anarchic world nothing was forbidden or sacred. Madeleine wondered how far she could travel on sheer audacity. Could she go through with a film? Money had never ceased to be an obstacle since she was a kid. Her mother had skimped on her, never giving her a chance. The years at Macy's dealing boxer shorts and undershirts were irreclaimable. The succession of actors who had dumped on her, used her, came back to sour her outlook.

"Wouldn't the nude pictures cut it?" she asked.

"I'm specking, sweetie."

Film! The idea that she would be portrayed in living color on a movie screen nurtured her fantasies.

"Would you be in it?"

"Did you take crazy pills? I'm the director."

Brockman had insisted that he was talented. Impossible to deal with for sure, but not a hack. She was up against a wall.

"Let's do the nudes, and can I think about the film?"

"Why think about it? Get your brain trust together. Jay Bernstein, Al Brockman, your lawyers, business managers. They'll work out your percentage of the gross and your billing."

"Shit, can't you be nice for five minutes?"

"You do it and I'll shoot your comp in another session and give it to you."

"Promoter."

He did half the last line of blow and saved half for her.

"Drop your pants, Scheherazade, and show us what the jerk-offs are dreaming about."

"You're pure romance."

He got her to spread her fingers against her pussy, grimace erotically as she simulated masturbating. Then he had her raise her breasts to her lips, flick out her tongue to suck her nipple. He made her kneel, spread her ass while turning to the camera.

"Wonderful, Madeleine. No lemons in the garden."

"I need an interpreter or subtitles."

"No pimples on your ass. My God, I've never met anyone meant for perversion as much as you . . . if only you had the brains to go with it."

His acrimony, she was beginning to understand, was defensive. He didn't mean half the things he said. His idea of a compliment was a sharp kick in the stomach. Talk about problems, Eugene Roth invented them.

"Good, good," he said encouragingly as he shot roll

after roll of film, moving to low angles, standing on chairs for high shots, working his tail off. "I got you off guard. Great. I like the innocence. Prices, am I going to get prices."

"How much more?" He had posed her with a hammer raised about to slam her privates, plying her with hits of the joint and tequila, more reserved with the coke.

"The world is waiting for you."

They quit at about one in the morning. She was beat, still indecisive. He stripped off his clothes, climbed the ladder and eased himself into the churning hot tub. No invitation for her. She joined him nonetheless, kept her distance from him on the opposite bench. He hadn't come on to her. Amazing. Certainly a new technique. He offered her a margarita, then recalled that his blender had suffered a stroke.

"Gene, how'd you reach this point?"

"Oh, transactional therapy in a hot tub? Suck on your thumb or give a primal scream, my neighbors are used to it."

"Hey, give me a chance to breathe. I mean making a film—like this is . . ."

"Right, you haven't read the script or approved your co-star. I'll give Donna Summer or Diana Ross a call. Motown can do the sound track and we'll have a book tie-in."

Is this what she had come to? What a way to begin her career. What would they say at acting class?

"Who goes to these films?"

"I'll see if I can get Ray Stark and Bob Evans."

"Come on."

"People who enjoy pornography. Men, women. They buy it, run it on cassettes at home when they've got vodka on the brain and limp dicks on their laps."

How could she get through to this man? Her body freaked out everyone. To Gene Roth it was commerce. He might have been riveting chrome strips on car doors on a Detroit assembly line. Wet, she liked the look of him and she now ignored his barrage of digs.

"Gene, why do you do this?"

"I should think about this for a good five seconds then come out with something that'll impress you." He stuck his head under the water for a moment and she became worried, but then he shot up, spurting water out of his mouth.

"You okay?"

"Yeah, I needed a schpritz."

"Back to you."

"I thought we did that."

"Come on."

"Well, I couldn't handle the pressure or rejections and I behaved like a prick. I fired Al and set up as a still photographer. I used to walk out of meetings, scream at studio executives in the commissary like Don Rickles when he hosted the Carson show. I started making a living doing comps and Al thinks that's what I still do . . . then I drifted into hardcore. The money's good. No pretensions and I don't have to romance people. I make a product and then walk away from it. Which is why you ought to think like me if you want to do it. You don't get your head involved and keep it uncomplicated."

What could he possibly think of her on a human level, she wondered, overcome by the savagery he displayed. His self-loathing was infectious and his attitude virulently attacked all the dreams that had been forming in her mind since she was an adolescent. It was one thing to have a roll in the sack with a man, but quite another to perform in public, feigning passion, exposing herself to an audience of deviates. What was a living for Gene would be nothing less than a desecration for her. She hurt all over, foundering, one moment rejecting the offer out of hand, the next convinced that this represented the first real opportunity she had been given since coming to Los Angeles.

But what if she could really act, give a performance, even on this level? Wouldn't it be a test that would help her shake off her fantasies or prove to herself that she possessed a spark of talent? For better or worse, she'd have a reel. The prospect of having herself on an actual film—never mind the subject matter—appealed to the narcissistic side of her character. Monroe and Mansfield, her idols, had done it, and it hadn't hurt them.

She had been a plain, fat little girl who had worked for years to lose weight, dieting, doing exercises, experimenting with makeup, clothes, vainly trying to attract attention, and here was this dissolute commercials director confirming that she projected sensuality and had something original. Could she go through with it, yet remain emotionally apart from the experience?

"Okay, okay," she said. "I'll do it."

"Funny, I didn't think you'd go for it."

Having made the decision, she was filled with remorse. Why couldn't she have had the luck to be spotted by a legitimate producer or an agent who recognized that she had a quality that would attract others?

"Do you like me, just a little?" she asked, drying herself. The question, she realized, serving to heighten rather than alleviate her insecurities.

He emitted an awful, derisive churlish sound and she was startled when it became evident that he was laughing at both of them.

"Would you like me to say that I thought you were something special?"

"Uh-huh."

He gave her a bleak, fatigued smile. "I'll let you know when the prints are ready."

Naked, traipsing through the battleground of grass, gopher holes, and beer bottles, he saw her to her car, uncaring about neighbors or passers-by.

"You don't want me to stay over and you didn't make a grab at me."

He kissed her on the mouth asexually.

"It's just our first date, Madeleine, and I'm respectable," he said mockingly.

"You're too fucking much."

On the drive back to the Hollywood Hills through the wasteland of the Valley, she did not allow herself to cry but rather marveled at the extent of his cruelty and her capacity to endure it. Within her she discerned only barren ground. Gene had been able to demonstrate to her that she had hit rock bottom and for a moment she rejoiced in stripping away the superficial morality she cloaked herself in.

She had come to realize that there was nothing within her, no rare spirit, no modesty, just a base, groveling hunger for recognition, as ignoble as it was pure. What she could not express or reveal even to Claire was how she felt when she passed one of the studios. Their proximity drove her crazy. Just behind the gates of Fox, Paramount, Burbank, the black tower at Universal, lay a world of wealth, influence, that touched every life on the planet. And she had been excluded, could never hope to enter those gates unless she forced her way through them.

She and Gene were a fine pair whom Brockman had allied. Maybe the agent had done her a favor by arranging her passage from captivity into the universe of darkness. Madeleine had left many men before, clasping at vague promises but still retaining her indefinite hope. Gene was yet another in the expanding list of benefactors who had clipped her. She was starting to see that in her line of work she was vulnerable, without a fullback position. Women were pulverized, kneaded into strange, unrecognizable shapes. It went against the grain, but she succumbed to her impossible visions . . . until Monday when she signed her time sheet.

15

Claire toweled off her face and neck and walked slowly to the bench beside the fence on the tennis court at the Beverly Hills Hotel. She had just finished her first lesson with Alex Olmedo. Giovanni was determined that she learn how to play and insisted on getting her a name teacher, a former Wimbledon champion, no less. Olmedo had been patient with her and was encouraging. She moved well on the court, lithely, and her reflexes were excellent.

Ed picked up his racquet, kissed her wet forehead, and said: "What a deprived childhood you must have had."

She took a drink of fresh orange juice, which he had brought in his picnic thermos. She smiled at him, grateful for the time and care he invested in her, and for a moment she was so completely overwhelmed by his generosity that she thought she could fall in love with him.

Although he was a fine player, he still took a lesson every week from Olmedo. She watched the fluid strokes of the master and his pupil, both hitting the ball with astonishing power, adroitly using the angles of the court. The splendor of Sunday with the sun shining, the horizon clear of smog for the first time in a week, outlining the mountains, gave Claire such a tangible sensation of exultation that she counted her blessings.

For a while she watched Ed play, then tiring of the endless cascade of yellow balls flying through the air, she skimmed through the Sunday *Times*. Labor Day was coming up and she couldn't wait for the long weekend. She glanced at a few ads in a desultory way, checked on the movie listings, then tried to separate the thick classified sections. She pulled out the social section. Her eye fell on a photo of a girl with long blonde hair and saucer-shaped eyes. The girl was smiling into space, communing with the infinite prospects within her grasp, and Claire was mesmerized by the name underneath the picture.

MISS HILLARY LANGLEY MARTINSON

A few balls rolled near her feet and one caromed off the fence beside her.

"Sorry," Ed called. "I've got to stop slugging," he told Olmedo.

"Step in, Ed . . . you're falling back a little."

Claire put on her sun visor and began to read the short article under the picture.

> Miss Hillary Langley Martinson, daughter of Mr. Leonard Martinson and the late Gloria Martinson of Bel Air, and Mr. Robert John Canaday, son of Mr. and Mrs. John Canaday of Westport, Conn., will be married at All Saint's Church in Beverly Hills on Saturday, September 8. A reception will follow at the bride's home. The bride's father is chairman of the Martinson Development Corporation and a well-known art collector and philanthropist. The groom graduated from the Harvard School of Design and is an architect with Hayward and Associates of Beverly Hills. The bride-to-be graduated from the Bishop School in La Jolla. She was presented at the Coronado Cotillion in 1975.

Claire released the paper and it dropped off her knees. She suppressed a groan, left the court, and wandered through the hotel garden. She found a shady spot under a eucalyptus tree where she watched in distraction as waiters wheeled room-service carts to bungalows, maids pulled hampers, gabbling in Spanish, couples arm in arm strolled to the pool. She made a vague effort to reason with herself. She knew that something of the kind would be coming, but there was no way to prepare for it.

Christ, she'd been doing so well, at peace with herself, freeing herself from the emotional attachment, divorced from the past. The pain she felt was so harrowing that she doubled over on the grass, clutching her stomach. She thought she was going to pass out. She heard her name called, then Giovanni spotted her. He bent on his knee, arched her back in his arms and looked at her with concern.

"What's wrong? Too much sun? Honey, you're white. Let's get you home and I'll call the doctor."

"No, I'll be okay," she said. She was fighting back, confronting the inevitability of the situation.

On the short ride back to Ed's house on Oxford Way behind the hotel, she was breathing heavily, and he remained silent, puzzled and giving her a chance to come out of it by herself. His houseman had laid out bowls of fresh fruit salad and yogurt for their breakfast. He asked Ed how they wanted their eggs while Claire settled into a chaise longue, grimacing unwittingly, eyes tightly closed.

"We're not ready yet," she heard him say. He sat down on the edge of the chaise, baffled and solicitous, stroked her ankles. He removed her tennis sneakers and peds. "Your color's back. Want to be left alone, huh?"

"I think so."

"Call me when you want anything or if you feel like talking."

She reached out for his hand and kissed it. His presence reassured her. Someone cared about her. Yet she was pleased to be left alone. Maybe the wedding announcement was what she had been waiting for, she reflected. It released her, canceled the debt. There was no need to maintain a subconscious vigil nor continue to grieve. The flame had been extinguished and in a way she couldn't quite define, she was relieved. Even though she had made no attempt to see Bobby, she had nurtured in the lonely recesses of her mind a glimmer of hope, remote as it seemed, that one day Bobby would find her again and beg her to come back to him. As long as that possibility remained, she was able to hold back a part of herself, reserving it for him.

The sun was frying her and she went into the cabana, put on one of her own swimsuits, and dove into the pool. She was no longer the wide-eyed girl dazzled by swimming in a heated pool at night, but a woman who had emerged from the most ferocious crisis of her life. She would have liked to think that she had been reborn, but it wasn't that easy.

Giovanni was on the phone in his den and he waved to her. Something had hurt her—and it wasn't physical.

"Any better?" he called out from the window.

"Absolutely."

"I've got a tennis game at the Dunlops' . . . okay with you?"

"Sounds good."

Events had moved so quickly for Bobby that he had difficulty aligning himself to an entirely new way of life. The Martinson house was filled with an assortment of people: Milton Williams the caterer, florists from John Patrick Burke, three women from shops on Rodeo Drive who were showing Hillary styles and materials for a wedding dress, a tailor from Bijan fitting him for tails. There were long-distance calls back and forth between him and his parents. One minute he was upstairs in Hillary's bedroom being shown swatches of material, the next called by Leonard down to the library to discuss the menu. Thematically Milton conjured up truffles and madeleines to go with the style of the house . . . the food ought to be Proustian but tempered by the slender virtues of La Nouvelle Cuisine. Leonard nodded sagaciously and revealed that Milton's creativity worked on such heroic metaphoric calibrations. One could make a pig of oneself, not gain weight, and still not blanch during cholesterol and lipoprotein tests. Suddenly he was an authority on cuisine? What next? Burgers and chili would be fine with Bobby.

The tailor finally completed his measurements, arranged three fittings for the following week. Bobby escaped into the deserted living room, found a loveseat in the corner by the window, slunk down and was grateful for a moment's solitude.

He didn't know what to blame for his state of physical exhaustion. Perhaps it was a combination of the demands Hillary made on him and the late hours he'd been working to come up with a design for Marine Mutual. Hayward and Leonard were constantly on top of him. He was lucky to get four hours' sleep a night before whipping into the office at seven to meet with draftsmen and model builders. He still hadn't found a design that he considered workable. He found himself on the defensive with Hillary when, at one in the morning, he diplomatically pleaded that he had to put in more time on his renderings.

She was supposed to be at Disegno Contemporaneo part of the week because of some new clients, but she found excuses to stay away and come to his office, interrupting conferences, dragging him to St. Germain or Le Restaurant for lunches that ran three hours.

He had suggested that they move into his apartment after the wedding, but she turned him down flat. She'd find a place for them . . . trust her. However, whenever he asked about her progress, she refused to be pinned down. His head was spinning and he believed his work was suffering. He couldn't lose this commission. Hayward had made it clear that this was the most important assignment the firm had ever undertaken. It was a happy, fulfilling, but frustrating period for him, shattering the order that was so essential to his work.

"There's my boy," Leonard said chirpily, spying him. "How about some air. These fittings can drive you nuts." His morning suit was out of fashion so he had undergone the same torture as Bobby.

"I'd like to find a bedroom with no one in it and sleep for two days."

"Come on, Bobby." Leonard handed him a Scotch on the rocks. "We never get a minute to talk."

Bobby hadn't had his hair cut in two months. He didn't have a barber. His refrigerator was bare. His laundry, mercifully, was now being done by one of the Martinson maids. He'd give his right arm for a quiet afternoon at his apartment, half watching sports and sending out for a pizza rather than Peking Duck at Mr. Chow's.

For once there were no guests at the house and he wouldn't be pulled around from one group to another, listening to drivel. Hillary's maid of honor, a twice-divorced stoned vampire, cloyingly pawed at him and, whenever they were alone, came at him like a linebacker. How was he expected to disengage himself or tell Hillary that the previous evening at dinner Kitty Oliver had asked when she could see him? She intimated that Hillary and she had been through a few scenes together, and that there was a group of old girls from the Bishop School who would welcome the couple into their midst. He didn't believe her. He was having serious difficulty getting his bearings in this open society. Not that he was a delicate flower or couldn't handle himself, but the naked aggression he was beginning to encounter wore him out.

Leonard put an arm around his shoulder, a not unwelcome and habitual gesture when they were together, while they strolled down beyond the pool to a small house about five hundred yards below the manor on the hill. It was a cottage with a newly shingled roof and had a singularly elegant shape because of the additions made over the years. Rather than a jerry-built anarchic structure, it had the charm of one of those English crofter's cottages that had been redone. As a boy, flipping through English architectural magazines that showed country churches falling apart and then restored, he would marvel at the ingenuity of English craftsmanship.

"I think we've solved your housing problem," Leonard said grandly, beaming with good cheer. "I can give you a townhouse in any of six developments"—Bobby scowled —"but, hell, they're not for you and Hillary."

"Thanks for the offer, but if Hillary sets her mind to it, she can find us an apartment. I told her she could go up to six hundred a month. If she makes a few commissions at her place, she might come out with close to fifteen or twenty a year. She mentioned something about an allowance, but that has to stop. I'm making a living."

The corners of Leonard's patrician mouth had a devious flange and his eyes narrowed, giving his countenance an iciness that made Bobby feel foolish.

"Hillary doesn't have any allowance. It's a trust."

"Same difference."

"No, Bobby, not at all." He raised his arms apologetically. "I don't have any control over Hillary's fortune."

They sat down on a couple of rattan chairs on the small lawn in front of the cottage.

"What's this got to do with anything?"

Discussions about money afflicted Bobby with insecurities. He found Hillary's wealth a source of embarrassment that struck at the roots of his manhood. He wouldn't be taken for a fortune hunter, no matter what other people thought, which is why a small apartment despite the crazy spiraling inflated property market appealed to him. He could cut the rent and like everyone in the country, they'd live on credit. His illusions of building a stake, buying fixer-uppers, could wait until he could afford it. He didn't want to parlay Hillary's capital into his nest egg.

"Leonard, I don't give a shit about money. I'm sorry to be crude about it . . . but I just don't care. Let smarter guys who're into shopping centers with their sharp-shooting lawyers and accountants get rich. It's not my ballgame. Listen, if this country turns socialist tomorrow it wouldn't matter to me. I'd do workers' housing or government buildings. I wouldn't like to be restrained by politics, but I'll still be doing my stuff. That's my story." He laughed. "Maybe U.S.C. won't take me on their faculty, but some little school will. I'll always be able to support Hillary."

They had carried their glasses down with them and Bobby would have loved another drink without climbing up the hill or having a servant bolt down with a tray to serve him. Leonard wandered into the cottage, which was stocked simply with comfortable, functional furniture. Bobby considered himself an intruder, since he was under the impression that these were staff quarters. There was a kitchen, two bedrooms, a poky den with a TV, and the ubiquitous backgammon table. Leonard pulled out a bottle of Black Label from a cupboard bursting with stock in the den. Obviously, this was his retreat.

"Let me enlighten you," he said gently, warmed by Bobby's directness and innocence. "When I married my late wife, I was just another guy who came back from World War Two—ever hear of that?—who built quonset huts for the army. So I decided to go to contractor's school, get my license, and build anything that would pay. Gloria's family were old money from San Diego. They were in hotels and land development. Her father didn't like me or trust me. So for the first three years we never even talked but as things got better with me, they accepted me.

"When Gloria was pregnant with Hillary in 'fifty-six, we'd been married for ten years and never thought we could have a child. The joy that filled our lives . . . Gloria's father decided to establish an irrevocable trust for Hillary. Although our relations had improved—the old man and me—he still considered me a freebooter." Leonard was on his feet, gesturing wildly as though he had incontestable proof for his father-in-law that he was worthy. "He put a million in trust for Hillary, which would provide something for her when she was twenty-one, and the formula was so fucking complicated and the trustees so competent that it keeps growing.

"When Hillary was three her mother died of cancer. My business was booming. I'd made it. I was trying to become old money in Beverly Hills—in our circles, Bobby." He paused and for a moment Bobby thought he was about to cry. "When I lost Gloria, I had a three-year-old child on my hands whom we'd spoiled rotten to a degree that we couldn't comprehend. And I went on spoiling her, maybe because I felt guilty because she'd lost her mother. . . . I didn't know any other way to treat her. So even though there've been women in my life and one I loved and wanted to marry, I never did. Hillary and I became a couple. So when you ask me about stopping Hillary's allowance, you're asking the wrong person. She'll come into her money when she's thirty and the checks she gets every month are beyond my control."

Leonard put the bottle of Black Label on the slickly glossed redwood table that had been shaped into one of those conversation pieces. There was ice if required, Bobby was told, but he poured them straight shots, clasped Leonard's hand and hugged him. They'd been transported to the plane of friendship, forming a real union.

"You can see my position then," Bobby said.

"Sure. Shit, yes. All I was going to do was offer you my old hideout for a temporary place. We can pull a few men off Alpine, decorate the joint in a week, give you a good place to work and eliminate a hassle. Hillary's not going to find an apartment. She won't even look. Be realistic. I can call Mike Silverman or Joyce Rey and get you a place in an hour. It's a joke, don't you see?"

He did and that was the problem. His affection for Leonard had never been so all-encompassing, so profound.

He loved the man. But something within Bobby resisted. Leonard, he realized, still needed Hillary with him. There was no way he was going to give her up, even with the blessing extended to the wedding that was about to take place. There was something that bound father and daughter that Bobby could never intrude upon.

"I accept your offer," Bobby said warily. Absurd to contest it. "We'll stay a few months until we can get located and I give Hillary a good shove," he suggested, belting back the straight shot and pouring them another. His prospective father-in-law and he would have an enduring friendship. The man had revealed his inner self, concealed nothing, and to Bobby this was a mark of a rare human being. However, Leonard was still uneasy, wrapped his arm around his shoulders protectively.

"Bobby, Hillary's a girl who had problems when she was growing up . . . and those engagements, well, I'd rather not go into details. She can be frivolous."

"And demanding."

"That's part of it. You've got to train her. Explain right from wrong."

The remark surprised Bobby, disturbed him. "I think she knows that."

"I didn't mean it like that. She's self-indulgent without realizing it. When she wants your time, there's no way I've found to put her off. It's my fault, naturally. But she doesn't understand what's at stake when you're working. She gets impulsive."

Bobby stretched out, thrust his legs on the redwood table. He was high and needed a confidant desperately.

"She's planned a honeymoon. Have you heard? We fly to Washington on Sunday and stay at some small cute place called the John Hay."

"I took her there when she was twelve. I was lobbying for FHA loans."

Leonard wiped the sweat off his lip and hit the bottle without filling Bobby's glass. He had become morose.

"Monday, the Concorde to Paris. Lunch at Lapérouse. She got us a suite at the Ritz. Leonard, it's like I'm the bride. The Gritti Palace in Venice. We're going to be away until November! She laid it on me this morning while one of the tailors was sticking pins in my ass. Doesn't she know

I'm working on a building and except for being born, nothing more important ever happened to me?"

"Talk her out of it," Leonard shot out obdurately.

"You do it."

"I'm not marrying her."

"We'll gang up on her," Bobby suggested affably.

Leonard winced, lurched to his feet unsteadily.

"Not me. I couldn't do it again. You're the boss, Bobby."

On Sundays Ellen Dunlop liked to cook, much to the chef's dismay. She burned pans while searing the beef, and added beer, Stilton cheese, bits of fat pork, cumin seed, and chorizo to Carroll Shelby's already perfect chili fixings. Out of his money the chef had purchased a set of Farberware pans for Ellen in the hope of preserving his immaculate copper pans, which were only to be kissed by flames when he was preparing a dish like Fettuccini Alfredo or Steak Diane *à table* for the abominable philistine Dunlops. A kitchen designer had installed a Fasar magnetic-induction job, which the chef, a Polish saucier, treated as he would an invading Russian infantryman. Frank adored it, showed it off, proud of the colorful tiles and computer-style buttons. No matter how many Cordon Bleu cooking lessons Ellen took, she couldn't use the damn setup and scorched everything, which was why she was nurturing the chili herself, never daring to leave the kitchen except for a tinkle while Claire guarded the fort. Ed and Frank were out on the court in another grudge match.

Ellen wiped her hands on her striped Gourmet Gallery *routier* apron.

"It's not just a question of being bored, because I've never been bored in my life, but I have to get off, Claire, know what I mean?" She hit the paprika, mistaking it for cayenne she was so dizzy.

"Not exactly."

Hands on her shapely hips, she turned away from the mélange simmering blissfully on the range, shook her ass in an arc, and remarked tartly:

"I'm Frank's third wife—his last one—and I love him. I know the kind of effect he has on other people but it doesn't matter to me. Just to give you an idea of the sort of man he is—he signed over three apartment houses he had in Beverly Hills, which I've taken condo. No premarital chicken-shit agreement up front. I can ring Marvin Mitchelson tomorrow and use Frank's corneas for earrings."

"Your chili's hissing."

"It's good for it. If I put the cover on now it won't reduce." She waved a wooden spoon over the pot and sternly commanded it, "Behave." Then she repaired to the electronically operated kitchen table, which dropped like a Murphy bed from the wall, and carried over a bottle of Sancerre. Frank bought names out of wine encyclopedias, but Giovanni had put him on to this jewel.

"I'm not interested in screwing around. I had my own employment agency in Chicago for six years. An apartment on Lake Shore Drive. I didn't need Frank, his problems, or his money."

She was defiantly thirty-eight and her figure was one of those unforgettable melodies that men could hum without finding tedious. Her skin was unlined and she had extraordinary naturally white teeth. She was Polish and her maiden name sounded like an off-brand vodka. The lines of her body seemed like the playfulness of a boy roaming around a piece of graph paper with his first compass. She was beautiful in a kind of indistinguishable way that gradually grew on one until it struck home that she was magnificent. Seeing Ellen was indeed a growth process.

"I really expected you to call me and in fact I'm a little pissed off that you didn't."

"Ellen, I had to find a job. I'm a working girl. Ed doesn't keep me."

"Well, what the hell're you doing at Minerva's? Frank'll never go in there after the way she spoke to him. He asked for an orange cashmere sweater and this woman—talk about nerve—came out of the back and told him to get in touch with Isaac Hayes." She gasped. "We couldn't believe it. Claire, for shit's sake, she says that to Frank Dunlop. Needless to say, he made a scene and this lunatic bars us. Frank was hysterical. Calls to lawyers . . . you can't imagine the madness this created in our household." She winked at Claire. "We've had a few, no, a lot of bummers. Frank was already paranoid but this got him completely bananas."

Oh, well, it was Sunday afternoon conversation. She had

thought of asking Ed to take her home and had phoned Madeleine, only to have the phone slammed down. No way of going back there, shelling peanuts and trying to compose herself. She'd have to go through the havoc of Madeleine's evening, then, depending on her mood, accompany her to the Imperial Gardens where she'd get them picked up for dinner at the sushi bar.

"I admit I'm coming on strong, but how does someone as smart as you work for Minerva?"

An image of Bobby and Hillary at the altar exchanging vows flashed through her mind.

She picked up her glass of wine and wandered out to the loggia outside the kitchen. It had become windy and the men were chasing lobs on the court below.

"Claire, I'm opening up to you. We have no friends. Our life here is a fiasco. Jesus, we had Rogers and Cowan for a while and that busted out. Charity dinners every night. Frank was giving away five thousand a week for us to eat chicken breasts stuffed with golf balls. We were used and we made mistakes. Socially it was awful."

Oh, for a dark peacefully quiet room where she could sleep and forget.

"What're we talking about? Your faithfulness? You convinced me. I believe every word. Or my job?"

"Claire, I want to go into business. I have to do something." She leaned her head on Claire's shoulder, forcing a disgruntled laugh from Claire. "I'm serious. I like you, dummy. Put something together."

The boys walked off the court, belting back bottles of Gatorade until it dripped on their faces and down their sweat-streaked shirts. Then they began to douse each other childishly. Kids after games on a Sunday afternoon.

"This isn't a good time for me," Claire said. She wanted Giovanni to hold her, squeeze her, assure her that she was loved. "I don't expect to work for Minerva until my hair turns gray."

"Claire, get on with it. Oh, now I sound like Frank. We've got money behind you . . . I just need a place for myself."

The prospect enticed her although she found it hard to believe that the Dunlops would ever really be persuaded to back a newcomer on a street as expensive and sophisticated as Rodeo Drive. After the shock of reading the wedding announcement, the afternoon turned out to have an unexpectedly bright side to it. Over chili and hot dogs and beer, Frank took up the refrain and Claire realized that she had to appear forceful and confident. Her future might be riding on how she handled herself. She was careful not to be overeager.

"Rodeo Drive doesn't need another boutique," she said. "So if you and Ellen are considering high fashion, I think you're on the wrong track." She smiled at Frank. "Upsetting as it might be, Minerva runs the business brilliantly. You'd have to go to six or eight different stores to find what she stocks."

"But her attitude toward people stinks," he replied irritably.

"That's part of the gimmick. Snobby, arrogant, it goes with the quality."

"She's right, Frank," Giovanni observed. "If I treated people that way in my restaurant, I'd be out in a week. Yet Studio 54 built their business on the principle of keeping people out. The London Club tried it, but L.A. wasn't ready for it." He held Claire's hand to indicate solidarity. "I've already told Claire that if she has something I could form a syndicate to back her."

Dunlop fidgeted. Although nothing was settled, the hint that Ellen might be undercut infuriated him. He knew all about these syndicates. A dozen or so wealthy people put up money, spent their time interfering, making idiotic suggestions, until they ran their toy into the ground. Uncle Sam picked up the loss in tax write-offs. More than anything, he wanted Ellen launched, appreciated by the society that had snubbed them. If she could have a presence on Rodeo Drive, it would open the social doors that had been slammed in his face.

He recognized that Giovanni was a successful businessman who had an emotional hold on Claire, but the syndicates, apart from causing vicious personality conflicts, were usually undercapitalized. Once the initial investment had been made, members were reluctant to come up with additional funds. Frank considered himself a good judge of character and there was a dynamism about Claire Stuart that intrigued him. He was an inveterate snooper and after meeting her, he had told his investigative department to run a check on her. The report he received was extremely encouraging, detailing her experience at Drake's. For the life of him, he couldn't imagine why she had taken a job at Minerva's, but there had to be a practical reason. If anyone was prime executive caliber, it was this beguiling girl. Armed with this knowledge, he had nagged Ellen to sound her out. He needed someone like Claire with retailing experience who could play a part in the coup he had conceived.

"What do you think would work, Claire?" he asked.

Why ask her opinion? Obviously this was a Dunlop hobby. She might as well cut loose to see why they'd bothered cultivating her.

"I'm a new girl. I've got a superficial fix on the stores and trade, but what I'm looking for"—she smiled disarmingly—"while we're spinning wheels, is something that would work throughout the country."

Dunlop unstuck himself from the back of his chair. Giovanni's face darkened with displeasure as though a mechanic had the prime booth in his restaurant.

"Come on, Claire, stop teasing us," Dunlop pressed her.

"A store is a reality, Frank. It's not like theorizing about the stock market or high finance, where pieces of paper shuffle from one office to another and profits run into millions." What the hell, why not bullshit with him? "This is goods . . . goods. You put a Minerva's in Cherry Hill, New Jersey, which is an affluent area, Beacon Hill, or Grosse Pointe—it might work, but could you take your kids there and spend five hundred? I'm trying to give you an idea of what might work. Since we're spitballing, the kind of store I'd like would involve the whole family."

"Continuity," Frank said, as though he were a statesman guaranteeing policy.

"It's called repeats," she said, observing Ellen's amateurish enthusiasm. "My feeling about Rodeo Drive is that it has to be used. Look around—Gucci, St. Laurent, Ted Lapidus are naturals. Dick Carroll still belongs to the village concept. He brought a Brooks Brothers operation to the street. Before Rodeo was anything, Dick Carroll had a *corner* and a clientele of men and women who wanted the

Eastern look and styles. If an operation like Courrèges had a few bad seasons, it wouldn't matter a damn because of the finance behind it.

"What I'm reaching for is a concept that would work on Rodeo Drive, make it respectable, fashionable, and at the same time, wouldn't change every three months. It would be a flagship that would lead the way to expansion. That was my problem at Drake's. Any way you look at it, it was another mall store in a class with Jefferson's in Florida, or K-Mart, the low end of the market. Now if I could find something on Rodeo Drive that would work at both ends, I'd have a real business. It would have to have a label because the public eats that up."

She loved discussing business and she felt flattered that the three of them had listened attentively. She had no illusions about Dunlop or Ed going to the well. It was idle chatter. Yet why in fact shouldn't Frank amuse his wife by investing in a business to keep her occupied? They were playing games, but she had enjoyed herself. At what she did, she was a true professional. They might have more money, but they would've been thrown out of her office at Drake's, which wasn't a think tank but a day-to-day battlefield outguessing the public.

The fantasy of having her own store with all its headaches and burdens stirred her ambition.

Giovanni behaved like a neglected child when he drove her home. She'd put him off earlier and he wasn't accustomed to this sort of frustration. The Dunlops also aggravated him. The fucking nerve they had, undercutting him in front of her. No wonder Frank and Ellen failed so wretchedly in Beverly Hills. Christ, the way they came on.

"No class," Ed advised her. He was really out of sorts.

"I agree. But she's serious and he has money and they're both unscrupulous."

He saw Madeleine peeping through the torn window shade in the corner of the mean, untidy living room.

"It's been some day, Claire," he said with disappointment. "You don't tell me what's on your mind. How'd I get involved with you?"

She was at the door and she too noticed Madeleine

spying on them. She would've liked to sneak around the back and boot Madeleine in the ass, putting her head through the screen.

"Ed, find yourself someone else," Claire said, more angry at Madeleine than him.

"I just might do that." He pressed up against her and she squirmed away. "But I'll call you tomorrow." He stalked back to his Jensen, mawkishly complaining: "The way you treat people."

16

Ellen started Claire's month off brilliantly by spending close to six thousand dollars on skirts, sweaters, blouses, and a few suits, and Minerva hummed merrily to herself when she checked Claire's book. She had offended too many people to remember that she had singled out Frank for special treatment. Visa approved the purchase, which was all she gave a rap about. However, Minerva had a short memory and when Claire called her the following Saturday morning to say she was ill and couldn't get to work. Minerva's voice had a callous stridency.

"I've worked with a hundred and three temperature and pneumonia."

"You're a better woman than I am," Claire rejoined.

"We'll man the trenches without you." She hung up brusquely.

Claire drove to Beverly Hills and parked her car on Bedford Drive on the six hundred block. She walked down to Santa Monica Boulevard and positioned herself across the street from All Saint's Church, surveying the fleets of chauffeured limousines dropping off wedding guests.

The sky was luminescent and it was a windless morning, in the mid-eighties. The air had a fresh lazy taste of promise and ripe late summer. A perfect day for a wedding. Earlier she had spotted a blonde girl in jeans driving a Rolls-Royce, followed by an entourage in other cars. In the sunlight, the girl's engagement ring had an overpowering brilliance. Shortly afterward, a team of photographers and news reporters belted out of three compact cars and Claire watched them take their positions on the portico of the church. The Spanish-style church with its tiled roof was small, romantic, with the intimate charm of a small-town chapel.

She couldn't allow Bobby to continue to live in her imagination and make the wound fester. Reality, her physical presence here, would be a palliative. She had no wish to embarrass Bobby or cause a scene. It was necessary to be a witness so that she'd finally be free.

At ten-thirty she saw a Fleetwood Cadillac pull up to the front of the church. Jack and Lynn Canaday got out and Bobby followed them. He wore striped trousers and severely cut pale gray tails with a white satin bow tie. He carried his black top hat. A couple of photographers asked him to stay where he was. He seemed surprised and bemused, then joined his parents. Lynn had a forced smile on her face and seemed to be sobbing. Christ knew how many Valiums she'd popped with her breakfast gin.

A Bach organ toccata carried mellifluously through the quiet street. Claire and Bobby had agreed on a Beethoven Piano Sonata, which would be played when she walked down the aisle. Claire leaned against a tree, gazing at the church, losing all sense of time.

The sound of raised, elated voices commingled with music from the church, and guests strolled leisurely outside, women in summer prints, men in dark suits, others formally dressed, elegant, rich, untouchable, rejoicing with the newly-married couple who emerged from the chapel.

Claire hurried to her car. She'd had enough of golden couples and yesterdays. He was married and she had been forgotten and what had linked them was buried. She had expected to be shattered and in a way she was disappointed that she had emerged unbroken, but in effect reconstituted, whole, at peace with herself for the first time during this long nightmare. She had passed through this emotional crucible and she would never again be the same. But maybe that was for the best, she thought, since there was nothing more she could lose.

At four o'clock on the afternoon of September 12, Leonard received a phone call from Ann summoning him to a meeting with her money man. In a state of agitation, he arrived at the bar of the Bel Air Hotel by four-thirty. Sitting at a window table with Ann was a sandy-haired man with a gaunt face, beaked nose, and harsh blue eyes. He stood up to shake Leonard's hand. John Blaire was deceptively tall, about six-two, with large freckled hands. He was in his mid-thirties, wore a gray pinstriped suit and a red challis tie. There was something decidedly vulpine about him and he had one of those overbred public school voices from which all trace of benevolence had been banished. Leonard could easily imagine him at a school like Eton, bullying and caning younger boys with a martial skill. He was drinking Guinness mixed with champagne, Black Velvets, an unspeakable combination recommended for seasickness.

"I wish I'd had a little notice," Leonard said, peering at Ann. "We could've arranged a dinner party for John. And you could've been my house guest."

"I came on short notice. Thanks all the same. Another time, perhaps."

Leonard ordered a Black Label on the rocks.

"I was at Slater Walker in the City. Then when it went bad, I set up shop for myself," he explained.

"That's when we decided to go to work together," Ann noted.

"I don't know much about English finance."

"Slater Walker had a merchant bank side and then went into a variety of funds and made some foolish investments. It was a debacle," Blaire told him.

Ann held Blaire's hand, more out of affection than sexual interest.

"John and I hooked up years before, when we were both clerks at Sun Life in the actuary department."

"Good God, Annie. I think we used to take home twenty quid a week," he reminisced. "Then I found out how real money is made. The Slater Walker experience was useful, made loads of contacts."

"So you're an independent financier."

"Hardly." He and Ann laughed, increasing Leonard's discomfort. "I made my first fortune as an asset stripper. I'd get control of a company with someone else's money, and use the shares to take over another company so long as it had valuable freehold property. Sell off the property to pay my lenders and find myself swimming in an ocean of cash, along with two shell companies. They can be very useful for companies seeking a listing on the stock exchange. John Bloom's Rolls Razor had nothing to do with the original company, for instance. He went into the washing machine business and out of it."

Blaire sounded thoroughly disreputable and took pleasure in recounting how he had gradually become more respectable.

"We've got a few offshore funds. Property and insurance bonds. We pay no tax in Lichtenstein, which is why we can afford to go higher than the majority of English funds. The Brighton Property Bond pays out about fourteen and a half percent."

Leonard asked who was behind Brighton.

"I represent a number of people in these private situations, as does Ann. You needn't concern yourself about their identities." He opened his attaché case and pulled out a file. He released a thick buck clip and showed Leonard a letter of credit in the name of Brighton Property Bonds for twenty million dollars from Barclays Bank to the Beverly Hills branch of Bank of America.

"Leonard, it seems to me that I delivered what I promised," Ann said mordantly. "However, I never claimed that I was empowered to negotiate for the rest of the loan."

Leonard had a sinking feeling. He could see that he was about to be whipsawed.

"Look, it seems to me that you people are getting a damned good deal. For five million you get half my interest in what's going to be a skyscraper in Century City. Fifty percent of Marine Mutual on your portfolio is a very impressive asset and our understanding, Ann, was that the rest of the money—five million to close escrow and fifteen million for the construction loan, which I can get matching funds for once this is closed—ought to satisfy anyone."

He could have saved his breath. Blaire wasn't listening, bored by the direction of the discussion.

"Leonard, I came here not to bargain but to inform you of the revised terms," he said mercilessly.

"We have a contract."

"It's an understanding," Ann corrected him. "John put

five million into the property on my say-so and he's shown nothing but good faith. It looks like you're the one trying to squirm out of this."

"Let him," Blaire advised her apathetically. "If he raises the money from another source within the next two days, he's welcome to it. He'll pay us back and we'll dispose of the funds elsewhere. Frankly, Leonard, we're getting thirty percent and a piece of the business for high-risk venture capital. We've also been very aggressive in the commodity markets. Most of the currencies are very shaky, as you know, because of high inflation. Give us back our five million and we'll buy gold."

He got up, signaling the waiter for the check, and Leonard turned ashen.

"You've just blown it, Leonard," Ann said sharply.

For a year he had failed to raise the twenty-five million he needed. How was he going to get it in two days? They were sweating him. He knew that he was powerless.

"John, give me a chance. I haven't said no to anything. Just what do you want?"

Blaire ordered more champagne and Guinness, then coldly laid down his terms.

"My dear chap, you do have an alternative. You can sue me for not fulfilling what you consider a contract but which is, as we understand it, an agreement in principle subject to a final review. We can litigate forever. Can you? In Lichtenstein? Have you the foggiest notion how difficult that would be? You lose your escrow and Marine Mutual sues you. Are you prepared for that?"

They had him skewered. When you dealt with private sources, he knew that you left yourself wide open for this type of flanking maneuver.

"What sort of additions did you have in mind?"

"Rodeo Puerta. Certainly it's highly speculative. Retail shops, but at least that would buttress our position until Marine is built and rented. If the building isn't rented in a year, we are going to find ourselves tied to a dead horse."

Leonard shook his head, recalling that when Ann had brought up the possibility he had been adamant in his refusal. "Five percent," he suggested finally.

"Do you think I'm an idiot? I want fifty-one percent!" Leonard's rockbed principle was never to give up a controlling interest in his projects. He was outraged by the serpentine tactics used on him. "Man, you're a bad credit risk. If you weren't, you never would have turned to Ann."

The utter ruthlessness of the proposal rocked him.

"Do you know what you're asking me to give up?"

"Rodeo Drive may be glamorous and puffed up by the media, but is there a guarantee you'll rent the stores at the sort of price you're considering?" Ann asked.

They went at him together, buffeting him back and forth. Christ, had he been set up. He saw it now all too clearly. The line beginning with Ann Shaw as a loan officer and her subsequent employment by him left him without any resources. She had been privy to all of his financial woes.

"How do I know that you won't change your mind by tomorrow and demand ninety percent—all of it," he protested.

Blaire pulled out the contract, turned to the last page. "I'll be happy to ring the bank now and go down there and sign it with you so you can rest easy." On the last page was a short paragraph describing Rodeo Puerta, with a note that 51 percent of the legally described property was to be given to Brighton Property Bonds A.C. in exchange for their total investment in the Martinson Development Company. He had no choice but to accept the terms. He found some small solace in the fact that Ann Shaw would be out of his life for good.

The dust-caked and sweating Mexican workmen Leonard had sent over from Alpine were still in the guesthouse when Bobby arrived there shortly after five. He was in a daze, running from place to place and apprehensive about an appointment he had at six with Dunlop to show him his first set of renderings. He and Hillary had been married just five days and his life had become increasingly complicated.

They had spent their wedding night at a house in the Malibu Colony, which Kitty Oliver had given them for the month. He hadn't completed the move from his apartment and he found commuting from Malibu yet another distraction. He couldn't work in the house. Sitting on the terrace, watching the waves roll in, drove him nuts. Possibly it was his mood or the pressure of work, but he could find no common ground with the neighbors.

Hillary had accepted the postponement of their honeymoon without grace and she blamed both him and Leonard for plotting behind her back. She brooded about it, unable to reconcile herself to the responsibilities Bobby faced, and he noticed the clever way she insinuated guilt on him. She had never learned to cook and had no intention of beginning a course in homemaking. When the maid didn't show up, the bed remained unmade, the towels accumulated on the bathroom floor. Although he was not enamored with the guesthouse, he would gladly exchange it for Malibu.

A white Mercedes 450SL was parked outside the house and a bare-chested Mexican sat on the front fender. His coppery skin was rippled with sweat. He had a large weight lifter's barrel chest, a tapered waist, thick-veined biceps, and a dark, scowling face. Bobby had a vague recollection of having seen him tiling the roof at Alpine. He didn't much like the man's defiant close-set brown eyes, which exuded the menace of a brawler.

"Do you speak English?"

The man shifted off the fender, ambled over to him, and gazed at him authoritatively.

"I should. I'm a Chicano. Born in Boyle Heights."

"Are you working on this job?"

"Yeah. Sort of supervising. Got to make sure that the boys don't mess around. You're the architect?"

"Right."

"You really ripped the shit out of the big house. Same thing here?"

"Christ, no. Some paint and wallpapering and a little carpentry."

Bobby led the way into the house and became violently angry when he saw Hillary sitting on the sofa with a margarita in hand. She had on high denim cutoffs that revealed the tops of her thighs and a flimsy yellow see-through tank top that framed her breasts. A few of the workmen were on ladders, scraping off wallpaper; another was under the sink in the kitchen fixing a leak, while a couple of others were in the bedroom. Music blasted from a radio in the kitchen.

"Hi, stranger," Hillary said. She rose to her feet unsteadily and wrapped her arms around him, still holding her glass. "Cocktail hour. Let me tell you, one of the boys whipped up a batch of margaritas. He can give lessons to the bartenders in town." She wasn't drunk, but slurring her words slightly.

Bobby held her by the waist and maneuvered her outside. She slid her fingers through the unbuttoned top of his shirt and he couldn't hold back, lambasted her.

"What the fuck is wrong with you? Walking around like that in front of these workmen, half drunk, waving your diamond ring in their faces." Leonard had given Hillary her mother's engagement ring, a massive solitaire diamond. No one had asked him how he felt about her flaunting an eight-carat ring.

"Relax. Jesus, have a drink and calm down."

"Hill, change your clothes."

"Forget it."

He'd never been so flustered with her and he found himself losing his self-control.

"You're begging for trouble, flashing your tits and ass."

She scowled at him.

"Don't tell *me* how to act. If you think I like keeping a bunch of guys company so that they don't tear the roof off, you're mistaken. I'm doing it for us so that we can have our little place."

"Can we stay in town tonight?"

"Okay. I'll book a table at Lucy's Adobe. I feel like Mexican tonight."

"Hillary, I've got to work tonight."

She swigged down the rest of her margarita.

"First no honeymoon, then you come at me like a wild man. You don't like Malibu . . . what's more important? Me or your shitty building?"

"I haven't got time to argue."

"You haven't got time for anything. Did you ever hear of something called F-U-N? When're you going to understand that we don't need the money? We can do anything . . . anything . . . Bobby, I'm offering you freedom from all the chickenshit you're chasing your tail off for."

He was so angry he could have struck her.

"My work isn't chickenshit to me. You've never done an honest day's work in your life, so what the hell would you know about it?"

She dropped her chin on her chest, subdued, vanquished, wretched in her failure to get through to him, and for a moment he wished he could establish some reasonable common ground so that they could come together. She stalked away from him, then turned. She reached into her pocket and pulled out a set of keys, then threw it to him.

"You didn't even notice, did you, or if you did you didn't give me the satisfaction of telling me you liked it."

"What are you talking about?"

"The car. I had it delivered and the boys waxed it because they did a lousy job at the dealer's."

He turned and realized that the plateless car had a DMV sticker pasted to the windshield and on the driver's door in dark brown script were the initials RJC. He had never seen anything so vulgar in his life. Now she was buying him off, bribing him. He flung the keys at her, enraged by pride.

"Do you think I'm some fucking gigolo? My work is chickenshit. You just took a wrong turn."

"Oh, you bastard," she snarled.

He'd never been so filled with rancor before, unable to think straight as he sped off in his Honda, then had to slow down for the electric gates to open. Shit, he hated the place. He was not going to let Hillary or anyone else imprison him. All that counted was the first rough set of drawings in his portfolio, which Dunlop would see in a few minutes.

His meeting with Dunlop had been brief and encouraging. "It's a strong maybe," he told Tim Hayward, who was waiting for him in a state of agitation in the bar of the Westwood Marquis. "We're almost there." Bobby wanted to review his work for a few days, then develop a more advanced and detailed set of renderings. He and Hayward had a pleasant few hours, exchanging small talk about the prospects emerging throughout L.A., and at around nine, rather than make a night of it, Bobby returned to the guesthouse in a spirit of conciliation. He abhorred domestic warfare. Maybe he could make Hillary understand his point of view.

The front door was unlocked and there was a noxious odor of glue, turpentine, and paint. On the kitchen counter was a pizza from Numero Uno, a deep-dish Chicago classic, and he realized that to please him—a junk food deviate of long standing—Hillary had picked up something he liked. The oven was heating on low. He went into the bedroom, found her in jeans, dozing on the bed, the TV tuned to *Quincy*. He bent down and kissed her forehead.

"Hi, tough guy," she said.

"About the car—"

"I drove it off a cliff." She giggled. She ran her hand up his trouser leg, pushed back the crotch and grasped his balls. "Bobby . . ."

"Uh-huh . . ."

"I'm going to do wicked things to you."

There was no point bringing up the argument, attempting to resolve the misunderstandings besetting them.

"Sure, let's go to work."

17

"I thought I would've seen you at the wedding," Ellen said over her seafood salad. They were at the Bistro, close enough to the store so that a traffic jam wouldn't prevent Claire from getting back in time. Minerva would not tolerate long lunches, even with good customers. "I was curious to see what you'd wear. I like the way you dress." Even in her black linen skirt and short-sleeved white cotton blouse with a tab collar, Claire managed to look attractive.

"I had other plans."

"Minerva, naturally." Ellen's eyes conveyed warmth and friendliness. "Ed came late to the party—and he was stag. I never would've believed he could go to a party alone and not leave with a tulip. Claire, you've got him."

"We're comfortable most of the time. What more could I want?"

"Do you love him?"

If her interest were not so well-intentioned, the question would have been impertinent.

"I don't give it much thought."

She found herself retreating, her mind flooded with images of Bobby and his bride. It was still dangerous territory for her to navigate.

"You don't discuss your background or personal life much, do you?"

"It's pretty much of a void. My mother settled in Vegas a few years ago. She's a cashier at the Sands. I keep meaning to get there. We've spoken once since I came to L.A.

We've never been close. Personality conflict. She's a free-wheeling woman—lives every day like it's her last—and we find it hard to make emotional contact." Claire hesitated. Maybe Ellen's sympathy could help her exorcise the phantom of Bobby. "I lost the man I was in love with," she admitted without experiencing humiliation or giving herself tragic airs. That her attitude was so matter-of-fact revealed to Ellen how profound the loss had actually been. "I may have been to blame, you know, innocently. Until I met Ed I was unworldly to a fault. I had my job at Drake's—the rising star"—she laughed sourly—"and my man. I was wearing blinkers. I had a tendency to oversimplify his needs. He wanted out and I let him off the hook."

Ellen was moved by the self-effacing recitation of Claire's disaster.

"You were loyal to him."

"Yes, it's a character defect. There are other men I can see now, but Ed's been very good to me and the single life doesn't agree with me. It's not even a case of being inhibited. I'm just happiest giving myself to one man. Maybe there's some young millionaire waiting for me, or a beach bum, but the problem of exploring these possibilities can wind up an end in itself. I live with a girl who's been on that track."

Ellen sounded her out about her relationship with Madeleine; without embellishment, Claire explained how, even though there was an underlying affection, the two of them frequently clashed. What began to emerge was a sense of rivalry between them that Claire could not halt. Claire looked at her watch. It was time to fly. She took out ten dollars and put it on the table.

"Don't be silly. Next time lunch's on you," Ellen said, signing the check. She walked Claire back to the store and sounded her out about moving.

"I'd give anything for my own place. Ed's asked me to move in with him . . . but then I lose my independence."

"I've got an idea." Ellen scribbled down an address and handed it to Claire. "Meet me here when you're through."

"Six-thirty?"

"That's good."

For some diehard natives, south of Wilshire Boulevard was the wrong side of Beverly Hills. It hardly mattered that one-bedroom apartments rented for eight hundred a month or that two-bedroom condos barely eleven hundred square feet with views of parking lots sold for a quarter of a million dollars. Any change would be welcome for Claire, and the three-story condominium with security on Camden Drive off Olympic represented paradise. Ellen was waiting outside the building in her bright yellow Rolls Corniche. The top was down and she had a copy of *Cosmo* spread over the wheel. She honked at Claire who pulled into the curb ahead of her.

Claire didn't know what to expect, for Ellen savored the game, and until she showed Claire into the third floor corner apartment, she maintained a tantalizing detachment.

"What do you think?" she asked when Claire stood in the center of the living room. The white thick-pile carpet under her feet was alien. Two navy blue sofas faced each other, separated by a mirrored coffee table. A wing chair in a light blue madras print closed in the area with a matching ottoman. The white marble fireplace was gas operated and filled with lava logs. Ellen opened the white drapes and pointed to a corner wraparound balcony.

"Are you serious? What do I think? It's a knockout. But they must be asking over a thousand a month for it."

"We'll see. Just look around."

There were two bedrooms with baths. One was a convertible den with bookcases, a sofa and armchair, a desk with pigeonholes set against the window. The master bedroom had a tufted powder blue headboard behind the queen-size bed, a frilly bedspread in a blue Provençal pattern and matching curtains. The bathroom was large with an ultra tub, a stall shower, and a makeup area. Time and effort had gone into the decorations. All the rooms had wooden moldings stained a honey color. The kitchen led to a dining area where there was a round glass table and four high-backed steel chairs with white leather seats. Ellen took a couple of Tabs from the side-by-side Westinghouse refrigerator-freezer and offered her one.

"So? Do you like it?"

"It's the prettiest apartment I think I've ever seen."

"It's mine," Ellen said, smiling broadly. "The building, I mean. I told you that I had three buildings. We used to put up executives who came in from Chicago here. But Frank prefers to have them stay at the house so he can have access to them day and night. I've thought about renting it furnished or selling it, but I'm glad I didn't. I like the place too much and the money I get isn't going to matter much. How much are you paying Madeleine?"

"Some months three—sometimes four. Officially two-fifty, but it depends on Madeleine's finances. I couldn't find a place for under that anywhere."

"You like it then?"

"Ellen, it's magnificent."

"You've got it for three hundred a month."

Claire was speechless, merely gazed adoringly at Ellen, opened her arms and kissed her.

"Ellen, this is real life and not some fairy tale. Why would you give this to me?"

"Isn't it obvious? Frank and I both like you enormously and what's the point of having a lot of money if you can't do things to please yourself. If I rent it or sell it, what the hell're we going to do with the money except pay tax on it? Marine Mutual is the sixth largest insurance company in the country. I don't even think Frank knows how much he's worth, but it's some sort of intimidating figure like two hundred million . . . The other side of the coin is that I'm in deadly earnest about breaking out in something of my own and I've got a good feeling about you. So, honey, set your mind to it and we'll start a business together."

From the terrace she could see the twin triangular towers of Century City, Roxbury Park, people walking on the street. She disliked the isolation of the Hollywood Hills. She loved the sense of being drawn into a city with an established neighborhood. She would no longer be at the mercy of her car, negotiating the tortuous hills and dodging wild motorcycle freaks who ripped up and down the canyons. She could walk to Rodeo Drive. Yet more than anything, the apartment would give her the sanctity of privacy, enable her to orchestrate her life, rebuild.

"Ellen, can I make a condition? There's an infernal middle-class streak in me. I like to pay my own way. If I have a good month, I'd feel better if I could increase the rent."

"Agreed. I'll have a cleaning crew come in tomorrow and you move in whenever you're ready."

Oddly enough, there was no one with whom she could share her good fortune. Giovanni would resent her independence. Depending on Madeleine's volatile frame of mind, Claire would either be accused of desertion or prevailed upon to take her in. She couldn't win, no matter which way she turned. By the time she reached the house it no longer mattered. She was going to please herself for once.

Madeleine was padding around barefoot, smoking a joint. Her eyes lingered on Claire's face for a moment, then she averted them, cleared a garbage bag off the counter, and reached for a half-filled bottle of Gallo Chablis. She held up an empty glass for Claire who told her she'd join her. The first thing she did was go to the bedroom, remove her black skirt and put her top into the hamper. The tub had a ring and she wanted to have a bath so she cleaned it with the last few specks of Ajax and the washcloth curled in the vanity cabinet like a rodent.

"Going out?" Claire asked when she returned to the living room.

"Yeah, in about an hour," Madeleine replied without enthusiasm. She handed her a glass of wine with a couple of thin ice cubes in it. "Have you got a minute?" she asked uneasily, fidgeting. Claire mentally composed a multiple choice of Madeleine's primary themes: another loan; a blind date for a hundred and should she go; or yet another two-hour analysis of Al Brockman's persistent avoidance of her. She had admitted to sleeping with him and wondered if it had been a failure of career strategy. If only she had someone like Lee Strasberg to mold her talents.

Actually, for once, Claire was way off line. This time Madeleine had really put herself in the shithouse.

"I think they suspect me at Gucci."

"Really? Since when is it their business who you sleep with? I thought they were in leather, not morals."

"Claire, it's not that." She was panic-stricken and Claire was puzzled and concerned.

"What is it? Tell me."

Madeleine's hands were shaking.

"I should've stopped months ago. But the money was

good and I'm always fucking broke. I've been ripping off bags returned for damages or repairs." Claire really shouldn't have been surprised, but she was. "I've got about a dozen women I sell them to for cash. Gucci's missing about three thousand dollars' worth of bags."

"Do they know it's you?"

"They're making it obvious, sort of . . . What happened at Drake's, Claire? Please, tell me."

She didn't want to frighten Madeleine. Drake's attitude was like Savonarola's. Burn the thieves at the stake. He had been fanatical about pilfering. It was bad enough he had to contend with shoplifting by the public; stealing by the staff was a Judas act. Drake forced prosecutions on flimsy evidence.

"Are you bonded there?"

"For sure."

"Oh, honey, you're so fucking dumb at times. How can Momma save you? Have they got cameras, surveillance devices?"

"Yes."

"If you're on film, you've got a chance. One girl at Drake's had it thrown out as inadmissible evidence. Her boyfriend was a law student and he happened to be right. Some federal thing." She took a hit of the joint. "What am I going to do with you, Maddy?"

"It'll ruin me—being exposed," Madeleine cried with high drama. "The media would crucify me," she sighed with wistful fear. "I'm human interest. It's a lifetime of notoriety."

"With bonding companies for sure. Take it easy, it's not as though Bette Midler got caught in the act."

"She could beat it. I can't," Madeleine said throwing her fists at an unforgiving universe whose design was to bring her to her knees, incarcerate her.

"If you're actually convicted, you'll get a suspended sentence." Claire pondered, screwed up her eyes. "You are a first offender?"

"Naturally."

"Okay, on the other hand you haven't been caught red-handed by more than one witness?"

"No."

"One girl's word against you is tough. Your defense is

that she's jealous and a liar. The store has to prove her case. Jesus, I feel like I'm on a tribunal. At Drake's, thank God I was out of that crap. The only way they can really nail you is if they picked up one of the women you sold a bag to and your client is prepared to be a witness against you. Drake had one like that in small appliances. He took the girl to the wall."

Claire had to rest for a moment. The grass had dazzled her. The last thing Madeleine needed to hear was that she'd be moving out shortly. She just couldn't go through with it. Madeleine could touch the guilt nerves at will, emotional acupuncture with perfect timing.

"Getting back to the bonding company. The store lays it on them with a claim, they then send out a snooper, usually a woman. She could be a sweet granny type or hyper like Joan Rivers. You never know. So if you haven't sold a bag to someone new, there's a chance."

Madeleine took no solace in Claire's scenario. She didn't even remember whom she hadn't sold a bag to. A round dozen was a conservative estimate. She worked by recommendation; her fan club of vultures functioned like a chain letter. Her Raffles-like masterpiece had been the shortstopping of a perfect crocodile Gucci classic with a loose clasp for which she'd received four hundred and eighteen dollars and a ticket to the play *Zoot Suit.* Madeleine had blown the money on one hit—a red silk trouser suit on sale at Hermès. Madeleine knew she wasn't merely into larceny—a case of fencing would be more appropriate.

"Oh, babe," she said, "I might have to go back East and work off-off-off-Broadway again." She raised her arm to her left breast to ward off who knew what, and then, to Claire's dismay, started to weep with awesome fury, making Claire jump.

"Madeleine, cut it out. I think I know what you should do." Madeleine rocked back and forth in her arms, heaving her chest against Claire's ear. "Force an accusation and then tell them you won't answer a single question until you speak to your lawyer. Don't chickenshit it. It's Gucci, not Drake's. They've got a reputation, which works against them." Claire became excited, infected by Madeleine's lunacy. "Threaten them . . . say you'll call the *L.A. Times* and *New West* and you're going to sue them for defamation of character and loss of income. Then demand severance pay. They'll do anything to get rid of you. I would."

Rapid eye movements suggested that the information was undergoing something like a mental digestive process in the buxom thief's mind. Madeleine squinted, sneaked a smirk.

"In another ten years you'll be the second Mrs. Archie Bunker," Claire said with encouragement.

"Not Meryl Streep?" She got the fixings and prepared to roll a fresh joint, a real event in their household since Madeleine usually dealt with clawlike holders for her collection of roaches.

"One other thing, babe," she said, winking at Claire in her most endearing style, the twelve-year-old bartering for an extra piece of pizza crust, "I've got a date tonight and I don't know if I can handle it. It's really weird."

Claire left the room, carrying a fresh glass of wine. Shit, she had to have a bath and get Madeleine out into the night before she drifted off the continental shelf.

"I'm not sure about this at all, Gene." Madeleine noticed that the director had in a liquor supply and a pane of glass, removed from his side window, on which he was cutting lines of coke with a Swiss army knife.

"Well, I realize that this is a major decision that you and the President ought to discuss and be as one."

"Come on, now, stop it." He poured some vodka into her glass. "By the way, I noticed a slight medicinal taste in the back of my throat from the coke."

"Is it disagreeable?"

"I'm not sure."

"When you are, write to the Consumer Union."

He was clean-shaven, neat in baggy white ducks, and he wore a tee shirt with MAUNA KEA printed on the front. They'd been discussing the Islands and Madeleine yearned to visit them. She kept referring to the South Pacific and Gene gave up explaining that it was Hawaii.

The fates had not entirely blighted her flight into future greatness. Gene had cropped some of the head shots, capturing a plenary cosmology of Madeleine's art. In a simulated toss-off sequence, she seized the manic postures of Gilda Radner, she thought, pouting slightly. Now, if only she had her voice, she'd be home and dry. Madeleine's loving gaze roved with narcissistic delight over the range of her moods: shocked, alluringly sensuous, cutie-pie giggly, aroused, orgasmically fulfilled. She really was something else.

"I kind of remind myself," she said pertly, "of Anne Baxter with Clift in *A Place in the Sun.*"

"All About Eve," he suggested. "You were Gene Tierney."

She nodded. "Exactly. You know your filmography."

"I know a fucking plowhead and dildo when I see one. You've never seen either film."

She was becoming accustomed to his barbs and flicked them off like gnats. He needed TLC, this barbarian. She softened, a maternal glint in her eye.

"Oh, Gene, what a rotten childhood you must've had to be so surly."

"Really? Both my parents were doctors. I had a great childhood. I had love, discipline, and freedom. I went to Horace Mann and finally to Yale where I was thrown out in my sophomore year for getting a blow job in the dining hall after it was closed. I'm on terrific terms with my folks. Where'd you get the idea that my childhood wasn't happy? From an astrology magazine?"

"You rebelled against it all," she observed, still scanning the glossies. "Marching, protesting . . ."

"That's enough. I'm a law-and-order man. I'd vote for Warren Burger for president." She looked blankly at him and roared.

"You're some character. Do you think I'd fall for that?"

"What?"

"Warren Burger. You just made that up. Didn't you? Admit it. There's no such person." He strode around the room, skipped, trying to remain in touch with reality, control his temper. "The pictures are tremendous. You're a very talented guy."

Coming from her, it was an insult, but he decided to be gracious about it.

"Considering I was just fucking around and not setting up for head shots, they're not bad. Wait'll you see what you look like after a straight session." He stuck his hand in his pocket, peeled out a hundred and fifty dollars, and gave the money to her. "I showed them to *Beavers and Boobs* and they bought two for three hundred, so we split fifty-fifty. Worth hauling your ass over here, wasn't it?"

She was astonished by his honesty and the generous impulse he revealed. If only he wouldn't keep her off balance. Perhaps this was his way. "You could've beat me for the money. I wouldn't have known. Does *B* and *B* want a profile on me?"

"No, they make up their own."

This was perplexing, tempering her thrust into celebrity status.

"What sort of thing do they do?"

"Since they like my stuff, you'll probably get a prime spot, opposite the bondage ads, and they'll make you foreign. Helga or something from Germany who was kidnapped by four truckers hitchhiking across America."

This was not at all promising. Among other things, Gene robbed her of any pleasure she might have had and she wondered how she could get through to him on an emotional level. She wasn't simply chattel and she resented his treatment. When she compared him to a man like Giovanni, suave and worldly, who courted Claire with such zealousness, she became exasperated. Goddammit, she was overdue for a run of luck. In the meantime, she settled for two lines of coke and her mood was quickly elevated to a high C. What a rush! He joined her, then rubbed a smear on his gums.

"I see what you mean about the blow. It's been hit with procaine. Still, it gets the job done."

Madeleine had another drink and was getting pretty well lit, he was relieved to see. He enjoyed teasing her and had no intention of drawing blood. Her hapless desire to make it infuriated him. However, she projected a rather touching, ingenuous human quality, which affected him. Unlike most of the hardhats he dealt with, she was so devoid of craftiness that he found himself taken with her. Although he was an aficionado of sport-fucking, he was glad he hadn't arranged for a guy to be in the act. In any event, the marketplace for his wares was demanding more lesbian material. Even straight people were growing bored with straight sex.

"What's going to happen tonight?" she asked. She might

have second thoughts. Her face pinched up and in her large brown eyes he observed distress.

"It's a lark . . . fun and games."

"See, I don't know what I'm letting myself in for."

"I've got an expert working with you. A pro. She'll love you. Just respond naturally. She'll do the heavy work because it's her trip. It'll be an experience. Treat it as a fantasy . . . a one-shot."

He sat beside her, placed his arm around her neck and kissed her.

"I honestly wish you liked me."

"Madeleine, I can't stand myself," he said forthrightly. "So what's left for anybody? But on principle, I do like you. If I didn't I would've tossed you out the first time."

She snuggled into his arms.

"I'm going to make you like yourself."

"Don't tamper with my pleasures."

Further discussion was abbreviated by the entrance of a smiling free-spirited piece of fudge called Alana trailing clouds of musk. She was exquisitely slender with an aquiline nose, and her hair twisted into corn rows. She was accompanied by a short-haired boy with bleached eyebrows and hair, carrying a large, battered case.

"Hi, I'm Jeremy, princess," he said to Madeleine. "We ready to make up the ladies, Gene?"

"Have a toot and let's go."

Actually, their presence reassured Madeleine. She was no longer facing the unknown. She was approaching her first film *call.* She rose from the tattered couch with a certain dignity. This was not the raw recruit painting a backdrop black, but a consummate professional. Her first role totally overshadowed her first screw. This she would remember if God spared her till she was eighty when, actuarially speaking, she might be considered the first lady of loops. Well, beginnings are seldom painless, she thought, accompanying her co-star and a future Percmore to the rookery that was Gene's second bedroom, a windowless cell in which paperbacks, records, old clothing, suitcases, camera equipment, a cot draped with a jagged hunk of yellow rubber foam, and a glass dresser set in front of a mirrored closet were the furnishings.

She'd do it as *The Turning Point,* a film she admired

inordinately because of Bancroft and MacLaine. She had taken her Superscope tape recorder to the movie the third time and pirated the dialogue. This was it, no holds barred. She'd act Alana back to Nigeria. Alana was in the shithouse against this scene stealer. Alana's agent would have to take it to SAG for arbitration before Madeleine was through with her. Gene would have a fit because Madeleine knew the tricks. She'd break scenes, demanding *takes*. Her first taste of the limelight, she thought triumphantly. She savored the moment, sipped a little white wine that Jeremy had brought with him. Never mind, just pour it into the empty vodka glass. She was not about to search for a clean glass in the director's kitchen—fuck that.

"It's because I'm black and a woman that the real estate is busting my ass," Alana said to her. "Man, they don't want me in Beverly Hills getting my license and selling my friends and taking home a thousand a week in commissions."

"That's interesting," Madeleine said. Way Bandy was unpacking his jars and tubes. "What do you do?"

"I'm a receptionist in a property place in Westwood. No names now." She touched the underside of Madeleine's breasts. "You got a full tank of gas. Who did them?"

"God." Madeleine was into short, trenchant dialogue. Long speeches bored the audience, except when Bancroft delivered them.

"Well, I'll find out soon enough. When they been done, they taste like yams."

Jeremy looked at Madeleine critically.

"Your smile lines are unused." He pancaked her face, neck, and forehead, used a brown eyeliner and shadow that appeared aqua in the light.

Alana smiled seductively at her.

"We're going to enjoy ourselves. I'll get her to smile. Oh, you can't take it seriously. Attitude is everything," Alana said. "Look at it as kicking up your heels and having a few laughs, really."

"I can live with that," Madeleine replied.

"Chosen tribe is all. Think about all them beautifully souled sisters out there with bad legs and acne. They don't get asked to do this. Fucking world is crazy anyhow, so what do we care?"

Gene entered and passed around a joint. Madeleine needed to be stroked.

"The first setup's in the bathroom," he told Jeremy. "I've got one side light and you'll hold the fill for the critical areas. Then we'll move it into the bedroom."

"What're you using?"

"Two overhead tungstens through a diffuser, a side and a fill. That should do it."

When she was ready, Gene slipped his arm through hers and for the first time since meeting him, she thought she detected a hint of concern, some vestige of common humanity binding them. But then it was gone and she was thrust back into the haunting feeling of being alone, her emotional domicile in L.A. It no longer upset her quite so much. Even though Claire was living with her, nothing could pierce that armor of solitariness, of living within her own skin. Maybe this was the kind of break she'd been looking for. But she refused to be a victim of self-deception. Perhaps Gene was priming her for something else. She'd have to be on her guard.

Gene led her into the bathroom and ran the bath. He poured in some bubble salts and the water turned a frothy green.

"Scared?"

"Uh-huh. Gene, what's a critical area?"

"Your pussy."

"How do you want us?" Alana asked.

"Dressed, as you are."

Jeremy came in holding a light meter while Gene choreographed the scene. Madeleine would go to the front door at a signal from him, open it to find her girlfriend there. Alana would be sullen, tearful if she could manage it. Madeleine would comfort her. Alana would soften and begin to gratefully kiss her friend. A bath might relax her. Madeleine was about to take one. Why not the two of them together in the tub like kids? They'd take off their clothes, frolic in the water.

A half hour later, after several stop-starts to change lenses, Madeleine's legs dangled over the side of the tub and Alana was squirting shaving cream over her pubic hair for what Gene called the bi-cosmic haircut—Persis Khambatta style. Alana had a mischievous, sensuous look on her face while Madeleine, as directed, smiled gaily. Alana deftly moved the razor in the creases of Madeleine's thighs, whisking off the hair, then she shaved her just below the navel while the camera whirred.

Gene encouragingly called out: "Good, good, you're enjoying it, Madeleine. You're getting turned on."

In another minute, all of the hair had been removed and Alana got out of the tub first. Gene stopped the camera and instructed Madeleine to stand up, covering her privates with a wash cloth, and then slowly drop the cloth. He wanted to cut on their reactions. When Madeleine performed the scene, she was helped out of the tub by Alana, who tenderly toweled her off. She began to kiss Madeleine's breasts. She stroked the nipples and Madeleine, against her will, found herself growing excited.

"Alana, put your hand on the naked parking lot," Gene bellowed. "Good. Now walk into the bedroom. Madeleine, you should be a little uncertain because you're not sure how you feel. Alana's turned you on but she's your friend. It's your first time."

Madeleine was becoming confused about how she actually felt.

They came into the floodlit bedroom. There was a red satin coverlet on the bed. Alana began coaxing Madeleine, her fingers grasping her hips. She stooped low, spread the pink lips of Madeleine's vagina and began to lick them. Then her mouth moved to her clitoris and unexpectedly Madeleine shuddered, knew that she was having an orgasm. She lay back on the bed. Alana's head was expertly on her thigh where the shot would not be blocked and she passionately thrust her tongue inside Madeleine. Again the juices churned and even though the thought of any lesbian relationship just a few hours ago would have disgusted her, she gave in to the moment, the fluidity of Alana's stroking hands and the manipulations of her infernal tongue. She had had head before, of course, from a man, but nothing that came close to this feeling, and she had an instant's panic. What if she were turning into a lesbian? The thought frightened her and in the midst of her uncertainty, her excitement became unbearable.

"Give it to her good," Jeremy cried, carried away by the undulating bodies, the unfeigned orgasmic cries of the two girls going at each other uncontrollably. "This is prime, prime!"

They continued for another fifteen minutes and Madeleine knew she had never before had such a powerfully exotic experience. She tried to separate her mind into compartments, but nothing could take her away from the sweet-tasting mouth of the black girl. Finally Gene told them that he was finished. The two girls lay sweating under the lights. Alana's brown eyes fixed on Madeleine's face and she leaned over and kissed her on the mouth.

"You're a honey," she said.

"It was my first time," Madeleine replied.

"Won't be the last for us, will it?"

"I don't know," she said doubtfully.

Gene paid both of them three hundred dollars in crisp hundreds and Madeleine put the money in her purse. She had left home that evening with only seven dollars and fifty cents to her name and she vowed that she'd never be that short again. She and Alana exchanged phone numbers and promised to keep in touch. Alana left with Jeremy, and Madeleine gathered her things and prepared to say good-night to Gene, who was in the developing room in the rear of the garden. He came outside, took hold of her hand and stared at her.

"You really turned my head around . . . was I okay?"

He didn't answer her question. There was a change taking place in his face. Gone was the scornful expression. He leaned over and lightly brushed her lips, then rubbed his hand down her thigh; she pressed her body against his.

"Think you'll like me as much as Alana?"

"Is that a proposal?"

"Certainly. I want to marry you. But my parents might insist on your converting to Judaism."

She pushed him away. "You never let up, do you?"

"Sow belly, when I get through with you, you're going to think you've been smoked."

She pondered her decision. She found him attractive and he fascinated her, but was there any future? Should she get involved and risk being dumped when some other girl came along who interested him? Perhaps it would be better to keep it strictly business, but she was curious, challenged. This was the closest he'd come to pursuing her and she wondered what kind of lover he'd be. She was enjoying the game.

"Do I get paid for it?"

"I only buy gifts . . . a mink coat or a five-carat diamond."

He put his hand between her thighs, dreamily propped his head on her breast and they dropped to the ground in a corkscrew movement. Her mouth opened and he slid his tongue inside and for once he was unguarded—at her mercy. Gone was the supercilious taunting manner, displaced by a suppliance.

"One thing, Gene. I'm through working in stores and I want you to use me whenever you can."

"You're really full of surprises."

18

Parting with Madeleine proved painless. No quarrel or trauma. Claire was even given two hundred dollars on the loan she had advanced her over the months. Found money. She met the new man in Madeleine's life, a wise-guy photographer who diagrammed her figure with his eyes and invited her to his studio for a body reading whenever she was in the mood. The fact that he made the pass so openly did not distress Madeleine. "That's Gene's way of being friendly. He's totally innocent," she was told. They seemed perfectly suited to each other, the aspiring actress and her Svengali. He was going to line up work for Madeleine in *Hustler* and *High Society* and Claire had no doubt that one day Madeleine would be leering out at her from the magazine rack.

The move into the apartment on Camden Drive was simple, considering that she had no furniture to cart. Ellen came by the first evening she was in; they cracked a bottle of Louis Roederer champagne and Claire had that sense of discovery of having found a friend whose affection and loyalty she could depend on.

Giovanni had lost his advantage and she detected a sour side to his possessiveness. They saw less of each other since she grew bored marking time with him at the restaurant. The independence Claire had sought, free from all attachments, was intoxicating. She loved the apartment and the time on her own allowed her to think about what she wanted to do.

Occasionally she caught six o'clock movies in Westwood, followed up by hamburgers at the Apple Pan, then returned home and made lists, notes on yellow pads in her search for the idea that would launch her on Rodeo Drive. There was no longer any challenge in selling off the floor at Minerva's. She had proved that she was better than just about anybody on the street and she found herself anxious to move on.

She would prowl the stores after closing, gazing at clothes, gimmick game shops, new miracle organic restaurants, or search the shelves at Aunt Tilly's health store, a tribute to the city's belief in alchemy. Bran and jojoba shampoo were in, meat definitely out, and jogging now had two schools of thought: those who believed it was good for the heart and others, equally vociferous, who were convinced that it enlarged the vessels and led to strokes. Tennis was fading, she decided. She saw fewer people in their pastel Head outfits on Rodeo, where it had once been a uniform. What was increasingly apparent was the fact that this society was attracted by whatever seemed to be new and different.

Some evenings she went downtown to the Fashion Mart, which straddled a pair of blocks and harbored hundreds of showrooms. Walking through seemingly endless corridors, Claire felt a surge of excitement. Owning a business and buying for it, testing her taste, was radically different from merely selling what somebody else selected. She missed the action of the market. She saw dozens of buyers scurrying past her with their order pads, their jammed handbags and briefcases, igniting the tensions within her. Images crowded her mind. It would be impossible to compete on a fashion level with Courrèges, Lapidus, and all the other multimillion-dollar companies who used a street like Rodeo as a showcase for their creations.

On her lunch hour while waiting next to Hunter's Bookstore to cross Little Santa Monica on her way to grab a sandwich at Le Grand Buffet, a charcuterie up the street, she found herself standing beside an angular young man in army jungle fatigues. The yellowish-green splays of color caught her eye. Rather than a small handbag, the man carried a knapsack. All he needed was a machine gun and grenades attached to his belt clip to lead his troops through the bush into combat. Unconsciously, she followed him for a couple of blocks, watched him get into a van painted a dizzying metallic orange with a signed mural on the side of it depicting a man fishing by a stream. The van was equipped with TV, a telephone, CB, and a sound system that detonated, filling the street with the Bee Gees' falsetto. The outfit must have cost a small fortune. Claire leaned against a car, mesmerized. Her destiny leapt out to embrace her.

Rodeo Drive catered to fashion. Her market would go a step beyond—to fantasy. Her shop had to be revolutionary yet realistically priced. It had to suggest that people were wrong to spend fortunes at the boutiques. The spangles and beads, the elegant French and Italian cuts, Minerva's classic English look, would not be displaced. There were enough people who bought price and nothing else to shore up their egos.

The fashion magazines were as confused as the buyers. No one was certain about what to do. Mini or no mini, bright colors or somber, baggy jeans or tight Mac Keens. Inflation was affecting the budget of everyone except the very wealthy, who in any event kept their clothes forever.

She was in a state of euphoria when she met Ellen and Frank at Pips that evening. Claire wore a hot pink trouser suit with a purple silk blouse and had taken trouble with her hair. She communicated an extraordinary excitement to them as they sat at the bar drinking Bombays on the rocks, waiting for their table. Music from the disco spilled over and there was a tumult of voices, people greeting each other, hurrying into the backgammon room in the rear to settle scores.

Ellen was carried along. She had never seen her fresh-faced, innocent protégée in such an overpowering mood. Claire realized that catching people unprepared was a treacherous strategy that might militate against her, and she tried to compose her thoughts. She had no illusions about the immense task that lay ahead of her. It was one thing to be told that they'd back her and quite another to have them come across. She'd have to lead them by the nose, step by step.

"Ever since I arrived here, I've wondered why people who own a Rolls and a Mercedes need a four-wheel drive or an RV. Beverly Hills is full of them. They're gas-eaters and the roads are in good shape. It doesn't snow here, and who drives on dirt tracks?"

Frank nodded with interest.

"We've got a Cherokee Chief. It's in the garage most of the time."

"Why'd you buy it?"

Ellen gave a guilty laugh. "For fun."

"But do you understand why you did it?" Claire asked.

"Not really."

"I like driving it," Frank said. "When we go up to the mountain lakes it's the perfect car."

"You're really playing a role though, aren't you? You and Ellen become just Mr. and Mrs. Blue Collar doing a grass-roots number. In a way you're trying to return to a simpler way of life . . . away from it all. The Marlboro Man is alive and well and living in Beverly Hills or Bel Air."

The Dunlops were both intrigued, but couldn't find a handle to her suggestions.

"Even when you're at home for barbecues you're casual; you're playing a version of the pioneer man. Everyone is. They're fed up with cities, their jobs, their small apartments. They want the outdoors. Elbow room. Rafting vacations. . . . Smell that clean air, taste the fish cooked over a campfire."

The maître d' called them to their table, seated them in a booth, and recommended the Chinese special of lemon chicken. The room was filled with familiar faces, but now that she'd seen Dustin Hoffman in Nate 'n Al's, Cher in Courrèges, and an unshaved Kirk Douglas window-shopping, she realized that none of them were designed heroically. This was just their territory.

"More and more people want to escape, find a little corner and pretend they're the great outdoors type. They'll still wear Givenchy originals and carry Louis Vuitton bags and the men will be decked out from Giorgio, but most of the time, people here dress like bums. What I'd like to appeal to is the spirit of adventure and Rodeo Drive hasn't got a store like it."

Ellen seemed unsure of her ground and did not react with enthusiasm, and Frank dourly scanned the wine list.

They weren't biting. They had everything and she'd fallen flat, but she refused to quit.

"There's no argument about your observations," Frank said, "but what do you plan to sell?"

"The store would be called Rodeo Wilderness and I'd sell army fatigues, Coleman stoves, compasses, tents, fishing gear, Zippo lighters, safari clothes, everything for camping."

"I have to admit thet I had something more high-styled in mind."

"Give her a chance, Ellen."

Claire had the dismal feeling of having lost them. After dinner, Ellen avoided the subject and went off to play backgammon with another woman. Claire was exhausted, battered by her rejection. Frank did nothing to encourage Claire and she decided to leave as soon as they'd finished coffee. Claire saw her chance slipping away, condemning her to years of slogging it out, working for other people. Minerva was probably right. She—or some other store—would have Claire's youth.

"If you put that kind of operation on an exclusive street like Rodeo, you'd kind of baptize it, give it respectability, wouldn't you?" Frank suggested incisively.

"I guess so." She was enervated, but she pressed on out of courtesy. Perhaps she could find out where she'd gone wrong and refine her pitch when she discussed it with Ed. "I never thought of this as one of a kind. The life style doesn't exist just in Beverly Hills . . . Dallas, Houston, New York." She forced a smile to her face, exasperated by the futility of her grandiose scheme. "Rodeo Wilderness would be a pilot for stores all over the country. Franchise and get rich, right, Frank?"

For a moment she was convinced that she had revived his interest, but she could see that he was just being polite. Despite his gruffness, he was patient, letting her down gently, passing the time.

"How would Ellen fit in?"

"I'd hoped she could do the promotion side. I'd run the business, sell, do the buying." This was becoming hopeless, demoralizing her. Yet she couldn't quite let go. "The beauty part of this is that we wouldn't be at the mercy of manufacturers . . . the government is only too happy to unload surplus. I'd have a few girls doing alterations. . . . Frank, I'm sorry, I really am. But Ellen's been wonderful to me and I took her too seriously about getting involved in a business. Maybe this doesn't belong on Rodeo Drive or Hollywood Boulevard, but I wanted to hit a different market."

"Ellen's my stalking horse," he said obliquely. "Naturally, if she wanted a little flutter in business, I'd finance her, but not for this."

Claire agreed. She was no longer the girl who took her lumps and spent her time sobbing into the pillow. It was a voracious, mean world. But she had the most valuable asset of all—an unshakable conviction that her time had come and that the idea would work with the right investor.

"There isn't a shop in the city, let alone Rodeo Drive, that would pose a threat, and this isn't a one-season gimmick but a way of life that's here to stay."

Christ, she wished she had discussed it with Ed first. At least he wouldn't have made her seem such a fool. With no one to cushion the blow, she was reminded of her last week in Westport. The evening with her mother at the Lobster Pot came back to her. Milly had pushed her to stand up for herself.

"Frank, would you mind if I left now? It's ten-thirty and my arches ache, I think I may be a late developer of flat feet."

He didn't believe her and lifted the tablecloth. Her feet were firmly in her slingback purple heels. It was a helluva combination to put together. Claire's presence electrified people. Physically, she was not his type. Ellen, with her rosebud breasts and slim contours, suited him. A lifetime of the finest class hookers had never satisfied him. Ellen's was the body he had fantasized about, searched for through two marriages. Ellen had the singular virtue of eliminating promiscuity from his days. He woke up five days out of seven with a hard-on and as an insurance man, he was loath to tamper with a 71.4 percent.

"One more drink, please." Frank was acting strangely and she was convinced that she'd be out of the apartment in the morning for failing them.

"I promised to give Ed a ring if I was still awake. He's so touchy lately."

"Don't talk business with him," Frank said, his voice quavering. "You don't need him for this."

She was taken aback. Maybe this was why Frank was hated, leading people on, then crushing them for the sheer bullying pleasure.

"Why keep it secret? Ed might be interested. Believe me, I'm going to give this a shot."

"Ed Giovanni," he pronounced the name acidulously, "runs a restaurant. He listens to people all day long promoting their harebrained schemes and he encourages everybody. He's got a great joint, but Claire, it's a restaurant. Understand? Linguini, white veal, kisses for the ladies and big hellos."

What a putdown. She got her second wind and would've cut loose. She was sleeping with Ed. She adored the man.

"Your idea is fabulous. I love it." He spilled some brandy on his chin. "Forget Ellen. I stopped her from becoming a decorator, buying a tennis complex, and hell knows what other craziness. Last year it was an exercise studio. I'm the one who always wanted Rodeo Drive. It's like the Boardwalk in Monopoly."

She was utterly confused. Frank sneered at the figure of Hugh Hefner standing at the entrance of the dining room. "Him I can buy for cash. Do you understand?" He waited for Hefner to depart, despising his celebrity. "I hated him in Chicago too," he admitted. "I'm building a skyscraper . . . Hefner holds charity functions and gets all the publicity . . . . Oh, forget it. The idea of franchising this is a honey. I'm a man who works in multiples, and when an idea is presented to me its growth potential is my primary consideration."

Claire bolted back her brandy and stared at Frank distantly. She'd seen Frank before when he'd been drunkenly effusive.

"You'll remember this conversation tomorrow?"

"Claire, I'll kick you in the teeth if you don't shut up."

"What's really in it for you?" she asked.

"First of all, I see a profit in it." He was stone sober and she became increasingly nervous. The sweet venom of his mouth told her he wasn't lying. "I want the publicity and all the credit for doing it. In other words, I made the baby, you had it."

He offered his hand and she shook it. Leading Frank, she said: "Let's dance. It's been a long time."

He gripped her by the waist.

"I don't dance."

"I'll show you."

It was eleven-thirty when Frank, enjoying himself and talking constantly, dragged her, mopping his brow, to the bar and collected ice water for them both; then, pulling her, he wiggled through the backgammon players in the back of Pips. Spectators were massed around several games in which the doubling and redoubling was frenetic. Ellen was involved in a small game for a hundred a pop, which included doubling. At other tables, thousands were changing hands between players who impassively rolled the dice, moved their counters adroitly, and scanned the room without interest. The wealth surrounding Claire had an overpowering effect, curiously ambivalent. At first it was intoxicating, then rank, malodorous. The boredom was infectious. These were the faces she encountered each day on Rodeo Drive, tough and finicky in stores, but at night their real faces crawled out of the sunlight: the cap jobs, hair transplants, bag and chin lifts, over-dieted bodies, a parade of decadence marching to the tune of backgammon dice and cocaine. When she was in the ladies' room, spoons, mirrors, gold blades, and platinum tooters were openly passed around among women of all ages. The brazenness surprised her. She occasionally smoked a joint with Madeleine, but basically she preferred a drink. She'd organized so many store parties, attended countless engagement parties, weddings, baptisms among the girls at Drake's that she was accustomed to drinking. She could hold eight good drinks, which enhanced her reputation among manufacturers as a tough buyer.

Ellen caught her eye and winked, enjoying the flutter, in her element. Claire had played the game several times and since no money had been involved and you could take forever before moving, she had played inattentively. She really preferred baseball and football games, crushed in the stands with thousands of fans, munching a hot dog and drinking a beer. Having missed those four felonious years of a college coed, a sorority, she frequently read articles about them, assimilating their adventures but not consciously imitating them. Still, their experiences lodged in her mind and she realized she was devoid of the symptoms of high society. Even worse than her feebleness at backgammon, she had never learned bridge, and tennis had been lobbed into her week by Giovanni only recently. Compared to California girls she had been bred on another planet. She had been a working girl during her adolescence. As an adult, she had assumed heavy responsibilities. She was aware that social graces depending on racquets, cards, counters, or small machines with voices made her eyes glassy. Let her get to the track before the doubles went off so she could bet a wheel and nurse a Bloody Mary was her idea of a diversion, not Kahlúa coffee in a glass as eyes framed in tinted glasses shifted counters.

She thought she ought to wait until Frank told Ellen he was going to be her business partner before departing. Just to get it on record, a witness to his folly. She had her back to a table a couple of aisles away and the conversation she overheard froze her.

"I couldn't help it . . ."

"That's all I ever hear from you."

"I was at a meeting. I couldn't get out. I haven't even eaten."

"Well, I'm stuck fourteen thousand dollars to some bum who can't play to save his ass."

Claire turned slowly, revealing only her profile. An angel-faced blonde with a servant problem seemed to be accusing one of the domestics of theft.

"Fourteen? How are we going to pay that?"

"That isn't your problem, buster," she said so vehemently that her words stung like a maddened hornet. "I settle my own debts. And, more particularly, you're becoming just a little too drag-ass for me."

"You're the goddamn limit. Come on, let's go home."

"I'm staying . . . so goodbye. I'll be home when I goddamn feel like it."

Bobby, stooping, had his hands pressed on the table. His skin had the hue of eraser chalk. God, he'd aged. His face was rigid with a tortured anger. She had never before seen this side of him. She hardly recognized him. Maybe they tested smog on him in some kind of chamber. How long had he been married, eight weeks, three months? The date hadn't stuck with Claire. He blew down the aisle, brusquely slamming into people. She said goodnight to the Dunlops and told them she'd take a cab back to the apartment.

Badgering an attendant for his car, Bobby caused a little dissension among the groups ahead of him. His manners had occasionally been scurrilous. She slipped next to him and when he saw her, he reacted as though he'd been shoved. She looked away and asked the attendant to call a cab. Bobby gripped her arm and shouted to the carhop, "That's mine." He flipped a buck at him while opening the door for Claire, then he rushed to the driver's side, thrust himself inside, and roared up Robertson Boulevard.

"I like your car, Bobby. I should always be driven around in a Mercedes 450. It suits me, don't you think?"

"When'd you get here?"

"Months ago. But I'm a native now."

"Where are we going?"

"Giovanni's."

The full realization that Claire was here, sitting beside him, gave him chills. She had changed so completely since he'd last seen her that the experience of déjà vu did not impose itself. It was Claire, and yet it wasn't. She was much prettier than he'd ever thought and there was no expression of accusation or even a sign of disappointment as she lay back on the headrest, stretched her arms, and tugged off her high heels. In fact there was a kind of wanton beauty about her serenity.

"What are you doing?"

"I'm going to open a store on Rodeo Drive."

He looked at her incredulously. "Drake's won't work," he said diplomatically, guiding a novice to confession.

"I didn't have that in mind."

"Jesus Christ, Claire." They were on Giovanni's corner and she directed him down the back alley. It was midnight and the front door would be closed. A disbelieving smile firmed Bobby's face, made him glad to be alive, filled him with wonderment. Claire rang the doorbell on the grated kitchen door and Pietro answered it. He had a napkin looped through his collar with a wine stain as faint as a bloodless vein. He and two other captains were sitting beside the range with the chef eating a carbonara and figuring out the evening's tip points.

"Any parties still here?" she asked.

"Just a two on the balcony. He's already been given the car keys. Fifteenth anniversary." He chuckled, returned to his pasta. "People, Claire. He got sore when I told him we don't sing in this establishment."

The captains and the chef nodded to Bobby as though they might have known him. It was like a doorman's flourish to a taxi.

"Mr. G's at his table," he said.

Bobby made a lunge for the door to open it but Claire had already flicked it open.

"You eat here a lot, I guess."

"With the staff," she said pleasantly, sharing the residue of many agreeable evenings with him.

" 'Ullo, Claire," Mario the bartender greeted her. He was a pudgy, balding Florentine who resembled Garo Yepremian. He'd been with Giovanni from the day the place opened. He gave Claire a pony with Strega and a side of Evian water. He nodded to Bobby. "Signore?" Bobby ordered a brandy, any brandy. Mario gave him a Bisquit. Mario was about to lunge into his denunciation of the Rams for deserting him personally when the cashier passed, carrying her Canon adding machine.

Ed was sitting in his alcove so that he could see the bar. He did not operate out of an office. His cashier wrote the letters and the duty captain took reservations. He had outgrown growth—just let him stay put in his El Dorado. European businessmen had heard that his place was difficult to get into and he squeezed them through. It was astonishing; they were spending two hundred for a party of three at lunch and paying cash or traveler's checks. The recession in Beverly Hills should last till he was ninety.

He closed the books, the checks were snapped twice with a rubber band. Pietro was up Wednesdays for the night deposit at Security Pacific.

Bobby wanted to keep talking to her at the bar, press her into a corner like the guilty husbands who slipped cash to their girlfriends for cashmeres at Minerva's. Ed had on his glasses, the hornrims. He'd left his wire frames at home. She'd picked them out, a gray frame, lightweight. They gave Giovanni a more critical eye, as though he might have been a film reviewer or the head of studio publicity.

He shoved his glasses up to his forehead, then slipped them into his jacket, rose from the table, conveying the warmth of an Indian summer. He hugged her.

"Hey—uh—Bobby." Bobby shook his hand formally. This was his third time in Giovanni's—dinner, redeeming his marker, and for shit's sake, now. Mario brought over a fresh setup of Poland water. Ed beckoned them both to the booth. "Slide in, Claire."

Carlo told him he'd turned in the last tab. "The loges finally left. I got the names, though. Let them slink through the net at Peppone or Adriano next time." He consolidated the captain's reservation list. Unlike Giovanni, he read the trades and was an abominable snob, upsetting people with bad tables so that they returned to the bar for drinks while waiting for another table and were forced to tip him just to get some attention. It was all relative: the food would still be excellent and the tips larger. Everybody was happy.

"Bobby, what're you up to?" Giovanni asked.

"Doing a couple of things."

"Hayward's, or have you moved?" He dealt with network and studio executives who stayed at their jobs as long as Vegas dealers.

Claire raised her glass and did half her drink in admiration.

"Your mind, Ed."

"It's a Rolodex. And I was at your wedding, Bobby. Right?"

"If you say so." Bobby's glass was not immediately refilled and he waved it. Mario was already in his street clothes, but he'd out-thought Bobby. He came to the table in his suede carcoat, bringing shots for the civilians.

Giovanni took hold of Claire's hand under the table. Bobby was far enough away from them. He leaned over and kissed her on the neck. "You're on your own for two weeks and we talk on the phone. Are we having a fight without a quarrel? When do I see it?"

"Tonight."

Bobby sat at the far edge of the table and pretended he was elsewhere. Facing in a different direction filtered the sound. He wanted Claire to get rid of this guy.

". . . I won't swim after dinner." Ed had a liquid smirk

on his mouth. He was so human, soft, that Claire hugged him. The surroundings were familiar. She was at home with him. They were company, friends. She treasured the magical good humor of his disposition. He was usually tired at night and read, but in the morning he squirmed into her with grace and it gave him a sense of worthiness.

"How'd it go with Ellen?" he asked quietly.

He didn't hold out much hope for his syndicate—two advertising executives, a film producer, and the business manager of a girl whose pilot floated between two networks and Andrew Wald's at ON-TV.

"She passed, but Frank's willing to go in."

"I don't believe it."

"We shook hands on it."

He was skeptical. "Don't give Minerva notice yet."

Bobby stood up and caught their attention. He wasn't so much hurt as baffled.

"Where'd you guys hook up?"

"At Pips," Bobby said. "I gave your girl a lift."

"Thanks, that was nice of you."

Giovanni turned to Claire. "Ellen's backgammon any better?" Bobby headed for the entrance. "Bobby, see you." Giovanni touched Claire's breast with the back of his hand and kissed her on the mouth. They heard the door lock snap with the large night bolt. "You going to keep giving me a hard time, or what?"

Claire hugged him when they got to the bar. He picked up his car keys from behind the bottle of Pastis on the lower shelf.

"Not tonight."

19

There were gradual stages, calibrations that manifested themselves in Hillary's mood. Losing infuriated her, and after she wrote out a check for fourteen thousand dollars to the slugger who'd chopped her ears off at backgammon, she drifted into the bar at Pips. She swooped in between Frank and Ellen and had a double brandy. Frank hadn't seen Bobby. He'd been too busy with his friend, Claire Stuart. "You've got to meet her, Hillary." Frank's enthusiasm stuck in her throat. She had recognized the name instantly. It was after one when Hillary phoned the house. There was no answer. She wasn't conscious of the depth of her rage until she picked up her car. The attendant had known her for years and informed her that Bobby had been in a hurry and left with a girl. She went back inside Pips and made a call at the reception desk. The voice at the other end was accommodating, even soothing.

"I wasn't sleeping. Sure, I'll take your check." He gave her directions. "Take Pacific and hang a right at Club Court Drive. It's very narrow. Take a left on the next lane to Westminster . . . La Guita. Got it?" She wrote down the address. She rushed into her car, slewed out of the lot, and shot down to the Santa Monica Freeway, running lights, hitting seventy. Bobby's act of apostasy transcended explanations or apologies. She had trusted him; now everything became nightmarishly clear.

The two of them had set her up . . .

Her anger dissolved into something like outrage and

when she reached the peeling stucco rooming house in a Venice back alley the slender pieties of their relationship had been washed away. The agony of it made her wince.

He might have played one off against the other—at least that—but to marry her, then continue with Claire showed a murderous structure of premeditation that reduced her to jelly. The work pressure he claimed was nothing but cheating. To do this to her in public, with her father's business associate the gulled witness, assumed a malevolence beyond coarse betrayal. The guilt she had felt about Claire evaporated. Christ, would she make him pay for this. Bobby didn't know it yet, but he'd made the mistake of his life. There wouldn't be recriminations, briefs of any kind. This was war. Yet although she fought against it, a part of her rebelled, sought a fragment of hope, a thread toward reconciliation.

The front of the house was almost dark. No place to park. She pulled in behind three shitbox pickups blocking a rocky driveway. The tail of her car stuck out beyond the cars on the street. Fuck it. She was wearing a red silk pleated skirt and a white silk blouse with the tab collar turned up. She'd dressed for dinner at nine with Bobby. She'd worn her hair down with a side part on the right, held back by two mother-of-pearl combs, Bobby's favorite style.

When Geraldo and his crew fixed up the guesthouse, she'd seen them pass around some blow. They gave her a few lines one afternoon and she wound up buying a gram, then an eighth.

She enjoyed decorating their first home, and did the whole place monochromatically in gray with various shades subtly accenting the den and bedroom. The kitchen had been retiled in a starkly bright Aztec motif and some of the decorators she knew brought over pieces on approval. Disegno Contemporaneo loaned her an L-shaped sofa in a smoky iron velvet. She was still waiting for more furniture but a few people who saw the house really thought it was different, interesting. It wasn't everyone's style, but she decided to move away from Leonard's fussy brothel mannerisms. She and Bobby would color it with their love.

There were five steps up to a squeaking wooden porch.

In a large square window a green sign printed by hand hung vertically: COCINA LA GUITA. A cluster of tables had chairs piled on top of them and a young boy was mopping the lino floor. She heard a man at the far end of the porch whisper. She peered through the darkness and the spark of a cigarette radiated.

"Hey, Hillary. Hi, you found it."

Two men walked languidly ahead, shaking the porch under her. They were young and slender and not the lumbering brutes of their footfalls.

"Geraldo. How you doing?"

"Great . . . just great. I was going down to Fatburger . . . I could've met you."

The lithe boys weren't boys, but in their late twenties, clean-shaven with short hair, denim shirts. They were expressionless, passive almost, dull-eyed, silently frightening—and thrilling. They wore shoulder-holsters packed with large bulky handguns. The man to her left gripped a sawed-off shotgun, pointed down.

"Surprise, surprise," she said gaily. It was awkward because he stood behind the two men.

"How about that." Geraldo opened the screen door. She went in first. The boy finished mopping, then replaced the chairs in the dry places. Behind the staircase she approached was a corridor leading to a rectangular public room with a fireplace, a couple of Naugahyde sofas, a TV, and three men passing a joint around while they played cards on a table a foot below them.

"Want a drink or are you hungry? I think I can still get you something out of the kitchen."

"A drink would do me just fine."

The two men from the porch edged into the card game, lighted cigarettes, and picked up a couple of beers from the floor. Geraldo walked ahead of her to a cabinet in the dining room. There were five circular tables with lots of chairs. It was a little restaurant, she noticed. On the tables were small plastic menus.

"A guy I know dropped off a bottle of Mezcal." He lifted the tequila, flicked it upside down so that the worm curled through the neck of the bottle, then poured them shooters in some counter Coca-Cola glasses that he lifted off a white plastic tray on the kitchen hatch. It was too homey for her to be scared. "You want a G?" he asked. He removed a pouch from the cupboard, picked up a knife from the cutlery section, balanced a fragment on the tip of the knife, then chopped it on the counter. He pulled a straw from a box, cut off all but about two inches of it and handed it to her. "See if you like it."

She blew one line. It snaked for about five inches. He'd given her a turnpike and she had to change nostrils.

"There's no rush. It hasn't been touched. So, Beverly Hills, what's happening? I haven't seen the architect at the house for a week. What's he up to?" He grinned at her warmly. He had a large jaw with fine teeth, too dainty for his mouth, and there was a look about him, even at two in the morning, of such personal care and self-centered diligence that she thought he might be off to a date.

"Fuck him," she said, leaning on the counter.

"You guys need a marriage counselor. You bring back a little for him. Works all the time."

"He doesn't do coke."

"Educate him."

Geraldo pulled a chair off a table, turned its back to her and sat astride it. A piece of flypaper the kid was trying to hang behind him caught their attention.

"Forget it," Geraldo said. The boy picked up his mop and pail and dragged himself out.

She looked at Geraldo, the tapered waist, the curly hair, his black vinyl jacket with its V-flange at the collar. There was a sureness in his eyes but the signs of promoting her, wiggling in romantically, were absent.

"I'd like an eighth or a quarter if you've got it."

"How about a kilo?" He was teasing her. She couldn't quite identify the internal gestures, but she felt that female sense of being where she wasn't supposed to be with a man who would guarantee her safety. "Come on upstairs, Hillary."

She followed him without trepidation up the stairs, through angles of hallways to a room at the end. She could see the ocean over TV aerials and rooftops maybe a few hundred yards away.

"It's my aunt's house. I bought it for her in seventy-one, then she took in boarders . . . friends of mine." He opened the door to his room, newly painted in eggshell. There were a few locks on it inside. "I'll weigh you a good quarter, okay?"

His room had two windows, a courtesy balcony with a few plants outside. A bookshelf had been built into the wall and there were some tapes, records, slatted in a corner. A dining room chair faced it with a laboratory scale in a Lucite case centered beside a Pioneer receiver. The familiar surroundings hovered about him.

"How do you get blow like this?"

"You're a very curious lady."

With his high cheekbones, seductive smile, she discovered a disconcerting fineness, a spirit that bolstered her. He was not about to rip her clothes off, blow a hole through her ear, and dump her on the beach. Geraldo was a honey. Just a trip to be with. He reached into a bureau drawer, wiggled out a pouch the size of a melon.

"You're a real dealer."

"This is a favor. I wouldn't even talk to you. I move weight. You're a gram buyer."

He was thirty-four and had served seven years in Duell Prison for second-degree murder. A parole had come through in August and his friends had found a construction job for him so that the parole case officer was placated and gave him a clean bill of health. This plunge into the underworld titillated her.

"Does it bother you to discuss it?"

"No. It was a straight hit and I got picked up with the piece. I plea-bargained for murder two."

Intrigued, she stared at him calmly weighing her quarter of an ounce on the scale.

"You killed the man intentionally?"

"There was a war and it's still going on. Between EME, that's the Mexican Mafia, and us."

"Who's us?"

"Nuestra Familia."

"But seven years," she said, confounded by his equanimity.

"It wasn't lost time. I recruited more men from inside." He tuned the radio to a jazz station, then finished weighing the coke.

She observed Geraldo's patience, the casual way he tilted his head like a bird listening for foreign sounds that would indicate danger. She had read about drug dealers, but only dealt with small-time hustlers who had to squeeze a few sources to come up with a quarter of an ounce. These people were very different, they were criminals, an organized gang, *professionals*. And it was clear that the man leaning on the windowsill was their leader. She was mesmerized by him and quietly asked if he had any pills.

"We're moving seven-fourteen Roers, the synthetic Ludes, but I've got a bottle of lemons." He opened the door and she saw a clean but spartan bedroom with a bathroom at the end. He handed her a bottle of fifty Quaaludes. She popped one immediately. He'd cut half a dozen lines on a mirror, tooted a pair of them, then held the mirror for her. In his restraint and dignity, he exuded an extraordinary mesh of intelligence and raw power. She couldn't imagine him even raising his voice. She couldn't leave him. The Quaalude began to daze her, push her into a wonderful relaxed state, and when she mixed it with the coke, the combination lofted her to a new plane of awareness.

"All that time without a woman."

"It was a problem," he admitted stolidly. "Duell is old-fashioned about letting the inmates get off."

"What'd you do?" She knew she was babbling, asking indiscreet questions.

"Jesus, you don't stop, do you?" He shrugged apathetically. "You develop relationships . . ."

It was as though he struck her between the eyes with a blunt instrument and pulsations charged through her breasts. Her panties were wet. It was impossible to conceive of a moment during her entire life when she had been more sexually aroused. She was seated in an overstuffed low armchair covered in a tacky floral fabric. He kept his distance. They were locked in a trap of anticipation and unsurfaced passion. The bedroom door was still open. She got to her feet shakily.

"Can I . . . use the bathroom?" He nodded. She crept through the bedroom stealthily. A lowboy cherrywood dresser with a tarnished mirror attached to it, comb, brush, cologne, a few religious pictures. There was a shower attachment in the high oval-shaped tub, Revlon Flex shampoo, a hair dryer, a stack of coarse towels on a wicker hamper. She let the hot water run in the old round sink, straddled it and douched herself. She could barely manage to touch herself without suppressing a yelp. She was so animally drawn to Geraldo that she thought she'd climb up the wall. She brushed her hair, put on fresh lipstick, and dabbed Fracas behind her ears and along her neck.

His admission vaulted into her mind. He'd had *relationships* in prison. Of course—that was logical, reasonable—his lithe muscular body coupled with another man's. . . . Where did they do it? In cells, the shower?

When he worked at the guesthouse she had watched him lying on the grass, smoking, sunning himself—the lazy dog—squinting when she passed by him. There had been no thought of contact then, only some amiable, unsuggestive bantering about sandwiches and six-packs, which was why she resented Bobby's goddamn puritanical dirty-minded bullshit about her cutoffs and tank top. She wasn't flaunting herself. Subconsciously she sensed that Geraldo's presence ensured her safety. His influence over the other workmen became obvious. The respect he was accorded shadowed the playfulness of the men. He was one of them but apart, yet he didn't make a big deal out of it.

Bobby—Claire—they could drop dead. The ignominy of her position asserted itself, then she banished it. Fuck them.

Floating with the Lude . . . oh, it was good, nursing the sweet salacious thoughts within. She smiled from ear to ear, like a teenager. He leaned against an old-fashioned brass headboard on his bed, not even queen-sized. She sat on a rocker jammed by the side of the window.

"You going to write me a check?"

"What do I owe you?" Her head buzzed.

"Seven for the coke, and I get six apiece for Ludes, an even thousand. Actually I'd prefer cash. Maybe I'll hold the check till you can get to the bank."

She went into the parlor, grabbed her handbag, located a pen on his lousy little desk, hating him, the miserable Spic bastard, fucking body-builder, probably pumping iron with all the fags in Santa Monica. Who did this piece of garbage think he was? In her anger, she wanted to take her diamond engagement ring, grind it against his face and make him bleed.

She wrote out a check for the wrong amount, canceled

it, then, snarling, she sat down in his chair, swallowed another pill, saw there were still two lines left on the mirror, did one and carried it in to him, balancing her purse in the crook of her arm, the checkbook below the mirror. She unloaded her bag, stooped to her knees and held up the mirror to his nose with a straw. His eyes had a misty chasteness. He blew the line. She placed the mirror on the knotty piece of rattan rug beside his feet. The lino was cold on her knees.

"You still going to Fatburger?" It was after four. "You want a burger or've you got a date?" She flung the check on his pillow.

"I'd like it signed."

"You're not a man . . . you make me sick."

He straightened her up quickly, brutally lifting her by the hair and throwing her down. She wound up on her shoulder with her legs hitting the floor heavily.

"Date with a guy, huh?"

He squeezed his kneecaps, sprang up from the bed, then walked past her.

"It's stupid to be nice to people." He helped her up with concern. "Hillary, go back to the architect. Don't mess around with me—my head."

She crossed her legs, tucking her feet over her thighs, an old lotus exercise in gym at school.

"I must really scare you." She took out her combs, ran them through her hair.

"What is this?" he asked with exasperation. "Come on, kid. You can't drive, one of my people'll take you home. We know the way. Hillary?"

The new Quaalude stormed into her head, blurring her vision. He took hold of her arm, pulled her to her feet. Her head drooped back and he caught it, shifted her to his bed, the fireman rescuing a victim.

"I'm seven years late," she said.

She leaned against him. In her stupored passion she wrapped her arms around his neck, pinched his ribs, then she gripped his hair, pulled his face down; he hid in the crease of her breasts. Her hand traveled to the center of his buttocks, backing into his balls. He lay beside her, inert, eyes alternating between anger and disbelief, then he bolstered himself with his arm, took her check, rolled it up, and squeezed out a mound of coke from her bag onto the mirror. She closed her eyes, opened them instantly since she was fading. Her fingers crept along his fly, winching open the sticky broken-toothed upper part until she could wield her hand into the slit of his jockey shorts and his steaming hot sticky dick was fettered between her thumb and index finger. She tortured it out of the slit and he watched her, cautiously, unadventurously. She fiendishly parted his tight lips with her tongue. He tasted of those rose-colored Swedish breath candies. The Ludes waxed her brain. His childish tongue backed away from hers.

"You're going home," he said apprehensively. "Hillary, please, be a big girl."

Her tongue was on the head of his cock, swirling around the tip. He had his hand on her shoulder, like a nervous gambler with his last few chips. Oh, shit, did she have his number. He started to get hard, alert. No, don't let this happen . . . to him. . . . He didn't need this shit . . . She anchored his fingers along the sides of her clitoris, guiding the motions, finding his middle finger, gliding it into the passage.

"You fuck around a lot?" he asked, shocked by his reactions.

"I used to."

"Rich and all that sort of—hey, don't, stop, please, stop it." He pushed her head to the pillow awkwardly, trying not to hurt her, merely to disengage himself.

"When did you have a woman last?"

"Jesus . . . don't."

He shuddered. Blearily she spread out his fingers and piloted him gently through her vagina so she could feel the pressure on her anus. She seized hold of his wrist, making him withdraw. His hand was buttery, evil. He was frightened, pulled away furtively.

"Rubia, no—" His words collapsed in the madness. She licked his fingers, straightened out the coke lines, blew his nose full of smoke. This time the treat was on her. She wiggled his small, firmly packed ass beside her head and did him, sucked off the premature drip. His balls firmed, encouraging her.

"Geraldo, taste me."

"I can't."

"Put your mouth on it."

"It's . . . disgusting."

She wriggled down the bed, rubbed the head of his cock into the canal for a moment. It gleamed like a sword.

"Taste it, taste," she insisted. He put his little finger on her clitoris, frowned, then held it by his nostril. "Don't be chickenshit, come on, come on."

He might have been placed on a line before a firing squad.

"It's eight or nine years . . . even before I went in . . . I didn't—"

She forced his head down, nurturing him, then grasped his balls and whipped his cock inside her, felt it growing. He came quickly, humiliated by the explosiveness.

"Don't worry, there's still more. It's so hard. Just don't let it drift, yeah, yeah . . ."

She raised her ass, constructed another erection, not quite false. She eased up, then withdrew it for him, jollied him on his side, kissed his mouth and flat broad chin.

"Guapa," he cooed remorsefully.

She was licking his balls, shunted him over to the side, then spread out his buttocks where a red butterfly had been tattooed below his hip.

His lack of experience and uncertainty were mortifying to him. He was a battle-scarred Roman legionary who had spent a lifetime among men at war. Camaraderie, loyalty, and not the arms of a woman had been the extent of his experience. She went down on him again, and again, violently, then squirreled him inside her, a child in a cave afraid of the darkness, giving him hope and the sweet imagery of a woman at his mercy. This was another of those dope accidents that she had encountered years ago when she was running wild, but this time, older, and expert at pleasure, the animal strain within her possessed some grace. He smiled at her with pride, sank his head on her breast tenderly.

"I never thought about it."

"What?" she asked.

"Being gay or straight."

She raised his head, held his face in her hot sticky fingers, searching for his character.

"You were straight all the time. You just didn't know it."

"I needed you to find out."

She blocked out everything in this first conspiracy of passion, the *folie à deux* on which they had embarked.

Leaving the Bagel Nosh without cream cheese on her top lip or lipstick on her teeth indicated to Madeleine that she would arrive at Gucci without another Neptune trident bisecting her Virgo rising. Christ, did she need cap work. She'd get to it when she had ten thousand in the bank, but what the hell, by then all dental work would be paid for by the government. She could hardly walk. She and Gene had gorged themselves for three days and she had no idea how she'd last the day on her feet. A red would keep her going.

For a change, she got into Gucci early, chary, aware of the danger looming. The beefy security man seemed to stare at her when she punched in. She smiled but his close-set eyes revealed no warmth and passed through her as though she were disembodied. She went to her counter at the rear of the store and he unlocked the showcase. If they accused her of stealing, she'd pass out.

Claire's suggestion of threatening a lawsuit belonged in a fantasy world. She'd fold up and her panic would be her undoing. She shook involuntarily when the guard greeted some other girls. Cleaners began dusting the merchandise and the assistant manager was bringing out gem cases from the safe for the rare gift boutique. She would have preferred to give him notice, but she knew she had to wait for the manager to come in. He was the one who had been suspicious of her and she would have to face him.

She had lived a lifetime since her first night with Gene and although it was hard to be objective about making the film, the experience had not really touched her. She had kept that secret part of her separated from the actuality. It had paid good money and she had finally, through it, met a man whom she cared for. Gene wasn't just another body passing through her nights. She found herself caring, thinking about him, involved emotionally. He gave her the confidence to quit her job. He assured her that he'd keep her in work, posing for stills, and that she didn't have to make any hardcore loops again.

God had given her a magnificent body and she knew now that she could use it. Gene had fixed an appointment later that week with Al Brockman at ICM to show him her composite and meet the agent who handled their clients for commercials.

The manager entered the store. He was a plump, middle-aged Italian from Milan who spoke perfect English and seemed more like an ambassador than a store manager. He was the sort of man you'd expect to find chatting with Henry Kissinger rather than examining cracks in customers' leather bags.

Madeleine caught his eye.

"Mr. Verona—"

"Yes, Miss Gilbert."

She suddenly felt safe, unafraid. He expected her behind the counter at opening. Maybe she'd been imagining the dossier he and his security people had accumulated on her.

"May I see you for a moment in your office?"

"Is it important?" he asked brusquely as though he were going to meet the Pope rather than make his daily call to the factory in Milan to check on deliveries of loafers.

"Yes, sir."

She followed him past his secretary. He placed his attaché case on the sofa and looked at the messages stacked on his desk.

"What is it?"

"I'm afraid I'm going to leave today."

"No notice?" He was outraged.

"Well, the thing is, I've got some interviews scheduled this week and, well, my future depends on them. And Mondays aren't that busy."

He did not invite her to sit. He sank into his highbacked chair. He had piercing brown eyes, slick black hair groomed in a widow's peak, and drab olive skin.

"How long have you been here?"

"Almost a year."

"Have you been unhappy?"

"No, but the thing is, I never expected to make a career working at a handbag counter."

"Gucci is not just a handbag counter."

"I'm aware of that, Mr. Verona. But I have hopes of becoming an actress."

"You too?" he replied sarcastically.

"You won't have any problems replacing me. There must be twenty applicants for every job here."

She was sweating through her thin cotton sweater. She sensed his anger building. Who would have believed that anyone, least of all the manager, would have considered her valuable to the store?

"I'd appreciate your mailing me my check."

He grimaced as though in pain.

"Someone tipped you off?"

Had she heard right? She pretended to misunderstand. His eyes never left her.

"Pardon me? Are you leaving too?"

"We would have had a search warrant to go through your place in a few days."

She decided that indignation or brazening it out would be too obvious. She was called upon to act, give a performance, but selecting the right role and interpreting it properly was crucial. She reached into the slender grab bag of resources she possessed. She couldn't simply appear dumb but surrealistic. In drama class, nothing was more disconcerting than a non sequitur.

"I don't do dope."

"What are you talking about?" he asked in a fluster.

"Well, some of the girls smoke grass and do coke, but I'm a health freak."

"I'm talking about the missing bags."

"Which ones?"

"You were at the security meeting."

She gave him a blank, uncomprehending stare.

"I never listened. I was trying to memorize a part I'm auditioning for."

He thought he was losing his mind.

"Didn't you know that someone's been stealing bags that customers return?" he asked in a thunderous, accusing voice.

"Where?" she replied unblinkingly.

"Here! At Gucci."

"If I ever spotted a shoplifter I'd turn her in without thinking twice, I swear, Mr. Verona."

He was about to explode, throw a tantrum as he did when he discovered a shoulder strap askew in the window.

"I'm not talking about shoplifters."

"Then who's taking bags?"

"You don't know that we've had internal pilfering and missing merchandise?"

"No," she said, raising her eyes and keeping them motionless on his face. An expression of surprise was frozen on her vacuous face. "I'm sorry about not giving you notice, Mr. Verona, but I'd feel so much better, kind of have a feeling that I had a chance, if I knew you were pulling for me and wishing me luck."

"This is intolerable. Goodbye, Miss Gilbert."

She walked down to the Beverly Wilshire and rushed to the ladies' room. She opened a stall and heaved. She washed her pallid face, put on some fresh lipstick and blush, and with rubbery legs barely made it upstairs to the Pink Turtle Coffee Shop. She sat down, giggled to herself while the waitress waited for her order. Christ, she *could* act. Anything was possible. She had triumphed and she regarded this as an encouraging sign in the ordeal that lay ahead when she met Brockman at the agency.

20

Everyone needs absolution, and Dr. Ira Parks of Bedford Drive in Beverly Hills had been Hillary's confessor, counselor, and psychiatrist for years. She visited his office three times a week and not even her father knew that the relationship still listed along, since she paid the bills out of her personal account. She couldn't return home to face Bobby so she spaced out the morning in a little outdoor cafe on the Venice bike path before going to her eleven o'clock appointment.

Her union with Dr. Parks had begun twelve years ago when her father had revealed his intention to marry and Hillary had run away from home. Leonard's romance had come to nothing that time, but five years later, when he again became involved with a woman, Hillary had disappeared for two months from the Bishop School and had been found living in a commune near the South Fork River in Humboldt County. According to Hillary, her father's disposition toward other women was a betrayal. She had given her very soul to Leonard and he repaid her with grotesque faithlessness. The moment her back was turned, he was running away from her to get married. Maybe down deep, he hated her and longed to replace her with another woman who would usurp her place in the house. She was the center. She had to be.

Parks was in his early sixties, small-framed with a wispy moustache, balding in the front. His eyes were magnified somewhat out of proportion by his thick-lensed glasses. Over the years she had been in and out of love with him. Now she thought occasionally about his dying and she would become disconsolate. Where would she ever find a friendship to compare with theirs?

"You don't exactly look like you started work at eight this morning." She had showered but her clothes were disheveled and her hair was lank, greasy, gritty with sand. She'd taken a walk with Geraldo at seven on the beach. Parks' mouth curled in a world-weary smile.

He had listened to a diatribe on Bobby's callousness, the plot against her launched by her husband's former fiancée, all of this rationally leading to a no-holds-barred orgy with her dope dealer who was surrounded by a gang of armed thugs. It was Thursday in Beverly Hills, no question of that. What would the weekend wreak among his population of mad hatters? He no longer asked himself rhetorically what the world was coming to. He knew.

"Have you confronted Bobby about this plot?"

"I'll spit in his face."

"That's a fairly mature approach."

"He married me for my money."

Parks referred to his notes. Since Bobby had been hired before meeting Hillary, asked her to move in to a small apartment rather than the guesthouse on the estate, and suggested that she live on a budget determined by his salary and not her income, Hillary's interpretation hardly bore discussion. It would serve merely to fuel antagonisms. All of her thought processes, quirks, and regressions manifested themselves. Emotionally, she was about twelve, and there was just no beating that. He had met Bobby twice and foolishly held out hopes that a guy like this would be the making of Hillary. Really smart and creative with a funny sort of idealism, which Beverly Hills would cure him of. For Hillary, he was wonderful.

"Hillary, why not have a free, open discussion with Bobby?"

"You don't seem to understand. The man's on half-mast with me. He neglects me. He's always exhausted. His work comes first. He's no fun. We didn't even have a honeymoon."

Parks recalled her visit after that episode with dismay.

She was his failure, his hopeless case. Although there had been periods when she responded to the melody of reason, controlled her impulses, she invariably reverted to the well-furnished dollhouse of her Electra Complex. No amount of analysis or therapy would alter the nature of her mind. Her love-hate relationship with her father had been shifted to Bobby. Extraordinary, with all of the property at his disposal, Leonard and she had decided that the guesthouse would be as much of a separation as they could tolerate.

Bobby's sexual indifference and inadequacies cropped up, along with his malevolent schemes. A nice, simplistic rationalization for her own infidelity and her desire to be granted pardon. In short, she intended to continue her crusading affair with the dope dealer in order to be close to the supplies. It was a pretty convenient solution.

"Hillary, the last time you got into drugs . . ."

"There were problems. I'm the first one to admit that. But I think you're trying to divert my attention away from these real problems with Bobby."

She telegraphed that reversal.

"On the contrary, you're trying to divert yourself and me away from the drugs." This she didn't want to hear. "You're allergic to cocaine, drugs in general."

"I don't believe for a minute it creates psychosis."

"Maybe I should pay you a hundred dollars an hour," he remarked, a laugh tinged with irony.

"I won't accept this. And just to prove it, I won't score again."

"Fine, I'll feel more secure. Hillary, this is no environment for you with the people you've described. Take my word for it. Can I have an understanding that this isn't going to happen again?"

She dithered for a couple of minutes, hating to have been outfoxed again. She still had her quarter ounce and Ludes secreted. They had done Geraldo's and he hadn't even collected the money. They were even anyway. Maybe coke could make life a bit more interesting for her and Bobby.

"I'll try, I really will." The minute she got into her car she opened her stash, used her nail to take a hit, and could hardly wait to get home to grind it up and feed it into gram bottles.

* * *

Claire made a real effort to concentrate, sitting across from Dunlop and his lawyer, a plump-chinned avuncular shark who flailed her with so many legal entanglements that she thought she'd pass out. Seeing Bobby had ruined her sex with Giovanni. Although she had tried to put Bobby out of her mind, she was appalled by the effect his physical presence had on her. She was cured . . . or was she? A fine time to find out. The small of her back pinched. She was on the eighteenth floor of one of those monolithic skyscrapers in Century City watching a couple of specks walk off the tee at the L.A. Country Club.

What the negotiation—and to dignify it as such would be absurd—afforded her was seven-fifty a week and expenses. After an elaborate formula was arrived at, on the net profits she would be entitled to ten percent. Her salary would be set against her percentage. Frank had ruled that she could not be represented by a lawyer, accountant, not even a friend. She would have been happy with three hundred a week and a fair share, but Frank was adamant. She was an employee who'd been thrown an incentive . . . nothing more.

Rodeo Wilderness, its name, trademark, label, all of it belonged to Frank Dunlop. However, she recognized an opportunity and she wasn't about to lose it. Frank was the money man. When he kissed her after she signed the deal memo, she vowed to find a way to make him eat it.

Her salary commenced on signature and she was obliged to leave Minerva without notice. Frank had insisted on that. He had even battled sinisterly for Claire to go to lunch and never return. She had won a real big point by refusing. An account for Rodeo Wilderness would be opened with Fred Gray at U.C.B. with an initial buying fund of a hundred thousand dollars. Her plans had crystallized and Claire was stunned by the responsibility of administering the money and the million and one things that starting from the ground up entailed.

Frank dropped her at Minerva's, gabbling happily about their union.

"I don't think it's right for you to come in with me."

His small-mindedness was pestilential. He was just warming up. The enemies he'd accumulated would be hearing from him. Nails would be driven into coffins. He had the temperament of Robespierre.

"I suppose you're right, but I'd like to see that bitch's face."

He double-parked in front of Minerva's.

"This might be premature, but where is our store? We've got three blocks, so it's got to be somewhere in the vicinity."

"I'll let you know by the end of the week. It's not your worry."

"It would also help," she said sardonically, "if you gave me some time period for the opening. Spring at the latest to catch the season."

"I'm sure that's in the ballpark."

"That'll give me enough time to buy, hire staff, arrange for shipments, and have the interior design done, I hope."

"Claire, you're on your way," he replied complacently, blissfully unaware of the realities.

She had arrived during the lunchtime lull, but nothing could save her from Minerva's mordant rasp. Beckoning Claire to her redoubt in the back, she flared up bitterly, preventing an amicable parting.

"Just who the devil do you think you are . . . ? This is the second time you phoned in at the last minute!"

"I've worked six days a week from the beginning," Claire replied, getting hot under the collar. The woman was tyrannical and she drank. Her gin breath wheezed in Claire's face.

"And learned how to sell on the best street in the country. The trouble I've taken with you."

"You had good material to start with."

"Don't be impertinent, damn it. You're a shop assistant."

"Would you like to make out my check now and we'll call it a day."

Minerva was totally unprepared for this act of rebellion, and attempted a strategic retreat. Claire had netted out thirty-five hundred the previous month. Bringing in another girl with Christmas six weeks away and taking the floor herself would be insufferable. She had to leave for London at the end of the week to check on deliveries and buy the summer line. She'd intended putting Claire in charge.

"You're a helluva business woman, Minerva, but you don't know how to treat people."

"I've reason to blow up," she replied, grumbling but accepting the rebuke.

"I had a whole women's wear department under me and there was none of this backbiting."

"You happen to be on Rodeo Drive and certain things are expected of you."

"I'll work out the week if you want me to."

Minerva's face drooped. She had gone too far, she realized. Claire wasn't just another shop assistant. The girl was magic with customers and had already developed a following. Minerva detected a request for a raise so she beat Claire to it, offering her another point. When Claire demurred, Minerva suggested they go out for dinner that evening to see if they could reach an understanding.

"The reason I have to leave is that I'm going to open a store on Rodeo Drive—with a partner, of course."

Minerva recoiled as though from a blow.

"Rubbish."

"It's true. I've just signed away my life for the finance."

"You've been undermining me from the day you arrived for this adventure, haven't you? Admit it. Beastly little traitor. I should have known."

"We're not in competition. I wouldn't do something like that to you. Give me some credit. You've got a lock on your market," she said, hoping to reassure the woman who was behaving as though she was deranged.

Minerva's face twisted in a grimace. "You can't do this to me. I've spent years putting this store together since I was closed out at Biba's."

No matter what Claire said, she couldn't persuade Minerva that she wouldn't be undercutting her, or stealing her clientele. The awful fear Claire inspired and the raging torrent of abuse that spewed forth astonished her. At the bottom of it all, she pitied Minerva. She quietly cleaned out her locker and left the dry cleaning receipt for her skirt and blouse on the register with a note of her new address and a request for her check.

She spent the next hour strolling idly up and down the street to drive the bad taste out of her mouth. Her life had opened in such a broad, unexpected way that she could hardly recognize the girl who had been publicly humiliated and did not wish to go on living.

Bobby had spent most of the day with a model-maker explaining his renderings. The structure he had devised needed a three-dimensional projection because Frank would never be able to understand his drawings. During this period, Bobby had reverted to his natural tendency of secrecy. He operated poorly in groups and since Hayward didn't press him—more out of fear than usual practice—he went his own way, finding a level of fulfillment that had escaped him in his personal life.

The essential part of romance and falling in love with Hillary was the mystery it had conjured up. What would they become, how would they shape their lives? The answers were now obvious and as he watched his design of the house on Alpine Drive nearing completion, he felt unutterable loss. There was no one he could turn to who could share the cold climate of his despair. The irony of his situation wasn't wasted on him. Now that his career was blossoming, the one aspect he had believed inviolate was caving in before his eyes. Like land under water, his marriage was becoming a reclamation project rather than broadening out as he and Hillary knew each other better. The magnificent courtship, the splendor of their affair, had no real foundation.

At about six he was tempted to join Gary for a drink. Rubin and his wife were back with their lawyers and as far as Gary was concerned, this time he was going to hold out for a divorce. Swapping stories about domestic warfare didn't fit into his present mood.

Hillary hadn't come home the previous night, nor had she phoned the office. He assumed she'd spent the night at Malibu with Kitty, bellyaching about him. Driving back to the guesthouse, he pulled up and parked on a side road to compose his thoughts. Against his will, images of Claire flooded back, haunting him. She had been unapproachable and he knew that she was gone forever.

She had picked an old smoothie in Ed Giovanni. Unquestionably she had come to L.A. to find him but had lost heart. The agony that he had caused her wrenched him and he didn't believe he could ever resolve the feelings of ambivalence her presence inspired. Trust Claire. A shop on Rodeo Drive. It was a natural. Nothing surprised him. If anyone belonged in Beverly Hills, it was Claire. Bobby had built his life on the rockbed of her misery and he could never forgive himself for the ghastly mistake he'd made. He had violated the basic laws of human architecture.

Claire and him . . . the two of them in L.A., living in a small apartment, the silent communication, the incorrigible enthusiasm she brought to any discussion of his projects even when he went off the rails. What was that worth?

His temper didn't improve when he found Hillary at home, the gray walls enclosing them in a snail's shell. What havoc Hillary must have created in the homes of the dummies lured into the showroom. She seemed tractable at first, fixed him a cocktail. He was glad there was no reunion kiss or an immediate desire to yank him into the bedroom for one of her special blow jobs, her technique for resolving all difficulties.

"How was your evening?" he asked without looking for trouble.

"The question ought to be reversed, huh? How was sugar plum? The two of you get it on?"

He resisted the impulse to grab her by the throat and bang her head against the wall. He felt rotten enough without an excursion into wife beating. She rehashed the bill of indictments against him: neglect, their shitty sex life, and now it was all clear to her. He was filling Claire's tank. A beautiful scam. In her bloodshot eyes there seemed to be a curious acknowledgment of pain. Even though she was the one who had stayed out all night, he was on trial. He marveled at her skill, the astuteness of her childish logic.

He tossed his jacket on a gray leather chair upholstered with brass buttons, sat on a gray suede barstool, keeping his distance from her.

"Would the truth be out of place?"

"Just coming from you . . ."

"Come on, Hillary, grow up. I had no idea Claire was here. I dropped her off at Giovanni's restaurant."

"Really? I grew up there. Ed closes at eleven. So don't tell me . . ."

He poured himself a monster shot of Scotch, jiggled it

around two lonely ice cubes, sipped it pensively, then regaining his self-control, said: "She's Ed's girlfriend."

"Oh, really? What's she after, free dinners?" She tossed her blonde hair venomously. "I suppose that's possible. She'd fuck anything . . . Dunlop, Giovanni. Jesus, Bobby, you were involved with a real animal. No wonder you grabbed me. I was the closest you'd ever come to a virgin." The prodigal vileness of her mind exceeded any boundary he might have contemplated. "You two have a very unusual relationship—deal would be a better word. Does it turn you on, or is it all strictly business? You think because this is a community property state, you'll walk away with half my trust? It doesn't work that way. Only earnings, not inheritance."

She leapt up from the sofa, rushed into the bedroom, slammed the door, daring him to enter. He had in one part of his mind returned to her, willing to make it up, open up, release their anxieties, and search for the common bond that had united them. Where was the romance? Had it been a cruel phantom that had never existed? What was happening to them? The outrageous passion that had forged their union shattered before his eyes. He was unprepared for this foulness. Maybe a couple of digs, or not even that. Forgive and forget. He was off the hook until the model-maker had completed his primary structure . . . five days, a week. Rattling in his head was a suggestion of a trip to Mexico City, a Club Universe quickie that he could afford.

Brought up with respect and a natural gentility enhanced by Claire, assaults of this kind were alien, withering. He was a strong man and once the shock of seeing Claire in her new circumstances had dissipated, he was prepared for a mild beef. Where were you? Maybe a couple of pointed remarks, followed by dinner, confessions, and some time off. The moment he had come through the door he had accepted Hillary's place in the time of their lives. But where was the girl who had changed his life, the golden princess in her castle?

She was in the bedroom, churning to an infernal racket of noise. He had come to hate music at the volume she played it—the squawking violence of sound physically hurt his eardrums. She lay across the bed in her aqua slit skirt, her breasts flattened by the position, sniffing cocaine through a solid gold tube.

"Ah, a dinner guest. There's enough to go around. It'll make you sexy, you can go all night." The phone rang but she ignored it for six rings until the service picked up. "It's just Kitty . . . we're going to roll. Two reservations . . . the Mandarin and Peppone's. See what we feel like, then the Daisy. I want to dance till they have to carry me out." She giggled. "Sound good to you, Bobby?"

He'd had a bellyful of Hillary. What in the name of God was he going to do with her? He saw no future for them, just a continuing series of abrasive arguments down the road. She treated him with the tact due a hired hand who could be turfed out at her pleasure. He was certainly no moral savior, nor one of those self-righteous prigs, but he objected to her indecent self-indulgence, which threatened to envelop him.

"Have I made you feel bad?" she asked kittenishly.

"Unspeakably." She was too volatile and exhausting for there to be any true prospect of a sustained relationship.

"Maybe you can understand how I felt when you took off with that bitch."

He couldn't cope with her. Reason flew out the window and in her company he felt disreputable. Yet he hated to quit on her this soon. Would it ever be possible to develop a normal social life, find common interests, forge links? He turned the stereo volume down, sat on the edge of the bed. Newly married couples always had problems.

"Come on, relax, for Chrissake . . . at least try it."

"I'm not into drugs. And coke costs a fortune," he said, mired in the chaos her attitude generated.

"The treat's on me."

"Let up, Hillary, will you, please."

"You don't dance, fuck, gamble, do drugs . . ."

"I'm a total write-off."

"You said it. Can't you cut loose?"

"If it means staying up till three in the morning all the time and blowing coke, the answer is no."

Inadvertently, he withdrew, found himself sinking into a hellish abyss. On the most basic level of human intercourse —how to live their lives together—deepening fissures had evolved, separating them, thrusting them into two camps, hurling recriminations at each other. They were no longer allies but vandals goring each other.

"Honey, do me a favor, cancel out Kitty and let's stay in, barbecue a few burgers."

"And do what? Discuss your drawings?" she snarled. "Or hear another lecture on architecture?" She packed up her drugs in a wallet-like petit-point compact, arranging the bottles, spoons, sniffers in various compartments like a mechanic on a repair call. "You never loved me. For once, admit the truth. It's always been Claire, Claire, Claire!"

He made no effort to prevent her from leaving, passing from innocence to guilt by the insistence of her accusation until he believed he believed her. He sat alone at the bar until ten. Then, driven by an overwhelming desire, he located Claire's phone number and address from Information.

He neither considered the consequences nor his condition when he drove to Camden Drive. One of the tenants was leaving and he walked into the lobby without announcing himself, spotted her name on the mailbox and took the elevator up to the third floor. He lumbered down the corridor, breathing heavily, listened outside her door for a moment, then rang the bell. He placed his palm over the peephole and in a minute she opened the door on the chainlock and regarded him indecisively, standing with folded arms, blocking his entry.

The signs were familiar when he had a load on. Hair tousled, eyes red-ringed, mouth gravely set, breath expelling fumes of Scotch. The scapegrace. In the old days, this usually meant he had been stuck with another office assignment he deplored and she would listen patiently, agree that his talents were being wasted. He was a most agreeable drunk, never abusive or violent. She let him in.

"The party's next week, but your invitation's in the mail."

"Claire, don't hammer me."

He wasn't as high as she had suspected. He groped at her face but she agilely disengaged herself without skittishness. She was no longer his property, nor anyone else's. He walked around the living room. The TV was tuned low to a news station and on the glass table stacks of catalogues and order blanks were spread out; a motley assortment of fabrics, clothes, canteens, hats, and outdoor equipment littered the floor. She had on a pair of jeans, tennis sneakers, and a blousy red top. She wasn't wearing makeup. He peered around the room, savoring the coziness of it, the warmth that she brought to it.

"I'm up to my ears, honestly, Bobby."

She had an innate graciousness, but she was in no mood to be magnanimous.

"Can we have a drink together? I'd appreciate it."

He found a corner on the sofa next to the fireplace, which she'd put on the minute she arrived home. His uncertainty offended her. She'd laid it on heavy with Giovanni, the mistress of a restaurant, the darling of a libertine whom she'd reformed. But sooner or later, their paths had to cross. When they did, she played her hand brutally, contrary to her nature. She'd flouted Giovanni and she regretted it, but no one was immune to the blandishments of revenge.

"I guess you're on Scotch. A couple of rocks, huh?"

His eyes tracked her in the kitchen. She still kept the booze in a kitchen cabinet beside the refrigerator, a jar of pistachio nuts, a can of pâté, smoked oysters. If he opened the refrigerator, he'd bet his life he'd find a slab of cheddar, an Italian salami, eggs, skinless and boneless sardines, a jar of pickles, and some Polish ham. He settled for J&B and a dish of macadamia nuts.

"Are you really going into business?"

Maybe he had an hour to kill before collecting his princess at Pips or wherever she was playing out her evening.

"Yes, the store's going to be on Rodeo Drive and God help me, I think I know what I'm doing. If it doesn't work, I can still shoot home to Drake's and cut my throat," she said without self-deprecation. She had given herself a cruel shot of vodka. If she got through it, she'd pass out from exhaustion. She'd spent the day running around downtown from the Fashion Mart to a bunch of government surplus warehouses, buying samples. The trunk of her car was loaded with everything from combat walkie-talkies to Primus stoves, which she couldn't carry up to the apartment. Her body ached. She switched off the TV, lowered her eyes to four days of the *Times* she hadn't touched and meant to throw away when she got around to it. She had put Ed off for the evening. Celebrations were premature. She had enough of screening parties, parties for their own sake, obscure award evenings in which speeches were made congratulating rich people for the marvelous talent of being rich. Ed catered many of these bashes and if she ever saw another plate of micro-cannelloni stuffed with spinach she thought she'd throw it against the wall.

The silence with Bobby suffocated her.

"Are you pleased to see me?" he asked tentatively, sliding into comfortable familiarity.

"Honestly?"

"For sure."

"Not especially. I think you know me well enough. I'm not contentious. Our scraps were never serious." She played with the ends of her hair. She'd wash it tomorrow. She was too tired tonight. "What about you? I never thought of interrogating you about your play time."

He jiggled his empty glass, then fixed himself another drink, making himself at home, which she resented. It showed no respect. His attitude inspired surliness. Then, without dissimulating, in a spirit of candor, he revealed the condition of his marriage without complaint. She was proud of him for not embroidering, giving himself the best of it, or cringing. She couldn't forgive him. It was easy to flail him, barbarously peel his skin off. He was so open that the malice Claire might have stored within her soul was transformed into compassion.

She shared, finally, the pleasure of his breakthrough as an architect. All the evenings discussing Mies, Le Corbu, Bauhaus, Saarinen's expressionist approach, Pei's functionalism, the history of his heroes, had paid off. Robert John Canaday was about to achieve his dream as Principal Architect on a major building and she wanted to embrace him benevolently.

She had placed ice in a plastic tub and the two bottles on the coffee table, so that they could help themselves. All that was missing was the late-night scrambled eggs on toasted English muffins and the mugs of instant coffee. Those shared communions of daily life would never disappear. They formed character, bound them.

"I'm happy for you."

"I believe you," he said, grasping hold of her fingers.

"Why shouldn't you? We're all so goddamn selfish that most of the time it screws up your head. Kids, no kids, down payments on homes, who do you borrow from? Shackles. What am I missing, right? My old Bobby is actually designing a building in Century City and I'm going to have a store on Rodeo Drive. You know what? Maybe we were meant to be out here. To cut loose. At the time, Jesus . . . forget it. But the positive side of it makes me feel good." She was high, no question about it, and they were smiling at each other. "The opportunity you gave us . . . And that's only one thing. I'm talking about other aspects. We were both locked into a situation . . . one of those plateaus and we were afraid to take chances. At least I was."

"Claire, I really want to talk to you."

"Hear me out."

She put on a late-night top-forty station like old times. The nearness of him enchanted her. Oh, what they wouldn't give for a week in the sun in the old days. How they used to plan vacations on Sunday mornings reading the New York *Times* travel section. Lighted tennis courts, barbecues on the beaches, Caribbean islands, free golf and scuba diving, exotic restaurants . . . Their big nights out were cocktails at the Sign of the Dove and dinner in Chinatown. She wanted to explain that a different person had emerged. She had changed and the quest carrying her along had no predictable destination. She might have signed on one of those tramp steamers that was at sea for two months or a year and because of cargo requirements docked in Yokohama instead of Singapore.

She brought out some cheese, lox, slices of rye bread, thick hunks of Italian salami, and a slab of terrine. It took a minute and she slapped it all on a coarse wooden board she had bought at the Akron.

"Maybe I was meant for finer things too and didn't know it." She hunched up her shoulders. The catalogues on the table could wait. He hunkered her close to him and there was no reason to resist his touch. The pain of it wafted out of her head. "Please, listen to me. You're an intelligent man . . ." His hand caressed her breasts. "Bobby . . . ? Maybe I wasn't created by God to hang your drip-dry shirts on my towel rail, sponge mustard stains off your ties, run out for pizza at eleven at night, stand in line at the butcher for a lean crown roast, dry lettuce leaves in paper towels or, while you're watching football on Sundays, dash down to the laundry room to wash your underdrawers and then scrounge for bleach because I forgot it and the stains won't come out without it."

He put down his drink, having ignored the food, and slouched back.

"Listen to me . . . Was I meant to pull in a paycheck so you could turn up your nose at tract developments or have stretch marks on my stomach and a houseful of kids with allergies? I mean, you're here now. Am I supposed to give you the paper to read and dash to the bathroom to douche myself and squirt in the newest feminine hygiene spray because you're ready to go and heaven forbid I should have an odor? Could there possibly be evenings when I want to read a book or write a letter or even think and what are you doing but waiting for me to go down on you? Where am I in all of this?"

He stared at her with disbelief, foundering, his face tight, listening.

"Don't take this personally or think I'm a disappointed woman who wants her pound of flesh and is sticking it to you. Maybe *I* wasn't really the one for you."

She had hurt him without intending to, and she pressed against him, kissed his cheek, put his neck into the comforting vice of her thumb and forefinger and massaged the kinks out of it. He had spent so many years leaning over drafting tables that he suffered from muscle seizures and pinched nerves. A light of comprehension shone in his tired eyes.

"Bobby, just consider the fact that I'm a person who believes in herself. I was meant for finer things too."

"All of this has been bottled up in you?"

"Maybe I wanted a relationship without you dominating it."

She moved away, rose, stretched, but he refused to take the hint, sitting stolidly in the corner, pulverized. Their failure of communication in the past jolted him. Claire had ascended to another level. She was untouchable, beyond him. He discerned another side of her and he despised himself for selling her short. He retreated, confused, humbled by his own obtuseness.

"All I ever cared about was making it as an architect."

"What's wrong with that? It's a little too late to condemn yourself for being ambitious. Believe me, I didn't want you to do any of those lousy projects. You better than anyone can appreciate what I'm going through. I'm going to find out what's inside me."

The cyclical speed of life was moving more rapidly than he could contend with. It wasn't as though he were left behind, but he strained to grasp the emblems of faith that were tearing him apart.

"It's over with Hillary and me."

She laughed with quiet charity, took the empty glass from his hand, guiding him to the door without animosity.

"It's too soon."

"I'm leaving myself wide open. I know that now. I can't take her." She had no intention of encouraging his folly. Let someone else referee this bout. She had a business to begin and the work involved was as much as she could handle. "I'm staying with a friend on Spaulding. He's in and out of a divorce. This time he's on the firing line . . ."

"Good night, Bobby." She saw him to the elevator, relieved it was on her floor and they didn't have to wait. She hurried back to her apartment and slammed the door. Her body was taut. She switched on the TV, found herself in a scene with Fredric March and Myrna Loy in *The Best Years of Our Lives*. She lay her head on the deep carpet, squirming, heard a car outside revving, which woke the neighbor's dog below who went out to the terrace and howled.

21

Presentations gave Bobby fits. The model-maker and an assistant carried the model into Hayward's office and it was a mess. The cement color was much too light and not the honey brown he'd asked for; the tower had a revolve like a goddamn Hyatt House bar and munchkin dummy people were seated at slatted windows. It might have been a model for some low-budget horror movie. No wonder Dunlop flew into rages.

The adrenaline charged through Bobby. He looked at the clock—five to three. Dunlop and Hayward were at lunch with Leonard. They were due back from the Bistro Garden any minute. A couple of secretaries aligned the poster-sized renderings, sheeted over with acrylic, on metal easels. Ten of them, showing exterior elevations, the interiors, Dunlop's office, hallways, the plaza entry, elevator banks, the imposing rotunda, conference rooms, an auditorium that could seat five hundred for a meeting and through the use of sliding panels could open north and south so that another thousand people could be accommodated for a major seminar.

He covered the model with a brown velvet cloth. Had he gone too far? Would they consider the design too revolutionary? Sweat trickled down his neck. The hundreds of hours he had spent from prelims to the final rendering had been thrilling. The joy of the work had been the most fulfilling experience of his life. Never mind that his marriage was falling apart and that he and Hillary hardly spoke. He had no idea what the outcome would be, but he dismissed these thoughts when he heard Hayward asking his secretary to hold his calls.

The three men filed into the room. Leonard greeted him effusively. He kept clearing his throat and his eyes darted over the table and the concealed drawings on the easels. An encouraging sign was Frank's boyish curiosity and obvious good humor. Hayward, the inscrutable chameleon, was prepared for all eventualities. The men sat down, waiting for Bobby to begin. If ever a man had been offered a chance to make his career, this was it, and Bobby was dazzled by the aura of confidence emerging from within. He had never run scared and possibly his whole life, the training, the studying, the frustrated belief that his chance would never come, had brought him to this point.

"Contrary to Tim's belief that I can sell my ideas, the fact remains that ideas sell themselves. With that in mind, and taking into consideration that Frank as chairman of Marine wanted a building that was highly original in concept as well as being functional, I tried a variety of approaches. But none of them satisfied me. I don't like the sharp angles and the shapes of the buildings in Century City . . " They listened intently and with growing concern. "I played around with arcs for a while because they convey movement and you remember at our first session I gave you my feelings about insurance companies and their images. They're all wonderful. Kemper's got the cavalry charging to settle your claims . . . Allstate are the good-hands people as long as you stay out of their clutches."

"I agree entirely with you," Dunlop said. "And I'm interested in the way you cut through to the problem."

"Monolithic structures discourage the public and you wanted something more than a container for human beings to be packaged in. Now the arc suggests an embrace"—he raised his arms symbolically to personalize his idea—"a working together. The form appealed to me. Until I took another look at the Century Plaza Hotel and realized that the shape didn't work and that there's a heck of a lot of legwork to get from one end to another, which hardly adds to efficiency." Frank beamed approvingly and Leonard and Hayward exchanged glances.

Bobby joined his hands. "What I've come up with in

human terms is basic and understandable . . . the circle! Now it grew in stages and the renderings and models have the unity . . . a wheel, a circle. I can't say I'm thrilled with the model, but it'll convey the impression of the building." He lifted the cloth and they beheld a circular glass structure with tinted windows, elevators that could be seen from the street and suggested a spiral look as they expressed to their separate floors.

"The tinted glass is an energy conservation device. I hoped by projecting the elevators, people could see the flow of human traffic, which will give the building movement, activity. Things are happening here." He lifted the acrylic sheets from his colored renderings. "With this kind of structure, you convey a universal image. The arc was incomplete and implies a partial welcome. It's too abrupt. The circle is a total form. It's modern, but a direct tie to the past."

For a moment no one uttered a word and he thought he was dead. The concept was too simple and not gimmicky enough for Frank, who probably visualized flying buttresses and a facade that Albert Speer would have dreamed up for the new Berlin. He had said his piece and was drained. Dunlop stalked around the model like a suspicious cat, then he turned to the renderings, which Leonard and Hayward were examining. Bobby's mouth was dry and tremors shook his knees. Christ, if he could just vanish, become invisible. The ecstasy of the actual work gave way to a sinking morbid depression. It was out of his hands, the energy of creation had expired.

Dunlop gripped his arm and gazed at him with admiration. He shook his head for a few seconds.

"Bobby, it's spectacular . . . everything I dreamed of but couldn't visualize or express. I'm not just pleased but thrilled."

The color returned to Leonard's face and Hayward beamed at him. When Dunlop surveyed his own office at the top, the space, the ceiling height, the curved desk like a Gemini control panel, the conference table near the entry, the private elevator, he was like a kid with his first train set. Bobby had read his character . . . the small, soured outcast who wanted the high visibility and social acceptance his wealth had not provided.

"When can we break ground, Leonard?"

"Once we get all the permits and building inspectors to approve. In about two weeks."

Dunlop shook Bobby's hand and told Leonard that he wanted to discuss some details with him and have a look at Rodeo Puerta. He left the office in a state of elation. All the pieces were falling into place.

"Bobby, this is a triumph," Hayward said. "You nailed the bastard."

It was a curious observation and Bobby felt deflated. He just couldn't get used to the duplicitous methods in which Leonard and Tim operated.

"I just tried to give the man what I thought he wanted."

Tim suggested some time off, a vacation on the firm, and when he returned they would discuss a partnership. Bobby no longer wanted to leave town. He had to get his life in some semblance of order. He cursed under his breath. If only he could go to Claire and share the greatest triumph of his career, the launching pad that would take him to the stars. But beyond this disappointment, he had an awesome sense of humility, and floating through his consciousness was the sacrifice Claire had been forced to make so he could realize his dream.

Frank Dunlop was one of those rare businessmen who still conceived of conquest. Let other men lie back complacently and mine their small fields. The startup of Marine Mutual would hit the real estate section of the Sunday *Times* with a photo of Bobby's rendering, Dunlop's name mentioned, but then it would be forgotten until construction was completed. Frank wanted more, a presence in Beverly Hills that would bring the notoriety he and Ellen had been denied. Meeting Claire had been yet another element that would ultimately feed his voracious imperial appetites. The long-term possibilities of a chain of Rodeo Wilderness stores had enormous growth potential. Claire might know how to run the business, but she had no understanding of the financial world. He had bought her cheap. The idea was a natural and he was convinced of her ability to carry it through.

Strolling leisurely with Leonard to the heart of the golden street, he saw his power increase, made manifest, crystallized by Rodeo Puerta, the door to Rodeo Drive.

Before engaging Leonard as his developer, he had scrupulously done his homework. Leonard was stretched too thin. Frank had seen the credit crunch coming in 1978, almost two years before it would affect the big borrowers. His experience in Europe had taught him that men like Leonard, hanging on a thread, would go under once the squeeze came. Leonard smiled as he strolled through the development, still in its shell state. However, Frank detected that scent that men living perilously above their limits gave off.

"Want to hit some balls at Bel Air?" Leonard asked. Leonard had sponsored him for membership, but he secretly hoped that Frank would be blackballed. He hadn't really pushed hard and his cronies picked up the clue. Leonard was simply fulfilling a business obligation. Frank Dunlop brutalized the people he worked with. He studied the pink florid skin, the shapeless blazer, the grotesque manners of the Midwesterner who thought he could just buy his way into society. Leonard detested him. Once they broke ground on the building, Dunlop would be scratched from his guest list.

"No, I'm just enjoying myself having a walk around with you. When do you think you'll be finished with this?"

"After the first of the year."

"Have you put any stores on the market yet?"

Leonard smiled malevolently.

"No way. I think when we're completed we might push rentals up to fifteen dollars a square foot with escalators after the third year."

Frank tramped over an army of carpenters, drywallers, and masons working under the arrogant guidance of several interior designers from some Italian outfit who hovered over the sweating men like bloodletting insects.

He stepped over a wooden barrier into the corner store. The concrete had been laid and it was rank. The location would be perfect for Claire.

"How large are they running?"

"Two thousand square feet."

"Shit, I like the sound of those numbers . . . thirty thousand a month if you can get that. I thought ten dollars a square foot was top dollar."

"Are you interested in a store for Ellen? Who knows,

maybe we could work something out. I'd give you first crack. I've got almost four hundred inquiries already, but I'll put you on the top of the list."

"You actually believe you can get this kind of rent?"

"It's a seller's market, Frank. The street is international and the most exclusive one in America."

"How're you carrying the paper on all the loans?"

"I'm managing." Leonard gave him a tight smile, revealing nothing.

"You know what I've always admired most about you, Leonard?"

"Tell me."

"Your line of bullshit and your ability to look like nothing worries you even though your house is burning down."

"It's a skill."

"That depends."

Frank enjoyed this process of feeling his opponent out. They were like heavyweights in the first round of a championship fight.

"Why didn't you come to me when you lost your credit revolve with the B of A? I could have picked up a phone and guaranteed your end."

Leonard began to squirm. How the hell did he pick up confidential information?

"You would have swallowed me up."

"Well, I knew how vulnerable you were from the beginning. That's why I accepted your bid."

"I guessed as much."

The clash of horns, the use of strategy to maneuver an opponent, was Dunlop's lifeblood. He had a genius for finding troubled companies, pumping money into them, and entrusting them to corporate doctors who reorganized them. Leonard was not an astute businessman, but rather an opportunist with no overview. Turnover was his principle, but when the market in property slowed, Leonard was stuck. He was a sucker for easy supply and demand ideas, but he never penetrated those sanctums in which men with Dunlop's power sat around a table and decided how to alter supply.

"So, Frank, what's your interest?"

"It's sure as hell not straightforward."

"Did you get the banks to close me out?"

"I suggested that they tighten up. They got the message."

"Why?" Leonard was groping for some explanation in this maze.

"Hey, my act is to behave like some jerk clumping down corridors. I'm supposed to be shallow, noisy, and not very interesting, remember? That image suits me."

Leonard searched for some hint of what was on his mind. He virtually gave away the jewel in his empire and now he'd make Dunlop hemorrhage on any store he would want to rent. God, this bloodletting would be delicious. He relished the moment.

"Frank, did you want me to go under?"

"Of course not. I just thought that if you had a case of the shorts from a negative cash flow, you'd go to outside sources to save what you had."

"I did that."

"Naturally," Dunlop said without emotion. "I orchestrated it . . ."

"You've lost me."

Dunlop joined Leonard on the street and gazed at the mall. Rodeo Puerta was enclosed by a series of winged arches that thrust to the sky. The poured concrete, painted a muted yellow, reflected a sense of elegant formality. It would be the most exclusive development on the street.

"Well, honestly, Leonard, I couldn't come right out and tell you how badly I wanted a piece of this little group of stores. What would you have done?"

"Asked what the traffic would bear."

"Exactly. You'd have a hot buyer on your hands and you would've stuck it to me." Frank's jeering laughter chilled Leonard and he grew cautious. "My dear man, you're fooling around with the big boys and we play hardball."

Leonard strained to make a connection, join links. Suggestions, implications, danced through his mind and he was mystified.

"Are you suggesting that I haven't handled myself well? Look at the financial climate."

"Sweetheart, you're a chump," Frank said, savoring the moment. "You're a developer who lucked into a parking lot a few years ago that you didn't know what the hell to do with until Rodeo Drive emerged as the fashion street in

America. So you build a mall, your houses aren't selling, and you run from one bank to another because you think of yourself as an insider. The banks prefer depositors to borrowers. Didn't anyone ever explain that to you?"

Leonard had a dizzy spell and he had difficulty breathing. His pressure was rising dangerously. The months of tension had wrecked his constitution. Everything was becoming jumbled. He sat down on the small wall outside the mall and Dunlop put his foot alongside him, resting his elbow on his knee.

"I just had to bide my time. I knew that you owned this piece of property and when you tendered for Marine, I constructed a scenario. You were overextended and I assisted your credit squeeze."

"Don't tell me . . ."

"I have an offshore company called Brighton Property Bonds with an excess of tax-free cash and a smart little bastard I picked up off the floor when Slater Walker got into trouble. Mr. Blaire was an asset stripper so I gave him respectability, a piece of the action, and he's my front. Well, Mr. John Blaire knows a sharp-witted money-hungry lady he worked with in London and she happens to be a loan officer who processes your application. She gets in touch with Blaire and he wires me. The banks have closed you out . . . so Ann finds her private source. You've borrowed my money, Leonard, to build my skyscraper because I wanted this piece of property. Now there was no way I could ever get my hands on the parcels you tied up in Century City or Rodeo Drive. What was I going to do, buy somebody's lease and pay through the nose for a little store?"

Leonard was in over his head, frightened and confused. How had this come to pass? Oh, yes, he knew his reading of the housing market had been wrong. Mortgage money had dried up and one side of the Martinson Development Corporation sucked another dry until a corpse remained.

"I gave you fifty-one percent of Rodeo Puerta."

"I took it, my friend, but look what you got in return . . . solvency. You can build Marine now. No fucking bank is breathing down your neck. You can relax."

"Am I supposed to thank you for this screwing?"

In Leonard's peculiar world view, Frank displayed the

attitude of a thief unjustly accused. On the rarefied level he operated on, he was a savior, not a villain.

"But is it a screwing? The people I respect like Charlie Bludhorn and Norton Simon don't actually screw people. They see a problem and they solve it to their advantage. We understand business and you don't. More than anything, I wanted a presence on Rodeo Drive because it was the *right* deal, the right place to be for the nineteen-eighties. The property is priceless, like owning a collection of Rembrandts . . ."

He tried to communicate his excitement to Leonard rather than treating him as the jailer who had his keys stolen. But that was precisely the trouble with this community. They never gave newcomers an opportunity, for they were so calcified in their ways and condign ties that their game was excluding talent and imagination. They had constructed a limestone wall of social graces, enfeebled dynasties—and this was California, L.A. no less!

In their uptight clannishness they had humiliated him. When Dunlop finally decided to make Los Angeles his base and home he knew that better opportunities existed in New York among the gracious partners of Salomon Brothers, or London, which because of the union warfare he could not abide for long periods of time—dustmen, postal employees, engineers were always striking—and no matter where he and Ellen were invited something spoiled their good time. Bombs in Harrods or Selfridge's, blackouts at Number Eleven Cadogan Gardens, their favorite hotel. L.A. was impenetrable to him. Either you were in the movie business or out of it. Yet scores of people he'd met excluded the entertainment business from their social lives. A hardrock inner circle controlled the city and he was tired of being a mug at charity evenings and he no longer responded to those invitations. He was determined to make his mark on the Monopoly board that figured in his calculations. The skyscraper in Century City might be home office for him in Bobby's view, but Rodeo Drive would be the carriage to drive him into a layer of society in which he made all of the rules.

"I never intended ruining you, Leonard, even though you think I'm a prick. Well, lots of people feel that way about Bobby Fischer. What was I supposed to do . . .

advertise that I, Frank Dunlop, wanted property on Rodeo Drive? Can you imagine the kind of numbers I would've been hit with? The real estate people—Mike Silverman, Jack Hupp, Stan . . . are they stupid or something? I could never go through them. My personal interest would have resulted in a further escalation of prices on the street." Frank never let up, just kept slamming Leonard. "It wouldn't have outpriced me, but for shit's sake, why not get in on the ground floor. You had a problem; well, I've solved it and you won't go under."

Leonard had recovered from the whipping. He was the boxer who fought valiantly only to have the fight stopped because of cuts in the sixth round, and Frank took his arm, raised him from the wall with dignity.

"Can I ask you a personal question, Frank?"

"You sound like Ellen."

"Why do you behave like such an obnoxious idiot? When the banks turned me down, couldn't you have come to me like a gentleman and laid it on the line?"

They walked up Rodeo Drive to Mr. Guy's window, filled with last year's English tweeds and tomorrow's Rodeo Drive splendid styles, herringbones, checks, one plaid.

"A gentleman is wealthy. I'm rich."

Leonard shook his head regretfully, coming to terms with this creature who was beyond any reckoning he could assign. Frank had walked far enough and dragged him back to the other side of the street where Rodeo Puerta was being built.

"I should have been satisfied as a developer. I had grander ideas," Leonard said, his bones aching.

"The first rule is knowing how flexible and strong your financial base is. That's your foundation. Which of these is the best location?"

"Again, it depends on what you're selling."

"I just want the heavy traffic spot."

He led Frank into a store that overlooked the escalator. The store had large domed skylights and a bright aspect.

A designer handed Leonard a set of plans. He explained that they only finished the stores when they had a tenant on a long lease. The store had a space of two thousand square feet, which did not include a gallery storage room.

"You'll get people coming and going here. They have to

pass the escalator even if they want to use the stairs. Frank, it has to be a class operation or else you'll kill the other stores. No fast food joints or pinball parlors."

"Don't worry about that."

Leonard again became alarmed. As the majority stockholder, Dunlop could replace him at his pleasure and the attendant publicity, the loss of face, would ruin Leonard's standing in the community. The prospect of being drummed out terrified him.

"What made you come out into the open now?" he asked.

"I was waiting for an idea that smelled of money and had growth potential. Why just give it away? So I had to make a decision to go after it now. I met the sharpest girl in town through my wife, and there was no way I could pass on this idea."

"Who?"

"Claire Stuart."

"I don't know her."

"Leonard, there's a lot of things you don't know. Why do delis advertise Chicago products? Simple, they're the best. You're a first-class manager, Leonard. Just about the best front anyone could ask for—on Rodeo Drive. You have the right contacts. There's no need to be frightened. I want to keep you."

Nobody had ever spoken to Leonard this way. He had become an underling, a hired hand, without real authority, and it was agonizing. Dunlop owned him, could shove him into a sewer and keep the stores unrented at Rodeo Puerta if it suited him and force him out. Everything would be lost, his house, his pictures, but more important than the stores or the unsold houses was Hillary. Who knew what she might be capable of doing to him? He didn't trust her.

"Frank, why go into your own store when the chances of failing are so strong?"

"I want to shake this place up."

Leonard wanted to hurt this man so badly that if they were at home, he would have shot him and then hired a lawyer to whip the charge.

"You know what people out here think of you—"

"I don't give a rat's ass any more."

"That's clear. But what's the difference between being wealthy and rich? Now, Mark Taper's wealthy and he's also rich. But if Mark had to come up with some real money—"

Dunlop patted him on the shoulder. All of these small men disgusted Leonard, petty bullies who enjoyed their games.

"I was the small ugly kid on my block on the South Side of Chicago."

"What does rich mean?" Leonard asked. Frank looked at his chronometer, scratched his ass, and pointed to the corner store, obsessed with it. "How'd you do it, Frank?"

"How? What a question. I have cash flow and the banks don't." He walked to his car, a drop-head Bentley S-3 that hadn't been washed in weeks. Disgusting to keep a classic car in that condition. The car wasn't even locked, and the seat hides had cracked so badly that prickly fillings oozed out of the driver's side.

"Leonard, you build the Marine Mutual." He slid into the car. He opened the glove compartment and seized a plastic checkbook cover. "I'm going home now and try to get my head together with some horrible dinner party Ellen arranged. But if you want to jump in the car with me and get a check from Western Union in three minutes, my cash position would work out to be two hundred and twelve million dollars. I'm not rich, just liquid."

Madeleine waited at the well of secretaries' desks at the ICM agency. She clutched the black portfolio containing her composites. Her palms sweated on the vinyl. She wished she'd been able to afford real leather, but everything she liked was priced around five hundred dollars. Maybe, just maybe, the astrological confluence of stars, planets, risings, had formed the right conjunction and she would be accepted by the agency. She regarded her escape from Gucci as an augury of good fortune. Christ, she might have been sitting in the detectives' room at the Beverly Hills police station, tearfully sweating out charges against her.

Seeing Al Brockman again made her nervous. Her stomach made strange rumbling sounds, which she hoped no one could hear. Brockman had agreed to interview her only after Gene had phoned him and assured him that the photographs had turned out well and that Madeleine would be a natural for commercials. She glanced at her compact mirror to check her makeup. It looked fine, not too heavy, ladylike but with a hint of alluring sensuality. Naturally everyone zeroed in on her breasts, the shape and size of them, but she had learned from Claire to be less blatant about what she had under her tight sweater; she'd taken to wearing loose-fitting blouses.

Brockman's secretary answered the intercom, motioned Madeleine to follow her. Madeleine's heart leapt into her throat, the saliva dried in her mouth, and her stomach roared like a symphony orchestra as she lightheadedly followed her down the corridor. She had a flash of Al lying beside her on his king-sized bed, groaning softly as she went down on him. What an idiot she was. How would he react to seeing his one-night-stand blow-job specialist? He'd come twice, then packed her off at four in the morning. Obviously the thought of waking up with her beside him was repugnant. The men in this town were strange creatures, filled with contradictions. They talked earnestly about meaningful relationships but simply wanted to drop a load and get rid of girls like her. All anyone was looking for really seemed to be advancement and an uncomplicated screw.

Al looked very relaxed, but businesslike. He was talking to a slender gray-haired woman with piercing intelligent blue eyes who had an air of authority and was dressed in a lime green shantung suit Madeleine had seen in Hermès' window. Al kissed Madeleine lightly on the cheek and unexpectedly gave her a hug, then introduced her to Sue Price, who handled commercials for the agency. Al had his secretary bring in coffee for the three of them, and as he sat back on his leather chair and smiled pleasantly, she began to relax.

"How's my boy, Gene?" he asked.

"Terrific." She had a tendency to sound strident when she was scared.

Al turned to Sue.

"When I came out here and started working, I had this kid Gene Roth who was the shit-hot commercial director in New York. He worked for BBD and O, Doyle Dane,

Grey. Utterly fantastic. Naturally he wanted to direct features. But in the meantime he had to eat, so I got him a hundred-thousand-a-year contract with Film Fare and after six months he packs it in. He claims the scripts I send him are crap, that he's getting nowhere, that he hates commercials. Talk about a cave-in, he stops working entirely. Then he takes ten backward steps and sets up as a freelance photographer. Gene doing stills . . ."

Sue was watching Madeleine's face and she knew it.

"He couldn't take the rat race," she said. "That's the difference between me and a lot of people. I've got nothing to lose and with that attitude, how can I be afraid?"

Sue nodded. She'd heard this a few thousand times.

"What've you been doing?"

"Working on Rodeo Drive. I gave notice at Gucci." She wondered if she ought to admit that that was where she first met Al but decided to let him volunteer the information. She noticed he wasn't taking the bait. "I'm also studying at the Actors' Workshop on La Brea and taking voice lessons."

"Why'd you quit Gucci?" Sue asked.

"I decided to gamble on this interview. I've got a little money saved and if I continued working at the store, I'd never feel that I'd given myself a chance. There'd always be a paycheck to fall back on."

"You've got guts," Sue said.

"Madeleine, to be honest with you, we're not sure if we'll sign you," Al noted abruptly. "I know that you want to act and do commercials, but as far as I'm concerned, since I don't know your work I can't send you out on casting calls. The reason you're here is that Gene said the photographs were very good and that you're one of the best models he's ever shot." He turned to Sue. "Gene's an artist and that's his problem. But in all the years I've known the guy, I've never heard him say a kind word about his work or any model. So it's up to you, Sue."

Madeleine struggled with the zipper on her portfolio. Oh, Christ, their eyes were on her and this cheap crummy zipper was holding up her life. Her fingers were growing numb from the struggle. She came over to the sofa, laid the portfolio flat on its side and opened it.

"It's brand new," she said, handing them the photographs. Sue took them, sat on the edge of Al's desk, and as she shuffled them she passed them to him. Madeleine had been completely transformed on film. The lighting, the angles, full shots in swimsuits were magical. There were closeups; in some of the pictures she was fully dressed; in others she wore lace panties and had her arms wrapped around herself so that only the swell of her bare breasts could be seen. She wasn't simply a buxom shop girl, narrow-waisted and swivel-hipped, sitting before them, but at least twenty different women.

"They're dynamite," Sue said excitedly. "Jesus, I've been in this business for twenty years and it never ceases to astonish me what a good photographer can do." She pointed at one in which Madeleine was dancing and the expression of animation and joy on her face jumped out at them. Basking in her moment of glory, the world had suddenly become beautiful. That was the secret of this town. Never quit on yourself, make yourself available to anyone who could help, be compliant. Nothing mattered in the end so long as she succeeded. She'd make ten porn movies, blow Al every day he wanted her, just give her a decent shot at the future that lay out there like a mirage.

Al was nodding his head encouragingly. Then he looked up at Madeleine, and he saw her in a different light. She was beautiful, zany, sexy, funny, and not just a piece of ass who'd snuck into his bedroom. He remembered how severely he'd spoken to her, treating her with contempt. He'd fobbed her off on Gene, never expecting to hear from her again. Case closed.

But now it occurred to him that difficult as Gene was, maybe he'd softened. In any event, Al recognized talent and he believed that if Gene Roth could be controlled, did not rudely walk out of meetings with producers or tell studio executives to fuck off, he could make it as a director, and he still badly wanted to represent him. Nothing was more frustrating to an agent than giving up on talent and in a short time find that they were signed by another agent who'd found them work and bingo, they were off getting a quarter of a million on a film or were in a series forever and collecting residuals. Every agent in town made mistakes and Al didn't want to lose this piece of tail with such an extraordinary range of characters within her. If Sue got her some commercials and she gained some visual recognition, he could get her a small part. All this girl had to do was walk around a pool in a bikini, ask a dumb question that would make an audience laugh, and she just might make it. Decisions made him irritable.

"Our representing you depends on Sue's judgment," he said. "If she can get you seasoned and in a few TV commercials so that we can build a reel, then I'll take you on. The thing for you to understand, Madeleine, is that at the beginning, I can't help you. It's up to her."

Sue easily picked up the ball and studied the girl's confused face.

"What we're attempting to do, Madeleine, is explain the realities of life at this agency. Now a small agency might be thrilled if after a year or two you were earning thirty to fifty thousand a year. As far as we're concerned, it would be a disaster. We couldn't put the resources and manpower at your disposal for a five-thousand-a-year commission. Our clients are big earners, which is why ICM and William Morris dominate the agency business. You can get lost in the shuffle with a big agency, but if there's any earning potential, we'll maximize it. So a few thousand a year in commissions might be terrific from your point of view, but we're looking for that hundred-thousand-dollar commission and because the agency is financially sound, we can afford to pick the people we represent."

Madeleine was perplexed and assailed by doubts. What were they trying to tell her?

"I decided to start at the top rather than make the rounds of the other agencies for just the reasons you mentioned." She had to demonstrate her belief in herself, for this was a business in which everyone felt insecure. "We're all on the same wavelength," she added. "Believe me, if you don't think I can eventually be making a million a year, then you shouldn't even consider taking me on."

Al smiled.

"Jesus, what chutzpah."

"Put me with good people, like Gene, and I'll wind up on my feet."

There was a daring and softness about the girl, Sue

thought. She was easy to like, a real person rather than one of those cap-toothed blondes who besieged her each day with pleas for interviews.

"I'll take you on for a year," she said, "and then we'll see where we go from there."

Madeleine was shellshocked. She didn't walk to her car, but floated like a bird in the air. She was so happy that when she finally got into her grimy, rusted Mustang, she lay down on the seat and cried.

22

For the past year, Ed Giovanni had been toying with the idea of accepting an offer for his restaurant. Periodically one of the large chains sent out an executive who would feel him out about selling. Although he had the operation down to a fine science, it was essentially a one-man business, molded by the force of his personality and his devotion. If he left it for six months he doubted that it would be the same place when he returned. It was a child that would never reach maturity and needed the constant nurturing of the parent to ensure that standards were maintained.

Restaurants were funny businesses and did not respond to the formulas taught in Geneva and Cornell. In the previous year, Lawry's had sought to expand. The Peterson company had bought Scandia from his friend Ken Hansen. Joe Stellini had opened a restaurant south of Beverly Hills, which attracted the New Hollywood and revived Pico Boulevard. Peter Morton, who had taste and imagination, bought an old antique iron store on Robertson and put in a delightful chophouse.

The night-after-night routine was beginning to wear Giovanni down and the prospect of a move to Palm Springs, buying a condo at Indian Wells or at Mission Hills, became increasingly tempting. It would afford him the leisure he craved.

Golf or tennis whenever he rolled out of bed. He'd keep the house in Beverly Hills, possibly rent it during the summer and travel to Europe. A sale of the restaurant would net him close to two million dollars and he could limit the tax bite by taking it with interest on deferrals. Still, a life without anything to do was an aimless fantasy and he considered opening a small restaurant in the Springs with a limited menu and a short week. A dinner-only setup from six to ten. But more than anything, the approach of his fiftieth birthday, that fortunate milestone, affected his thinking.

It wasn't too late for him to have a child. The doctors had tested him and found him fertile. He didn't want three or four kids, just one, and he found in Claire the woman he wished to share his life with. This love business for an old philanderer like him was certainly strange.

He had persuaded her to drive down with him for the day to Palm Springs. The clean desert air and the glorious sunshine appealed to her and she liked the starkness, the slatey mountains, the proximity to L.A. During the drive he had told her what was on his mind and she felt that she owed him something, but her attitude was sympathetic rather than passionate. He hadn't pressed her. She recognized that he was groping for a permanent relationship. She saw through his worldliness, the cowl of sophistication adorning him. He was an intensely lonely man who had been foraging for too many years within a closed society. Her attraction was not as singular as it might have appeared. She was an outsider, essentially a small-town unspoiled girl, and as such she represented an inverted type of exoticism, divorced from his own experience.

Giovanni's life was circumscribed by guys blowing a few hundred for dinner at his restaurant and the mobs who filled L'Esplanade for lunch. His acquaintances were always rushing to meetings or to catch planes, searching for an element of reality that Beverly Hills lacked. Claire understood that Ed was fighting to break out. He had convinced himself that she possessed a secret that would expose the brittleness of his world and make him whole.

They were outside a model house on the fifth fairway at Mission Hills, asking price, $320,000. The agent had suggested that they look at various locations. The course was filled with an assortment of older people, men in Bermuda shorts, women with sweeping, truncated backswings who hit woods every shot.

"What's wrong with me? I'd really like you to tell me, Claire." The question took her by surprise. His extraordinarily handsome face was sapped of all vitality, his mouth hung limp. "It's worrying me. I never expected you to become a problem in my life . . . you know. When I met you, I thought, well, this girl's warm and innocent—not like the sharpshooters I've run into for years—and I could get serious. I am serious."

They skirted along the fairway, walking on the cart path, and she gripped his hand tightly, fighting a battle within her.

"I've been terrified of getting involved or letting any man get a hold on me again."

"You were burned once. Broken engagements are common enough. It's your ex's hard luck; don't make it mine. I'm not a kid and I don't like running around any longer. I've had it. I just want to know that when you get over this hangup you'll be prepared to make a commitment." His earnestness and the disappointment he generated touched her. She put an arm around his waist, leaned her head on his shoulder, almost as though he were her father and was seeking to share her burden.

"You're the only man I've been with since I came out here. I'm not terribly experienced sexually and I never thought I'd be able to go to bed with anyone but him. You changed that. But it was a bitch of an adjustment. If you give me a chance, I'd like to fall in love with you. There's no one I'd rather be in love with than you."

They were seeing less of each other and the future worried him. She had a business to start up and she would flog herself to make it work. Her ambition was yet another snare. He sensed that it would fragment their attachment and he realized that the fact that he was twice her age militated against him. The emphasis they each had in constructing their lives was in opposition. Yet he was profoundly affected by her admission. She'd rather be in love with him than anyone else, and he found himself filled with such love and confusion that he had to move away from her.

"I want to give you everything," he said softly. "Are you over the other man?"

She tried to be honest but her disavowal fell short.

"Most of the time." The grimace that accompanied the statement was made more poignant for him by Claire's lack of awareness and the way her eyes filled with inexpressible hope. Was this the image she saw in the mirror, revealing an infinite capacity for pain that she couldn't conceal? The girl embodied all of the fine, valorous notions he had once possessed, then lost when his experience ran counter to such ideals. In Beverly Hills such women were in short supply and he began to understand how Claire had gained such a powerful hold over him. Nothing she did was premeditated, and he felt compelled to protect her against herself.

He was overwhelmed by the range of his feelings, the elegant tonalities of his emotions, the tenderness she invoked. He was not a man usually given to sentiment or such subtle revelations of his own sensibility, and it came as a shock to him that in his role as Claire's protector he was as enchanted with her wound as she herself. He had always associated good health and vigor with the capacity to love, but now he was succumbing to the malaise it could inflict, the poisoned roots of her past.

Leonard had been too distracted by salvaging the Martinson Development Corporation to pay much attention to the domestic climate prevailing in his daughter's household. He had enough on his plate and finally Hillary had another guardian, whom he had come to regard as the savior fate had personally placed at his disposal. As things worked out, he wasn't far off the mark. Bobby had demonstrated what amounted to genius in his revival of the spec house and his design for Marine Mutual. Bobby's handling of the power-crazed Dunlop confirmed to Leonard that God was on his side. His attachment to his son-in-law had grown in stages until it assumed an almost mystical veneration.

Yes, Dunlop had skinned his hide, but he was prudent enough to count his blessings, for he was alive and for the first time in over two years solvent. In a celebratory mood, he invited his "children" up to the house to catch up on family matters.

They came separately. Bobby was withdrawn, tight-lipped, and they covered the timetable for permits, excavation, the sessions they would hold with the structural engineers. Hillary followed about a half hour later. In contrast to Bobby's work pants, she was dressed in a high-waisted red velvet skirt, boots, a cowl-necked cashmere sweater. She hardly looked at Bobby over drinks, and Leonard discerned in her a disconcerting, hyperactive energy, which alarmed him. She glared at Bobby contemptuously.

"If all I'm going to hear is more and more of this crap about architecture, then I'm leaving." She had seen Geraldo twice that week and the attraction, rather than dissipating, had grown more stimulating and erotic. Her life had been split down the middle. During the day she was a respectable Beverly Hills aristocrat and at night she was privy to secret plans of cocaine shipments, men who might have to be blown away.

In the basement of La Guita, Geraldo had secreted an arsenal of weapons, handguns, automatic rifles, which at first frightened her, then intoxicated her. The previous night on the beach she had fired for the first time a nine-millimeter pistol with a silencer. She had potshotted the doors of a couple of cars, and when she inspected the results, she had been transfixed by the degree of damage. The psychological wallop coursing through her mind revealed her omnipotence. No one was going to spoil her good time. She put Dr. Parks on hold, canceling her appointments until further notice. She wouldn't be pulled up short.

Bobby finished his drink impassively. He'd wandered back and forth that week between the apartment and the guesthouse, oscillating, perplexed, winding down from the intensity of the work he had done on the Marine design. And for the first time he could remember there was a kind of aimlessness, a drifting, that crept over him, annihilating the pleasure he should have taken from his achievement. He desperately needed a break but he didn't know where he wanted to be. Possibly a week back in New York, or a few days in Hawaii. Hayward had mentioned a condo development in Maui the firm was being considered for. What caught Bobby's imagination was the possibility of working on his first marina. Waterfront developments presented unique challenges. Yet he couldn't bring himself to take off without resolving his situation with Hillary.

He could no longer gauge his feelings about his wife. Was it one of those three-day wonders in which the parties admit defeat, walk away without bitterness? The sanity of cutting one's losses seemed the way to proceed. But he was held fast by the destruction this engineered. The breakup with Claire had to be worth *more* and it festered in his gut. His perspective of the situation was obscured by internal conflicts. He had never been a quitter, but as he faced his wife across a sea of acrimony, he had no distinct course to take.

"You've never wanted to do anything with your life, so how could you understand what I've been going through," he observed, losing his cool.

Hillary puckered her mouth, as though tasting a bad oyster but with no place to spit.

"That's the sort of shit I've been putting up with," she told her father. "Can you believe it?"

Leonard assumed his natural defensive role. He flew off the golf course when lightning began. He'd made reservations at L'Orangerie and they would be due to leave in ten minutes. He pulled out a Sotheby-Parke Bernet auction catalogue he'd received last month. Did they want to attend it with him? There were a couple of Hepplewhite pieces that might be interesting.

"Don't change the subject, understand, Leonard?" Hillary said, glowering at him. She pointed an accusing finger at Bobby. "This . . . did a number on the two of us that's an all-timer."

"Great, Hillary, let's bring it out into the open," Bobby said.

Caught in a crossfire, Leonard recommended that Bobby grab a jacket and he'd pick him up at the guesthouse in five minutes, but he was ignored. Sitting in the palatial room, surrounded by his collection of Vuillard, Bonnard, and Soutine, he should have felt invincible, but Hillary made him cringe. He saw the intractable, willful teenage girl who had manipulated him, taunting him, possessed of such wiles that he groveled at her feet. Her vindictiveness was beyond human endurance. She had twisted his personal life, creating an unsavory code between them that reduced him to pulp. He couldn't allow her to do this to Bobby. It was time to stand up to her, peel away the years of tyranny.

"If we're going to be late, then I'll have to phone Virginie at the restaurant."

In public, Hillary avoided clashes, preferring to make entrances, smile graciously, focus attention on herself.

"You spend enough money there, so let them wait."

"That's not the point, Hillary," he asserted. "I've been fighting a battle to survive. It's a miracle I didn't go under. I came out of it. Honey, I want to celebrate with the two most precious people in the world. My children," he added emotionally. He raised his hand majestically, calling for a truce.

"If you were in that much trouble, you could've come to me." Hillary raised her chin regally. "I would've bailed you out."

"I'm sorry I brought it up." Leonard retreated.

Bobby watched the flagrant way Hillary maneuvered her father, keeping him off balance, one moment the devoted child, the next auditioning him. What a creature! The ultimate bitch. Strike, counterattack. The games they played.

"Maybe," Bobby said in the tenor of a surmise, "there's been too much money in this family."

Leonard laughed bitterly.

"One of the nicest things about you is that you don't understand money. I've lived so far beyond my means that money's a kind of abstraction until you run into a pig-faced animal like Frank Dunlop and he makes you appreciate the force of it . . . its dominion. Hillary knew that instinctively."

Why run to the powder room and hide from these mugs? she thought. She had passed those stages of acting a role. She opened her purse, took out a gram bottle of coke, sprinkled some on the glass table, formed thick caterpillar lines, shaped them with a platinum blade and defiantly snorted three of them. Her supply would never run out and if she *chose*, Geraldo and a couple of his people would come over and kill Bobby and her father. She possessed the power of life and death. Geraldo would fake a robbery . . . she'd be locked in the bathroom, the servants bound, herded into a room, only Claude would be on duty and these absurd niggling problems would vanish. Dr. Parks was wrong. Drugs agreed with her, delineating the structure of her power. Her friends and collaborators in the boundless freedom that she was reaching for. Her position was unassailable.

"Hillary, don't," Leonard implored her. He left his chair, cuddled her face, reestablishing the old alliance. "The two of you have the world. Bobby"—he drew him into the conspiracy of courtiers attending Hillary—"don't take all this seriously. Right, honey?"

Bobby got up, found the booze tray on a table beside Leonard's chess board. Without guests, the rule was help yourself rather than have staff hovering. Leonard had a selection of malt Scotches, all of them Glen something or other, and Bobby found a clean glass, poured himself one, and turned his back on Leonard's whispered cajoling. Leonard's voice was like a satin lining in a silk purse, striving for unseen supremacy.

"It's sort of a relief to have a witness," Bobby said.

"I'd rather be somewhere else."

"I'll bet you would," Hillary snapped. She stood up, leaving her father in his slouching position on the edge of the sofa. "This marriage is a fraud . . . we were both sucked in. He brought his girl out here. What do you think of that?" Leonard raised his hands in a gesture of surrender. "Want to hear about that? We've been used."

"Hillary—"

Leonard was shouted down by the reverberation of her scream, or was it a jeer, a mad, howling laugh? That she was beautiful hardly counted, bursting with that sensuous ripeness heedlessly invested by nature on some women. But she was planted in soft eroding soil, and the rains that naturally occur would not contribute to her blossoming, Bobby thought, but rather lift the roots up, wash her down a gully. The caprice of destruction was something Hillary had been born with.

"While I've been trying to make a home out of your old whorehouse, he and Claire have been doing their number. I guess they planned to grab a hunk of my money and then drift somewhere else. We're suckers."

Leonard was beside himself, foundering, searching for the magic that would impose a semblance of order on this lunacy.

Bobby took his glass and wiggled onto the sofa. He looked at the shape of the remaining cocaine lines, their zigzags, like a spine curved, destroyed by scoliosis. He picked up the sniffer, ran his thumb along the spherical entry, shoved it into his own nose to investigate the sensation. Cold metal in his nostril. He was carried back to his childhood, the after-school meetings in Labell's drugstore near the school. Doc Larry used to fill prescriptions and tell the kids jokes, just so long as they didn't mess up the soda fountain and fling ice cream at the Breyer's sign or dip pretzels into the milkshakes and shove them in the ears of the little girls. Ah, the sweet impulsive vandalism of those days . . . Bobby put the straw in his mouth, sucked out a bit of the pale Scotch, then, when it reached his lips, he placed his forefinger over it, creating a vacuum, locking the Scotch in the tube. He waved it over the cocaine while Hillary, aghast, moved toward him. Then he let the Scotch spatter on the mound of white powder.

"You just bought it, brother." She seized Leonard's arm. "This was a gesture on my part . . . of being honest, rather than hiding and slinking. I'm through pretending."

"You started this, Hillary," Leonard shouted. What he wouldn't give to put her over his knee and spank the hell out of her. "You provoked him—both of us."

Bobby jumped to his feet as Hillary closed in like a gunboat about to fire at him.

"I'm not going to stand for this gang-up." Bobby was not intimidated, she saw; Leonard, her foe, the sniveling, gutless whelp, who needed her more than she did him, received the full blast of her scorn. "That you, my father, would allow this. We're finished."

She scrambled for her purse, opened it, and triumphantly jiggled two bottles in her hands, snake eyes in dice.

"Hillary, hang on for a minute," Bobby said, then he blocked her from leaving. "Just so it's perfectly clear, I'm sorry about us and what I did was a dumb shitty grandstand thing. I don't love you." For a moment she fell into one of those doelike, flighty, hurt, back-against-the-wall, tormented debuntantes, sloe-eyed, vulnerable, squeezing the defecting beaus she had strung out.

"You don't mean that. . . . Leonard, explain the facts of life to him." Then she was off. Bobby stood by the door while she slid into her Rolls, slowly nurturing the accelerator until it started and then cruised down the hill into the next frame of her evening.

Claire paced out the store with a set of blueprints. It was almost square, forty by fifty with sixteen-foot-high ceilings. She could afford to lose half the height, install a gallery where she could display tents, backpacks, rafts, and increase her selling space by another fifteen hundred feet. But how would it look? The double window facing the street and the location itself couldn't be better. But would the gallery add the visual dimension she hoped to create? The two designers Leonard had sent over from Disegno Contemporaneo only abetted the confusion. They didn't know what they were talking about and she had politely but firmly insisted that they give her some time to think through her concept.

A temporary phone had been set up in the rear of the store and she had bought a bridge table, four chairs, and a desk lamp at Sears. But she found herself in a ghastly muddle and she was running scared about making a decision. In her desperation, she had phoned Hayward's and left a message for Bobby with his secretary. It was four o'clock and if he didn't turn up shortly the light would be lost.

It was more than a week since he'd marched into her apartment, shaking the foundation of her peace of mind. She had rejected him and if she had to do it over, without malice or vindictiveness, she couldn't find it within herself to react differently. The hunger for him, however, still remained, unabated and unforgivable, resisting logic.

He appeared shortly after four, muddied, his face and hair caked with dust and flecks of grit on his eyebrows. He had been on the Marine site with surveyors and earthmoving caterpillars. He was in a good humor, jaunty, and the joy of being out of money meetings in the office communicated itself. The plot survey had been screwy, he told her.

"I could use a shower, but since I was in the neighborhood . . . how're you doing?" He restrained his inclination to put his arms around her, kiss her. The track conditions had changed. Yet he was the same person she would've married. They had erased their history.

"I need a personal favor. I know this isn't your line of country, but I have to be able to trust somebody. The people Leonard has working for him are high-pressure designers. They don't know a damned thing about the retail business and whenever I make a suggestion, they just knock me down."

He loosened up, laughing, and their past was frighteningly evoked. She had stifled her feelings. Nothing could put her on the firing line, at his mercy.

"You want a freebie."

"You said it, I didn't."

"I'm not much with stores and this thing is built. Leonard should've brought in a demolition company." He chortled. "But I suppose it sells."

She was genuinely worried about falling under his spell. She explained her problem and he scanned the floor plan. "What's the most important thing?"

"Space. I have to be able to show my stuff assembled."

He walked around, commenting on the lousy shape. Well, she had to live with it, nothing he could do about that. She saw in practice the fierce driven side of his personality, a taskmaster.

"If you go two floors it'll make the place a coffin," he said.

"I have to compromise and I know what you think about that."

"Simply put, by gaining space, you'll lose space. It's for outdoor people. Keep it open and informal. You put stairs in and you lose the effect. If you box out the walls in barnwood you can have storage space and still display your gear on retractable rails."

She nodded approvingly. She was concerned about cluttering the center of the store, losing aisles that would run into counters.

"Have you got another set of specs?"

"No, these are mine," she said, clutching the drawings as though they proved her legitimacy.

"Oh, I'll get some from Leonard or ask at the office. There must be a bunch of them kicking around." He tilted his head up, his neck ringed with grime. "Tents, rafts, camping gear . . . maybe . . . ?"

"What?"

She followed him outside, up a metal staircase to the roof. He picked up a handful of stones, then caustically said: "Tiles in front and a tar and gravel roof. Cutting corners like this."

"I don't understand."

"It's a flat roof, babe. If there are heavy rains, you'll have leaks."

Christ, he caused more difficulties than she had anticipated. He walked around, hands on hips, nodding to himself and excluding her.

"You know what might be nice for this?"

"Let me in on it . . ."

"Suppose with the rafts and tents and other displays you had up there, you replaced these instant module skylights with slanted ones, do them asymmetrically at different angles to break up the monotony, so that when customers looked up, they'd see the sky and feel it. Isn't that what you're aiming for?"

"And when it rains, you're in a tent. Oh, I love it."

"You will be. Not me." He agreed to do some sketches, then shuffled uneasily down the staircase. It was a dark evening, December, the air had a snap but lacked the frost they had known. No snow or sleighs or people jump-starting their batteries. A shared hardship that the cold imposed would never be theirs again. He hinted at the fact that he was straightening out his situation without delving into it. She couldn't bring herself to draw close to him, but tacitly joined him in repudiating their ties, and the monumental screwup of their present circumstances. It was certainly more comfortable, this vital awareness, something like fatalism . . .

"Can I buy you dinner? No funny business."

"Another night."

"Plans?"

"Business. Credit applications to a bunch of manufacturers. References. Forms."

He didn't press her and she loved him so deeply for not lashing out, arousing desires. It was a bitter moment for them both, holding a match until their fingers were burnt.

Gene was busy rolling a joint from the new Sinsemilla that had just arrived in town. Two hits and you could talk for an hour without pausing; three and people began to dissolve before your eyes; four and you were off to the emergency ward with Leonard Bernstein leading the orchestra of your paranoia. Gene told her to take it easy.

"This Arab offered me a thousand a week and an apartment at the Sierra Towers just to be there when he was in town," Madeleine said.

Testing the waters with his own serpentine technique appealed to her. Shit! She was an actress. What actually occurred happened to be not quite so lucrative and respectable. A horny dude at Joe Allen's bar where she'd stopped for a drink bought her a round, picked up her tab, squired her out to her car, flashed his roll, and offered her lobster at the Palm.

"You should've grabbed it, turkey. I could've met you there as your brother and we stick him with a tab that requires the paramedics."

He refused to allow a woman to get into his system. Unfortunately, it was a little late with Madeleine. Her dumb persistence, the goddamn size-four wrench she contorted her pussy into was worth thirty days at Chino. Madeleine's eyes widened apprehensively. Gene was the ultimate hard case and she was crazy about him. Another winning ticket.

"I may've let myself get fucked over before. No more." She closed her eyes, a small-theater Tennessee Williams heroine who hit the sour mash a little hard. "I care about you."

He reached for her breast like a headwaiter for a tip.

"Oh, we're in an honesty session." He switched on the JVC portable TV to a religious fanatic on UHF threatening rape, arthritis, and doomsday scenarios if money wasn't phoned in pronto for his book.

"Gene, turn it off, will you?" He was the master of his own electrical appliances. She didn't mess with his tone controls.

They were laying out on the hot tub shelf on Gene's selection of Ramada and Holiday Inn towels under shimmering sunlight, the sky cross-grained with cloud. The L.A. weather had a fretful unpredictability. No smog, drizzles, the inferno season over, tourists on the Strip and the cruel paradox of Christmas decorations braying in the wind promised another crowded December 25 for Madeleine, with strangers jostling their half-gallon Paul Masson Chablis in the kitchen and picking ice out of dead glasses. Last Christmas she had worked a hospitality suite for paint wholesalers at the Bonaventure and wound up at a table for eighteen in a Chinese restaurant at a real pig-out. A guy had groped her under the table all evening with sparerib sauce under his fingernails and offered her fifty. She wouldn't've balled him on a bet. The next time she needed six thousand gallons of ecru special mix, she'd phone it in.

It was becoming obvious that no matter what she did, she could not rouse Gene from the apathy he had succumbed to long before they met. She had spent the last week finally going out on interviews and she was optimistic about getting a job. The casting director at Doyle Dane had asked her to come back after Christmas for a second interview.

Sue thought she had made a good impression. With a new girl, the second interview meant that the sponsor would be present. He had already bought the agency's ad campaign for Soothe Aide, a fizzy new poison to relieve indigestion and heartburn that they were about to market nationally. Only a small warning: Ingesting too much of it caused night blindness. But if she was picked up for the launch in the campaign, she would be in the print ads as well as a series of TV commercials. Apart from the fee, she could collect residuals! A breakthrough. Al had wormed into the act. He had suggested Gene as the director, but the Doyle Dane account executive had wired *no* from New York about Eugene Roth.

It started to drizzle. Gene carried his TV into the bedroom while she switched off the tub. The towels didn't matter. He'd steal more. He gave chambermaids five bucks, backed his car up to their linen wagons and they loaded the trunk. Oh, his dignity and calculated petty thievery.

But, shit, what a stockade. Sexually he'd bagged her, she could go no further—or who knew, maybe she could, depending on what he dreamed up. His inventiveness molded a cause: She was the woman, she alone, who could reform him, restoring the career he'd abandoned.

"You've got to do straight stuff."

He was taking a leak, turned his head and splattered the seat.

"Wonderful, my mentor. I just know that I'll come out of this wearing Armani." His gay voice, not funny, just grating. "Tits and ass pay the bills."

She now memorized the trade papers, could do the Travel Log from the *Reporter* or Who's Where from *Variety*. Brockman wanted to represent him. Naturally, he preferred Jeff Berg. His bloodshot eyes filled with outrage. "Madeleine, don't promote me. I like you as you are."

"If I get this job, I'm through doing beaver."

"Plenty of herrings in the barrel."

That was it, beyond the earthquake faults or the Great Continental Divide. He rolled his fingers on her outskirts. Her pubic hair had shot through her skin like pikes, hurting, itching, and tickling. Nothing to be overjoyed about when they snagged into panties. She shoved him away.

"I'm talking sense to you."

"Call the Arabian Embassy. Emirates . . . this is a waste of time and a valuable hard-on. I don't believe in myself. If I have to do shit, let me pick it."

She made her move. On with the bra, the panties she couldn't find, probably soaking in his tub, into the elderly but dignified narrow camel trousers she'd bought at a Bonwit's sale, her English look.

"If I'm only another piece of ass, then fine. Let's forget it. I just can't handle a guy without any self-respect."

He wasn't quite sure what to make of this rebelliousness.

"Leaving?"

"I'd rather eat with an Arab and screw him than you."

"Well, it's a redistribution of petro-dollars at least."

What possessed her? She craned her fist back and slugged him. She banged high on the forehead into bone. Her knuckles were mashed, devilishly painful. Her eyes were gorged with tears, hot, prickly on her skin. She railed against the injustices of her life. He had recovered from the shock of the blow.

"You walked in and I knew that sooner or later you'd be trying to lick me into shape. God protect me from aspiring actresses and big dumb tits." He put his arms around her waist and cooed to her. "Burn some steaks for a change." She grabbed the seat of her existence, her handbag. "What do you want me to do?"

"See Al and go to work."

"Why? I've been through this nonsense."

"Not with me, you haven't. I'd like to see you put your ass on the line."

23

The appearance of a U-Haul trailer, proclaiming that an "adventure in moving" was about to take place, might have gone unnoticed in virtually any part of Los Angeles. However, when the U-Haul is attached to a Mercedes 450SL and is careening around the scenic byways of Bellagio Road and stops in front of the estate of Leonard Martinson, it can only mean that a burglary is going to occur. The neighbors in this verdant paradise ensconced behind hedges as formidable as a seawall are not by nature curious. They have millions locked in their property, nubile daughters, a rage for privacy; and behind their wrought-iron electronically operated gates they are simply frightened to death.

Their private police force, the Bel Air Patrol, are as a rule affable and always cautious. But when they receive three phone calls from those nice people who keep starved Dobermans chained on their grounds, or those charming Iranians who have short men in residence strolling around with automatic weapons, as well as those actors with alarm systems in their pockets, the cops get nervous. They approached Bobby with guns drawn, demanded his ID, and they glanced with skepticism at the possessions he had stacked on the U-Haul—suits, two valises, drawing boards, T-squares, cartons of oversized reference books on architecture. No Sony, mink, or diamonds were on view.

The small drama of proving who he was amused Bobby. He had come full circle and was cast back into his position of interloper. It required an appearance by Leonard to subdue the wolves. There was evidence that Hillary had been in and out of the guesthouse, but neither of them had seen her; Dr. Parks was put on alert, but he had not heard from her either. A couple of her suitcases were missing, along with part of her wardrobe. None of her expensive formal wear had been removed.

Leonard stood before him, crestfallen, aching. The union that had begun so promisingly was ending in tragedy. If Bobby were the kind of unscrupulous fortune-hunter Hillary had asserted, the blow of his departure would have been mitigated. But on the contrary, Bobby had proved to be independent, a man of character, old-fashioned in his allegiance, worthy of trust. Leonard loved him. The loss of his daughter and son-in-law devastated him.

"Tim got my Honda back from the leasing company, so I'm giving Hillary back the Mercedes." No one returned a thirty-five-thousand-dollar car. Not only was such a gesture unprecedented, but it was also debasing.

"You own it legally," Leonard remonstrated feebly. Everything that happened seemed to make him feel worse.

"Oh, come on." He extended his hand. Leonard grasped it, holding on for dear life. The hideous void he was plunged into matched the gloomy cold afternoon. "Don't take this personally, for Chrissake . . . I've got to move on." He halted. Leonard's suffering upset him, but he had to cut loose cleanly and not give him false hope. "I'm using Bob Mayer for the divorce. It'll be quiet and dignified. No money or kids are involved. I have no property and I certainly don't want Hillary's, so when you see her, ask her to find a lawyer and let them wrap it up."

One of the supreme joys of the single life resides in its unaccountability. Bobby spent the evening sorting through his cartons of books. One of his heroes was Sir Basil Spence and he never tired of reviewing the plans and photographs of Coventry Cathedral, which had been destroyed in 1940 and rebuilt in 1962. The brilliant union between the old and the new seemed to Bobby the highest achievement in architecture, symbolizing Spence's artistic humanism. It was a far cry from his own design for Marine

Mutual Insurance. Would he ever really grow in the soil of Los Angeles and realize those high spiritual elements his faith had been built on? He visualized an infinite progression of office buildings, remodels, futuristic homes on unbuildable hillsides, conventional homes in the flats for millionaires.

It was dangerous to question his newly found acceptance, but he needed answers and he could find them only from within. Would his development as an architect be over in five years, ten? And would he regard his work as worthless, commercial, inconsequential, as Rubin did? Would he have a firm like Hayward, a tie-up with a Martinson, bash out designs on an assembly line? It was almost a relief to have had his personal life crash down so that he could concentrate on the quintessential vision that had drawn him to architecture.

He made himself a hero sandwich out of a Gallo pack, half watched a Dick Cavett interview, then fiddled around with some sketches for Claire's store; the design problem made him feel useful. He'd do the work for her with love, as a gesture to the pure decency of the past he had squandered.

What had begun as an act of defiance, following the familiar pattern of her life, had turned into yet another form of imprisonment for Hillary. She was recovering from the drug binge she had been on for weeks, but the downers she'd been popping destroyed her will to act. She existed in a hypnotic Quaalude limbo and as she stood under the shower she fought to break out of the drug haze that enclosed her.

She thought of Bobby with a rush of fondness. She missed the forbearing gentility that had been part of her attraction to him. He was a beautiful guy, filled with ideas, ambition, and she had discarded him, lured by her own weakness to a grotesque season in hell. She had unleashed Geraldo's dormant tormented sexuality and what had begun as a game budded into an addiction for him, a love so wantonly dependent that it disfigured the entire landscape of the civilized life she had once been part of. Earlier that morning, Geraldo had left for a drug buy in San Diego.

She'd had her taste of low life and wanted to escape. She put on a pair of cheap recycled jeans and a shirt she dimly recalled Geraldo's buying for her at an outdoor stall beside the Venice bike path. Her large, staring, bleary eyes mocked her in the cracked mirror, giving her face a blanched pallor. Dressed, she passed through La Guita's grimy living room. Even though she was getting chills, her forehead dripping with oily cold sweat whining through her skin, she was determined to stay off drugs. She'd been shooting a deadly recipe of coke mixed with speed.

When she pulled off the San Diego Freeway onto Sunset Boulevard and headed toward Bel Air, she peered out of the window like a tourist at the houses with their protective greenery. She drove through the gates of the estate and had a heady sensation of jubilation when she spotted Bobby's Mercedes parked outside the guesthouse. He was home! She'd crawl on her knees to him, plead with him to stay with her, but first she had to confess the truth. They'd agree that she needed psychiatric help. They'd fight it together. She'd convince Bobby that she belonged to him. They'd build their lives together, move to an apartment, she'd go back to work.

The cartons on the floor of the foyer disheartened her. She grew panicky, looked around, noticed the empty bookshelves, the open closet doors.

Guardedly she walked to his study and called out, "Bobby, Bobby, baby, I'm home—for good!"

A contrite smile played on her face. It wasn't serious, just Leonard's little girl guilty of a harmless prank, seeking forgiveness. She had a singular relapse, gloriously returned to those sunny, spoiled days of her childhood when all she had to do was run to Leonard and he would make everything better. She knocked several times on the door, then pushed it open. The curtains were pulled back, the room bathed in blinding sunlight.

Every trace of Bobby was gone. His work table, books, slide rules, calculators, drawing paper. The room was stark. Hillary ran into their bedroom, screeching repetitively: "Please don't go, I'll be good, good, good, I promise, please." She yanked the closet door open, the dresser drawers. No hint or relic of the man she had married remained.

A sealed envelope Scotch-taped to the bathroom mirror welcomed her back.

Dear Hillary,

Here are the keys to the Mercedes, trunk and ignition, and also the keys to the guesthouse. My attorney is Robert Mayer, 553-8111. I suggest that your lawyer get in touch with him. Mayer thinks that the details can be worked out quickly. I haven't taken anything that we received at the wedding. I hope that unlike our marriage we can avoid complications in our divorce and act with discretion to avoid upsetting your father. He's taking this very badly. Compared to you, my funds are limited and I can't afford to run up large legal bills, so I'd be grateful if you could take this into consideration.

Find whatever you're looking for, and may it bring you happiness.

Good luck,
Bobby

The generous, rueful tone of his letter shattered Hillary. All hopes of a reconciliation appeared doomed. But she was prepared to fight to get him back and she knew that she could count on Leonard's help. She telephoned her father's office and learned that he was at a planning meeting at Hayward's. Perfect. She'd get a chance to see them both and throw herself on their mercy. They wouldn't let her sink!

How in the name of God had she let this happen to her? She'd loved Bobby. There was some grass on a shelf in the bathroom, but she couldn't handle it. She scooped some water into her cupped hand and swallowed a pair of blue Valiums, then hastily poured some Visine into her eyes and smeared blush powder on her cheeks.

She waited patiently in the reception room at Hayward's for her father and Bobby to come out of the meeting. This was a new Hillary, she told herself, sweet, guileless, the child of two men she had defied. They'd forgive her once they realized she had changed. She'd fit in, be a loving wife and daughter, have Bobby's child. They'd have quiet evenings at home. Leonard would come for dinner once a week, or perhaps they'd have a big Sunday lunch the way people did in England. She'd go to cooking classes at the Cookstore. They'd buy a dog.

She sat in a stupor, smiling through her hallucinations at the receptionist. Seldom given to optimism, she was possessed of a thunderous calm. She had made a life decision that had come from within and had not been imposed on her. She was already changing, reformed. The old Hillary would have barged past the receptionist, interrupted the meeting, and blurted out whatever came into her head, no matter who was present.

Her body shuddered when she saw them, a subdued wan smile desolated her face. She looked as though she were in the throes of a chronic illness. Leonard put his arms around her and cuddled her. Her eyes were transfixed on Bobby.

"Honey, you don't know how worried we've been about you," Leonard said. She slipped from Leonard's embrace and dropped her head remorsefully. She held up Bobby's letter.

"Do you mean it?"

"I'm sorry," Bobby said. They left the building together and stood on Cañon Drive, at a loss as to how to extricate themselves, both father and husband.

"Won't you give me a chance?" she asked plaintively.

"It just won't work."

"Maybe a vacation—Europe—the honeymoon you missed," Leonard adventurously suggested, then retreated when Bobby glared at him.

"Hey, this is awkward as hell. Hillary, we both made a mistake . . . life goes on. You need some time to straighten yourself out. You'll meet the right man. Just don't rush into anything," he added in a tone of condolence. "We're not enemies . . ." He was no longer part of her tragedy.

"Please, please," she whispered. "Take me back."

"Hillary, this isn't doing anyone any good," Leonard said benevolently. "It wasn't meant to be. These things happen. I'll look after you."

"Daddy—" Leonard seemed shocked by her tenderness. "I'm in the mess of my life."

Ruthless in her emotional demands, Hillary's penchant for finding trouble offended Bobby. Although he could forgive her, he despised those treacherous wiles she fell back on to get her own way.

"There's no hand to play out, Hillary," Bobby said. "We both lost."

Leonard grimaced, the keeper of his daughter's anguish, the old partnership still intact. How could he put his princess's world back together? Hillary had bottomed out and Bobby excused himself before a scene developed. Crossing the street, he tried to forget the puffy face, the swollen protruding veins, the vacant eyes, the trembling mouth of the girl he had married.

A pack of salesmen loitered outside Claire's store while a couple of them had her cornered in the back, draping clothes over themselves, revealing the wonders of Kelty's Anoraks and parkas. The precarious familiarity of her days at Drake's rushed at Bobby, cast him back to last Christmas, the store party, dogs in blankets, cheese puffs, the personnel guy caught with his pants down in the packing department, then the two of them stoned at the Cheshire Cheese piano bar, their ghoulish hangovers the next day. How had she dragged herself out of bed the next morning and gone to work? She arrived home at three, however, with ground filet steak and she blended the best steak tartare he'd ever eaten. Craig Claiborne's mixture, she said, served with a pitcher of fiery bullshots that shrouded the hangover. Then she passed out till six when he woke her, sat on the toilet seat watching her in the tub, shaving her legs. He dried her off, rubbing the towel up and down her back, between her legs. Then they made love, rushed out to another cocktail party and got embalmed again. The sweetness of those memories was part of him, worth preserving.

Salesmen scowled at him as he approached her. She explained that business was suspended until two. She'd be out to lunch. They walked a couple of blocks to the Bread Winner on South Beverly Drive, which specialized in do-it-yourself salad bar health concoctions. They had a pair of ham-and-cheese sandwiches. She examined his drawings, marveled at his compulsive neatness, the fluid lines of his pen, the exquisite clarity of his mind. There, on paper, were people shopping in the store, racks, counters, a second-floor gallery, a kayak as a mobile, a section for fishing gear, and in jungle green ink, a leaf with the name Rodeo Wilderness inscribed in it. She reached across the table, squeezed his hand, and gazed at him reverently. He had signed the drawings "From Bobby to Claire, with love."

"You've behaved like a real friend. The things you can do . . . incredible. I don't think I ever appreciated it. I said I did."

Her approval gave him a degree of satisfaction that had the charm of a student grading a professor's paper. He cautiously told her about the divorce proceedings, omitting Hillary's last attempt at a patch job. Why bother? Claire seemed inattentive and the chord resounded vagrantly like someone accidentally banging an elbow on a piano keyboard.

"I want to sleep with you," he said. "Badly."

"I've given it some thought." She was genuinely afraid of falling under his spell again. What was it that made her as the injured party choke with guilt? An uneasy yielding came over her . . . the need for him.

"Do you want to kick ass?"

"Not any longer," she admitted. "I'm much too enterprising for that. Let's just not make any conditions and see what happens. Okay?"

"You're not holding out," he said with surprise.

"Isn't life too short, or something of the kind?" She'd stopped eating and drank her black coffee.

"What're you up to Christmas?"

"I'm not sure."

They were the only family each possessed in the mutinous rootless latitudes of Los Angeles. He wrote down his phone number at what had become the divorce-action-pending male preserve. Divorce, though, was the wrong word. Mayer had explained that a change in the law in favor of neither party had been newly baptised "dissolution." He thrust the card with the number into her hand, but she let it fall to the floor at the cash register.

"I know the number." Her face was placid enough. "I used to phone you there and leave messages with Mr. Rubin." She hugged him, clutching the drawings under her arm. "See you."

* * *

Madeleine couldn't believe what the advertising agency's art director was putting her through. She'd washed her hair in some mucky shampoo that gave it the texture of chewing gum and had towel-dried it so that it stood on end in lank patches. False eyelashes were glued on which made her eyes tear and she was bundled into a frowsy bathrobe with lint-ridged knobs.

"This isn't a commercial," she protested. "It's an execution."

"Eat another candy bar and let the chocolate melt on the corners of your mouth a bit," she was ordered by Richie Wald, a plump, hirsute man who had been assigned by Doyle Dane to prepare her test for the Soothe Aide commercial.

The product was a foul, lemon-flavored salt that brought her out in flushes, caused such rapid-fire belches that she sounded like an automatic weapon. It made her diaphragm feel as though someone had kicked her with a hobnailed boot.

They were in a large professional studio on the Strip and Wald kept hammering at Madeleine and her co-star, a merry bit-player with a receding hairline and a beer belly. Madeleine was *playing* a pregnant woman—her dedication to the craft insisted that she walk with the slightly backward tilt that pregnant women use to offset the extra weight in front—whose nauseating yen for morbid food combinations would make cannibals ill. She was cued by Wald and, stomach forward, she reviewed the menu for dinner in the mock kitchen setup:

"Just wait till you taste the oysters in prune gravy and the cold radish soup . . ." She paused while Howard Adler, her putative husband, recoiled. "But leave room for the meatballs braised in strawberry vinegar. It's the new cuisine." Adler seemed to lunge at her, while she blissfully munched on a candy bar and stirred the concoction on the stove.

"Doll," he began in a croaking voice, "I still haven't digested the banana and tuna fish soufflé."

"Just have some Soothe Aide and it'll make everything better," she cooed to the survivor of her cuisine.

In a moment, Adler had poured some of the elixir into a glass of water. There was a moment's relief while, as

Richie explained, a voice-over would comment on the product's miracles while it was shot in close-up, fizzing, pack behind it. Then Adler swallowed it and beamed at her in relief.

"Couldn't we have something like roast beef tomorrow?" he pleaded.

"Of course. I've been meaning to try it out with my yogurt and olive sauce."

A victimized resignation crossed the doughy features of Adler. They gave each other a loving cuddle while his eyes sought the bottle of Soothe Aide.

Wald switched off the video camera. Before going to film, he'd have to show the tape to the client.

Despite looking like a pregnant cow, Madeleine was elated to have her first legitimate acting assignment. What an achievement. She couldn't wait to retail the wonderful tribulations that all actresses accumulated when they were on the set. The playback had such a ring of authenticity that while she dressed and made up she was no longer troubled by the fact that she would be unrecognizable to anyone who actually knew her. She wasn't going to be typecast! Adler, who when not working "straight" was a sort of Yiddish troubadour who farmed the wedding circuit, singing, cracking jokes, making up poems, knocked on her cubicle.

"Madeleine, you were just terrific."

"Thanks, I appreciate that."

"Timing was spot on."

"Why didn't Wald say anything?"

"He's agency. They're all noncommittal. If the client likes you, he'll kiss your ass and then your agent can jump on his head because then he's really out on a limb. See, they never pay compliments unless they got Farrah or someone like that who already has her deal with a company. Advertising art directors are all the same. They're not anything. They cheat on expenses and spend their weekends in drunken stupors because they're afraid by Monday morning they'll find somebody else at their desk."

Wald's sullen eyes testified to this observation, for when Madeleine passed him on the way out of the studio he merely nodded perfunctorily and informed her the tape would be sent to New York by express air package. L.A.

had become increasingly important as a commercial center, but New York regarded it as a casting base and the decisions were made and checks written there.

"We'll take it from there," he noted, peering over her shoulder to the parking lot where his metal gray 1973 Porsche 912 reaffirmed his reality and debts.

She decided to make him sweat because he'd been so high-handed.

"Any idea of when you'll know?"

"We'll be in touch with your agent."

"Good, she'll give you a better idea of my availability."

He blinked nervously. His head would be on a griddle if the client approved her and she was not available. So much of this business was built on bluff and chicanery, and she knew her only chance of surviving was to affect independence and the bland apathy of a girl in demand.

"I've got a women's hygiene product and an Avis that've been confirmed," she lied. "I'm also supposed to do a second audition for Toyota, national." The truth of it was that she'd be moonlighting at the convention center as a demonstrator at an RV show. She'd be climbing into Winnebagos with heavy-breathing men to explain the pleasures of showering on wheels. It was twenty-five dollars an hour and she'd be roaming around in a lime green bikini and a baseball cap. Wald at last focused on her.

"Your agent's going to get an earful from me, Madeleine."

"As long as you don't blame me, Mr. Wald. I'm just in the cargo bay," she added, needling him.

Gene's truck was in the parking lot and Madeleine rushed to her mentor. She was beginning to understand him. He'd spent years in this phony advertising world until he could no longer tolerate it. Amid the Mercedes, Porsches, Jags, his battered grimy pickup represented a misguided integrity. Gene had lived in this world of gleaming empty symbols and had rejected them. She got inside the cab and he ran his index finger affectionately along her cheek.

"Well, how'd it go, Jugs?"

"My co-star thought I was great. A guy called Richard Wald shot it on videotape."

"Richie's still at it," he mused. "Well, the tape camera's

got automatic lighting so at least he can't fuck that up. I knew him years ago when he was trying to make it as a director. He couldn't light. They called him the prince of darkness. People came out in silhouette. He's great at print layouts, though."

"He's a bastard."

"What do you expect? The guy's been walking on eggs for ten years. His wife left him for another chick. Wells, Rich gave him his walking papers and he busted out of his own agency after six months. Went in with some flaky copywriter he was screwing. The man's a basket case."

"I rattled his cage."

"Pick on someone your own size." He leaned over and kissed her, then pulled away abruptly and gave her an embarrassed smile. "I just saw Al Brockman and signed. Looks like I'm going to be doing one of those Kotex numbers for active women and then interview for a pilot in Hawaii."

"Fantastic."

"Let's go to the Palm. I haven't eaten lobster since the night before my Bar Mitzvah."

The image she had toiled for burgeoned forth. A reel would be born. Even more tangible was the power she had demonstrated over Gene. She loved him for a variety of reasons, but in some respects, the transcendent one, committing her to him, had to do with the fact that he was living proof that she could influence another human being. Gene would hardly agree, but he had become her triumph, her acolyte.

"Gene, I was thinking—"

"Don't. It'll affect your brain."

"Come on. If I really truly start rolling, is there a chance someone might crawl out of the woodwork and blackmail me about the movie?"

"You should be that lucky. We'll give the *National Enquirer* an exclusive on it. I'll hand over the neg so they run it."

No more Joe Allen's chili and spinach salads with the house dressing. The Palm! Avis . . . a Kotex, if she could get it with Gene. Lobster, L.A., wonderland. She embraced it. The carhop pegged her face. She nodded coolly. Celebrities always did.

24

Christmas was closing in and the prospect of a renewed relationship with Bobby haunted Claire. She didn't kid herself. There was still a deep underlying residue of feeling that she couldn't suppress. She thought about him constantly and despite her independence she was beset by an uncontrollable longing for him that resisted her natural distrust. She was not really the kind of woman dedicated to revenge, but a small voice from within kept her from facing her doubts. She drove by his apartment on Spaulding. His car was parked outside. The temptation to see him was overwhelming, but she gritted her teeth, drove away in disgust, and the moment passed.

She would have ample time to regret her decision, for when she reached her apartment she found Hillary sitting on the fire staircase opposite her door.

"What are you doing here?"

"I . . . had to . . . see you," Hillary said, strained by the exertion of even talking. She lurched toward Claire, who moved out of her way.

"What's the matter?"

"I'm a little dizzy . . ."

Claire leaned against the wall indecisively. What made Hillary appear even more pitiable was the attempt she was making to invest herself with a shade of dignity. Her eyes couldn't focus and her voice had a winded rawness.

"Please, can I come in?"

"Why?" Claire asked, losing her temper. "This stinks—

you're unscrupulous. What the hell do you want from my life?" Her anger was so harrowing that for an instant she could hardly believe that she had been capable of such animosity. She, who had never been able to rebuke anyone without feelings of guilt, now had a clear perception of how people mindlessly committed murder. If she'd had a knife she could have plunged it into Hillary's chest. The realization sobered her up.

"I don't blame you—"

Claire ignored her, unlocked the door, hesitated before walking in, then slowly turned.

"Say what you have to, but don't expect any favors."

"You're right to hate me."

"Don't tell me what's right, sister."

Hillary stood awkwardly in the anteway while Claire tossed her keys and bag on the hall table, then went into the kitchen and poured herself a straight vodka from the freezer. She tried to compose herself but the pulse throbbed in her chest and the moment she banged back the vodka, she had a nasty burning sensation in the back of her throat that made her think she'd swallowed acid.

"I'm involved with a man . . ."

"Really. Am I supposed to care?"

This girl was off the wall, or simpleminded.

"I'm in trouble," she said, with eyes cast down, unable to meet the severity of Claire's gaze. "It's serious."

"Why come to me of all people? Do you think if you live or die it'd make the slightest difference to me?" The lash of Claire's voice did not alter the beaten, wan expression on Hillary's face. Claire realized that the aura of defeat Hillary gave off had neutralized her from all forms of abuse.

"Don't let Bobby divorce me—not yet."

"What? Hey, I think you better get the hell out of here right now." She should have dismissed Hillary the minute she had seen her. "Talk to Bobby or your lawyer."

Hillary nodded, then continued as though Claire and she were confidantes of long standing, girlfriends who had shared a common experience.

"Let me explain." She gripped the table for support. "I wanted to escape from my father and Bobby and I met a man who just got out of prison . . . he turned me on.

He's dangerous . . . he deals drugs. What started out as kicks for me is an obsession for him. I'm afraid of him."

"Can't you pick yourself up and leave?"

"It isn't that easy. He knows I'm pregnant."

"I don't understand and I'm not sure I care if I do," Claire replied. A cloudy, inexplicable sorrow knotted Claire's emotions. The longer Hillary remained, the more cutting and devious the sensation. She had to get rid of her.

"Look, this is tough for me . . . I feel humiliated coming here. This man sees me as some kind of goddess. He worships me. Once I'm divorced, he's planning to marry me."

"Tell him you don't want him," Claire replied, baffled.

"I'm not strong enough. If I run out on him, where do I go? My father's had all the problems he can tolerate with me. And if this man and my father ever meet, he'd kill my father. He's outside the law or society. Human life doesn't matter to him. He only cares about his own wishes. So I thought if Bobby could hold off, not push things, it'd give me some time. Geraldo doesn't want his child born out of wedlock. On the one hand, he's prepared to kill whoever gets in his way, and at the same time, he wants a respectable married life. It's insane, but that's what it's like for me."

Hillary pulled a capsule from her pocket and swallowed it without water.

Claire hardly knew how to respond. This macabre situation was completely outside of her range of experience. She motioned for Hillary to be seated and the two of them sat side by side on the sofa. "Do you want a drink?" She regretted the offer. Pills and alcohol didn't mix.

"Sure, anything . . . please."

What possessed this beautiful girl, the daughter of a millionaire, to destroy herself? What could have drawn her to a murderer? Claire went to the bar, poured a vodka on the rocks. She handed Hillary the drink and sat down again.

"What makes you think for a second that I could get Bobby to change his mind?"

There was an artless tenderness around Hillary's mouth, a poignant emblem of better, more innocent days, an unfeigned trust that unsettled Claire. It was much easier to despise the Hillary who had informed her fantasies. But face to face with this abject creature, the inclination to protect her preyed on Claire. She was torn between anger and a disconcerting compassion. It was impossible to hate Hillary.

"Bobby loves you. I felt it all along. We got carried away. I thought about you, but you didn't have any substance. You were the girl back home the soldier on leave forgets. Then, I don't know what happened. It got out of hand. I sent him back to you . . . ruined. All we had was a kind of craziness of the moment, but we were completely wrong for each other and so I started getting edgy. Oh . . . was this going wrong, off the rails. Let me tell you. It never started . . . sitting next to you and . . . well, I feel suicidal. I'm in no man's land . . ."

The horror of hearing Hillary's side of the story almost broke Claire. Her betrayal hadn't been viciously engineered by two callous people. They had their lawless magic and then it vanished in the thunderous chaos of everyday existence.

"I couldn't persuade Bobby to do anything he was against. I never could," Claire admitted finally.

"He loves you," she insisted, and the words hung in the air, a bitter incantation of lost souls. "He does."

"I wish the hell you'd stop saying that." Against her will, Claire's sovereignty diminished. She had to bring some comfort to this girl. "Don't you see the position I'd be in? Bobby would be doing this for me! Even though it's for you . . . I'd owe him." The situation she found herself in filled her with apprehension.

"Does it matter? . . . he loves you."

"You want too much."

"Claire, somewhere inside me, I know that I have to save myself. Only I can do it. Give me the time," she pleaded.

They sat in a pall of silence, empty glasses, Hillary's fingers squirming, Claire so wound up as to be immobilized by the collusion, the captive linkage. On Hillary's docile hapless face was the cloistered hope of what . . . redemption?

"I'll think about it. Do you feel anything about what I went through?"

"You have to ask that?"

"What was it like . . . the two of you?" Claire asked, shivering.

"Difficult. He was being unfaithful to you. That made him uptight . . . guilty . . . then it was over . . ."

Claire had encountered the enemy and after Hillary left, she agonized over her role in this affair. Her, theirs, whose? She was landlocked, a conspirator to the breach of faith conducted against her.

Christmas came and went unceremoniously for Claire. She had difficulty feeling a holiday spirit, even though Beverly Hills was crowded by ten in the morning with frantic shoppers searching for parking spaces, buying, buying, lists of mere acquaintances in hand for whom they should buy gifts from Pierre Deux or David Orgel or Geary's. Others who would receive wine or cheese baskets from Jurgensen's. Green and silver stars and Santas in their sleighs with reindeer hung over the streets, encouraging the Christmas feeling—the commerce of it all. The pace was frenetic, but Claire could not associate Christmas with the unseasonably warm temperatures. She gave thanks to the fact that she could walk to Rodeo Drive from her apartment and not have to face the "Lot Full" signs adorning the parking lots.

She attended several parties with Ed, met new people through him, among them a few journalists from *New West* and *Los Angeles Magazine* who showed a good deal of interest in Rodeo Wilderness. Giovanni had a small dinner party on Christmas Day. A few of the men from the restaurant stopped in for a drink. When the day washed into evening they were alone and he was deciding which other parties to hit, making a token appearance to drop off some presents.

The ground under them shifted, then suddenly cleaved open. She had given him a russet and sand-colored Winter Eagle jacket made by Jansport, whose line she would carry. He had bought her a few things—a pink cashmere sweater from Juschi, a Gucci handbag, and a Donnay tennis racquet. She'd been using rentals until then. Shortly before they were due to leave for a party that columnist

Dick Kleiner was holding with his P.R. wife Chicki, he disappeared for a few minutes, returning smiling with boyish aplomb, and asked her to close her eyes. He placed a box in her hand from Fred, the jeweler on Rodeo Drive. With reluctance and trepidation, she opened it while he waited, his face a repository of the spirit the season strangely lacked. The black velvet box sprung open at a touch and she beheld a Piaget wristwatch with a snaked platinum band, the face of which was sprinkled with diamond chips.

What did she think, the donor inquired graciously, attending her reaction like a courtier. Her first view of the purlieu of King Solomon's mines. Funny question. When he raised the cuff of her blouse to snap it on her wrist, she committed one of those ghastly follies of honorable women. She refused it. He mistook the rebuff for that small-town modesty that endeared Claire to him, but when it became apparent that this was not a case of maidenly humility, he got really pissed off with her. Her gesture was disdainful.

"I've been insulted by experts, but you're in a class by yourself." She fell silent. Was it merely a question of the price, the label? What the hell did she want from him? Wasn't it natural for a man to give the woman he loved and planned to marry something reflecting his high esteem? The thought, not the price, ought to be her primary consideration. "I feel like somebody bashed me with a baseball bat." She remained taciturn, emotionally delinquent. "You've got me against the wall. Where do you want to push me?"

She put her arms around him, hugged him, and regretfully told him that the New Year's weekend at the Tennis Club in Palm Springs was off. She had agreed to see Bobby. Giovanni was flabbergasted. He might have just had a call from the fire department advising him that his restaurant had burned to the ground. He communicated such a profound grieving impotence that she dropped to her knees with bowed head. The look on his face was unbearable to behold, for it was without sentimentality. She might have shoved him through a window and he'd risen to his feet blindly with slivers of glass ridged in his face. The revelation of Bobby and her past, the marriage to

Hillary, elevated him to a state beyond shock. He was impaled.

That she could be capable of such an emotional whipping, brutalizing a worldly guy like Giovanni, tormented Claire. At the annual office bash Hayward held for his employees and clients at five-thirty on New Year's Eve, which showcased the firm's achievements—the progress of their year—in models and renderings, with Dom Pérignon and Delights by Denis, she was so depressed that she drifted through the exhibit and sat on a desk in the reception area while the guests babbled about money, plot locations, materials, divorces, reconciliations, and property shelter hedges. Having performed an execution and listened to her phone ring all day, she was unable to overcome the lethargy seeping through her bones.

The tumult of force-feeding a good time on New Year's Eve—greeting a new decade, no less—did not touch her. Occasionally she spotted Bobby in the throng, looking for her. The view was terrific as far as she was concerned. People searching for the bathrooms along with bar waiters stopped beside the exhibit of Bobby's model displayed in glass at the entryway of the office. A brass plaque had been made:

Marine Mutual Insurance Building
Frank Dunlop, Chairman
Architects: Robert J. Canaday
Hayward & Associates
Builder: Martinson Development Corporation

Tributes no longer were meaningful to Claire. All she could visualize was the batch of unopened telegrams she'd signed for, which she'd shoved in the hall closet along with the rest of the junk she'd had shipped from the storage warehouse in Westport. She'd read one telegram from Ed, and that was enough. It made her weep inconsolably the day after Christmas and her behavior made a bad impression on the sales rep from Tumbleweed Transit whose backpacks she wanted to handle.

Trying to keep up with the store and her emotional situation was wrecking her. She fell into the slothful ways of staying up till three, fending off the alarm at six, wriggling through the days, fighting her way into showrooms closed to retailers, driving to army bases to purchase souvenirs to furnish the store, arguing with the contractors and Leonard—who objected to another level, which would set a bad example—calling Frank, leaving messages, jawing with Ellen whose interest in the store was becoming a nuisance.

Bobby asked her to make any New Year's Eve plans that would be comfortable for her. Drinks and cold cuts at her apartment to baptize the new decade. Madeleine and Gene would join them. Just the four of them. Bobby had no objections. They'd be together. What else mattered?

With an Italian heiress glued to him like a garden slug, Bobby wriggled his way through the room.

"What's up, babe?"

"I can't breathe in here."

The Italian lady hung by him, speaking English spasmodically, roping him into a purview of his model just outside the room, but visible, so that she could receive a personal tour of his office in the rear and hand him a commission. She and her husband, the fat raffish thug in the black Brioni suit who spoke no English, had discussed hiring him to do exactly the same building in Milan. Of course, it would be corporate headquarters but just carry on the roof an orange neon sign announcing the founder's product.

"Scolaro," the owner's wife advised her, was a brand of informal shoes for school children that all the kids wore in Italy. They cured, or prevented, fallen arches or something of the kind. Signore Scolaro, who smelled as though he'd been marinated in Aqua di Selva, seized his wife's arm and pulled her back to safety. He and Roberto would, his wife explained, convene at the Polo Lounge after New Year's to discuss shoes.

Bobby held Claire's waist, guiding her outside. His touch was strangely alien, yet protective.

"Buyers," he said. "You must know what it's like. Are you sleepy, babe, or what?"

"Just a little high."

"Let me say goodnight to the others."

"I'll meet you at my place."

"Claire . . ."

He'd had his hair cut short and he appeared younger. He wore the navy blazer she'd picked out for him at a Paul Stuart sale and a baggy pair of blue hound's-tooth trousers that he'd had since college, which made him look like a golf hustler. His face had taken on a gauntness. His belly was flat—no more corned beef sandwiches at the Blarney Stone or midnight pizzas. He might have been ten pounds lighter than the last time she'd seen him stripped. Hard to tell. He escorted her to her car.

"It's winter, Bobby," she said out of the blue.

"Next year we'll have cards printed by Francis-Orr." She rolled down the window and he stroked her face. "Claire, I love you."

Madeleine and Gene were due at ten. Claire stacked up some platters in the kitchen, glasses, then threw herself into the shower for five minutes. While the water pounded on her back and neck, the damned phone rang with repetitive vehemence until she ran out, dripping wet, and took it off the hook. Then, chilled, she rushed back into the shower.

She hadn't lied to Giovanni, small comfort. She switched off the blow dryer, jumped into a pair of panties when the lobby intercom pierced her ears, then the doorbell. She was running in two directions like a crazy woman. She spoke through the intercom and heard an apology. A bunch of people had hit the wrong button. Bobby was at the door, ringing a third time. No time really to be modest, so she let him in. Real romance. She told him to bring out the ice, open some wine, and she dashed into the bedroom. She put on some blush and mascara, that was it, flung her boots and jeans into the bottom of the closet and pulled on a black wool skirt and a white V-neck lamb's-wool sweater, the first combination that hit her.

Bobby pressed the switch to light the California fire—lava logs with gas flames—lowered the lights, switched Ellen's McIntosh to K-Earth, releasing the cleansing voice of Barry Manilow into their lives.

"You're looking skinny, babe."

"I thought you were too," she said. The telephone had released a squawking signal and their attention focused on it. He replaced the receiver. In a moment it rang again and they listened until it harped on their nerves.

"Are you going to answer it?"

"I'll take it in my bedroom."

The cord was wrapped around her feet. She was sitting on the floor and Bobby stood in the halfway house of her bedroom, beyond the dresser where some handbags were stashed beside the lowboy, which was faced with credit card slips. Claire wasn't wearing shoes and she was speaking in a low voice. He heard nothing but—

"Yes, yes, I know . . ." Silences. Her eyes riveted to the wall. Then a whisper: "Okay." An interminable pause. More words Bobby couldn't hear. "I have to go now. Happy New Year . . ."

The look of agitation suffusing her face was an unuttered indictment of him, but regrettably she made no comment. He would have preferred to clear the air. There was obviously a deep affection between Claire and Giovanni and she had been struggling to sever the tie. The New Year would be beginning on a melancholy note. If he could have erased time and returned to the funny relaxed evening they had spent with his college roommate and his wife along with a bunch of the guys from school he knew, despite the first flower of success he'd experienced, he would have sacrificed it. Since the break with Hillary, he had come to see the dimensions of the wound he had caused.

"Claire . . ."

"Skip it."

The D. J. on K-Earth was doing a retrospective of the hits of 1979 and they listened to Billy Joel's "Fifty-Second Street." Bobby had brought a couple of bottles of Dom from the office; he popped a cork on one and stuck the other in the refrigerator. He handed her a glass and was on the verge of proposing a toast, but she had started to drink.

"Have you seen Hillary?" she asked.

The question cheered him, would demonstrate the forcefulness of his decision.

"Once . . . weeks ago. My lawyer's pushing to wrap up the divorce."

"Maybe he ought to go easy," she observed enigmatically. He listened with growing bitterness to the story she related about Hillary, appalled at the way Claire had been manipulated.

"Oh, I'm supposed to be the martyr because she got knocked up. Her stock in trade is the little-girl-lost number," he said vehemently.

"I couldn't turn her down. I promised I'd mention it to you."

The world had fallen off its axis. Bobby reeled at the twist. Claire didn't hate Hillary, was acting as her advocate.

"What difference would a few months make?"

He was furious at her offhand manner. Was she testing him, consigning him to a permanent limbo, protecting herself from him? Or was there, underneath all the maneuvering, a secret sisterhood, a point of union among all women? He saw himself being neatly mousetrapped. The resurgence of his love for Claire was deeper than he had perceived. A fatalistic gloom settled over him. He hated Hillary. Her slyness undermined his future with Claire.

"If I hold up the divorce, where do *we* stand?"

"Don't press it. I'm not going anywhere," she said.

He smiled at her, and the tension evaporated. She had that rare ability of imbuing whatever she touched with her spirit, a vivacity that uplifted him. He reached over and held her, then tentatively pressed his mouth against hers. The warmth of her flesh against his had an enchanting familiarity and he luxuriated in his good fortune. To have the chance to regain what might have been irrevocably lost was a miracle.

Madeleine and Gene arrived shortly after ten. Claire had put out a cold spread of pâté, cheeses and French bread, and some sausage. The reunion marked a new beginning and Claire was elated. There was no current of estrangement between Madeleine and Bobby and she discovered that Gene Roth wasn't nearly as she'd remembered.

"I never thought I'd be starting the year with this kind of sprint." He'd been hired to direct a pilot in Hawaii. "It's a teenage actioner for the family hour. Adventure, scuba diving, three girls and two boys, tits and ass for the under twelves. Know what I mean?" He passed around a pipe filled with Turkish hash. "Lots of surf and beach sequences, no sucking but petting around the campfires. Each week our band of detectives does some rescue work and good deeds."

He was antic and so disarmingly unpretentious that

Claire could understand how Madeleine had fallen under his spell.

"We start with them coming to the aid of a beachcomber who's about to be dispossessed by a condo developer. He won't move, so he's strong-armed. The kids pull him out of a rowboat where he's been jugged and they find out he's a great painter. A closet Gauguin. One of the little chicks has a father on the police force, another's mother is a reporter on the Mahi-Mahi *Bugle*. Oh, yeah, there's an aquatic wonder dog . . . the Mark Spitz of shepherds. He's the big acting talent in this bunch . . ."

Bobby had loosened up and listened to the whimsical recitation, breaking up uncontrollably. Gene had nagged him to have a hit of the hash and eventually Bobby took a couple of blasts. The mixture of champagne and hash made him giddy, and his troubles were left behind.

Madeleine watched the two men with Claire from the dining room and she generated that companionable trust that had bound the two of them for years. Claire had arrived in L.A. in the middle of one of Madeleine's worst periods, which, she explained, accounted for the rift in their friendship.

"See, I've always been promiscuous, but I'm not a whore, and Christ almighty, Claire, I don't know what possessed me to think I should charge for it."

Soothe Aide had not yet come through for a campaign commitment, but Budget Cars had picked her for a thirty-second spot and Demure Douche was offering more money than Kotex, and her book was filled with prospective advertisers from NyQuil to Ex-Lax. But the fact was she had a great deal of spare time that she had no way of filling.

"Is there any way I can help you with the store?"

Claire hired her first temporary employee on the spot. She'd get Madeleine a couple of hundred a week from Dunlop. It would give Claire the freedom to cover more ground and not tie her to the store at inconvenient hours. Eventually, the conversation shifted to Bobby.

"I wish I could be diplomatic, but are you heading for a fall again?"

"I hope not."

"Claire, I've been burned lots of times and I can rebound. I always have. But, babe, after what you went through, I worry." She embraced Claire. "You're not built for these setbacks. Getting fucked over was my daily bread until I met Gene and even now I'm not sure of him. He'll be off on location . . . knowing him, anything can happen. You and Bobby are small-town people with those old-fashioned values and you won't change."

She had touched a pressure point. With Bobby back in her life, Claire thought, could she let go again? She was stronger now, more independent, a woman who had just ended an affair, and was starting a business that would be enormously demanding. Bobby's career had been launched. He'd never have to scramble for commissions again. Could she adjust to a domestic life with him?

"I'll have to find out."

The second bottle of champagne was opened and the four of them joined hands, sang "Auld Lang Syne" as the new decade of uncertainty came forth. Bobby held her in his arms, kissed her passionately, and for that instant her doubts were dispelled. The shimmering crystal image of their love thrust them back in time, but then the mood was broken for Claire.

The four of them sat around until two, making small talk, sharing confidences. The edge that Madeleine had, Gene explained, was her ability to accept disappointment, come back and fall on her face again. He himself admitted that his fears were so all-encompassing that he never expected to rise above them again.

"I needed someone who didn't know any better to pull me together," he said, holding onto Madeleine for dear life as they were leaving. When they were gone, Claire sat down beside Bobby. They were drinking coffee and brandy and he seemed abashed and solemn as though too many ideas were fighting for expression and he was afraid of them, or of making a move, in case Claire rebuffed him. He'd been attentive and restrained all evening.

"Madeleine thinks I'm a shit. She didn't come out with it. She sort of looked at me a few times and . . . well, I sort of agreed with her. What right do I have to push myself on you again? I blew it, forced you to give up Ed. Well, I didn't actually force you, but the pressure was implicit. Oh, Claire, what the hell am I doing to you? I can't live with it . . ."

Madeleine had not pulled punches and had told him of Claire's suicide attempt. He was distraught.

Claire possessed an innate sensitivity regarding his predicament. She took his hand, steered him into the bedroom and smiled receptively. She stretched out on the bed, taking her usual side by the window, for he couldn't ever fall asleep unless he was on the male preserve by the door. She had learned of this endearing vigilance when they had started sleeping together. After the breakup, she had gone over to his side, subconsciously reserving it for him. With Giovanni, it didn't matter where she slept. Bobby remained withdrawn and she stretched out her hand to him. He shifted uneasily, guilt-ridden.

"I want to hold you," she said, her blue eyes wide with invitation.

His head came to rest on her shoulder. They lay for a moment in profile, looking at each other, then he hugged her and they kissed with a playful adolescent delicacy. Her fingers were on the back of his neck, gently stroking him. The desire for him had never been absent and she was able to block out their last evening together, when he had turned her down. He reclaimed his place in the center of her life and in a curious way it was as though he had never been gone.

The party in the dining room at La Guita was losing steam at four-thirty in the morning. Geraldo as host had provided two ounces of uncut Bolivian rock, which had been placed on a small wall mirror along with a jackknife and a glass straw for his select group. Only four men and two women remained, dancing drunkenly around the mass of empty tequila bottles. Hillary had been on a speed excursion most of the evening, popping Preludins and blowing coke. She dare not shoot up in front of Geraldo. He had a singular antipathy for the needle.

Hillary sat beside him at a table in the rear. He drank his San Miguel straight from the bottle and his lynx brown eyes hovered over her adoringly. She smiled at him. The smile had become a nervous mannerism. He kissed her hand; then, when she put a cigarette in her mouth, he flipped open his Zippo lighter, always the gentleman. A radical transformation had occurred in his personality which she found both thrilling and intimidating. The ascetic, restrained side had vanished and an indulgent, half-mad, licentious greed overtook him. It was a voyage through uncharted waters, a glimpse through the portal of hell so profligate that she almost longed for the austere, inhibited man she had first discovered.

He had been very drunk before the New Year and had cajoled her to leave the party for a while. They had gone upstairs and he had stripped her, tied her hands to the bedpost and, although he did not hurt her, he played a rape game with her, demanding that she cry out, beg for help, then ultimately resign herself to her fate. Then afterward, he had sobered up sufficiently, cried, begged her to forgive him. They returned to the merrymakers before midnight.

"I'm going to have to go up to Fresno for a while. And I don't want you to be around here by yourself." She had half listened to a beef a couple of his men had about being stiffed for a half pound by a small dealer there. The dealer had sought the assistance of Geraldo's rivals in EME, breaking the fragile peace that had been established between the two Latin gangs. "When I get back," he continued, "maybe we'll go to Florida. Get some sun. You're not looking good. Skin's too white. Maybe you should see the doctor. I'd like you to be checked out, eat proper, get enough rest. We're going to be parents. A family!" he added proudly.

Hillary recognized that her opportunity had arrived. She'd return to Leonard, kick the drugs—for good. It wasn't too late for an abortion. She clung to these tenuous plans, hoping that she could keep her resolve. She knew that if she didn't make her move as soon as he left, she'd never escape from him.

"You'll stay with your father when I'm away?"

"I guess that'd be best," she replied tentatively.

"It'll give you a chance to tell him about us. Your father and I have to meet to discuss our plans. You get him to light a fire under your lawyer, or I will."

Geraldo, the outcast, the cold-blooded murderer who'd spent half his life in prison, had certain eccentric notions of society. As far as Hillary was concerned, he had an obligation to do things properly, with decorum. She could well imagine her father entertaining Geraldo in his French château. In two minutes Leonard would hit the alarm and the place would be swarming with cops and security men from the Bel Air Patrol. Yes, it would be quite a scene. Geraldo coming to make a social call, asking for his daughter's hand, while his men sat in the Lincoln clutching their grease guns.

"I'm not sure. He's very possessive and—"

"You do it," he commanded. Geraldo was adamant. "I'd like him to understand me. That I'm not after your money or his connections. We're from different ends of society but that doesn't mean I don't love you and won't protect you."

There was a taint of lunacy in his earnest desire for social balance and acceptance, and at such moments, motivated by pride, he was at his most dangerous. "Your father and I will work it out. We're both leaders. Believe me, there's a common ground between men like us," he rambled on, sowing his fantasies in this grimy cantina in Venice while Leonard, only a few miles away, lay on silk sheets in a seventeenth-century Jacobean bed. For a moment she contemplated the encounter. Leonard would reach for his checkbook and offer to pay him to get out of their lives and at precisely that moment, affronted by the developer's brusque officious manner in doing business, Geraldo would take out his .357 magnum and blow Leonard's head off.

In bed, a short time later, Geraldo grasped her in his powerful sinewy arms and delicately stroked her breasts, which were growing larger and firmer. The nipples swelled and he kissed them tenderly. The expectant father emerged from his cocoon.

"I didn't hurt you before, did I?"

"No," she said placatingly.

"Every night when I fall asleep, I imagine myself holding our baby. I've wanted this my whole life . . . *una familia.*"

She swallowed two Seconals. Soon Geraldo would be away. She was drifting off to sleep when she felt him slipping into her. The encounter had no meaning for her any longer; she was entering another world, ruled by his madness.

"Happy New Year, *cariño,*" he whispered lovingly.

25

In her dreams, Claire heard the pounding of nails, buzz saws, the churning of cement mixers. The faces of the men working in the store merged with those of sales reps and Leonard Martinson, to whom she took her complaints about the slow progress. He'd make a couple of notes, bawl at his foreman, but he was distracted, spread too thin, in constant transit between the Marine Mutual site and Rodeo Puerta. His personal problems with Hillary were never mentioned, but his face was wearied, hangdog, and Claire hated herself for vilifying him but her future was at stake.

Workmen didn't show up and oftentimes their work was unacceptable. Walls had to be rebuilt, the building inspector found code deviations, issued citations. Dunlop had provided her with the capital, but found his big toy in Century City more interesting.

Partners were death. Ellen came by occasionally, bombarded her with idiotic suggestions. However, the Dunlops were riding a curling wave of publicity organized by a P.R. at Rogers and Cowan and they reveled in their celebrity. Articles in gossip columns praised their ingenuity and one of them referred to Claire as the manager of Rodeo Wilderness. The manifold difficulties of starting a business from the ground up and her slavish devotion to it made her short-tempered and brought out a hard-driving, ruthless streak in her. If she heard one more excuse for a late delivery, she'd climb a wall.

When Madeleine was available, she let her keep an eye on the workmen and sign for deliveries, check the invoices and organize everything in the closed-off storage area, which she had managed to get the workmen to finish. This allowed Claire to take trips up to Edwards Air Force base where she bought a job lot of test-pilot suits and worked out a deal with a larcenous stock clerk in the quartermaster corps. She paid him a bounty of ten dollars for unusual gear. She raced down to Camp Pendleton outside San Clemente and purchased a batch of Special Forces camouflage outfits. The naval base yielded nothing, but she was put in touch with a jackal-like creature who had a large warehouse in L.A. with an enormous selection of brand-new equipment and clothing.

Marv Baker sold his merchandise only for cash or bank checks. Credit and terms were alien to his business practice. He refused to deliver, take returns. His big accounts were mining camps, chemical companies producing pesticides, large out-of-state army-navy stores, and some mail order.

He sat in his closetlike office drinking Diet Rite, chewing on his fingernails, and scribbling orders on his desk blotter. He was a short, thin man with a high shiny forehead, close-set avaricious brown eyes, a ferret-like nose, and pasty white rough skin on which his beard made absurd arbitrary patches. On his sour curled mouth was distrust and the sorry arrogance of one who detested people.

He grudgingly agreed to give Claire a tour of his cavernous dusty warehouse. His merchandise was stacked in mildewed cartons: oilskins, sleeping bags, knapsacks, sling bags, camping equipment, clothes, boots and shoes; all gave off a rank greasy odor. Some tents were assembled and a couple of rafts had been inflated and Claire tried to visualize how she could display them. She rooted through boxes of overalls, camouflage jackets spotted with jungle green, checked sizes, found battle jackets, khaki shorts that could be cut off so that they had the right camping outdoor look.

"First order has to be a minimum of five thousand dollars in cash or a bank check. No deliveries and any damages you find you live with," Baker said.

Claire had been tempered by her stint in Drake's bargain basement when she'd been a junior buyer and had to deal with scavengers. The experience had proved invaluable.

"There's only one condition on my side if we're going to do any business." He scowled at her. "Just don't give me any crap. My initial order could run fifteen to twenty-five thousand."

He'd heard those stories before and she had to wait while he phoned the bank to check her credit, while she continued to root through bins and made notes in an order book. Baker found her in the camping section. His attitude had altered discernibly.

"I spoke to the bank and I heard music," he said.

"Good." She was perfunctory. "These stoves are rust scarred."

"Take it easy. They're for mail order. New ones are coming in."

"Marv, if this isn't going to be hit or miss and you want volume orders and there are no terms . . . you're going to have to tell me what the discount is."

"I can live with ten off."

"I can't." She packed up her attaché case and order forms. She was walking. He was accustomed to the easy graft he had with company purchasing agents and petty kickbacks.

"I'll work with you, Miss Stuart."

The magic phrase. Once a supplier committed himself, she took him by the throat.

"Start writing, Marv, and we'll see what the numbers look like." When the order was totaled, she would be in a position to scale him down and press the deal. Getting back into action was intoxicating and she realized how much she'd missed the pace of business. It was in her blood. Rodeo Wilderness was her vision, her taste would shape it.

In the evenings she spent her time correlating her orders, working on the books, writing letters to suppliers; the all-consuming drain on her energy continued to foster misunderstandings with Bobby. The two of them were out of step, and although they shied away from arguments, it was becoming evident that the combination of mutual exhaustion and his inability to respect her independence was leading to a confrontation, the point of no return.

With only a tattered Sav-On vinyl bag that she'd found in the basement at La Guita, Hillary drove up the long tortuous familiar road to her house. Geraldo had admired her Gucci luggage, so she had made him a gift of it. She had been waiting anxiously since the New Year for Geraldo to leave for Fresno, but he had constantly delayed his departure.

He had finally left that afternoon and she'd taken her Rolls to a car wash. Despite the cleanup, the car looked ready for a body shop. The batteries in her remote control gate opener had run dry and she searched for her keys. This furtive entrance at night was preferable to seeing her father in daylight. She prayed that he was out so that she could go to her room in the main house rather than take up residence in the guesthouse. Leonard would regard this as a sign of good faith and not interrogate her. When she stopped in the driveway, she found the housekeeper and butler standing in the entry.

"Something wrong?" she asked when she left the car.

"You tripped the silent alarm, Mrs. Canaday," Claude, the butler, said. He turned the key in the alarm system to cancel the police call, then walked down the steps to the car and took the bag from her.

"Is my father in?" she asked tremulously.

"He's in the study," the housekeeper informed her.

Hillary had a sense of homecoming when she walked through the hallway. The dining room was dark, a light shone in the kitchen, and there was a fresh smell of lemon oil, coddled furniture, rare objets d'art. The serenity of wealth. It would provide a protective barrier, a chasm, that Geraldo would never dare cross. For the first time in years she was grateful to Leonard for his strength, the blindness of his adoration, and his predilection for smothering her with affection.

The princess had returned from exile to her kingdom. How, she thought bitterly, had she turned her back on her birthright? She passed the study. The door was open and Leonard lay stretched out in his leather easy chair, dozing in front of the television. A glass of milk and a plate of chocolate chip cookies were on the table beside him. He frowned, rubbed his eyes, and blinked at her. He made a move to rise but she rushed to him, threw herself in his arms; he touched her face with infinite gentleness, then cradled her tenderly.

She was afraid that he would begin to cry and she said sweetly: "Daddy, I've come home. I want to be with you . . ."

He remained speechless, caught in the throes of an inexpressible emotion.

"Honey, it's been so long since you called me Daddy."

She switched off the TV and had to sit down. She was shaky on her feet.

"I'm in trouble," she said. Music to his ears.

"You look tired. Come on upstairs. Your room's always been kept ready."

As they walked up the wide staircase, arm in arm, she asked in a tired, disillusioned voice, "Where did I go wrong?"

He did not want to rehash the past record of her follies for fear of alienating her.

"You're back. Nothing else matters."

After months at La Guita, her majestic suite and its creature comforts were all the more inviting. She opened the French windows and noticed that it had begun to rain, a fine, feathery drizzle that smelled clean and fresh.

"I've given you a hard time."

He was not in the mood for recriminations. Logic had no place in their lives.

"I've never wanted to be anything except your friend." Her demoralized condition worried him. He had had sleepless nights since she'd been gone, but it appeared that Hillary had suffered more.

"I trust you," she began, "but you're not going to like what I have to say." She was listless and he did not want to press her.

"Why not get some sleep and we'll talk about it in the morning?"

She was a driven woman, ruled by a demanding spirit that fed her self-indulgence.

"It can't wait." She gave a terrible, eerie moan that was

so intensely oppressive that his pressure rose with explosive suddenness. She was crying, gasping convulsively. He'd seen her cry many times, usually in pique or to impeach his authority, but this was a new Hillary, this forlorn beaten creature.

"Honey, I beg you . . . don't . . ." He stroked her hair, then sat on the edge of her bed. It had been years since they had shared this degree of intimacy. She had come down with scarlet fever when she was ten and he recalled sitting on her bed—the room had been soft pink with lace curtains and filled with dolls in those days—and he had fed her Campbell's tomato soup, which had been her favorite food. He had taken pride nursing her during those days when her fever had been a hundred and four. His little girl.

"Hillary, I'll help you. I'll do anything," he beseeched her.

"Daddy, I'm pregnant and I don't want it." Tears coursed down her pallid cheeks.

"We'll get you to a doctor tomorrow. I'm with you, darling. I'm with you."

"I've ruined my life," she said, pointing a finger at herself.

"Don't be silly. We'll have good times again. I promise. It's just a phase. It'll pass."

"Geraldo will kill me when he finds out."

"What are you talking about? Hillary, I won't let anyone hurt you. . . . You're my baby . . . you always will be." He'd waited years to say this without any demurral from her. It was a moment he would always cherish, he and Hillary together, united in love. He had never wavered in his devotion to her and he would not relinquish the hold fate had established. Hillary needed him.

"He—Geraldo—murders people," she said starkly.

"You're safe now," he assured her. He was more upset by Hillary's paranoia than the imaginary threats of her lover. "I'll send you away if necessary. He won't find you."

"Yes, he will. He'll come after you and he'll make you tell him where I am."

"I'm not exactly helpless." He held her at arm's length and looked with acuity at her. "Don't you think after all the years I've lived here, I have *connections* too? Hillary,

I've done favors, sold homes, carried the mortgages for quite a few people. Homicide detectives, top brass from the FBI. We're not exactly without friends."

"Daddy, he's crazy. He's been in prison most of his life and he thinks he's some kind of king—a ruler. He commands people."

The strategy of battle intrigued Leonard, would enable him to demonstrate his prowess. Hillary's return, so long in coming, would not be abandoned without war. He'd call Ira Parks, explain the situation, ask him for his advice.

"You know something, Hill, I've had tough guys try to put the bite on me. Don't you think that syndicate people have wanted to launder their money in the property business? I've had my share of threats. But I never let them in. Honey, nobody's going to walk into my office and tell me what to do. I'm not some piker off the street. These sort of people are going up against a man with some resources. I've taken a helluva beating financially this year, but I came out of it in one piece."

She stretched out on the bed and her fatigued eyes reflected the pale failure of rebellion. She wanted to retreat from life, find herself, and reenter society.

"I'm going to change. This time I mean it . . ."

"Don't make promises. It isn't necessary. I'll go to the wall for you because you're worth it. Hillary, I love you and I always will."

Her contrition overwhelmed him. She wanted to pay penance to him and he was merely relieved to have her home safely.

"I'm sleepy." She extended her arms. He bent down and kissed her forehead, her hair, her cheeks. He'd never share her with any man again.

It was well after midnight when Gene burst through the door, startling Madeleine. She had been watching John Garfield in *Body and Soul*. The movie enthralled her. Usually when Gene arrived home this late he was hungry and they'd troop down to Canter's, the all-night deli on Fairfax, where he gorged himself on a five-course meal. It didn't matter how late it was. Except for his renewed dedication to his career, he was irregular in most of his habits.

Lately, she thought he was losing interest in her. It made

no difference whatever to him whether she worked or not. In fact, he was keeping her, making her car payments, and to make matters worse, he had taken over her lease. She wondered if he might have been fooling around with the models in his commercials, but was afraid to ask. It was a matter of no small concern to her that at a whim he could dump her, have her repossessed, move another girl in, and if she didn't like it she could tell her story walking. She was in love with him and her dependence on him manifested itself in destructive resentment.

"You're coming to Hawaii," he announced in a booming voice. "The network okayed you as my piece of ass. All expenses paid."

"Thrilling." She glanced at the TV. John Garfield was taking a terrible pounding in the ring.

"You're my P.A., Madeleine. How's that for a title? You can hold the stopwatch or wear my viewfinder." She sulked, tight-lipped, preserving her dignity from his vandalism. "What the fuck does it matter? It's a freebie for us. Kahala Hilton, first-class tickets, a car with a driver!"

Unmoved by the offer, she appeared glum, detached, and when he said, "Some fucking reaction. You're really a pain in the ass," she did not answer. "Come on, give me a smile and let's go grab some salami and eggs at Canter's."

"I don't feel like going. Why don't you take someone else? You shouldn't have any trouble. Call someone from your loop book."

He had still not lost his good humor. He picked up a joint from the table, lighted it, took a few hits, and beamed with affection at her.

"You're starting to sound like the wife I didn't marry five years ago. I left her. Hey, listen, when I get back, I'm going to do a Movie of the Week for ABC." He opened up his briefcase and flapped a buff-colored script against his thigh. "I read this and it's a beauty. Mother dying of cancer, daughter doing Angel Dust, and Dad's a homicide cop who's having a thing with his daughter's best friend. It's *Soap* as *Police Story*, or the other way around. I may be able to cast you as the social worker who goes undercover and reunites the family. So kiss my feet and stop behaving like a dildo."

All that remained of the porno-photographer who had

seduced her was his rough language. Gene had mellowed out. He was buying his trousers at Mr. Guy, Bally shoes, Michael Rosati had civilized his hair and he wore it in a fashionable short cut. He looked years younger. He was svelte, off heavy drugs, drinking Lite, gobbling vitamins, and pondering the purchase of a Mercedes. All of the trappings of success he had previously spurned he had repurchased from the pages of *L.A. Magazine,* and he attended to his new faith with the zeal of a convert. Shit, Gene Roth was finally making it.

"What's this new moodiness, Jugs? A little while ago you would have fallen down the stairs for a trip to Hawaii." He peeled off five crisp hundred-dollar bills. "Go bananas. Buy yourself a few things." She ignored him. "Madeleine, don't turn your ass to me. I'm talking to you."

Garfield was in close-up, held passionately by Lilli Palmer. They were magic. A languorous kiss, the two of them breathless. Garfield was champion.

"I'm not going."

"A threat, Madeleine?"

"No. I'm waiting for a Tegrin commercial."

"Forget it. I turned it down and the director they hired is using his old lady."

His scornful eyes infuriated her. "This fucking business . . . I'll never survive," she whined.

"If you're a quitter, then I can live with it, but can you?"

The hell with it. "Claire's opening her store and I think I've reached the point where I'd rather be working with her."

His mouth dropped and for a moment she thought he might strike her. He puffed on the joint, then stabbed it out in a saucer.

"Listen to me! I didn't let you pull me out of the shit to have you wind up a salesgirl again. Claire has a business head but you, you're a dummy. All the time and effort in drama classes, your reel and me behind you, and this is what it comes to. Make sense for once, Madeleine."

Her anguished face served only to enrage him.

"I'm a nothing. I've had a few jobs, but what am I really? I'm your housekeeper and piece."

"Since when was a prime pussy unworthy of respect?"

"Let up," she shrieked. "I have no self-respect. I live like a goddamn mooch." Whatever Claire paid her vanished. She'd blown a couple of hundred that day on a skin treatment at Aida Thibiant and a pair of boots. Everything she earned disappeared. "I have to come to you for gas money. It's starting to happen for you, Gene, so cut loose. You've come back from the dead."

He put his arm around her and she pulled away as though from a spider.

"What gives you the right to be this down on yourself?"

"I've stopped kidding myself. Maybe I'll have a future with Claire."

He was outraged, beside himself with frustration. He had believed in her whacky optimism, her dumb airs; her ignorance provided him with new hope. The insanity of it was that Madeleine had been his inspiration to fight back and he realized how fragile his own grip on life was when she caved in.

"Don't do this to us, Madeleine. The miserable facts of life are these: Al had you signed as a long shot to get me again. The director is the key to this business . . . you can package your clients with him. They'll keep sending you on calls and interviews as long as I'm working. It was a mousetrap to suck me back. I'm your chance in this business and *I* need you."

The revelation was so nefarious that she groaned helplessly. The truth tainted her aspirations, made a mockery of her dreams.

"Go along with it," he insisted. "I'll stick you down their throats. And with all the interviews, something'll break for you."

She passed through shock, depression, and panic until she achieved the splendid instantaneous insight in which her self-respect finally gripped her, seizing hold of her with the righteous power of a religious conversion. At last she understood.

"Gene, you're doing a fine job holding your own balls," she said calmly. "You don't need me any more. This business—you can stick it up your ass."

"Don't talk like a fucking scrubber."

"So long."

He stalked out of the house and did not return that night.

Los Angeles abounds with private clinics, serene asylums for drinkers, dope freaks, crackpots, and people whose brains have been frazzled by the natural disasters of their own everyday existence. None, however, is more private, exclusive than Melody Park in Encino, and it was here that Hillary had her trouble-free abortion. Her course of therapy for drug addiction under Dr. Ira Parks' guidance proceeded with surprising results. His patient's cooperative disposition toward the treatment encouraged him. Hillary was fighting back.

Leonard sat with her in the garden, elated by her progress. He had succeeded in eliciting a number of facts from her during her stay about Geraldo. Hillary was pliable and candid to a fault. His rebel had turned out to be a wounded victim who regarded him as a faithless lover. Leonard was by turns guilt-ridden and disconcerted by the view from Hillary's side of the fence. They had spent years locked in a strangle embrace that was the source of their consuming, dazzling ignorance.

As Leonard regarded her face washed by sunshine beside the clinic's therapy pool, he could not imagine a sweeter, more compliant girl. He had discussed Geraldo with a homicide detective he had known for some time. He had learned that Geraldo Flores was a monster, had instigated a deadly gang war. His group, Nuestra Familia, were not people to meddle with. Geraldo had been rousted in Fresno for a parole violation but was due to be released, courtesy of an ACLU lawyer. Apparently Geraldo's civil rights had been violated. Coincidentally, two Mexicans associated with EME had been executed during Geraldo's visit.

"Still, I wouldn't lose any sleep. Flores is more interested in dope than his love life," the detective revealed.

Despite the facade of confidence Leonard displayed, he dreaded Geraldo's return to L.A. He hoped the detective was correct in assuming Geraldo's priorities, despite Hillary's fear, but Leonard was taking no chances. Once Hillary was on her feet, he was going to take her out of the country. The Far East. A cruise on the *Princess*. Flores had no passport. They'd disappear, wait for him to break parole, be picked up for a murder. They would return when he was safely in prison.

"I'll have to see Geraldo . . . and explain," Hillary told her father.

"Explain what?" Leonard was outraged. "Hillary, this episode is over. Don't give it a second thought."

The sun had brought out the golden natural highlights of her hair and he remembered how, when she was a child, he had rubbed cream on her skin so that she didn't burn. She had been a delicate, docile little girl. Then suddenly something inexplicable occurred when he planned to marry. She had developed a quirkiness that made her ungovernable. But now they were back together again, presenting a unified front.

"Don't worry about Flores. You're Hillary Martinson and nobody's going to threaten you while I'm around." There was a suggestion of muscle, sinew, which money had built, and in his clear gray eyes, the set of his jaw, she found her security. "You know, honey, I haven't seen you looking this well in months."

"I'm riding again . . . sleeping without Seconals."

"Maybe we'll buy a place in Santa Ynez, keep some horses," he suggested.

The idea appealed to her and they discussed going to Ireland for bloodstock auctions. He'd sold the Alpine house for two million eight, and a million of it in cash was waiting for him in Zurich. The conversation drifted aimlessly, but then she was betrayed by her failures.

"I've been thinking about Bobby lately. We overreached at the beginning. If we'd known each other a little better . . . I was afraid to lose him and I grabbed him." She had regrets. Tears gathered in the corners of her eyes. The sanity of her lament gripped him. "For a while I'm sure he almost loved me. He's not the sort of guy who could fake it."

"He wasn't for you."

Leonard had observed Bobby with Claire. Hillary's beauty, glamour, and sophistication had snared him. A two-day wonder. They weren't right together. You couldn't treat a man like Bobby as if he were a two-bit fortune hunter. Sooner or later Bobby would have made his mark.

Leonard recognized talent when he saw it. Bobby didn't need Hillary to further his career. He had been infatuated with her, totally overwhelmed. And, Leonard was sure, Bobby had loved her then.

"Would you ask Bobby to come and see me?" Leonard hesitated, then Hillary's rueful smile undermined him. "I just want to apologize and work things out."

He kissed her on the forehead, tasted the silky sweat on his lips; while driving back to Bel Air, he knew he could not deny his daughter the opportunity to make amends. He worshipped Hillary.

Bobby wore a yellow hardhat and goggles to keep the mud and cement threshing through the air from getting in his eyes. His khaki overalls—a gift from Claire—were coated with hardened gray pellets from the giant mixers. The foundation of Marine Mutual was being laid, and Bobby stood in the gigantic hole, five stories deep, while around him fleets of construction trucks, dredges, and bulldozers were stacked like linebackers in some arcane defense formation. Hundreds of men were on the site, digging, shoring up the walls of the immense parking lot, and although he had been there for ten hours, eating a ham sandwich from the catering truck with the rest of the boys, he had a feeling of exhilaration.

But the great excitement for men like Bobby lay in the concept. The circle, unity itself, which would grow above this massive hole, had magical properties.

His elation was dampened when he spotted Leonard coming toward him. The harmony of his day had been disrupted. He wished Leonard would let his contractor run the job. It was a maddening relationship. Before the client accepted the design, the developer and architect would wear each other's socks. Once the deal was signed and construction began, the developer's insidious role would be revealed. He might have hired the architect and contractors, but he represented the client. On the site he became a dumb cop, woolgathering, a spy, and the men despised him.

Leonard scanned the work brusquely, armed with a set of plans he couldn't decipher. He arbitrarily interrupted a meeting with Bobby's staff of engineers and spread the plan of the substructure out on the tailgate of a Jeep that was being used as a drafting board.

"Why are you going so much wider than the original plans?" he asked. Bobby dismissed the men to spare Leonard the embarrassment.

"Ten percent sway factor. You've heard of earthquakes, haven't you? Your geologist's survey explains it. This isn't granite here. See for yourself. It's mud. Clay. And we've got to buttress it with fill."

Leonard gave him an awkward smile. "I'm running in too many directions."

Bulldozers lumbered around them, shifting mud. A developer, Bobby thought with contempt, doesn't give a shit about anything but his fees. Over and out, on to the next ruin. It would have been unthinkable for a man in any other business—computers, cars, tanks, whatever—to survive without practical knowledge. Developers were goddamn marriage brokers, nothing more, who absolved themselves of all responsibility once the client had been sold. Leonard was just a dealer in buildings, houses, shopping centers.

Give the client anything he wanted. If the guy were crazy and thought of building a hundred-foot toilet on a site, Leonard or one of his brethren would bid the job for a price and let the contractor find a way to bring it up to code. They asked no questions, except about the cost overruns and labor disputes. They played golf, went to parties, seduced potential clients, preyed on the innocent who had grandiose schemes, then hired men like Bobby and dumped these ill-shaped ideas, these misalliances between vision and economic necessity, on their laps. They didn't care and in a way they were worse than the Dunlops of the world, who at least had the ego to make a statement.

"Bobby, can I bring up a personal matter?"

"Clay isn't personal."

"Hillary is."

They walked up the steps of the site trailer and slipped into the back room. Bobby pulled a bottle of Scotch out of a cupboard. He poured two shots into cone-shaped paper cups.

"You're being very understanding about Hillary," Leonard began with difficulty. "I appreciate it."

"Yeah, well?" Bobby softened his tone. "How's she doing?"

"She s changing—for the better. There was a beautiful quality in her once, as you know," he said emotionally. "Today I saw it fighting to come out. It won't happen overnight. We have to be patient. She's been through a very rough time these past few months, Bobby."

"Are you including me?"

The phones jangled and his beeper kept up its whine.

"Hillary made her own problems. But you cared for her once, Bobby. You want to see her recover."

"Naturally," he admitted. "But I have to cut loose sooner or later. For my own sake."

Leonard lowered his eyes and seemed positively frail when he addressed Bobby again.

"I have to ask you for a favor."

"What?"

"Just visit her. She wants you to forgive her, Bobby. It'll make a tremendous difference. Jesus, I'm not asking you to try again. I don't expect that. It's just that, well . . ." he fidgeted with his tie. "It'd give her the confidence to find her way back."

It would be ignoble to crush Leonard. The man's hand was played out. He was whipped.

"I'll think about it," Bobby assured him.

"You're a damn nice guy," Leonard said, and then left.

Leonard's plea had made Bobby lose his concentration. He spent another hour at the site inspecting the foundations, then, bone-weary, returned to his apartment. Now that Claire was back in his life, part-time, inconclusively, he found himself gnawed by jealousy.

She had allowed him to stay the night at her apartment only once, on New Year's Eve, refused to go to his place except to have a drink before dinner. They'd meet at restaurants, whenever she was free. She wasn't merely independent but a law unto herself. What ate at his gut more than the time she allocated to him was the overpowering sexuality she inspired. He had become possessive and she made it clear to him that it didn't suit her. To make matters worse, she was still seeing Giovanni. He and Claire were down to once-a-week afterdinner fucks. The true horror, however, was her casual honesty. She was not playing games with him or frustrating him vindictively.

The previous night, nearing eleven with the news about to begin, they had both been in her bed, naked, relaxed, and he had rolled over, kissed her smooth, flat stomach, and indicated that he wanted her again.

"I have to be up at five to call New York, so let's make it another night."

He had not taken her at her word—he'd continued kissing her, arousing both of them until she firmly pushed him away. It had been so unexpected that he lost his temper.

"What am I, some stud you can unload whenever you get bored?"

She glared at him, her face registering indignation.

"It's my life. I'm the sole owner and proprietor. You're a guest, so act like one."

The authority she exerted over him was intolerable, objectionable, and he distrusted her. She brought a poise, knowledge to their lovemaking that robbed it of romance. In some respects, despite his satisfaction, he formed the impression that she regarded him as someone to work out with. He couldn't quite identify the sensation. He'd thrown her to the wolves—but that was over and he yearned for their old times together, which had been displaced by her rules.

"Are you expecting someone—a late date?"

"What kind of remark is that?"

"Just curious." He was dressing.

"If I was, I'd tell you about it."

"Ed drop by after he's finished at the restaurant?"

"Sometimes. Not lately."

He yanked her up from the bed, seized her by the shoulders, and shoved her against the wall.

"Are you sleeping with him too? He's a fucking guinea pimp."

She picked up her flimsy bathrobe and put it on. She was not a woman who taunted a man, but Bobby had overstepped certain boundaries. He didn't own her and his claim was from their past. She objected to being roughed up and she wanted to be sure he understood that she wouldn't stand for any bullying.

"It's my life and I do what I want with it."

He raised his hand, about to strike her, then he let it fall to his side and picked up his shoes.

"I don't remember you being so pushy or with a temper," she said from the bathroom doorway. "What're you getting so crazy for? I told you the truth. I've got to be up early."

He hated her with such passion that he thought he was capable of murdering her. She had taken away his manhood, forced him into a subservient position. She was paying him back ever so skillfully, he thought.

"Claire, you're fucking me around."

The conversation clearly bored her. "You're an ass."

"Shit, isn't there such a thing as good faith between us?"

"I thought I'd demonstrated it. You make demands like you used to. I don't know what it is with you. I'm not the girl who used to handwash the argyle socks your mother knitted. Don't you push me around."

"A fuck is a fuck?" he asked bitterly.

"Not exactly. But it's not a cataclysmic event in my life. It has a place . . . sometimes, when the mood is right, it's important. What I'm trying to tell you, Bobby, is that we're not an old married couple. You're taking too much for granted. You get what you see. I don't belong to you but to myself. We're starting from different points, so either we understand each other or let's go our separate ways. No big deal. The world isn't going to change. I see who I like and you do the same thing. Don't make this whole thing an obligation we have to live up to. No either/or, Bobby."

The fight went out of him and he came toward her with an expression of doleful acceptance.

"You're right." He kissed her and was encouraged when she squeezed him. "Want to go away for the weekend . . . just for a change of scenery?"

"If I can."

"Santa Barbara . . . we can rent a sailboat."

"I'd love to, but let's see." She walked him to the door and kissed him affectionately on the check.

26

When Madeleine read in "Who's Where" that Gene was in Hawaii, despite the fact that she could have continued working for him, she could have croaked. He was scouting locations, another snippet in the *Reporter* revealed, while for two bills a week she was unpacking Tumbleweed backpacks with names like Piggyback and Caboose, "a perfect companion for that first day at school, or exploring the wilds of the backyard. Recommended for 3- to 5-year-olds." Her exasperation peaked and she fell into her old junk-food ways—pizza, hefty falafel pouches, burgers, and burritos were mindlessly shoved into her face, making her feel even worse. Her flaccid lack of direction was a source of torment. Working in a store repelled her, even though she had opted for the Rodeo Wilderness.

Life in the fast lane of show-biz had slowed to a crawl and Madeleine grew increasingly discouraged. At the last minute, Soothe Aide did not pick up her option for further commercials and scrapped their campaign.

She persevered and found some catalogue work for a mail order outfit who thought she looked terrific in their Beautifully Big Girl bras and mistress negligees. Trapped, stymied, she went to every casting call for commercials and series in her category (young mother/career girl). Ultimately she scored with a few days' work at scale pay in a horror movie shooting in the Valley. It was the first legitimate acting job she could list on her résumé. Her head and limbs were hacked off by the film's star, a quiet, maniacal high school youth with a fetish for Black and Decker equipment. The boy appeared familiar; Madeleine finally recognized him as the pimpled youth who had made such an impression in *The Castoffs,* the TV series that had never been picked up, and who had propositioned her at Al Brockman's party. He didn't remember her and Madeleine was not about to remind him of their previous encounter.

He attacked her along with three other women at their weekly bridge game, photographed and preserved their parts in the plant he worked in, which manufactured frozen TV dinners. Her photograph, a decapitation still, was then shown several times by the detective investigating the case. Eventually an old codger recognized a plaster cast of Madeleine's head, which was hooked onto a hindquarter of baby spring lamb destined for the stew vat. So in a remote way, his favorite face, Madeleine's, led to the youth's apprehension. Some credit!

Claire had given her time off for her screen debut. In fact, her generosity toward Madeleine was the only way she recognized her old friend. Claire's energy, her ruthless determination, were like barbs, tearing Madeleine's flesh. One minute she was barking orders at carpenters installing racks and counters, electricians putting in track lighting and dimmers; the next, seeing manufacturers' reps and decisively explaining why their stuff was unsuitable; or, if she liked it, she made her order contingent on a delivery date that had to be confirmed by the factory. She wasn't going to tie her money up and be stuck waiting for merchandise.

At the end of the day, when she and Claire left the store, Claire insisted on a walk up Rodeo, pausing at every window to check on any changes, then she would return for a final examination of Rodeo Wilderness. The store had the clean flowing lines that Bobby had captured in his design. The progress never failed to excite Claire. It was their creation.

"Claire, I have to talk to you."

"I understand what you're going through. Working with me isn't permanent . . . you're just helping me out until—"

"Until when?" Madeleine grimaced. "Oh, Claire, it's worse than ever. Now that I have an agent, a SAG card and I've actually worked, it's harder on me than it was before. Auditions, calls, readings, phone calls . . . and it ends up by me being turned down. I don't know how strong my stomach is any more. The rejections are just unspeakable. I know I shouldn't take them personally but there's always some goddamn reason why I'm not right. My tits are too big, my face is wrong, they don't like my smile, I don't project properly, they want a different type or any number of reasons. But the real agony is when no one bothers to explain. My agent just says, 'They passed.' That's it. And I'm back in the store trying to figure out what the fuck they want from my life."

She persuaded Claire to spend the evening with her and although there was a pile of letters stacked up requiring answers, Claire couldn't refuse. Returning to Madeleine's house was like finding herself in a time warp, familiar but strange, and Claire found it difficult to recognize herself in these surroundings. The room she'd slept in was small, cramped, filled with Gene's photographic equipment and cartons of girlie magazines. The temperature had dropped, rains were coming, and Dr. George, the eccentric personality weatherman on Eyewitness News, recommended sandbags for hillside residents due to the incipient danger of mudslides.

Madeleine lit a fire while Claire opened a bottle of Soave.

"I can't tell you how much I appreciate your being here." Madeleine's nights were oppressive. Without Gene to lash out at her, discuss his work and her indefinite prospects, she was foundering, wretched, cut off.

"Come on."

Madeleine had developed, late in life, a culinary skill that astounded Claire. She could make an omelette. Gene liked them and had bought one of those foolproof pans that a seven-year-old could operate. The cheese and green onion omelettes came out perfectly and they ate them on trays in front of the fireplace. Madeleine's mood of despondency persisted. In some respects, she reflected, neither of them had changed since their early time in Westport. But here they were, a dozen years later, sitting in the Hollywood Hills without husbands, children, or determinable futures.

"You dug a hole for yourself," Claire said. "I don't see why you didn't go to Hawaii with Gene. Isn't it a little late to discover artistic integrity or whatever the hell it is?"

Madeleine didn't want to hear this. "I thought I was breaking through on my own. The worst thing that happened was I developed some self-respect—not artistic integrity. I don't even know what that means. Now I don't bother with acting class and I've stopped calling Sue at ICM. Maybe I don't really believe in myself . . . all the ranting I did when you lived here was a performance. When I got a shot with a few commercials I thought I'd never stop working and then, to find out I was nowhere without Gene . . . it was like cutting my legs off. I had to show myself I had some dignity." She shook her head forlornly, fought back tears, which had been threatening for weeks. "I'm twenty-four years old and I can't tell you what I've been through since I met Gene and things started to *happen*." Lately she'd been having nightmares about her hardcore loop. "Claire, when I was working for Gucci, I could dream, play games with myself, tell myself I had inner motivation. God, I've been rehearsing Academy Award speeches since I was fifteen, for Chrissake. Well, I am a dreamer. I always have been. But it's a void. This is *Hollywood*. It's full of shit and all the people are dreamers, drifters, some bigtime but mostly peasants like me who bullshit at Joe Allen's bar."

Claire vainly tried to reason with Madeleine but she was so down on herself that nothing could dent the fortress in which her depression was imprisoned. This was no self-pitying act. Madeleine had discovered the gruesome truth about herself, about making it, and it neither elevated her nor established a path of freedom.

"I'll probably go back to New York and jack around off-Broadway. I'll wind up in the East Village with some kid who'll screw my brains out and then throw my clothes out the window when he finds someone who'll boost his career." She was not far off the mark. It had happened to her before. But Claire couldn't imagine Madeleine returning to that lifestyle, any more than she could see herself back at Drake's.

At ten, while they were doing the dishes, the phone rang. Madeleine ignored it, told Claire to forget it. It rang a dozen times, then started again. Then again. Claire finally picked it up.

It was Gene, shrieking infernally from Hawaii. Where was that lowlife bitch? Claire held the receiver away from her ear.

"It's your lover, reciting Browning."

"He's so rank. Hang up," Madeleine said, slipping into her *Long Goodbye* debutante voice.

"Madeleine, I'm not an answering service. You hang up on him." Gene's threatening, raucous voice crackled through the room with maniacal curses.

Madeleine stared at Claire, then plodded to the phone apprehensively. Claire tried to block out the droning, agonized sound of Madeleine's protests, the repeated refusals, the remorse in her eyes. She impetuously hung up. A moment later the phone renewed its relentless ringing. Claire persuaded Madeleine to be reasonable, forced her to speak to him.

"Madeleine, I've got a yeast infection on my balls, herpes on my cock, ticks in my ears from the cunts out here."

"Nuke the sharks, Gene. I'm not inheriting your diseases."

"I've booked you on the one A.M. American five-six-three. And I got ABC to approve you."

"Why didn't Al or anyone call me?"

"They're probably at Ma Maison holding Ray Stark's hand or something important. Now, do what I tell you or I'll fix your ass real good."

"How?"

"I'll screen your loop at the Adult Film Festival." She thought she'd faint, wavered on her feet. "Madeleine, ABC loves my dailies and I forced a fight with the actress they pushed on me. She's been fired. You're getting twelve thousand dollars for this and an 'Introducing' billing."

"Have you really got the clap?" she asked vaguely.

"Yeah, a one-handed one. Now, I'll pick you up at the airport . . . Be there, scrubber . . ."

Claire helped her to pack. Madeleine was in no condition to drive. She cleaned out her purse—sixty-three dollars—and put the basket case in a taxi for LAX.

"It's on to greatness," Claire said, amused.

"If the script's any good," Madeleine replied moodily, then hugged her.

The moment Leonard saw the hypnotic, commanding eyes of the man sitting on his bed, he knew that he was face to face with Geraldo. Leonard's chest tightened. He thought he might have a heart attack. The evening had started so pleasantly. Hillary had called him from the clinic, then he attended one of a series of cocktail parties the Dunlops had organized for Rodeo Wilderness.

Geraldo motioned him to sit on a chair opposite the bed. Leonard thought of speaking, defending himself in some way, but the profound calm of the man's face destroyed his will. It was like coming face to face with some silent jungle beast. Geraldo moved closer to him until their faces were mere inches away.

"Hillary is pregnant with my child." Leonard nodded. "Where is she?"

"I'm sorry to be the one to tell you that she had a miscarriage three weeks ago." He had a newfound respect for Hillary's judgment. If Geraldo became suspicious, he was dead.

"How did it happen?" Geraldo rubbed his hands sorrowfully, then a sudden impassiveness took over his face.

"She came back from the beach. I hadn't seen her for ages. She never bothered to get in touch with me. You must know that," Leonard rambled nervously. "Her husband was suing her for divorce. The miscarriage . . . it must have been from the drugs she'd been taking . . ."

Geraldo seemed bored, dissatisfied with the answer. He angrily stalked around Leonard's bedroom. His fury gave way to resignation, which was even more harrowing. Leonard licked his lips nervously.

"Where is she?"

"In a private clinic."

"I'm going to see her."

"Can I ask the doctor if she can have visitors?"

"No, you can't," Geraldo said peremptorily. "I don't need anyone's permission, Mr. Martinson. You take me there tomorrow. You keep your word with me and you won't have any problems."

Geraldo backed against the windowsill, perched on the edge. He wore tight black jeans and a coarse blue turtleneck sweater; there was a grotesque handsomeness about him. His face had a violent insecurity, which Leonard chose to ignore. Judging from the powerful upper structure, he might have been an athlete gone to ruin. But the eyes were vulpine, untrusting. Leonard felt a gradual return of his strength. He'd see how the man played poker, deciding that Geraldo might back down if he were raised.

"Are you threatening me? I've got friends in the police, the FBI, the D.A.'s office . . ."

Geraldo shook his head sadly. He might have been one of those secret police torturers whose atrocities one read about in the papers. "I thought this would be straight, man to man, but you're trying to pull shit with me." He sighed despairingly. Then he pulled a long thin metal coil from his back pocket and laid it across Leonard's shoulders like a snake. "That's a piano wire. You ever mention cop and I'll wrap this around your neck and while you're still breathing, I'll personally pour gasoline on you and light a match. Right here, in your fucking bedroom." Leonard's eyes protruded as if this torture was already taking place. "I'll be here tomorrow night at six o'clock and we'll see Hillary together." Geraldo's shoulders slumped forward. He walked to the door with lowered head. Before he left the room, Leonard heard him mutter disconsolately, *"Mi niño—mi niño se murió."*

The weather had been foul in L.A. all through February. Driving rain storms blanketed the city and after the summer fires, unseeded hillsides collapsed, unleashing violent walls of mud that cascaded down, destroying homes, washing out roads, creating a besieged helplessness among people. It was as though nature had been disturbed and settled a plague on the city.

Bobby had lost days of work in these conditions, but the foundations were at last laid on Marine Mutual. When he dropped in on Claire at the store, he was decidedly uneasy, fearing that something would come up that would prevent her from leaving town. She was in the rear of the store on her knees, unpacking goods. She'd hired a few women to press garments. The air was filled with the hiss of steam irons and the skylights were pounded by furious rains.

"They're not leaking," she said, looking up and smiling.

The barnwood paneling had been hammered in with rusted nails she'd bought in Bishop. Carpenters had installed the display cases, coaxed the rustic wooden clothes racks into place. Bobby climbed a ladder to the gallery, spoke to a carpenter aligning storage cabinets. The floor had no sway and would pass a code inspection.

"You're early," Claire said. She hadn't seen him since their blowup. Married or not, the bond between them was permanent. If they could only reach an understanding that allowed her to function unfettered by his conventional notions. He still didn't appreciate how deeply she was committed to making a name for herself.

"The scaffolding's being unloaded at Marine and nothing's going to happen till the beginning of next week," he said.

He cast an appraising eye at the entryway and shouted down to the mason. "It's too symmetrical. Slop-joint it. Man, these bricks weren't manufactured yesterday." Nothing in the store ought to appear too smooth. The image he sought was the antithesis of the fussy, overdressed street. He paid attention to small details.

"At times I wonder why you bother with the store. Your work's done."

"What the hell. It's for you. Frank may have put up the money, but you're my client."

At times there was such a luminous charm about Bobby that she fought to resist. With so much to do, it was impossible for her to go away for the weekend. She didn't quite know how she was going to beg off.

"What time will you be ready?" he asked as she accompanied him to the front. He noticed her avert her eyes. "Windy, but the storm isn't due till Tuesday. I managed to rent us a catamaran for both days. We can sail to Santa Rosa through the Santa Barbara channel. I hear it's an incredible trip. There's a wildlife sanctuary . . ."

"I don't know."

She walked with him to his car. The wind threshed her hair. She put an arm around his waist.

"I thought we had a date. I made a reservation at the Biltmore."

"I've got staff interviews tomorrow—beginning at seven. People are coming in from all over. I can't stand them up."

A melancholy anger, almost censure, seized him. "You've done a wonderful job kicking my ass . . . I'm grateful. We'll always be friends. But somehow or other you've lost sight of where you are. You're caught up in all the bullshit of Rodeo Drive. Maybe I'm the wrong one to tell you, but, babe, you don't know what's important any more. One weekend isn't a matter of life or death. Claire, I'm going."

The rich vein of guilt that existed between them had a reciprocal quality. Lately, she had experienced an almost nightmarish humiliation because she had come to the conclusion that she was the stronger. Still clinging to him was the blemished innocence that touched her at the deepest emotional level. Maybe it was the way he carried himself, or the knowledge that he had never stopped loving her. She floundered, incapable of resolving the conflict between the career she wanted and defining the position he'd assigned to her. There was nothing demeaning about marrying him but, somehow, becoming his wife—or anyone else's at this stage—was a demotion. She saw nothing ignoble about succeeding, recognizing an opportunity, exploiting it. She was human, she had a hunger to be recognized, and she knew that she'd never be happy with him until she had established herself.

"You're one of them now," he said contemptuously.

"People change," she said wistfully, "not always for the better."

He stood beside his Honda. She'd never seen a dirtier car. Of course, he was always outside. He disliked offices, routine, haggling. For a man with such remarkable physical attributes, he was surprisingly antisocial. He had always been a loner. He had formed no close male emotional alliances since college. He was possessed by a vision of himself as a titan of architecture and this made him unhappy and dissatisfied with himself—and naturally with Claire. All of this flashed through her mind when he got into the car, started the engine.

"I'll try to make it. Suppose I meet you for lunch tomorrow at the hotel . . . I need the morning here, Bobby. I can't help it. Marv's also bringing some stuff he bought at an auction for me. He says there's no limit to what they could sell for."

"What's the matter with you, Claire? You sound so goddamn greedy," he said disgustedly.

Leonard nervously went to the Steinway grand sitting in the corner of the living room. He put his highball on the piano and sat, tinkling the keys, remembering when he and Hillary used to play duets and sing at the top of their voices or hammer the piano playing "Chopsticks." His finger hit a dead key and he stiffened involuntarily. He walked to the side of the piano and gingerly lifted the lid. A wire had been severed.

It was one thing to be outfoxed in a business deal by Frank Dunlop, and quite another to have a man threaten him in his own home. The image of the long piece of piano wire Geraldo had dangled in front of him was horrific. That people like Geraldo actually existed and could snuff him out in an instant petrified him.

Hillary had explored the lower depths and emerged with a demon. She had gone too far. At the same time, Leonard knew he would never again be given an opportunity like this. He could save his daughter, form an unbreakable alliance with her. What complicated the situation was the native intelligence Geraldo had revealed. It was raw, untutored but effective. Leonard had always been a clever talker. Perhaps there was some way he could persuade Geraldo to give her up. He fingered the Chippendale table alongside his chair and groped for a cigarette in the gold filigree box. As he was about to light it, he had a shuddering awareness of a presence behind him. He was afraid to turn. Yet he could not afford to behave as though nothing were wrong. He moved his head slightly. Looming before him, wearing a respectable blue business suit and a wide silk tie, was Geraldo. He looked like an office manager, a petty bureaucrat, the organizer of typing pools. Leonard emitted a short grunt.

"How . . . ?"

Geraldo came toward him and Leonard flinched, anticipating a blow.

"The same way as last night," Geraldo said, as though explaining the facts of life to a child. "I met Hillary when you were redoing the guesthouse," he said. "She was some piece of work but I never came on to her," he added, governed by a singular propriety that puzzled Leonard. "I was a cat burglar when I was ten and at fourteen I organized my first gang. I cut a hole through your cyclone fence the other night, then covered it with the ivy. The alarm wires are obvious. For it to go off, you'd have to be robbed by amateurs. No way to keep me out," he explained academically. "I went to prep school at Soledad and graduated from Duell. You want any advice about protecting your joint here," Leonard's putative son-in-law continued, "I'd be happy to tell you. Can't be too careful. Ready to go?"

Leonard tortured a smile to his face. "You don't have much respect for fine things."

"Just Hillary."

"Let me offer you a drink then. It's the least I can do. I've got some Mortlach—a malt Scotch. It's as pale as Manzanilla."

Geraldo nodded warily. "Go. You're a smart man. No cops."

"How do you know?"

"My people've been around here since this morning."

Leonard laughed unwittingly. "And are my staff all dead?"

"No. They're cooking up a storm in the kitchen and watching TV."

Leonard went to the small corner bar and poured a shot in a graceful pony glass.

"It's meant to be drunk straight. You can taste the peat."

Geraldo extended his palm gracefully. It was such an incongruous aristocratic gesture that Leonard was rewarded with a sense of confidence. The tension slowly dissolved. A man acting as host, providing his guest with the best of his bar stock, would not be trussed up with his own piano wire. Yes, there might be a basis of negotiation, he thought, so long as he maintained his composure.

"Please sit down." There was a velvet lime green Empire couch with a carved back; it had been recovered since Hillary's wedding. Geraldo looked at it suspiciously, then moved to it, sat down delicately, crossing his legs.

"I don't understand. I've threatened you. Doesn't it worry you?"

"We have something in common. We both love Hillary and we want to do what's best for her. Her marriage was a washout"—Geraldo's dark eyes indicated assent—"which was a pity. It was one of those things that look good on paper—at least to her it did. Hillary can be overpowering. But sometimes she acts without thinking of the consequences." Geraldo remained taciturn and appeared to be considering these observations. "How much do you actually know about Hillary?"

Geraldo was embarrassed. Society, manners, confused him. He was being accorded respect and he felt that he had done Leonard who, after all, was his *novia*'s father, a grave injustice. But it was his way. In his world, people responded only after intimidation and it was Geraldo's custom to locate the center, then enforce his demands. Nothing was more valuable than one's life. It was an unchanging article of faith that he had learned in prison and on the streets: People fell in with him when he made it clear that he would stamp them out. This foreign society operated on a different level and he was intrigued by Leonard's graciousness. He had taken Geraldo seriously. Leonard raised his glass.

"To Hillary."

"To Hillary," Geraldo repeated. "You asked what I know about her. I love her. I want to marry her as soon as this divorce garbage is over. I would like her to have my children. I will protect her."

Leonard nodded approvingly, suppressed a sigh.

"It's good to know that there are still men around who believe in old-fashioned notions like that."

Geraldo was disconcerted. He'd acted like a savage and he was dealing with a prince, a man who accepted him as an equal and whose manner disarmed him.

"We think alike," Geraldo suggested, claiming a kinship that Leonard did not disavow.

"Hillary stole another woman's man and when she imagined he didn't love her enough or there was divided loyalty, she cracked," he said miserably. "She had these problems, even as a girl." Geraldo listened, spellbound. "Then she found you. I wasn't completely sure—after we lost contact —if she lived with you just to spite Bobby, or maybe it was to punish me. You understand, don't you?"

"Yes," Geraldo said wearily. "But maybe she lived with me because she loves me, do you understand that? And, of course, the drugs. That's my business. Pills, coke, even dust—whatever she wanted. Before I left, she was smoking freebase. I could have prevented her, but it meant hurting her, locking her in a room. Humiliate her, beat her? She loves me, as I do her. I know the drugs were not the entire reason she stayed with me, but she'd walk through fire for some blow."

"We're in complete agreement then," Leonard replied. "The clinic she's in is helping. Hillary's been clean for almost a month. If she sees you now, she'll get emotionally upset."

"Then when can I see her?"

"Soon."

"That's not good enough, Mr. Martinson."

"Next week."

Geraldo nodded. "You just made a deal. Don't forget."

27

The traffic jam from the mud slides along the Pacific Coast Highway stretched for four miles and Claire was at her wit's end crawling along. She should have taken the Ventura Freeway but the prospect of driving along the ocean on such a fine day was too seductive. She had forgotten about the devastation caused by the storms. She couldn't even cut through Topanga Canyon to get to the freeway because the damage had been even greater there and the road had been washed out.

She wouldn't let go of Bobby without one final effort. She just didn't seem to do anything right when the two of them were together. Her strength caused antagonism between them.

She reached the Biltmore after two. A few people lingered over coffee on the terrace. Bobby was not there, nor in his room, and no message had been left for her. She wondered if she ought to wait for him or drive back to L.A. He had registered them as husband and wife, and the card she was shown with his signature had an eerie, taunting sang-froid.

She was shown to their room, a small suite with a fireplace, in the main building, which overlooked the beach. She changed into jeans and a windbreaker and stood for a few minutes on the balcony, watching the sailboats jibbing, seesawing in the blustery wind. The sailing conditions were perfect. She decided to drive over to the club and wait it out with Bloody Marys.

Bobby had signed out at ten in the morning and she sat on the pier, squinting in the sunlight, hoping he hadn't sailed to the island. She realized that he had a legitimate grievance. She had made a choice . . . Rodeo Wilderness had taken precedence over her personal life. She wished at times that she could revert to her former self, compliant and filled with girlish passion for him. All he had to do was snap his fingers and she'd be there. It was an easier and in many ways more sympathetic arrangement. But she feared that her capacity for yielding to Bobby could never be regained.

There were changes in herself that she did not entirely approve of, but she was incapable of altering the conditions that had forced her to recreate herself. She had a business to build, an opportunity that would never again present itself. She knew that she still wanted Bobby, but it would have to be on her terms, and they would be dictated by the time she had available. Giovanni had understood her situation and was waiting it out.

Claire left a message for Bobby with a steward at the club and wandered down to the beach. A cold wind howled, blowing sand into her face. The joy of being on the beach compensated for any momentary discomfort. She pulled her windbreaker closer around her and felt totally free of responsibilities or the decisions confronting her. She had, she knew, fallen head over heels in love with California and hoped that one day she could afford a place at the beach; even if she fell short of her ideal financially, she had the prospect of independence at her fingertips. She had made a life for herself and she was not prepared to give it up.

"It's a selfish world," she told herself, "and I'm part of it, flowing with it." She sat on the sand, watching the yawls, ketches, and cats gliding low with full sail beyond the channel. In a way she wasn't sorry she'd missed Bobby, for she had come to cherish these private solitary times when nothing was expected of her. The curl of the waves, the hum of the wind, the absence of demands, no one to talk to, relaxed her.

At about four, she located Bobby in the club bar. There was a hurt, saturnine expression on his face. He had come in an hour before. She sat down alongside him.

"You finally made it." He sounded peeved, as though she'd stood him up.

"Don't make a guilt trip out of this."

He ordered a drink for her, played with a cigarette pack somebody had left, declined cheese and crackers offered by the bartender and shook his head angrily.

"You screwed up my day . . . I suppose you've got to leave at eight tomorrow morning." She didn't take the bait and remained silent. She fondly touched his ear with her finger. "Claire, what the hell is it with you?"

"I got here when I could."

"Where'd you go?"

"Just sat on the beach. There wasn't much else to do."

"Did you freeze your ass off?"

"Not as much as you did out on the water." She smiled gently at him. "I see I finally made it as Mrs. Canaday in California—unofficially, of course."

He realized that she wasn't out for blood. "Aren't you impressed?"

"Well, it was sort of déjà vu. It reminded me of a lot of weekends we had before. Motels," she added without enthusiasm. "The Biltmore's an improvement over our bottle of Relska, setups, ice from the floor machine, three towels, no maid, plastic rooms, plus dinner at the local roast beef emporium."

"Did you hate them—all those times?"

She decided against hedging. "I didn't know any better. I wanted to hop into bed with you and wake up as your wife. You never used to talk about *us,* just about all the hack work you were being forced to do at the office and the skyscrapers you were destined to build. So here we are." She laughed at herself. "Life's been just great, hasn't it?"

"All this resentment. Why'd you bother coming in the first place?"

"Just because you don't understand me doesn't mean I don't love you."

He smiled, relieved that he could still inspire her with feelings he'd feared that she had abandoned.

"It's different, though, isn't it?" There was a desolate power in his face, the pellucid blue eyes, the flat nose, his tousled, streaky blond hair. He was the best looking man she'd ever seen. Adversity merely emphasized the glory of his looks and she never lost sight of the radiant ingenuousness he displayed because he never thought much about his physical attributes and was indeed modest about them. "I wish to hell we could go back to what we were . . ."

"Come on. Let's get room service to bring up some drinks—and make love."

The suggestion was agreeable. He paid the bar bill and she followed him back to the hotel.

They always seemed to be in different cars, she thought, when she parked behind him. She walked to the embankment next to the hotel. The sun was low, a molten orange ball dropping into a cast-iron sheet of water, a planet on fire. He took her arm. They kissed and she felt the tyranny of her passion for him returning, then she shook it off. He was just a man, a mortal who made mistakes, lived with regrets. They were no longer people drifting but caught in the currents of competition, and she too wished for those simple elements that had been part of their common experience.

He ordered a bottle of champagne while she set some logs in the fireplace. There was such warmth in his smile when she lighted the fire that the moment she was off her knees, she threw her arms around him and kissed him. The conflicts separating them dissolved and they came together with spontaneous ease. Smoky blue fumes of dusky light filled the sky and with the crackling fire resounding, she knew she could never again love anyone as she did him.

He led her to the bed, held her hands in his and she leaned her head on his shoulder. He filled their glasses with champagne and asked if they should make a toast. She was caught up in the moment. A spirit of renewal, a belief in their future together, filled her mind. She didn't know how to respond and she broke the slender thread of romance.

"I'm not sure I believe in toasts anymore."

She hadn't intended to rattle him. He frowned and the spark left his face.

"Broken promises, right?"

"I didn't mean it to come out that way."

"It doesn't matter."

She despised herself for forcing him to retreat. Against her natural bent she'd become a bully.

"I love you, Bobby, but I can't seem to say anything right."

"Don't worry about it, babe. It'll take time before you trust me again. I'm prepared." He stretched out on the bed and she pressed against him. He toyed with her hair and they smiled awkwardly at each other. They seemed to be sharing a belated honeymoon without benefit of marriage but there was a barrier of irresolution that held them apart.

"Do you think once the store's open and you've got it running, that you could get away for a few weeks?"

"I'm not sure. Why?"

"Oh, you know me. I can't resist competitions and there was one in an architectural journal last month that I entered."

She looked at him, thoroughly bewildered.

"I don't follow you."

"Well, I've always been an admirer of Basil Spence's Cathedral at Coventry and, well, Claire, to get right to the heart of it, the University of Hull in England is planning to build a chapel and they invited applicants without nationality restrictions." She reached for the champagne and sat up, unnerved. "They've invited me to an interview and I thought, whether I get the commission or not, we could spend a few weeks in Europe and I could get to see what they're doing there."

She was incredulous and she strained to contain her disappointment. "You'd leave Hayward?"

"Well, you don't think I want to spend my life doing office buildings . . . and stores."

"But, Bobby, I don't understand. You've got everything in the palm of your hand."

"Really? Hey, getting rich in Beverly Hills and designing boutiques on Rodeo Drive isn't my idea of a challenge. You think I'm the sort of guy who's going to be hustling at the Bistro or Le Restaurant every day with guys like Dunlop and Leonard?"

She was shaken. They had not merely drifted apart, they lived in different worlds, isolated from each other. She observed a dreamy, faraway look in his eyes. "If you get this—chapel—would you expect me to go to Hull with you?"

"Naturally. By then the divorce would've come through."

"Honey, you're throwing everything away, chasing rainbows."

"No, I'm not," he said firmly. "It's just that I think there's something very wrong in a place where a decent four-bedroom house goes for half a million dollars plus and where people can spend four hundred bucks for a sweater." He began to laugh uproariously. "And everyone thinks it normal." He waited for her to react, but she decided to hear him out.

"Claire, this is you and me and it's real life. The Spanish house I finished on Alpine . . . Leonard cleared more than a million. I'm not pretending to be a moralist, but it's all getting out of hand and I don't like being a part of transactions like this. It offends me. I won't even go into the kind of profits involved in building Marine Mutual. They were stuck for a design and I came up with one that Frank Dunlop, who doesn't know his ass from a hole in the wall, approved! He thinks the sun rises and sets on me now. So the possibility of doing a chapel in a university doesn't exactly demean me. What's wrong with designing a place of worship? Big bucks aren't involved except for the donors, and if they hire me, I'll break my back trying to create something beautiful instead of making the rich richer in Beverly Hills."

She was bewildered by the vehemence of his argument, the contempt, the detestation he held for what in effect were her goals. She refused to give in.

"Can't we both be right?"

"How?"

He had lighted a cigarette, rolled over on his side. She caught a glimpse of his white, almost diaphanous skin. Imagine, he had not had a chance to sun himself for almost a year except today when he'd been out sailing. The charm and beauty of California had turned sour for him.

"What's wrong with opening a store on the most exclusive street in the country, selling people something I believe they'll buy and, with luck, building a national chain of stores? Was selling junk at Drake's, pretending that a twenty-two dollar dress we bought for ten at a job lot was high fashion? I want to give people what they think they want and I hope to God I'm right. You make it sound like a crime."

He rubbed her cheek lovingly and kissed the tip of her nose.

"I hadn't thought about it, but I guess you're right."

She was filled with uncertainty; the blood rushed to her face. She wished she could reach out, get inside his soul, reveal the practical side of human affairs.

"You're suggesting that there's something wrong with making a success out of myself."

"No, not at all. It's what the people out here stand for. The emphasis on money is like no place else in the world. For me it's being a fashionable architect, courting clients, being well-liked, making more and more connections, living behind walls, insulated from everything that goes on in the lives of real people. That's what's bugging me. Le Corbu once told a group of students that bad architects hide all their mistakes behind elaborate facades. You're going to be selling things to those people . . . I feel good about the design I did for you, babe, but I wouldn't do it again . . . Claire," he said with the soft guile of someone who has found a place for optimism and is prepared to be unrepentant about his decision, "I want out."

There seemed to be a willful, self-destructive element to his idealism that was not amenable to emotional persuasion. He was almost twenty-nine, he had designed a major office building and could write his own ticket, and he was turning his back on it. She had a vision of him returning to a college environment and she remembered all those evenings when she came in to Manhattan to meet him after class at the New School. What had possessed him to teach non-credit adult education courses to a mixed bag of people who wanted to learn something but could do nothing about the way they lived? He'd been a wonderful teacher, sympathetic, humorous, and informative, and yet he knew that he was not about to light any spirits and that he was an apostle without honor, anonymous. If ever a man was worth loving and suffering for, he was that man, and she embraced him with such affection and enchantment that she thought her heart would break.

"What're you crying about? Don't tell me I've hurt you."

"You just make me cry." She slipped under the covers

and looked at his old sneakers, cutoffs, and the gray underwear that men who use laundromats wind up with and she wanted to assume all of those domestic caring concerns a loving wife develops when a couple is able to remain lovers and not have to defend their rights. They were past that sort of thing, clinging together like tarred flotsam washed up on a beach after a shipwreck.

She wiped her eyes with the corner of the sheet. His hand spread out on her belly and in the shadows it looked like a fern.

"Claire, come with me. It'll be a new beginning for us." He didn't understand any of her motives or her desires, and there was a childlike hope in his eyes that moved her. "You can get out." He described pub dinners, the digs they'd find, the way they'd bum around Europe like kids. They'd buy a Mini and be able to get fifty miles to the gallon. They'd visit museums, take side trips to Venice and Florence. He'd recently reread Ruskin's *Stones of Venice* and he'd teach her all she needed to know about the Venetian Renaissance.

"Stop!" She could tolerate it no longer. "You're daydreaming." His brow furrowed and there were fine wrinkles like calligraphy scriven on his pale skin.

"Don't you love me?"

"Too much," she asserted. He embraced her, felt her trembling. "We're headed in different directions, don't you see?"

"It's not too late to change."

"Oh, Bobby, I can't stand it. You're killing me."

They had dinner at a place called the Olive Mill and after the waiter rattled off the endless number of specials, fresh catches, they ordered and sat in silence. A wistful smile played across his mouth and they found themselves drinking too many cocktails without gaiety. Memories of other dinners at Peter's Backyard in the Village flooded back to her and she grieved, yearning for those evenings when she could share his thoughts, encourage his plans, support the reckless visions he had designed for them. But now it was different. She could no longer humor him at the expense of her own destiny. She could barely touch the sea bass and picked indifferently at some French fries just to do something with her hands.

"Couldn't you try to see things from my point of view?" she asked.

"I have," he observed kindly. "But I can't let myself get caught again. It'll destroy me."

They had coffee and a couple of brandies. The intensity of her suffering astonished her. If she could only make him realize what was at stake, that rather than selling out he would be in a position to become the master builder he had envisioned. Yet some compulsion drove him to give it all up and drag her into some indefinite future where they would be scrabbling for money and his reputation would elude him again. There was about him, she had begun to see, a tragic self-renunciation of which he was unaware. He'd come to California desperate for a job and found himself thrust into the center of power and he was prepared to walk away, lurch toward the unknown, obscurity. In all the time they'd been together, it had never dawned on her that he was reaching for a goal he could not define.

"You're an artist. The real thing," she said, gazing at him.

"You sound surprised."

"You enjoy being unhappy," she accused him. "You'll never be satisfied with your work."

"That's the attraction."

"Bobby, you're crazy."

"Not crazy enough—yet. When I am, I'll be able to do great work," he said carelessly as though it were just a matter of time. The image he had of himself was so heedlessly romantic, so filled with the anguish of achievement, falling short, starting over again, that she found herself flabbergasted by the callous innocence of his scheme.

"You're courting failure."

"Not in so many words." His face shone with anticipation. "But look what a challenge a chapel would be, provided I get the commission."

"And if you don't?"

"Something else'll turn up and it won't be a Savings and Loan squatting in the middle of nowhere."

"You want me to sweat it out with you—just airily dismiss the chance I've got."

"There's nothing wrong in taking risks, is there? If I ever get really desperate or bust out, I can come back, point to my triumph in Century City and grind out shitboxes. What have I got to lose? There'll always be a place like Hayward's and cranky millionaires like Frank. Or I could start my own firm and build townhouses at a marina somewhere. California's loaded with them. I just have to look at what they're putting up along the coast and in Santa Barbara to know that I can do it better." He paused, kissed her hand. "Let's roll the dice and see how we do."

"Mysteries."

"Of course."

They walked back to the hotel listening to the roar of waves, freedom, infinity, the thunder of primal forces. Claire had a perception of how deeply he was committed, pushing himself, pulling her along in the riptide of his adventures. He renounced security, deplored success, and turned her world upside down. Either she had to share his obsessions or destroy them, because if she let go of him now there would always be something missing, something left undone, a hazy insecurity and a straining to hear the faint distant bell reminding her that in rejecting him, she had lost all that was truly valuable.

There was an inconsolable ache within her when they got close under the covers, their naked bodies entwined, the whisper of his warm breath on her neck. She had the sinking realization that they would both stand their ground, and in a short time he would vanish like a wreath of smoke.

She always responded to his touch, the delicate almost puzzled way he explored her body that was unconsciously erotic. She was no longer the captive and she wanted to push forward with him, the two of them charting each other's progress through a tough dynamic society. It was madness to run away, toss it aside for the amorphous quest he wanted to pursue.

"Bobby, don't leave me again," she pleaded.

"We'll go together," he replied, responding to his own voices. "I don't want to be without you."

She couldn't go on, gave herself to the moment, the thoughtless clash of bodies. His erection pressed hot between her thighs and she had a presage of the agony she'd suffer when Bobby was gone and there would be another man beside her in bed. The prospect was unendurable.

"Let's think about it, please," she said, clasping his face to her breasts and enjoying the sound of his breathing, his closeness, the unique stamp of the man trying to force her to reshape her life again. They'd both gambled and won and now he was ready to leave his chips at the table.

When she drove off alone the following morning, she was left with the image of Bobby still asleep in bed, finally at peace with himself. And for that matter, the burden of her choice no longer assailed her.

There was a spacious visiting room at the end of Melody Park's dining hall. Visitors were not permitted to see patients in their rooms. Amid the flock of well-heeled, mostly middle-aged wives visiting their wrecked, anxiety-ridden husbands who had flipped out, and the distinguished, concerned captains of industry assuring their aging, drying-out wives of eternal devotion and love, Geraldo fit in surprisingly well. He looked like one of those discreetly dressed gorillas employed by the establishment to attend to assaults that sometimes occurred when a washed-out, bleary-eyed former executive vice president on sick leave learned that his wife thought that he could take the news that she was divorcing him to marry the BMW salesman with whom she'd been carrying on for nine years.

The visitors, Leonard thought, would certainly think that Geraldo was on the staff and placed in the room to prevent any negative reactions from husbands so informed.

Hillary came through the patients' doorway wearing jeans and a pale blue cashmere sweater. Although she wore no makeup, she radiated good health. She was rested, her eyes clear, and there was a confident attitude in the way she carried herself. She hadn't used any drugs or touched liquor for over a month. She slept well each night, read and watched TV, cooperated with Dr. Parks who visited her five days a week and reported to Leonard that he was convinced that a new person was about to emerge. Hillary had cast off her rebellious ideas and she was eager to do something with her life. She had suggested returning to interior designing but this time properly building a career. Music to Leonard's ears. She was convinced that her prospects for the future had never been brighter. She wanted to succeed.

A lambent smile crossed her lips when Leonard waved to her from the sofa beside the garden windows. She hadn't yet seen Geraldo. Leonard embraced her and the warmth between them was genuine.

"I left the books and magazines you wanted in the car. I'll get them before I go."

The smile on her face froze and an expression of utter desolation came over her when Geraldo turned away from the window and confronted her. He extended his hands and stalked toward her.

"He insisted on coming. You were right. There was no way I could refuse."

"It's okay. I'll handle it. I think I'd better see him alone."

"I'm here if you need me."

She met Geraldo before he reached them and inclined her head toward the garden. There were several patients strolling with family members. Geraldo took hold of her arm, and Leonard had a sinking sensation as this force beyond his control exerted itself, crushing him.

It had rained earlier that day and the lawn was sodden, patched with mud in spots. The sky was mottled with umber-gray clouds that hung low on the horizon and gusts of wind blew Hillary's hair into her eyes. They might have been a million miles from the life they'd known.

"You're not glad to see me," Geraldo said when they stopped by a corral fence. Some of the patients rode and enjoyed the therapy of working in the stables or tending to the vegetable gardens in the fields beyond.

She knew Geraldo well enough to avoid compromising her position. Any sign of weakness would be seized upon and wreck her plan to escape from him.

"It's over," she said firmly. "You left me to go to Fresno when I was pregnant. I'm not going back with you."

He had never imagined that such a forceful side of Hillary could emerge from the quirky, drug-hungry woman he had loved. Rather than being put off, he was impressed by the new steadiness he found within her.

"The separation's been a good thing. The atmosphere wasn't good for you. You didn't have me to lean on and we can come together as equals now. If you think I liked watching you blowing an eighth of coke a day, taking pills—you're wrong. I gave in to you because you were in trouble and your weakness was more than a match for me." He gripped her hard and swiveled her around so that they were facing each other. "Now, what happened to the baby?"

"I lost it. I started to hemorrhage. I had no place to go."

His mouth curled scornfully and he stared at her so truculently that she backed off.

"Whenever I deal with your kind of people, they imagine I'm some dumb Chicano who'll swallow anything you tell him. Don't you know better by now? Suppose I just visit the doctor who saw you . . . and ask a few questions. Do you think for a minute if Jorge shoves a nine-millimeter down his old lady's throat, he won't cough up the medical records? Hillary, I had to go to Fresno to find out what kind of support I had. I couldn't back down. While I was there, I got rousted and dumped into the slam for a few weeks. It was chickenshit and they had to let me go. It's ridiculous." He laughed. "Unless I get caught with a smoking gun standing over a body, no one can touch me. The lawyers fall over themselves protecting my constitutional rights. We've got a license to kill and nobody can stop us. I took it real easy on your father. Should I get the doctor's address from him and make him drive me there? You know what I do to people who lie and try to fuck me around."

She closed her eyes and felt his fingers tenderly rubbing her neck and face. There was no escaping from him. She was filled with self-loathing for having put her father in jeopardy, thrusting him into the depths of the lowlife, the violence she had condoned.

"Tell me the truth—just lay it on me. I've been your lover, your anchor, your protector. What am I going to do? Hurt you? See, my situation's no better than yours. I'm hooked on you and you have to hang in with me. There's no other way. You can't play games with me, call a cop or get a lawyer. All that's behind you—the normal stuff." He shook his head impassively. "You're involved with me. This thing with the Mexican organization's coming to a head. We can't go on killing each other. It'll be one group in a few more weeks. Then we can get out of Venice, buy a place, get married and live like everybody else. I'm just doing what I have to. I didn't do all that time to come out and let other people walk into what we built. The Italians and blacks are out of it. They don't come near our areas, so how could I let these people from Mexico come into my barrio and take over my business? They're not even Americans. Let them stay on their side of the border and get rich because we'll buy whatever they can supply, but understand what this is all about—it's power, control, and pride! I built an organization and no one can knock it down."

She began to cry silently and she fell into his arms.

"Don't, don't, Hillary," he pleaded.

"I had to leave you . . . try again." Her face contracted with pain. "Another chance to see if I could pull myself together."

"It's too late to go back, Hillary. But you'll pull yourself up—with me. The night you turned me around, it was over." He cradled her head on his shoulder. "The baby—what happened?"

"I had an abortion."

His head dropped. He stood motionlessly, then whispered: "Why . . . why? Oh, sweet Jesus, why did you take that away from me?"

She was overcome by the poignancy of his suffering, the strong man humbled, grieving, beyond solace, and she felt the heady excitement of supreme power, a high beyond drugs, the accession to a place above all others in a small, spiteful world of grasping, confused people.

"How could you do this?" he asked in a quavering voice.

"I'm sorry." She clasped her hands around the back of his neck, smelled the rose cologne he used after shaving. "There'll be other chances—another baby, I swear. I was afraid for this one—the drugs I'd been taking. The first three months are so important, you know? And I didn't have enough faith when you went away. What if you were killed or sent away again? I wasn't strong enough."

He nodded, rubbed his red-rimmed eyes, convinced that destiny had removed the blight he feared of a childless life, a dynasty bereft of heirs.

"Let's go," he said.

When they saw Leonard's twisted, worried face, they fell

silent. There was nothing they could say that would explain or alleviate the agony of this loss. When Hillary passed by him, she stopped, turned, and looked directly at him with the softness that had captivated him in the child he had tried to reclaim. He was convinced that Hillary would work out a way to escape from Geraldo. He had faith in her. Her mind was not fogged with drugs and her determination was clear. He had met Geraldo and understood the detour she had to take, but in his heart he believed that she would come home.

Leonard started for his car and Geraldo caught up with him on the path. As though in a daydream he listened to the softly endearing words of commiseration.

"You're a better man than I thought," Geraldo said. "I'll take care of her and maybe one day you'll understand what we have."

Leonard watched her approach Geraldo's motorcycle. She straddled the pillion of the 750 Honda, wrapped her arms around his waist. He revved, then the motorcycle flew down the driveway like a rocket.

He wove in and out of traffic. The wind whipped her hair. How she'd missed the thrill of high speed. It was better than coke or an ammie rush, the air blasting into her face. Her heart pulsated wildly. It was better than flying, better than skiing. Speed, speed, she thought exultantly. It was what her life was all about—what it had missed.

"Man, can you drive this fucker!" she shouted, pressing her head against his shoulder as he zoomed down the San Diego Freeway.

"You like it, *guapa*?"

"It's blowing me out."

She had to tune into Geraldo's mind, and was prepared to play along until she found her way to escape. Denying the thrill that Geraldo gave her as they ripped past the commuters on the San Diego Freeway would be a travesty of the moment, she thought. In the back of her mind she would certainly remember the things she truly wanted. But if she were ever to get away from Geraldo, she had to make him feel completely secure with her.

Geraldo sped down Westminster Avenue against the one-way signal, past La Guita. He cut the engine at the bottom of the street next to the beach. She could see that the beach was empty, hear the rough surf, the waves spewing foam a few hundred yards away. She wanted to rip off her clothes and run across the sand to the water.

"You're okay?" he asked with a thin smile.

"Yes."

She ran across the bike path in the freezing wind and he zoomed after her on the bike, which stalled in the sand. He leapt toward her, wrestled her down. They lay entwined, speechless, trying to catch their breath. His hand slid down the small of her back and his nails dug into her buttocks. Her face was positively angelic. She was going to win this battle.

28

Bobby was on the move again. He hated packing. It was easy enough to place the blame on L.A. for his transience. But to tell the truth, the city hadn't really played any significant part in his decision. He'd written three letters of resignation to Tim Hayward that still hadn't been sent; he'd given them to Rubin to read. But Gary was aghast. "It's like leaving a pregnant woman. You can't build a temple, then strike it down. You're the Principal Architect on Marine Mutual."

The foundation had been laid and the building was beginning to take form above it. Anyone could stand guard over the construction. The fruit of his work had been completed.

He was dropping off his cartons and books and most of his clothes at Claire's apartment. She'd given him a key and painted it red with nail polish so he couldn't confuse it with the others on his ring. It was something she'd always done. He planned to store his gear in her hall closet until he had a permanent address. Afterward, he decided, he'd hit the office and confront Tim and leave honorably.

The closet was deeply angled, set back properly to give maximum storage space in a condo apartment, and he pushed aside a few of Claire's dresses, embalmed in plastic, to shunt in a box of books. Shoving in his old portfolio, a carton carrying a model that he'd designed as an undergraduate, destined never to see the light of day, saved for a posterity of some sort, he found a zippered see-through bag, different from the others.

He carried it out, laid it on the sofa, and stared at it. He unzipped the bag and pulled the dress out. It was Claire's wedding dress. Italian lace with a high waist, a velvet sash. He touched it gingerly. It was as though for an instant her body had joined his. With shaking hands he replaced it in the dark end of the closet.

Should he stay, continue working, pick his projects, dedicate himself to Claire and wait until she was ready for him? He could not persuade her to give up business. Rodeo Drive had taken her over. The intensity of her ambition was every bit as great as his. It had been forged in desperation and sorrow and had guided her to a new self. That was precisely the problem. He had tasted a degree of success, knew that it would never be enough for him. He was compelled to stretch himself so that he could grow and find out what was at the core. The struggle within him darkened his hopes and made him aware of how selfishly he had behaved.

He was, however, certain of one thing. He had to quit working for Hayward. His time with Hillary had already been washed out. It was as though he had never met her, never been married to her. He had come to Los Angeles, had reached the pinnacle of success—too soon? he wondered—and now there was nothing left for him.

He waited for Tim out in the reception area. Last year he had sat in the same seat, trying to detect from the secretary's immobile face if he had any chance for the job. Corseted in his three-piece suit he had sweated it, wondering if he had to give up his profession and face life as a disappointed man.

Hayward came out of his office, smiling beatifically, opened his arms to embrace Bobby.

"Am I your date for Claire's opening?"

"That's the best offer I've had today," Bobby replied affably.

"Have you got a surprise coming." They passed into the office. Bobby saw a new glossy model of Marine Mutual on a table in the center of the room. Beside it was a small black plaque engraved in gold letters: "Architects: Robert J. Canaday and Hayward Associates." Tim opened the liquor cabinet and offered Bobby a drink. "Do you know how many office buildings we've been offered?"

"How many?"

"Six! I've had to put out feelers in *Architectural Journal* for more people. You take your pick . . . conduct the interviews—develop your own team. Scotch okay?"

"Sure. Just ice."

Tim's spirit of bonhomie and conplacency had about it the clumsiness of a department store Santa.

"A partnership goes with it, Bobby. In the time you've been here, the business has changed dramatically. We're going to the Super Bowl: city centers, museums, prestige commercial buildings." Hayward banged his glass against Bobby's. "Give it a couple of years and you'll be in here, running the firm. We're going to expand enormously."

"Sounds terrific."

"I thought you'd be pleased."

"I am. But, Tim . . . it's not for me."

Hayward appeared slightly irked but took it in stride. Bobby was not an administrator, a solicitor and entertainer of new clients.

"I'll do the lunch stuff at the Bistro . . . we'll get Gary to do the day-to-day follow-ups. You'll handle the projects you have a feel for."

Bobby shook his head. Hayward smiled, afraid to open his mouth. Whatever he offered, Bobby rejected, and he had no idea how he could appease the firm's genius.

"Name your terms. Suppose your lawyer sits down with me and we structure a contract that'll make you happy." Hayward's pale blue eyes retreated.

"I'm leaving."

"I don't understand. Look, I know that things didn't work out with you and Hillary and that Leonard can be a pain in the ass, but that's over. You're beyond all the pettiness."

Bobby stared at the model on the table. It no longer interested him. It had occupied him day and night for months and now it might have been anybody's design for all he cared. He regarded it with serene detachment. An office building, a shelter for Frank's employees. He had achieved his objective of providing a home. He knew at that moment that he would never again design another office building. One was enough. It no longer represented a challenge, engaged him emotionally, and he realized that these elements were the lifeblood of his being.

"It's pretty," Bobby said with mild contempt.

"You're wrong. It's original, special," Hayward countered. "Look, after you design a building, the work's a bore. Think this out properly. You and Hillary had a mess. That was nothing to do with anything. Listen to me, Bobby . . . People have personal difficulties like you and Claire . . . then they're resolved. It's a new life. Give it time."

Bobby appeared distracted. He regarded the Marine Mutual model with distrust.

"The work in L.A. isn't for me," he said finally. "There are so many young talented people who'd be perfect for you. Develop them. You did it with me. You're a salesman with an architect's stamp and you gave me a chance when I needed it. You didn't interfere. You supported me down the line, but, shit, what sort of guy do you think I am? Just some hack who's in this to get rich? You and Leonard are in tune with your market."

Hayward nodded dumbly. He placed his hands on his hips and strode around his office, gesticulating wildly.

"What do you want . . . ? There has to be a basis of negotiation. You're hot, don't you understand? Write your own ticket. Millions are involved. Shit, Bobby, I can get us a quarter of a million for a fucking house plan." His skin had become pallid and he seemed thoroughly frightened by Bobby's intention. He was losing his golden goose.

He liked Tim, his slick flimflam whorish technique. At lunch Hayward always ordered caviar—so what if it cost fifty bucks a hit. Oh, God, what people wouldn't do for a client.

"I think there's something wrong with the people out here," Bobby responded. "Tim, I passed a house on Rexford the other day. Three Rolls-Royces in the driveway. So I parked for a few minutes out of curiosity. Two kids who couldn't've been twenty get into two of them. Then Mama slips into hers. What's Daddy drive? The QE2"

"Maybe they worked for it. Bobby, you're going too far. This is an insane discussion. You can't condemn people for making it. This is America . . . capitalism."

"Something's wrong, though. It's sick. It's not the American dream I see out here, but some strange perversion of materialism. So fuck it, fuck it, Tim."

"Millions of dollars are walking out the door with you, you bastard."

"That's your problem."

A phase of his life was over. If Claire could have heard him, she would have backed him all the way . . . or would she?

The fanfare of an opening party for Rodeo Wilderness was a necessary evil. The Dunlops had insisted, or rather their P.R. from Rogers and Cowan had demanded that, in spite of Claire's protestations, it be an event. So Giovanni's first team were hired to cater: micro-cannelloni, prosciutto rolled around melon thumbs, shrimp and, Claire observed with irony, crab claws of course. Juschi and Cecil Gee had spent fortunes on parties and Neiman-Marcus with all of its clout, having had more press than any ten stores put together, was as deserted as a morgue most of the time. There was, Claire knew, a professional group of guests culled from the client lists of P.R. companies who showed up at these unmomentous occasions . . . a couple of nobodies from canceled TV series, a few store owners, jewelers from South Beverly Drive, but certainly not Jerry Magnin or Dr. Aldo Gucci. Unless everything was going to be auctioned off for the Friends of the Music Center, they could forget about the Chandlers and the Ahmansons. They'd collect the matrons who came to look but never shopped. If they lucked out, there'd be two lines in the *Times'* society column, a sneer from Jeff Silverman in the *Examiner*, and some pictures in George Christy's column in the *Reporter*. Even a day before the opening, Claire had pleaded with them: "Rodeo Wilderness has to be discovered and a party for freeloaders isn't the way to do it."

"Whose money is in this?" Frank asked. Ellen's suggestion of a safari party with live animals had been vetoed. She'd overlooked the fact that, with handlers or not, they might crap on the floors. It had happened to Johnny Carson often enough.

"Who's the retail expert, you or me?" she countered bluntly. "Give me mentions in the papers and in *New West, Los Angeles Magazine, California Good Life,* the trades . . . send out a press release about the stuff we're selling, not about the people who came to drink. That's all I need." Deliveries were still coming in and her staff of four, two outdoorsy guys in their mid-twenties and two girls who were professional campers, were rearranging the stock. "The merchandise and the look of the place will draw people. Word of mouth, not hype. Frank, a party could turn into a fiasco and hurt us. Let's open to business and not bullshit. We've got a choice location, people will find us."

Her reservations fell on deaf ears. Having been snubbed since their arrival the Dunlops were determined to fight it out to the bitter end. Those who did *not* attend the opening included Henry Berger, Hugh O'Brian, the Kreisses, Clint Eastwood, Patrick Terrail, all of the fashion editors, Britt Ekland, George Hamilton, Alana and Rod Stewart, and every studio executive in town.

However, on the evening of April fourth, Good Friday no less, the place was mobbed. Maybe it was because the weather had finally improved and people on the list had nothing better to do with themselves. A disco group engaged by the Dunlops honked miserably on the balcony and the only celebrity of note was that rising young star, Mrs. Eugene Roth, now hyphenated as Madeleine Gilbert-Roth, sporting a suntan and a marriage band. People gravitated toward her and her eminent director husband.

"Who are these people?" Madeleine asked, squirming past the bar.

"Beats me," Claire replied angrily. Her dream had soured and she was so livid that she was prepared to walk out. She had no real authority and since she'd made her pact with the devil she regretted it. She had signed on for ten percent of nothing, a salary and a seventy-hour week. She spied Bobby near the entrance, trapped in a mob grabbing hors d'oeuvres off trays. She stood on the steps of the gallery and frantically signaled him. He needed the Rams front four to open a seam for him. He caught sight of her and she pointed to a corner beside the window for them to reconnoiter. It took five minutes and a few spilled drinks for them to reach each other.

His eyes were ablaze with happiness. She hadn't seen him this relaxed and tranquil in months. She embraced him.

"You've really done it, babe. I'm so proud of you. I just stopped by to wish you luck."

"Bobby, it's not working. I'm miserable. Frank's responsible for this vulgarity."

He appeared surprised.

"But people're enjoying themselves," he observed.

"They're the wrong people. I've been used. I have no control."

"Stick up for your rights, babe. You've gotten damn good at it." She had never been more confused. He told her he'd resigned and was going to San Francisco to an architect's convention. The people from Hull University would be there. They'd meet him then but he suspected they wanted to shop around. She was tempted to walk out right then, give it all up. But he remonstrated with her. "Claire, don't quit. You'll never be happy if you leave now. Take Frank to the mat . . . you've got him by the throat." His encouragement buoyed her spirits but now that he had made his move, she was thrown into even greater turmoil. Why not bum around Europe, get her bearings? They'd be together. The crowds were thinning out and he looked approvingly at the store.

"You've put too much into this," he counseled. "I believe in you." He'd see her when he came back from San Francisco.

By ten the store was empty, the caterers and cleaning crew had reestablished order, and she was left with the Dunlops. They'd made reservations at Stellini's. Just a quiet dinner for the three of them. Frank in his khaki jumpsuit and Ellen in a safari outfit were elated with the party. Claire opened her purse, removed the keys to both the store and the apartment.

"I'd suggest that you get in at eight-thirty to open," she said.

"What're you talking about?" Ellen asked anxiously.

"You bullied me into this party, which I don't think is going to help one bit and frankly, I'm unhappy with our arrangements, so I'm pulling out."

Frank was appalled by her attitude.

"You can't do this to me. We've got a contract."

"Sue me. You're the banker and I'm the business. You pared my share down to nothing. You haven't contributed a damn thing to this business except finance and a lousy party."

For once it seemed to him that his Caligula-like tactics had misfired. He was dealing with an individual.

"Have I been too rough with you, Claire? I backed an idea when you had nowhere to take it."

"You didn't give me the chance. You wrapped it up so fast that I didn't know what hit me. But the facts are that I conceived the idea, did the buying, spent months here handling every problem while you guys ignored it. I'm not some glorified manager. Hire someone else and see how you make out. If it doesn't catch on, what does a failure mean to you?"

In a hushed voice, Ellen said, "Frank's never failed."

"Well, Rodeo Drive might give him an opportunity. It cleanses the soul. When a store goes bad, the gossip starts with the other shop owners, then it moves real fast to the customers and you begin a nose-dive. You start asking questions about the stock, the prices, wonder if you should have an opening sale. You can absorb the loss. It won't put a dent in your fortune. But the reason I didn't want a party with a bunch of nobodies is that they aren't buyers and if we don't do business immediately it'll look funny to the street. So, unnecessarily, you put the pressure on me, went against my judgment. I have to carry the can. My neck's on the line and that's more important to me than your investment."

The Dunlops huddled in a corner, thoroughly taken aback by the severity of her argument. Maybe they'd pushed her too hard. For once, Frank Dunlop found himself on the defensive. If the store opened strong, they could move fast, tie up locations around the country. Claire's departure would force them to start hunting for a manager whose competence and honesty could not be guaranteed. Their little flutter on Rodeo Drive would backfire. Nothing could be more humiliating to the Dunlops than failing in Beverly Hills. Frank would sooner return to Chicago, drive on ice, dive into Lake Michigan. He'd made too much of his association with Rodeo Wilderness to be able to ignore the consequences of a failure. Had he remained a silent backer, he could have dropped Claire, but the fatal attraction of social mobility had boxed him in.

"Suppose we revise the terms of your deal? How does seventy-five/twenty-five sound to you?" he asked in a cajoling voice.

"It stinks."

He was outraged. "Are you suggesting a fifty-fifty split?"

"That's commonly known as justice."

"What exactly do you want, Claire?" Ellen asked. Frank was losing ground, getting them nowhere. The horror of being there on Saturday morning without any knowledge of the way things were worked was too horrible to contemplate.

"Sixty-forty in my favor," Claire demanded. "And the title of president and chief operating officer."

"I'll sleep on it."

"No you won't, Frank. You're going to be in here at eight-thirty tomorrow morning with your attorney and I don't care who's got a golf game or tennis date."

No one had ever spoken in those terms to Frank Dunlop and he wasn't sure how to react. He knew that he was hated. But men like him, Harold Geneen, Bludhorn, had to risk unpopularity to achieve their goals. The little guy who operated his small-potatoes business and knocked out a living did not have the courage to be despised, but rather depended on the goodwill of his minuscule clientele. Being loved was a weakness. To be feared and detested was the mark of supremacy and Frank Dunlop was not about to change.

This little girl, whose sweet charm had attracted him. had turned out to be tougher than he. The transformation in Claire petrified him. Was she bluffing?

"I don't see how you can reject a split down the middle."

"I just did." She handed Ellen the keys. "This is the front door key and be sure to close the window in the toilet. You don't want a cat burglar cleaning out your stock before you've opened. I'll have my stuff out of the apartment by tomorrow afternoon."

Dunlop pursued her into the street, agitated, ranting, pleading.

"Claire, Claire, please. You've got a deal."

"It better be in writing tomorrow, Frank."

Geraldo seldom left Hillary alone. He treated her with extraordinary tenderness but his domination had become so oppressive that privacy, a harmless shopping expedition, a visit with Kitty at the Colony and lunch, required endless discussion and the presence of one of his men. Hillary, who had always sought control over those close to her, was being stifled by Geraldo's possessiveness. She thought of her father, of Bobby, and she sent silent apologies to them, hoped they would understand.

Geraldo kept her away from drugs and made an effort to enforce the conditions of what, in his estimation, represented a normal life. Movies, bowling, riding dirt bikes, a walk on the beach. That was it. She should be happy. But her confinement was total, without reprieve, except for a Saturday visit with her father, overseen by Geraldo. Leonard had achieved the distinction of being on Geraldo's approved list. Martial law had been established in Hillary's life. Defying him carried intolerable consequences.

One night, in desperation, she had hit his drug cache, grabbing the first thing she found, which turned out to be an acid tab, leading her to a wasteland of paranoia. She could have accepted a beating for her disobedience but instead was stripped naked, handcuffed to the bed, and permitted to go to the bathroom only under his supervision. Solitary confinement lasted two days. He took his responsibility, the pledge to her father to keep her off drugs, with an insane dedication.

"You fuck up, you get thrown in the hole," the professional inmate curtly informed her. "That's the way the world works when you break the rules."

A day after she'd been released from the handcuffs, he took her to brunch around the corner at the Sidewalk Café on the Venice bike path. She gazed at the bizarrely dressed assortment of roller skaters, the combative bike riders fighting for their turf against them, the dog walkers, the blinding sunshine, the ambience and the uncertain harmonies of a nascent spring rising from the deadly winter rains.

He held her hand, kissed the tips of her fingers romantically.

"Hillary, the best thing that ever happened to me was meeting you. You're the most precious, beautiful . . . well, I can't put it into words . . . I want to preserve you," he said. She nodded, pulled her sunglasses down from her head, over her eyes.

"I made you happy," she said distantly, vague about the details.

"Too happy. So happy I won't ever give this up." She nodded and they were quiet. They ate omelettes, she listened to the plans he made. "The battle with EME is over. We're all on the same side. They supply, we sell. They make their profit and so do we." He layered his bread with butter. "I always wanted to meet a girl, have a bunch of children . . . get it?"

She was afraid to go against the grain. She needed a joint, a toot, a Lude, anything to prolong the mood, the flaky unrealizable plans that men made and women discarded.

"We're going to have that, Hillary." She was watching the skaters. "A houseful of children . . . three, five maybe. You'll breastfeed our babies, give them your health and love. And they'll have their grandfather . . . your father. I don't want his money. But he'll be proud of his grandchildren."

"Geraldo, I want to skate. Let's rent some."

"Hillary, you're not paying attention." She looked at him through her dark glasses, hating him, his absurd illusions, his barrel chest, the flowery scent he wore. "Your father is your trusty and you're doing time. If the prisoner escapes, then the trusty takes the punishment." She lowered her head, listening to Geraldo's graphic description of the potential torture that his future father-in-law might have to suffer if she were to step out of line again.

"I can't live with these threats," she implored him.

"You murdered my child because of the drugs you took! You'll never do it again. You owe me . . . a family belongs to me."

Later, sitting across from Leonard on her very best behavior, she smiled demurely, acquiescent when Geraldo said that he would be back later to take her to dinner with some friends.

She was drinking a light gin and tonic, approved by Geraldo. Two of them were her limit. She went to the window, saw him chat with his men. He drove off in a Caddy, leaving them behind. She picked up the bottle of

Bombay gin, poured herself a stiff shot and Leonard pursed his lips warily.

"You're not going to get loaded."

"Oh, no." They sat silently regarding each other.

"Have you discussed my suggestion with Geraldo?"

"What?" She was detached, drifting. Nothing like a shot of gin for a fast, easy lift.

"Getting an apartment in Beverly Hills. I ran into Joyce Rey today and she sends you her best. She's in charge of Rodeo Realty now . . . but the thing is, she heard of a honey on Oakhurst . . . a condo . . . I should've built it instead of my tracts in Mission Viejo. I never thought they'd sell at that price."

Hillary shook her head. There was a regality to his daughter, in spite of Geraldo. She wore a fashionable pair of black trousers with a pleated waist, a black cowl neck sweater that set off a single pearl on a gold chain, which had belonged to her mother. Her rich blonde hair was pinned up a little too messily and casually to suit him. It didn't matter what Hillary had gone through, she still retained an inbred aristocracy that reminded him of her mother.

"Why're you so negative? Maybe you could go back to Disegno. You'd have to be serious this time." The sour fumes of obsequiousness and dread throttled him. He'd need Geraldo's permission. The humiliation she'd subjected Leonard to made her cringe.

"Do you see Bobby at all?" she asked.

"No. He's leaving L.A. He resigned. Tim couldn't believe it. The man blew himself out of everything." She seemed apathetic. "It's got nothing to do with you. It's just Bobby. The important thing is his design. Tim hired a group from Philip Johnson's office to see it through . . . the world goes on."

Hillary moved to the sofa, laid her head on her father's chest. Awkward for Leonard. He withdrew and there was such a studied diffidence about him, a renunciation of their former private emotional reserves that she was hit with shakes. He watched her get up and pour another drink, relieved by the amount of ice she placed in the glass.

"Daddy, was I always a monster?" she asked.

"No."

He allowed himself to slip into her mood of easy confidences.

"Oh, you wanted to be like your mother to please me. I couldn't deny you anything. It was a kind of game. You'd imitate her and I'd encourage you, lead you. We were so damned silly. You never stopped asking questions about the way she pronounced words, or her favorite colors." He beamed, puckered his lips and enunciated the syllables of his dead wife's name. "Gloria . . ."

"I couldn't let you marry anyone."

"You're telling me. Well, maybe you were right. I'm past having a wife now." He sighed gently and there was such great friendliness in his face that Hillary felt united with him then. "It's so damned old-fashioned and silly, but your mother is what used to be known as a lost love."

Hillary and he inadvertently cuddled, reviving his memory and her role, and she put her arms around him and pressed her lips against his cheek, but it made him uncomfortable and he withdrew. The smell of gin disagreed with him. Geraldo would be back in an hour. Hillary had passed from his life.

He'd spend the spring in Italy, buy some pictures. He was solvent again and the property business no longer had any meaning. Frank Dunlop had skinned him in his own territory. A Midwestern peasant, gross, vindictive, had taught him the difference between shallow games and the violence of a consuming appetite. Leonard had had enough of it. He was out of hock. His properties were in the hands of another operator. He'd walk away from the table with his self-respect and live. Perhaps in a few months Hillary's fanatical suitor would have lost interest in her.

"You put me first and it was a mistake," Hillary advised him.

"I'd do it again." It was apparent to Hillary that he was lying. "Anyway, it's a little late to start worrying," he snapped with unexpected bitterness. He looked at his watch. "Suppose I clear out and let you and Geraldo meet on your own. I've got a dinner date with someone *I* like. I guess the pictures will be safe . . . naturally . . . Geraldo can beat the alarm any time. No small talent." Leonard extricated himself. "When I have a robbery, I'll know who to contact." He kissed Hillary's forehead. "I'll be in the study. I've got some calls to make."

She accompanied him to the hallway, grasping his arm like a deb about to make an entrance at her coming out. What would they think of her? She was lightheaded when she walked upstairs to her room.

"Hillary," he called. "Stay here if you want. I've missed you. Get us the hell out of this." She stopped, midway up the staircase, turned to him with a sibylline smile and waved.

When she opened the door to her room, she knew that she wanted to stay. Home, the smell of it. The linen on her bed was pale pink and the pillow shams were trimmed with lace. She'd always loved the view from the end of her bed, which overlooked the old French fountain Leonard had brought back from Grasse. Eucalyptus and pine trees surrounded the fountain and behind them were thickets of climbing roses on the brick wall that ran the length of the property.

She opened her handbag and took out the heavy, greasy-smelling revolver. Geraldo had a fetish about cleaning his weapons. She unsnapped the safety catch, held her eyes fast on the Japanese gardener who came into view in the dimming light with his net to clean the leaves out of the fountain. She sat on the end of the bed, intrigued by the gardener's deftness, the fastidiousness of purpose. She placed the barrel of the Walther against her left temple and, just as Geraldo had instructed her when they pot-shotted on the beach, she squeezed the trigger slowly.

Bobby didn't hear the news until he arrived back in Los Angeles late on Monday night. A group of reporters were camped outside his apartment, among them a surly aggressive Englishman with rotten teeth from the *National Enquirer*. He immediately began taking photographs. The questions were so fast, baffling, and personal that he hardly knew how to respond.

In rapid succession he heard:

"Did she kill herself because you were divorcing her?"

"Was she broken-hearted?"

"Was she taking drugs, do you know?"

"Do you know if she was seeing a psychiatrist?"

Bobby slammed the door in their faces, rushed to the telephone and dialed Leonard's number. A maid answered the phone and, after he identified himself, he was put on to Dr. Parks, Hillary's psychiatrist. He sounded exasperated and despondent.

"Can you tell me what happened?" Bobby asked.

"It's awful . . . Hillary was having a drink with her father on Saturday and when Leonard went to make a few phone calls, she went up to her bedroom and shot herself. It was totally unexpected. She hadn't appeared suicidal . . . nobody suspected anything like this could happen . . ."

"Where's Leonard?"

"Asleep. I've been keeping him on tranquilizers since it happened."

"I'd like to come over."

"I wouldn't advise it. It's a madhouse here. There are reporters all over the place. Taking photos of everything they can. It's disgusting . . ."

"They're here too."

"Bobby, the funeral's tomorrow at twelve at St. John's Memorial Park. It's off the San Diego Freeway on the way to the airport."

"What about a church service?"

"Leonard's not up to it. Just a simple gravesite service. It's such a terrible waste, Bobby. It had nothing to do with you."

Bobby heard the psychiatrist's voice crack and he gently replaced the receiver. He sat at the dining room table until three in the morning with a bottle of Black Label. On the floor beside the table was a picture on the front page of the *Times* of Hillary in her wedding dress outside the church. The headline said "HEIRESS SUICIDE." He couldn't bring himself to read the story.

Why had it turned out this way for her? There was no inkling of any self-destructive tendencies when they'd first met. She had been vivacious, vital, full of life and fun. He preferred to think of her that way, the fresh ebullient girl rather than the overbearingly possessive woman who emerged during their marriage.

What in the name of God had been going on in her mind during that crucial last minute? Had she thought of him, or felt that he had not given her a chance? Yet the incontestable evidence was that she wanted out of the marriage. She had left him. He had been unfulfilled, paranoid about Claire. But guilt overwhelmed him. If he had taken Hillary back when she had made her last appeal to him, would it have changed things? If he had responded, maybe she'd be alive now. Or would it have just delayed the inevitable, brought more unhappiness and anger to them both?

The shock of her suicide gripped him, would not respond to logic. He saw the soft contours of her body, the bulging breasts, thought he could touch the crescent-shaped lips with his forefinger. The smell of her hair teased him, filled the room. He looked around the apartment and the memory of the first night they spent together haunted him, the passion he had felt for her, which defied all rational thought.

What had killed Hillary? The society she was brought up in, the doting father, the knowledge that there were limits to her control over him? Something had gone dangerously wrong, years before they met. Some spring within the human mind, like the mechanism of a watch, recoiled and finally broke.

He had expected to find a great horde of people in attendance at the cemetery. Instead, there was only Leonard, a minister, the psychiatrist, and a dark swarthy man he dimly remembered seeing when the guesthouse was being redone. He had been her lover.

Dr. Parks, the competent doctor he had met at Leonard's house before he married Hillary, was now pale, harried, and broken. Leonard stood slump-shouldered, his face gray and unshaven, a caricature of the elegant, urbane millionaire Bobby had met when he first came to Los Angeles.

The minister was the same one who had married them and Bobby nodded to him. The minister said a few words about Hillary. They echoed the thoughts that Bobby had had the previous night. A beautiful girl . . . a glorious life abruptly terminated . . . she was a child of the Lord and her act was directed by a higher authority and she must not be judged by legal or temporal standards. Then he recited several verses from Ecclesiastes, ending on a troubled note that epitomized Hillary's life:

"And I gave my heart to know wisdom,
and to know madness and folly: I
perceived that this also is vexation of
spirit. For in much wisdom *is*
much grief: and he that increaseth
knowledge increaseth sorrow."

Dr. Parks had arranged for the interment to take place after the mourners had departed. In many ways he seemed as shattered as Leonard, and Bobby sympathized with the guilt that was consuming him.

Leonard raised his eyes to Bobby; they had an opaque, filmy quality as though he were drugged. He was helped into the car by his chauffeur and Parks. Bobby waited for the Chicano to approach him. He was carrying a small bunch of violets. He laid them beside the casket, which rested above the large dark hole that violated the green hillside. Then he removed a crucifix from around his neck, placed it on the coffin, and made the sign of the cross. Hillary had found her avenging angel. The man gave off a lofty sense of dignity and it was impossible to gauge his true feelings.

In clipped Spanish he said to Bobby:

"*La vida es sueño* . . . so everything is permitted."

For a few minutes Bobby watched customers examine the store windows with curiosity, disbelief, and finally, enough interest to go inside. The originality of Claire's concept thrilled him.

Behind him, a couple of Rolls-Royces, a phalanx of Mercedes, a Jaguar or two, and an occasional Stutz curb-crawled to see what new phenomenon was taking place on Rodeo Drive. He had returned his car to Hayward the previous day and rather than have him take a cab out to the airport, Claire had insisted on driving him.

The energy and vitality she demonstrated as he watched her moving from customer to customer assured him that she had made the right decision. She couldn't give up Rodeo Drive for him or anyone else. She belonged there. She had found her place.

He went inside, noticed that a number of the racks had thinned out. She had been open only three days and the store had a flavor about it. Everything from canteens, cooking stoves, to trout waders and barbecue cookbooks as well as the clothing caught one's eye, forced one to pause, pick up a Swiss Army knife, a safari hat or compass. It was fascinating. The Boy's Own Dream come true. Thus, right in the heart of Beverly Hills, one could imagine being on a raft, cooking trout by a stream, bedding down in a sleeping bag, drinking a few beers, reading by a lantern in a tent. Claire wasn't selling fashion but a mirage of freedom, communing with nature, survival, self-reliance. The temptation to purchase something, share the fantasy, was irresistible.

Claire was at the register, writing out a Visa slip for an elegant matron who had purchased several pairs of ribbed knee-high socks, a backpack, and a tin of snuff.

"How are you, babe?" he asked when he came up to her.

"Busy, thank God," she said, handing the woman the slip to sign and putting everything neatly into a plastic carry-bag that was imprinted with Bobby's leaf design, Rodeo Wilderness's trademark.

It was almost five and they'd close in an hour. His flight was at seven. Claire picked up her leather jacket from the brass hatstand behind the desk and told one of the staff to close up.

She remained poker-faced through the heavy rush hour traffic to the airport and for most of the way they were silent. Bobby glanced toward St. John's Memorial Park but didn't say anything to Claire about the recent event there. When she turned onto Century Boulevard the airport came into view. Jets thundered overhead in a clear sky.

"I miss you already," Bobby said.

She dodged the sentiment, fearing she would cave in. She pulled into the lot and found a spot opposite the TWA terminal. He took the trunk key and brought out his single cheap plaid airline case. He carried a camel's hair coat over his arm. He was checked in at the curb by a porter; he'd received his seat assignment when he bought his ticket. There was a pained smile on his face and his luminous blue eyes repeatedly focused on her. She took his arm and accompanied him up the long passageway to passport control. There was a line of people and they were forced to have a quiet moment together. They found a corner by the newsstand.

"I hope you find what you're looking for," she said awkwardly.

"Claire, I love you."

Claire lowered her eyes and he put his arms around her. She was afraid to kiss him. She would have preferred to turn her back and walk away.

"We'll see each other. I'm probably going to Europe on a buying trip in August. Who knows? You might be back before then."

"We'll hook up somewhere." His face was alive with excitement and optimism and she could see all of the bright fine things in his soul that she would always love. He was, for all his searching, the most beautiful human being she had ever known. Her devotion and love had not been wasted, for Bobby would always be the boy in the high school hallway, bemused, his head in the stars, unaware of the small realities of life. But perhaps it was better for him to remain unspoiled, to reject the security of a career to work on a church for a pittance.

There was only one woman on line at passport control and his flight had been called twice. The "Now Boarding" signal flashed insistently on the TV monitor.

Claire took a small package out of her handbag and gave it to him.

"Do I open it now?"

"When you're alone . . ."

He put his arms around her and with an awful sense of anguish kissed her. For a moment when they came apart, she was frightened she couldn't let go of him, that if he began walking he would be dragging her with him. Finally, with a stinging smile graven on her lips, she watched him present his passport and receive his boarding pass.

He turned and waved at her. He stopped at the entrance to the gate to see her standing, watching him.

He opened the box and took out a silver compass, which was engraved on the back: *"Love, Claire."*

When he looked up, Claire was gone.